Dear Ones
Hope you
love

Blue Turquoise, White Shell

♡ Virginia
August 5, 2007

Author's photo (back cover)
Courtesy of
Hollye Schumacher

Cover Layout and Text
Lee Emory

Treble Heart Books
1284 Overlook Dr.
Sierra Vista, AZ 85635-5512
http://www.trebleheartbooks.com

Printed and Published in the U.S.A.

ISBN: 978-1-932695-58-8

Other books by Virginia Nosky

Kachina
Chance Encounters
Pima Road

The Navajo

In the north is Big Sheep Peak in the La Plata Range, Colorado; in the south Mount Taylor, near Grants, New Mexico; to the west, near Flagstaff, Arizona, Mount Humphrey in the San Francisco Peaks; to the east, Pelado Mountain in the Jemez Range—the sacred mountains of the mythic Navajo Holy People. These four mountains encompass Dinetah, the Land of the People. Here a Navajo walks in beauty. He follows the Navajo Way. Separate a Navajo from Dinetah and he falls out of harmony with his universe. He no longer walks in beauty.

The Navajo were relative late-comers to the southwestern United Sates, a branch of the Athabascan peoples who began migrating from Asia about a thousand years ago. Hunters and gatherers, they drifted ever-southward, taking their culture with them. As they moved into northwestern New Mexico around 1400, they found that others, Pueblo cultures, had preceded them. The Navajo were a fierce, intelligent, ambitious people, and when they came to the end of their long migration, to the empty, beautiful land between their sacred mountains, they brought with them skills they had picked up from the tribes they had been exposed to along the way: farming, crafts, and husbandry.

To the southwest in the middle of the sixteenth century, the Spaniard Francisco Vasquez de Coronado brought three stupendous changes with him: horses, sheep, and Catholicism. The Navajo embraced the first two with startling adeptness and vehemently rejected the third.

Never more than a razor's edge from starvation, the nomadic Navajo saw the prosperous Pueblo farms and the flocks of Spanish sheep and herds of horses. Ever adaptable to innovations that appealed to their eye for the practical, they watched their Pueblo neighbors and learned. The women set about planting fields in their new land and the men set about stealing horses and sheep. They kidnapped male craftsmen, captured Pueblo women potters, weavers, and cultivators. The fields flourished, their horsemanship became legendary, and the herds and flocks grew. Navajos never became skilled at pottery, but their woolen rugs were unsurpassed, as later their silver jewelry would be.

To the degree that any Navajo eventually accepted Christianity, it was a religion, to all intents and purposes, super-imposed upon his own.

The record of Spanish domination in the New World is rife with stupidity, cruelty, and greed. Coronado's disastrous legacy would continue for two centuries and nearly annihilate the native cultures. In the beginning, scattered across their isolated lands, the Navajo could remain relatively unnoticed. But as Spanish domination moved to include them, they reacted with fury. They would attack, then cannily enter into peace treaties, only to gain time to prepare new assaults on the representatives of the Spanish king and the Spanish god.

With Napoleon's subjugation of Spain in 1808, the opportunity arose for Mexico to throw off the yoke of Spanish suzerainty. In the following decades, in the Territory of New Mexico, now Texas, Nevada, Utah, parts of Colorado, and the large expanse of Arizona, New Mexico, and California, the political situation was fluid, with many clashes between the encroaching white settlers and the Mexicans, as well as the Native American tribes. In 1845, the United States annexed Texas, precipitating the Mexican War that would change the course of the region's history. The annexation of Texas was the immediate cause, but the inexorable pressures of western population expansion and the influx of English-speaking peoples restive under Spanish rule and covetous of the vast, empty lands ripe for settling, made the war an inevitability. With the Mexicans riven by bitter internal disputes, the American prevailed handily. On March 10, 1848, the Treaty of Guadalupe Hildalgo ceded two-fifths of the Mexican Territory, plus an indemnity of $15,000,000 to the United States.

To the Navajo, the change in their oppressors made little difference. Their women and children were still victims of the slave trade, the Catholic priests still fulminated against their deities, beliefs, and ceremonials. The Americans were, with few exceptions, just as corrupt, stupid, duplicitous, and greedy in their dealings with the Navajo and the other tribes as the Spanish and Mexicans.

In August, 1846, under Brigadier General Watts Kearney, the Army of the West had taken possession of the Territory of New Mexico. In a proclamation he issued from Santa Fe, he declared: "The undersigned has instructions from his government to protect the religious institutions of New Mexico...also to protect the persons and property of all quiet and peaceful inhabitants within its boundaries against the Utes, Navajos, and Mexicans."

The resolute Navajo would fight the Americans just as grimly as they had the Spanish and Mexicans.

From 1851 to 1854, the epicenter of the Navajo struggle against the Army of the West was the area around Fort Defiance, in northeastern Arizona. In 1864, under Colonel Kit Carson, a scorched earth campaign decimated the Navajo people. They were interned in a bleak concentration camp at Fort Sumner, New Mexico after what is now called the Long Walk, a forced march odyssey that left thousands dead. After four years of hunger and disease, the Navajo signed a peace treaty with the United States government and were allowed to return to their lands. Fort Defiance became an administrative center of the modern Navajo tribal government. The political capital of the Navajo Nation is Window Rock three miles to the south, in northeastern Arizona near its border with New Mexico.

The Navajo Codetalkers

In 1942 the United States Marine Corps recruited 191 young Navajo men, each in good_physical condition and fluent in English and Navajo to be assigned to the codetalker program to send messages between troops over telephone and radio circuits in the Pacific Theater of World War II. There were eventually 420 codetalkers. They had regular Marine training at San Diego Marine Corps Recruit Depot. Finishing boot camp they were assigned to the Field Signal Battalion Training Center at Camp Pendleton in Oceanside, California.

Navajo is known as one of the "hidden languages" in that, at the time, there was no written form and no alphabet or other symbols. The Navajo tongue was confined to the area of the Navajo Nation, and complicating things, there were dialect variations among the clans, and sometimes within the clans themselves.

It was the first group of recruits that devised Navajo words for military terms. For example, names of birds denoted different aircraft: chicken hawk for dive bomber; hummingbird for fighter plane, eagle for transport plane, etc. A quotation mark was "hanging earring."

The commanding general was *war chief*, a major general was *two star.* Each letter of the English alphabet was given three forms: a=ant, ax, apple; b=badger, bat, barrel, and so on down the alphabet. It was essentially a code within a code.

All code talkers had to memorize primary and alternate code terms. Fortunately, peoples without written languages necessarily have excellent memories.

Acknowledgements

Much gratitude to all my family, who love what I do. And to the Scottsdale Writers Group for their unending support and sharp eyes. To Deborah Ledford, Marcia Fine, Judy Starbuck and Michael Greenwald. And special thanks to Skip Feinstein who had the inspiration for my cover.

Dedication

For Mother, who loves this book.

About the Cover

The "Navajo Wedding Basket" is an important vessel for the wedding ceremony. The traditional red and black pattern on neutral ground: its symbolism is difficult to translate from the Diné culture. The red open circle represents the womb and the source of life. It is bordered by black peaks inside and out: home, motherearth, the sacred places. During the wedding ceremony the basket is filled with a porridge of blue corn meal and ashes mixed with water, which is eaten by the wedding couple and guests in a ritual communion. The design opening is always kept facing east, the direction of the sunrise, new beginnings, and new life. The Japanese were never able to unravel the Navajo codetalkers messages.

Blue Turquoise, White Shell

Virginia Nosky

Treble Heart Books

The Creation

The Navajo. They call themselves Dineh. The People. Their myths involve their beginnings: the ascent from the four lower worlds into the fifth world, The Glittering World, their present home. The myths tell of First Man, *Alte Hostiin,* and First Woman, *Do Honootinii,* from ears of corn. And how they found their daughter, Changing Woman, who is also called White Shell Woman, *Yoolgai Asdzaa,* on a mountaintop in a cradle of clouds and rainbows interlaced with sunbeams and lightning. They tell of the union of Changing Woman and the Sun and the birth of the twin boys, Monster Slayer, *Naayee'Neizzghani,* and Child Born of Water, *To Bajish Chini.* And how the twin boys slew the monsters of the earth to create the mountains, lava flows, and rock formations of the gouged and corrugated land that lay between the four holy mountains of Dinetah: *Dibentsaa, Tsoodzil, Doko'oosliid, Sisnaajini* (The mythic Land of the People.)

Prologue

June 26, 1943 New Georgia, Solomon Islands

Captain Donald Kennedy looked at his watch. "At twenty-three hundred hours my native scouts will take your patrol through the channel. Keep your heads down, lads, and be quiet. You'll be under the Japanese guns at Viru."

The Australian officer's laconic accent was muffled in the fetid jungle humidity. The nightly rain had settled into a miserable misty drizzle as the reconnaissance patrol shuffled restlessly in the sodden sand. They were part of two companies that had been put ashore at the clandestine camp at Sego Point, ordered to attack the Japanese at Viru from the land side, to coincide with a seaborne attack on June 28th.

The shadowy figures of the native guides moved soundlessly, readying the stubby outriggers that would carry the Marine Raiders to a point above the Japanese outpost at Viru Harbor, 45 miles above the main objective: the big guns and airfield at Munda Point. They had to take out Viru before the assault on Munda could begin.

The drizzle slowed, then stopped, but the air was so wet it was almost impossible to tell the difference. Imperceptibly the sky began to break up and the brightest of the stars became weakly visible. A pale, milky three-quarter moon swam in and out of the hazy clouds.

"We're ready to push off, men," Sergeant Hodges said quietly. "Chase, you'll be with Begay and the radio equipment. We'll dig in and radio our position as soon as we find out something. Now, let's move out."

"Hey, Sarge. Are these guys really headhunters?" a wide-eyed private whispered hoarsely.

The sergeant grinned. "That's what the captain says. They take your head, shrink it, then pop it down. Like a grape."

The boy stared at a husky native, whose wide mouth split in an affable grin showing a dazzling set of brilliant white teeth.

The private reflexively gripped his M-1. "Jesus."

The rest of the men laughed uneasily.

Chase and Begay strapped the radio to their backs. It was a routine they had gone through many times before.

They were an unlikely team. Corporal Cabot William Walker Chase was the scion of an august Boston family. He had enlisted in the Marines from Harvard Medical School early in the war, afraid his family might pull strings and keep him from the adventure of the century. Corporal Nicholas Begay was a reservation sheep camp Navajo Indian recruited to an elite band of *code-talkers*.

Nicholas didn't talk much about his training, but after long discussions during the endless, inevitable waits of war, Cabot pieced together a sketchy background of his friend. The codes that he broadcast were based on the complex and guttural Navajo language. Nicholas had been sent to Fort Defiance on the Navajo Reservation, a relic of the old Indian

Wars that served as a government administrative center for the Bureau of Indian Affairs. Navajo men were trained in the codes there, then dispersed to the South Pacific. Cabot had listened with fascination as Nicholas would direct gun barrages and call bombsight coordinates to another of his tribe in the strange nasalaties, glottal stops, clicks, and rhythms of his impenetrable language.

Cabot had asked about the codes once, but Nicholas had answered, his hawk-like face expressionless, "The Japs ain't caught on yet, but if they do, you don't want to know."

In the company Cabot Chase was called "Doc." Nicholas was known as "Ears."

The outriggers moved silently away from shore and the men crouched tensely, not speaking, warned their voices would carry over water. Cabot glanced over at Nicholas from time to time. They were all nervous, but he knew his friend hated to be outside after dark, like all Navajos afraid of the ghosts and witches who stalked the unwary at night. And as for being on the water, it was totally out of his experience in the dry and rocky land in which he'd been raised. Nicholas caught his glance and smiled wanly.

The stocky natives beached the outriggers a couple of miles east of Viru and the Marines scrambled ashore, anxious to be off the vulnerable coast. It was midnight. They had thirty hours to get inland behind the Japanese installation—twelve miles through a matted jungle, obstructed by vines and creepers so dense you might lose sight of your buddy five feet away. Or imagine things that weren't there. Or, more dangerous still, miss things that were.

Cabot had thought the tropical forest was exotic and beautiful when he'd first seen it on Guadalcanal. He'd been enchanted with its brilliant birds, butterflies, and dazzling flowers. Now he despised it. The earth stank. It rotted. It clung and clutched at you, its fauna stung and chewed and bit, burrowed and crawled on human flesh. Awful, outsize creatures: venomous snakes as big around as a man's arm; spiders as big as dinner plates; huge, pale scorpions; giant centipedes with their poisonous footprints; leeches; crocodiles; the silent parasites, fungi, molds. Thick, disease-carrying clouds of mosquitoes. He loathed the jungle's debilitating diseases: malaria, dysentery, skin ulcers, dengue fever. Any one of dozens of filthy fevers. He shuddered with dread as they began to fight their way through the clinging, seething growth, the life force gone berserk.

After a night of anxious rest stops they plowed through mangrove swamps that sucked at their boots, crossing and re-crossing a scummy, meandering river, heaving each other out of the viscous, sometimes chin-deep water time and time again.

Their unit surprised a small Japanese patrol only moments before they would have been surprised themselves. It was a sharp, vicious fight with a touch of panic. Cabot had never seen hand-to-hand combat before and he lashed out blindly with his bayonet, surprised at the sound a Japanese made when the blade sank into his gut. Nicholas was calmer, ever protective of his radio equipment. At the end of the skirmish the patrol moved uneasily. Cabot wondered if they had killed them all. In the thickets of green murk it was impossible to be sure.

By twilight of the second day Cabot and Nicholas were on a ridge with a good view of the harbor. Exhausted, they dug in and opened cans of C-rations, ate scraps of cheese and chocolate bars.

"I'm so tired I don't care if a Nip cuts my throat while I sleep," Cabot groaned. "Wake me up, Ears, when the fun starts."

He settled into his ditch along with Nicholas, who grunted in agreement, still tinkering with his radio. Nicholas would be directing the destroyers' big guns in the morning. If the destroyers got into the channel.

Cabot was awakened by an unearthly crunching sound. He cautiously opened his eyes. Nicholas leaned against the other side of the foxhole, staring out into the black jungle, his Indian face impassive in an eerie glow.

"What the hell is that noise," Cabot whispered.

"Land crabs," Nicholas answered. "Big fellas, I understand. They tunnel through the sand."

"Jesus, what an awful sound. How do you know about land crabs? They have 'em on the reservation?"

"Nah. Not like these. Not sand like this either. Navajo sand is dry. It moves around, man. Blows up from Window Rock, maybe, then over to Chinle and down to Ganado. The dirt does, too. But we don't have all that much dirt. Just enough to grow grass for the sheep. What we got is rocks. Big, beautiful, solid rocks. Oh, we got trees, up in the mountains. Juniper, pinon. Cottonwoods, aspens along the creeks. The grass on the prairies. But it's mostly rocks, all in the prettiest colors you ever seen. It's clean there. So clean. It smells so good. And you can see for miles and miles and miles."

Nicholas looked inward at his revered homeland. A night bird screeched, counterpoint to the constant breeps, whines, and hums of the teeming insects.

"You know about land crabs. What's that spooky glow? There. Over there."

"Rotting log. Phosphorescence. God, Doc. I hate this place. Everything is decaying, dying here. I got to get home soon as this war is over. I got to. I got to dry out. Clean this stink out of my lungs. Even the stars are wrong."

Cabot knew of his friend's dread of dying away from his

homeland. It had nothing to do with the ingrained Navajo fear of death and dying. He knew Nicholas had courage. He'd explained to Cabot what it meant to a Navajo to be a warrior. To be a warrior was to be as the Twin Sons of Changing Woman, who slew the monsters that endangered his people in the ancient legends. But to die away from Dinetah, as he called his land, he would not have the ceremonies. It would mean he might return as a ghost to do evil.

"Ah, you'll get there," he said, wanting to reassure Nicholas. "Tell me again about Laura. Always helps to talk about a woman." They'd both told each other their stories many times on these endless waits in the darkness.

Nicholas grinned and settled back. "Laura. Well, we've known each other all our lives. She's beautiful. I guess she always was, only I just got to noticing it right before I had to go. We'll get married when I get back. When we found out I was being deployed to the Pacific, we both broke down and cried." He stopped and grinned. "You lookin' at me funny 'cause you think Indians are taught not to cry? That's only in the movies. Indians cry like everybody else."

"I wasn't, Ears. Honest."

"Well, all right then. Anyway, Laura was in nurses' training at the Public Health Hospital in Fort Defiance. She didn't tell me when she up and joined the army. Wanted it to be a surprise. They told her she'd most likely be sent to Guam, then we'd maybe get to see each other sometimes." He snorted. "But, typical government screw-up, they sent her to Europe. Get a letter every month or so, if I'm lucky. And she writes every day she can. Like I do." He looked off into the night. "Don't know if my letters ever get through."

"Sure they do, Nick. Tell her the next time you write you're going to bring me along to be best man. Tell her she'll like me a lot. Tell her I'm a relative."

This was an old joke between them. They'd often remarked that though Cabot's hair was a true red, and Nicholas's was very dark auburn, their eyes were remarkably the same odd gold.

At first Cabot had teased Nicholas. "You gotta be a half-breed, right?"

Nicholas had been testy at first, but then he answered, "I guess we got a white man somewhere back. Maybe one with red hair, like you. Say, you ever have a relative come out to Arizona, mistreat the Indians?"

The idea intrigued them and they played around with it on the long nights. After the war, Cabot said maybe they'd find out.

June 28, 1943 Viru

All eyes swept the harbor continually. And then, ghostlike, the two destroyers emerged in the misty morning half-light, gray and menacing.

Orange flashes signaled the first salvos, and in seconds the heavy thump of the hits reached the Marines. Nicholas connected with the radios on the ships. He began the strange coded messages that directed the naval gunfire as Cabot and the sergeant followed the barrage, scanning the Japanese installation with field glasses.

The coastal guns began firing, but the destroyers stayed out of range as they pounded Viru. A flotilla of supply ships appeared in back of the destroyers, carrying the two infantry companies ready to mop up what the Navy and the Marines had begun. Except the rest of the two companies of Marine Raiders hadn't arrived yet, bogged down in the miasmic jungle.

The Japanese soon realized there was a radio above them directing the destroyers' fire and turned the guns landward.

"Here we go, Doc. Keep your head down. The Japs know we're here."

The young private crept up. "The first platoon is here, sergeant." he whispered. "They got to be briefed. The others are about twenty minutes behind."

The sergeant signaled Cabot to take over as spotter, and crouching low, followed the private into the underbrush. A large explosion shook the ground under them. Another sounded farther away.

The morning passed, the artillery ebbing and flowing. Viru was a haze of smoky fires. The Marine Raiders prepared for their assault as the infantry readied the landing craft offshore.

The Japanese, not expecting a full attack from the rear, began retreating, running squarely into the advancing Marines. Gunfire became so general it was impossible to tell who was where.

Nicholas continued to direct the destroyers' fire as the landing craft advanced toward shore. As soon as they landed, the destroyers would leave and the battle would belong to the Army and the Marines.

"They're almost ashore, Ears. We'll be packing up in a minute."

There was the whine of a sniper's bullet. Cabot dropped the glasses and whirled, fumbling with his M-l. Nicholas was firing wildly into a tangle of ropy vines. There was a grunt and a Japanese tumbled from the green web of creepers.

Cabot's heart was crashing in his chest, his eyes straining to penetrate the undergrowth.

"You okay, Ears?" He glanced down.

Nicholas was slumped over his radio, a ragged hole in his throat, the severed carotid artery pumping his life away in gushes of blood.

"Ears? Oh, my God, Nick?"

Cabot fell to his knees and tried to staunch the river of red, desperate to save his friend. "It's not so bad, Nick. Don't you worry. You just take it easy for a minute. It'll be fine. Hey, I'm almost a doctor, remember? It's just a scratch."

Hot bright blood spread through his fingers.

Nicholas turned his head and tried to smile, then slumped against Cabot's chest.

Cabot clung to him, not believing, rocking Nicholas gently.

The sergeant appeared.

"Jesus, they got Ears?" The man kicked impotently at a thick creeper. "Shit. Oh, shit, shit, shit." He looked to the shore. "Doc. You got to leave him, Doc. The destroyers are leaving. The grunts has landed. We're moving in."

Cabot raised his agonized face to the sergeant. "He's got to go back to his Dinetah. He has to."

"He will, Doc."

Cabot's eyes blurred. "I'll make it up to you, Nick," he wept. "He saved my life, Sarge. I'd be dead if it wasn't for Nick."

The sergeant eased his hands away from Nicholas. "He was a good man. The best. Now we gotta go, corporal. Please, Doc."

Cabot carefully laid Nicholas down. Black flies were already attracted by the blood. He began to disassemble the radio.

The sergeant turned to go, then turned back and his voice was rough. "Doc, maybe we all got a Dinny-tah."

Chapter One

March, 1992, Marblehead, Massachusetts

"We made a bargain, Lily," Cabot Chase said quietly. "I'll hold you to it." He watched his granddaughter struggle to suppress her bitterness at what she considered an unreasonable demand. An unwelcome blip in her heretofore uninterrupted plans.

Rain ticked against the long windows in the gloomy late afternoon light, making rivulets that zigzagged down the leaded diamond panes. Lily Cabot Chase toyed with the stem of the sherry glass. The small fire, lit against the damp spring chill, threw small darts of light through the spirals of her dense thicket of coppery hair.

"I didn't think you'd make me go in the end, since you knew how reluctant I was. Am." she said unhappily.

"I've never hidden the reasons from you. You know that. You might not agree with them, or like them, but you knew from the outset, and you agreed."

"Oh, yes. 'My dear Lily,'" she sing-songed. "'You look at medicine as an intellectual challenge rather than a compassionate calling. Not good in a doctor. You don't look beyond the problem to the person who is sick. You've never been very patient with the weak. A year on the Navajo reservation with truly needing people will temper you.' Temper me! As if I needed tempering after the life I've spent with Mother and Daddy."

"I know you've been more parent than child to Ben and Mariella. I've asked myself a thousand times and more where I could have headed off Ben's woolly-headedness. The only thing I could do was bring you here with me when they went too far afield."

"Too far afield? Too spaced-out, you mean."

"It was a difficult time for that generation."

"It was a difficult time for your generation," she said, with exasperation tingeing her voice with resentment. "Mine as well. You turned out okay and I'm coping pretty well."

"Still, there were stresses...unprecedented..."

"My parents are self-indulgent cop-outs."

"I'm not disagreeing with you. Ben's my son, my only child. I daresay he's been a bigger disappointment to me than he has even to you."

"Well, at least they're into 'My body is my temple' macrobiotic mumbo jumbo instead of jumping into every new reality-altering substance that came down the ashram," she said, giving in slightly as she sensed a sorrow in her grandfather she had not felt before. She smiled ruefully. "Why, if the reservation gets too heavy for me, I can even scoot over to their crystals-cum-rice polish-cum-Tarot card shop in Sedona and experience a harmonic convergence, whatever that is. I wonder if Daddy still has a ring in his middle-aged nose."

"Lily, don't wear yourself out trying to compensate for their unwillingness to face responsibility. I'm afraid that's what medicine means to you."

"Grandfather, all I want to be is a first-rate surgeon. It will be hard enough as a woman. Even today women are at a disadvantage in the surgical fields. But I won't be. I won't be discounted. I'll be one of the best. I'm so close. What I don't need is a year wasted out in some dusty, sun-baked hospital in the middle of nowhere on an Indian reservation just because you had an epiphany there after the war."

His fingers tightened on his martini glass, but he said mildly, "I know you'll be the best, Lily. I also want to have the feeling it matters to you if your patients survive your care."

"That's not fair."

"Maybe. Six years ago you conceded I might have a point and you agreed to my condition...grudgingly, I'll admit. I offered to pay for your Harvard Med tuition. All I asked was this one thing. A year isn't going to lose you anything. And it might gain you a great deal."

He watched the wave of impatience that swept over his granddaughter's face before she spoke.

"Just because you fell in love with some gorgeous Indian woman and then felt guilty that you walked away from her and married grandmother, you insist on sending me off to work with the noble savage just to plump up your conscience."

His voice tensed with anger. "Now you're not being fair." He walked over to a dark, polished sideboard and refilled his cocktail glass from a crystal pitcher. He studied the cold gin and vermouth, picked up a dark bottle and turned. "Or maybe you are."

He came back to his granddaughter and carefully poured a gold Spanish sherry into her glass. "All I know is I want you to go there. I know it will be good for you. And you may not like it. You may refuse to do it. But we made a deal that I would pay for your schooling as far as you wanted to take it. All I asked of you was a year with the Navajo. That was the deal. I thought that was fair and you said you did, too. I will be very disappointed if you now walk away from that obligation to me."

She swirled the sherry gently and he watched it catch the firelight.

Without touching it she set it on a table. "Oh, you know I won't. I'm not that dishonest." She smiled. "But you probably knew I'd make a last ditch struggle not to go."

Cabot Chase relented and chuckled. "I did."

Lily walked over to a well-used leather sofa and picked up a tan Burberry thrown across the back. "Now I've got to get back into town. Larimer's taking me to a reception at the Gardner Museum. Then I'm on duty at the hospital for the rest of the week. Payback time for playing hooky today."

"I suppose Larimer thinks I'm an autocratic old tyrant sending his fiancée to the end of the earth."

"Better you don't ask. But you can imagine how much a Boston banker thinks of his almost-but-not-quite-made-up-her-mind-yet fiancée going to an Indian reservation. He doesn't think of you as an autocratic old tyrant. He thinks you're insane."

Cabot Chase set his drink down. He crossed to her and put a hand on her shoulder. "I know how busy you are. Thanks for coming out to Marblehead this afternoon. We needed to talk. Your internship is up the first of June. They'll be expecting your confirmation letter in Fort Defiance." He raised his hand and brushed his thumb under her chin. "Are we still friends?"

Lily looked up, then put her arms around him. "Of course, we're still friends," she said into the fine English wool of his dark suit. "But I'm not sorry I tried to weasel out of the deal. I would always wonder if I could have beaten you down. You're a hard man, Cabot Double W Chase."

He laughed at the name she'd called him from childhood and patted the springy mass of curls. "I love you, Lily. I know you won't regret this. I know it." He looked down into the gold-hazel eyes the color of his own.

She smiled and gave him a small hug. "And when am I going to get you to stop calling me Lily? I use my middle name now."

"Cabot? I sound like I'm talking to myself. Can't understand you girls now, wanting men's names."

She looked up, made a face and patted his cheek. "And I'm not a girl."

Lily Cabot Chase left the dark paneled library.

Cabot went back to the sideboard and emptied the martini pitcher into his glass. He hesitated, then drained the glass. Preoccupied, he walked over to the rain-streaked window and gazed at the darkening garden below, then raised unseeing eyes to the gray choppy waters of Massachusetts Bay.

It was almost fifty years ago and he remembered it as if it were yesterday.

Nearly an hour later, Cabot Chase realized he was staring at his fractured reflection in the diamond windowpanes. It was now fully dark, the garden and the ocean swallowed up in the black, rainy evening. He looked at himself carefully. Had he repaid Nicholas for saving his life? Had he even needed to? He'd thought so at the time. He remembered when the idea occurred to him. He hadn't been back in medical school long. A few months at most. He had recalled a conversation with

Nicholas, one of the hundreds they'd had to kill the endless hours of waiting in chowlines, on troop ships, in foxholes. Nicholas was talking about life on the reservation. He told Cabot how his mother had lost one of his infant brothers in childbirth and when Cabot questioned him further, Nicholas just shrugged.

"Well, there wasn't any doctor to come. Don't have many on the reservation and they're spread pretty thin. My mother was afraid of the hospital. The women, the medicine man, they tried their best, but...well, it happens."

Nicholas looked uncomfortable, then said, "Ah, Doc. You must think I'm pretty primitive. Right? But our ways have been with us for a thousand years. Longer. Change will come, but it'll be slow. Us guys who have been in the service, we'll bring back new ideas.

"Me and my friends, Laura too, graduated from the Indian School in Phoenix. We hated having to go to boarding school, all of us did. But they came and got us, the government did. Now I know it probably was a good thing. Education is the only way for the Indians. When the Navajo signed the peace treaty in 1868, we were promised a teacher for every thirty children. The government never lived up to that." He was quiet for a moment. "I'm going to college, I swear. Law school maybe. I'll learn how to make the government live up to the promises. Others will, too. Then we'll use the hospitals, and the doctors. Hell, we'll even *be* doctors." He laughed. "Whatta ya think, Doc? Maybe I'll go to medical school instead. What do you think of that? Would they let an Indian into Harvard Medical School?"

The idea had struck Nicholas as being outrageously funny and he'd roared with laughter, but Cabot hadn't thought it was funny. He wanted to pursue the idea, but they'd had to move out and the subject wasn't brought up again.

There had been Sego Point. Then Viru.

After the wrenching experiences of war Cabot had some bad moments trying to settle into being a medical student again. There was an air of unreality about the whole thing that stayed with him for months. He'd be sitting in a classroom taking notes, then zero in on his clean, cared-for hand, and memories would flood back to when that hand was filthy. And bloody.

A lot of the other veterans felt the same way. They'd all seen too much, their innocence and idealism tempered with the brutish things they'd seen. And done.

It had hardly occurred to Cabot until his conversations with Nicholas that all Americans were not within easy reach of medical attention. Maybe it was simply that he had survived the terrible war when so many hadn't that had made his sense of obligation to the Navajo who had saved his life so persistent. Vague at first, his plans to go west began to form. His parents had been aghast at the idea, anxious now that he take his place in the continuing line of distinguished Boston physicians. His father had been so shattered when Cabot didn't want to join his practice after his residency that Cabot promised he would come back to Boston in three years.

And so he'd begun his medical career at the Public Health Service Hospital in Fort Defiance on the Navajo Indian Reservation. And met Laura.

Chapter Two

June 14, 1992 Route 40

The blue Porsche convertible sped westward down the straight arrow of Interstate 40 as it cut through the ripening wheat fields past St. Louis. The car had been a gift from her grandfather when Cabot was an undergraduate. He told her she'd be better off trading it in on a four-wheel-drive, or at least a pickup truck, now that she would be driving on the reservation, but she dismissed the idea. How bad could the roads be in Fort Defiance? She wasn't going to be driving off main roads. That hadn't been part of the deal. She'd practice medicine for a year, work hard at the hospital, learning everything she could, then she would leave. Period. She had her surgical residency waiting for her at Johns Hopkins. She would get back to her life.

Thoughts of Larimer intruded. Larimer Madison, who wanted to marry her.

"Really, Cabot," he'd said. "I can't imagine what you're

thinking of, taking this wild scheme of your grandfather's seriously. Going to some backwater nothing hospital in the back of nowhere in the middle of a band of Indians. A reservation! My God. You've had the finest medical education in the world, interned at one of the best hospitals in the country. Who will want you after you've thrown away a year of your professional career treating a bunch of savages for God-knows-whatever primitive afflictions they're prone to. You must let me talk to your grandfather. I'm sure I can dissuade him of this folly."

The picture of Larimer up against her grandfather made her smile. "Get over it, Larimer. I've got to go."

"You're mad. Stark, staring mad. And so is that grandfather of yours. Why, not only that, it's dangerous. I can't imagine he'd jeopardize your safety."

"They haven't scalped anybody in a hundred and fifty years, Larimer," she said dryly. "And a year of altruism hardly disqualifies me from the medical profession. I still have my place at Johns Hopkins next year."

"Why don't you simply refuse? He'd get over it."

"The Chases don't renege on promises, Larimer. They also don't get over broken promises. Besides, I've got a conscience." She smiled crookedly. "Yes, I have a conscience, but apparently I have no heart. That's why Grandfather wants me to go. I will find my heart there, he says. Like the tin man."

Larimer groaned and pulled her close. "No, you don't have a heart, or you'd let me get you a ring and promise me when you'll marry me."

She'd danced away from the issue again. To be honest with herself, her year with the Navajo had actually been a good excuse to put Larimer off about marrying him. Which she wasn't sure she wanted to do. Not yet anyway. Oh, she probably would in the end. Wasn't he the calm, dependable, conventional man she'd planned for after experiencing the shambling waste of her parents' lives, chasing their gauzy rainbows? Seeing their dreams in smoke. Silly, useless, aging flower children. Larimer was steady, good-looking, polished. Though he was older, they liked the same things. He wanted her to succeed as a surgeon and would ease her way as much as he could. He was perfect for her.

Yes. He was perfect. Yes. But a life partner would have to wait. There would be time enough for all that in a year or two. Or three.

Cabot and the sleek blue car sped across the monotonous expanse of Oklahoma, dotted with black, crouching oil wells, like mantises rhythmically dipping to feed in the yellow, hot earth of the plains, shimmering in the early summer sun.

She didn't think she'd ever seen a bleaker stretch than the Texas panhandle. She roared through Amarillo, hardly noticed when she crossed into New Mexico. She stopped for gas in Tucumcari and put fifty cents in a beat-up cooler for a Diet Coke. She pulled the tab and took a quick swallow. It was glacially cold and made her eyes water. When they cleared she looked around and realized she was *west*.

Weather-beaten men in blue jeans and cowboy hats stood around the station, their dusty trucks sat at the pumps or stood yawning with their hoods up in the greasy garage. A tinny, country-western lament wailed its tale of heartbreak from somewhere in the back of a stack of cheap tires. The wind blew, sending a dust devil swirling through the station with gritty debris that stung her face and left a beige film over her car, and she supposed, herself.

As she hung up the nozzle, a large tumbleweed rolled across the road, into the station, and tangled in her legs before lodging itself in the Porsche's front wheels. She looked in dismay at the tiny scratches it left on her shins.

"God, even the bushes are attacking me," she muttered.

Cabot ignored the stares of the men while she signed the credit slip. She was six feet tall and, with her cascade of crinkly red hair, was used to being looked at. She bent and pulled the tumbleweed free. While she cleaned the windshield of the car, one of the younger cowboy types sidled over and leaned against the pump with the supreme self-confidence cowboy boots seemingly bred.

"How fast you go in that car there?" He switched a toothpick from one side of his mouth to the other.

He had bright blue eyes and an open smile, so Cabot suppressed her irritation and tried not to snap. "A hundred and thirty if I'm not in a hurry," she said as she slid under the wheel. She winked and squealed the tires as she shot back onto the access road to the Interstate.

Somehow the exchange depressed her. "My God, I suppose that passes for witty repartee in this part of the country. However will I survive a year here?" she pleaded with the blue sky. "They're all so *sunburned.*"

The dead flat landscape began to change and Cabot looked ahead with grudging admiration as red sandstone rock formations began to appear, then beyond Albuquerque, the humps of the Sandia Mountains. New England never looked like this. Wind-eroded spires, cave-pocked mesas glowed against a sky so intensely blue its very molecules swam in her eyes. It was a wild and unforgiving landscape that shimmered in a remorseless sun.

She stopped at a gas station in Gallup to ask for directions to the turn-off to Window Rock and Fort Defiance. A middle-aged Indian man came out of the garage, wiping his hands on an oily rag. Cabot told him to fill the tank and went to the Coke machine. She couldn't get enough to drink in the clear, dry air. She felt her cheek. It felt gritty, hot, and dry. The skin would definitely have to be taken care of in this withering climate, she thought. Bleakly, she hoped they sold moisturizer in Fort Defiance. Would they even know what it was?

A pair of small, wide-eyed Indian children peeped around the Coke machine, giggled shyly and held out some beaded trinkets. Cabot had been an only child. She had no idea how to behave with small children. It had been her experience that the most efficacious way to deal with them was to pay them off as quickly as possible with what they wanted and hope they would go away. With great ceremony she solemnly selected a key ring and gave them four dollars. They gasped at this largesse and, emboldened by her lack of sales resistance, ran into the station and brought out several pieces of silver and turquoise jewelry. She was about to smile and shake her head, but her eye was caught by a wide bracelet, set with three large, veined, irregular stones of a soft, greenish blue. It was similar to one her grandfather occasionally wore. He called it a *ketoh*, formerly worn by Indian men to protect the wrist from the snap of a bowstring, but later popular as simple adornment.

The Indian man, seeing her interest, came over. "Hope the grandkids aren't bothering you." He indicated the bracelet. "It's a nice piece. My son's a silversmith. The turquoise is real good. Comes from Morenci. Southern Arizona. Some of the best comes from the mines there."

"The markings are interesting."

"Spiderweb turquoise. Those reddish lines there are hematite. That's an iron oxide." The man wiped his hands again and traced his horny finger across the surface of the stone. "The more yellowish ones are limonite, a hydrated iron oxide."

Cabot concealed her surprise. "You're very knowledgeable."

"Did some silverwork myself, but decided I liked working with engines better."

"My grandfather has a bracelet very similar to this. It's Navajo, I'm sure. He worked at the Fort Defiance Hospital forty years ago. When he finished medical school after the war. World War II." she added.

Cabot turned the bracelet over in her hand, liking the slippery warm feel of the silver. She turned it over onto her wrist. "How much is it?"

"Three hundred and fifty."

"Can you put it on a credit card?"

"Sure can."

While he was writing the sales slip, he asked, "What was your grandfather's name?"

"He was a doctor. Cabot Chase."

"I remember him. He used to bring his vehicles in here. Had a red Chevy convertible for awhile, but he got a truck then. Roads of the Rez can beat up a car."

"The Rez?"

"Oh, that's what we call the Navajo Reservation around here."

"That's amazing you'd remember him from that long ago."

"Well, we got to be kind of friends. We were both in the war. In the Pacific. We'd go out and get a beer sometimes and tell war stories. He'd had a buddy killed that had been a friend of mine, another codetalker." The man was silent a moment, looking back. Then he turned to Cabot. "So you're his granddaughter. You just visitin' here?"

"No. I'm a doctor. I'm going to work at the hospital in Fort Defiance, too."

"Well, now, how about that. You come back and get your car fixed here then. I do good work, though it might take some doin' gettin' parts for that fancy car."

"Well, I won't be driving it hard."

"You go anywhere on the reservation, you'll be driving it hard." A squeal made him turn. "Hey, you kids get outta that car."

The two children, a girl about five and a boy about four, had insinuated themselves silently into the convertible and were ecstatically working the steering wheel, eyes glowing at the miracle of being in the sleek car.

Cabot smiled. "It's fine. They're not hurting anything." She signed the charge slip. "This isn't the reservation yet, is it?"

"No. Not far, though. Take a right at the next light. You'll run into the road to Window Rock. It's divided highway all the way. Three, four miles from Window Rock to Fort Defiance. You'll be there shy an hour."

"Thank you. Tell your son I really like the bracelet."

"I'll do that. His name is Emerson Yazzie, so you'll know. Your piece'll be signed on the back."

Cabot opened the car door and the children slid out reluctantly.

She started to get in, then turned back. "I'm Cabot Chase, same as my grandfather. And I'll remember about the car."

He pointed to a sign over the garage door. "Marcus Yazzie. Best mechanic between Albuquerque and Flagstaff."

As she drove away she glanced in the rearview mirror. The children were waving goodbye. She waved back, feeling better than she had for weeks. Maybe it wouldn't be so bad here. The Indian man didn't seem at all alien. He was very nice, as a matter of fact. Friendly. She hadn't expected that. Dour, that was the word that always came to mind when she thought about Indians. Always mad at the white man. Her grandfather had tried to convince her that the Navajo were friendly, funny, and very witty. She hadn't believed him.

She touched the bracelet. She really shouldn't have gotten it. It was too much to spend. The impulse had struck her so quickly. She wasn't usually so impetuous.

Cabot smiled. "Shut up Grandfather. It's just one bracelet."

Chapter Three

TÁÁ'NÁAZNILÍ' TÁÁ'

March, 1852, New Mexico Territory

Daago suppressed a giggle as she peeped through a small chink in the mud plaster of the hogan. She watched her Uncle Chii surreptitiously adjust himself under his breechcloth. She knew why he was uncomfortable. She'd just seen Hanabah dart from behind a tree and slip- her hand playfully under the small leather square that covered her uncle's private parts. Really! Hanabah was her friend, but even so, Hanabah was shameless. You weren't supposed to even think those kinds of thoughts about a man in your clan. She knew that a lot of girls thought about her handsome Uncle Chii that way, though, and that it made his wife furious.

A girl wasn't supposed to be spying on the men's council, either, but if the men decided to go raiding, there would be a

Squaw Dance after they returned, and she would get to meet a boy from another clan, and she could think those kinds of thoughts which seemed to occupy her more and more since her coming-of-age *kinaalda*. Daago simply had to know what they decided. And it wasn't as if she were spying on somebody else's house. This was where she lived. Manases, her father, had called the meeting tonight.

The men gradually filled the hogan, the firelight glinting off copper, ropy, lanolin-glossy thighs, as they hunkered down for the meeting. A long, reddish clay pipe was passed from man to man.

Chii beat a tattoo on a small hide drum to quiet the council. "Manases will speak," Chii said.

"We need horses and women," the headman intoned, giving weight to the severity of the situation.

The fire and tobacco smoke had turned the interior of the hogan into a stifling, eye-searing oven made pungent with the reek of men and sheep.

There was a low rumble as the warriors of the tribe nodded, a sheen of perspiration sharpening the shadows of each bronze, firelit face.

Ute and Mexican raiding parties had carried off many of their women and decimated their herds of horses and sheep. Their own raids had not replenished their losses. They would have to become more aggressive or risk being overrun.

"We are surrounded by enemies," Manases went on. Tall, even for a Navajo, he was their headman, leader of their clan. "We must grow. If we become strong, we can lead the Dineh against those who strike against us. We must have many children. Each man must have at least two wives. Our girls must marry as soon as they begin to bleed. Only by increasing our numbers can we grow in power and defy the Mexicans and the Americans and the tribes they use against us."

Each man was given his chance to speak. Manases glanced around the ring of somber faces, inviting comment.

"I agree with you, Manases. We must go farther than we have in the past. It will be dangerous. But we have no choice in the matter now," a solemn young warrior spoke and struck the ground with the flat of his hand for emphasis.

"We must go all the way to the Rio Grande, to the Mexican *rancherias*, where there are many horses, many women," Manases said, knowing the peril involved in the scope of his proposed plans. The wealthy *rancherias* nearby were well-guarded. They had lost too many men to their guns. They would have to go where they were not expected. Away from the protection of the United States Army at Fort Fauntleroy and the new Fort Defiance.

There was a murmur among the men as they squatted around the small, dying fire in Manases' large hogan. To go as far as the Rio Grande would be a dangerous undertaking. It would take over a month to get there and longer to get back if their raids were successful. Captive women were devilishly hard to transport if they were to be brought back in good condition, ready for childbearing and fieldwork. And it would be a long time to leave the camp only lightly guarded, their women and herds vulnerable to attacks from neighboring tribes. And the Mexicans and Americans. In 1852, a Navajo woman would bring two hundred dollars or more on the slave market, a child somewhat less. Horses were even more a source of ready money, in dollars or pesos.

"It is still early to move up to the summer camps, but it will be safer for our families and herds. They will be protected in the mountains. Lookouts can be posted to warn of marauders. It is best we go now. We will be less expected to make a major raid while there is still danger of snow."

It was necessary for a Navajo council to be unanimous, so each man was heard, each had an opportunity to express his doubts, but in the end, Manases' decision stood. The men of the Todachiinii clan would go raiding for horses and women on the Rio Grande *rancherias*--six hundred hard, dangerous miles across the *Malpais,* the rugged, inhospitable badlands to the southeast.

They would leave the day after tomorrow.

The tempo of the village intensified. More arrows had to be made, knives sharpened, bowstrings tightened. And then, there were the rituals to be performed. The medicine man asked the gods for the success of the raid—the gods of the bears, snakes, thunder, winds. The powerful deities of the East, West, North, and South were enlisted, with offerings of corn pollen. The men who were to go on the raiding party cleansed themselves in sweat lodges, where, in the searing heat they sang the sacred songs of purification to make their journey acceptable to the gods.

The party left before dawn. Before each man mounted his horse, he threw a small offering of turquoise or white shell into the sacred spring in a clearing near the village, then with his shout, his horse reared and he thundered out of the sheltered valley he might never see again.

When the last man had gone, the women and those men too young or old to go turned with heavy hearts to the business of moving the camp to the hidden valleys of the Chuska Mountains, some of them still deep in snow.

* * *

Daago sat on a small rise absently watching the sheep daintily cropping the small shoots of grass that were springing up under the melting snow. Several lambs had already been born, and many of the ewes were ready to drop. It wasn't a large herd, but her family's was bigger than most. Raiding Utes and Mexicans had taken a heavy toll and everyone hoped the men would bring back a few sheep at least from the Rio Grande, as well as horses and women. A goat or two would be nice.

The girl stretched and yawned. The sun was deliciously warm, though the mountain air still had a bite. Daago slipped her brightly-colored shawl off her shoulders and let her mind play on the scenes ahead when the men came back. After contact with the outside world, there would have to be ceremony to purify the men who might be contaminated with evil spirits. They had asked a neighboring clan to help in the performance of the Enemyway Ritual.

What set Daago to daydreaming was the Squaw Dance that always accompanied the Enemyway Ritual. The Navajo lived isolated lives and looked forward eagerly to all occasions to socialize. Marriage was forbidden within one's clan, so ceremonies served as meeting places for young people of different clans. Daago had had her *kinaalda*, her elaborate puberty ceremony, late last autumn. She was now eligible for marriage, but in the hard winter months she had had no chance to meet a young man from another clan and any interest in members of her own clan was forbidden.

She sighed. She knew she would be a highly desirable prospect. She was the daughter of Manases and she would bring a fine dowry of blankets, horses, and sheep. Daago tried to suppress the thoughts that she was pretty. It wasn't nice to be vain. It wasn't proper to think of oneself as better than someone else. But she had seen herself in the glitter of the sacred pool. She had seen her heavy hair gleam with bluish highlights, seen her large, black-fringed eyes, high cheekbones, and pointed, dimpled chin.

She opened her eyes and languidly held up a slim arm and wiggled narrow, tapered fingers. She glanced around. Of course, there was no one else anywhere near, but she was self-conscious about looking at herself. She inched her skirt over her knees and looked at her long, smooth legs.

Daago cupped her hands under her breasts. Yes, they were plumper than they were last week. She was sure of it. That meant they were still growing. Daago wanted large breasts because she noticed that the men always looked at the women with large breasts, even when they were nursing their babies and men weren't supposed to notice. Yes, she would have big breasts and at the Squaw Dance the men would look at her. Her toes curled inside her moccasins. She was nice to look at, really better than Hanabah. Who was pretty, too, of course.

Surely there would be a handsome young man of the Deeschiinii Clan who would smile at her when she asked him to dance. What would he give her when the dance was over? A piece of turquoise? That would be best. Yes, much the best. Although if he were special, anything would do. Even a piece of colored yarn.

Daago shivered, though not from the chilly air. She pulled her skirt back down over her legs and stood. It was time to take the sheep back to the camp for the night. She made a small, clicking sound in her throat that aroused the black and white dog on the periphery of the herd. The two of them began to move the flock down to camp and the brush corral that sheltered the sheep after dark.

Chapter Four

June 14, 1992 Navajo Reservation

The road was good and there wasn't much traffic, just an occasional pickup truck. There were mountains always in the distance, rocky outcrops of colorful sandstones that faded to grays, then silvers, before they vanished over the far-off horizon. Nearer, it was rutted, scrubby juniper and pinon-dotted landscape—the windswept Defiance Plateau stretching empty and vast to either side of the road.

The good feeling Cabot had after her short encounter with Marcus Yazzie and his grandchildren evaporated in the clear, dry air that whipped around, tangling her hair. Huge haystack-shaped rock formations appeared and a sign announced she was in Window Rock. Window Rock? This was the Navajo Nation's capital? Her eyes swept over the town. Everything seemed so...so *scattered*. A few buildings here and there, a couple of gas stations, a small shopping center. Down another road, in the distance, more buildings with a couple of flags flying that were apparently the administration center. Away, in the other direction, there was what looked like a school. Judging by the stadium it was probably a high school.

There was a small sign that pointed to Fort Defiance. She passed a pre-fab sort of building that announced itself as the police station. It looked deserted and tumbleweeds bunched against a neatly trimmed privet hedge, the only effort at formal landscaping in evidence.

The Window Rock citizens seemed to live in what looked like trailers over the surrounding hills in isolated groups unrelated to the town itself. Cabot reminded herself that the Navajo were not village dwellers like the pueblo tribes, but this seemed so random...unfocussed. Nothing remotely like New England, with its manicured village greens and main streets lined with self-consciously picturesque little shops.

At the faded stop sign by the intersection where the road led to Fort Defiance, a herd of cows grazed undisturbed in the shaggy weeds. Cabot turned and looked into the soft liquid brown eyes of a taffy heifer, her cud moving rhythmically, a bright green grass-foam flecking her peach-colored nose. She swished her tail at a bothersome fly and regarded Cabot serenely. Cabot had never been as close to a bovine as she now was, at the wheel of her sporty blue Porsche. There was a sinking sensation around her stomach and she had never felt so lonely in her life.

Cabot stared at the red sandstone block facade of the Public Health Hospital. A backwater hospital at the ass-end of nowhere. That was what Larimer had said. The hospital appeared through the leaves of great old oak trees that lined a silent street. There were yellow metal railings along the curbs, to discourage parking she supposed, though Cabot couldn't imagine why. There was no traffic. Around the hospital grounds, aging wooden government buildings nestled under the trees in what could only be called natural landscaping. Wild grasses and weeds, some bright yellow flowers grew in profusion, untroubled by mower or hoe.

Cabot saw a parking lot through the trees and pulled in, parking the Porsche between a pick-up and an old blue Pontiac, the first actual car she'd seen since she entered the reservation. A small wooden walk led over a ditch and across a shaggy park toward the hospital.

"I'm nuts. Grandfather, Grandfather, what have you gotten me into?" she muttered as she climbed out of the Porsche and headed for her first look at what would be the center of her life for a year. She waited for a rickety wagon pulled by a lethargic mule team to pass. What looked like a load of firewood teetered precariously at each bump in the dusty, tree-lined street. Cabot gave a hopeful wave to the driver, an old Indian with long silver earrings and a black, stovepipe hat. The man ignored her and she felt rebuffed. A sign of encouragement would have been welcome, she thought morosely.

She crossed the street, then looked back at her car. She wondered if it would be all right. She was sorry she hadn't put the top up and locked it. She made herself turn and walk up to what looked like the main door.

The middle-aged Indian woman behind the desk in the lobby was typing erratically on a battered Underwood, frowning in fierce concentration. Cabot cleared her throat and the woman looked up and cocked her head

"I'm Dr. Cabot Chase. I'm to be on the staff here."

"You the new doctor? 'Bout time. They was expecting

you last week." She looked carefully at Cabot. "Thought you'd be a man."

"Last week? I was very clear when I would arrive. I had to drive across the country." She was dismayed. What a lousy way to begin. She stifled her irritation. Her letter had been quite specific, if they'd read it. She had to assume they could read.

"I get Jane Manyfarms. Dr. Schiller, he's over to Ganado."

"Jane...uh, Manyfarms. She's in charge? Yes, would you get her please?"

Cabot looked around while she waited. There were several Navajos in the sparsely furnished lobby. The chrome and turquoise chairs were fairly new. The walls, she guessed, were an attempt to echo the red sandstone of the building and its surrounding geography. They were rather more a blushy lobster, but they were freshly painted and cheery. Cabot could hear none of the usual undercurrent of hospital noises—intercoms, telephones, the constant hums and clatters of a busy medical facility. A fly buzzed lazily in the rosy atmosphere. The overall ambiance radiated a kind of benign somnolence.

Cabot began to pace, half nervous, half impatient.

"It's all right, Pete. We won't stay long. Russell wanted to hear all about the meeting. You're a medicine man. They'll let you into Intensive Care."

Nicholas Nakai and Pete Price hurried up the steps of the Indian Hospital to pay a surreptitious call on their tribal chairman. One was dressed in a business suit, the older man in a typical navy velvet shirt, blue jeans, and heavy silver and turquoise jewelry.

"I abuse my privileges, they'll keep me out," Pete Price grumbled.

"You have your pouch of corn pollen. If Jane catches us just tell her you're here to say a couple of prayers over the chairman," Nicholas said. "She can't complain about that. Russell will be going out of Intensive Care in the morning anyway and a couple of prayers won't hurt."

"What about you? She'll know you're here on business."

He winked at the older man. "I'll tell her I'm here to pray, too."

At the desk Nicholas gave the receptionist a dazzling smile. "Annie, we're just going to run up to see Russell. We won't stay long. He wants to pray with Pete here. Uh…me, too."

Annie sniffed. "You boys'll do what you want around here, won't matter what I say. Just don't let Jane Manyfarms catch you. Last time you pulled that stuff she be mad as hell. Huh. You'd sure be better off prayin' for yourselves."

Nicholas laughed and the two men started for the elevator. Nicholas stopped and turned. It had suddenly registered that there was a very pretty female with explosive red hair who had watched their exchange at the desk with oblique curiosity. The tan skirt and white shirt were well-cut, looked expensive. She looked edgy and out of place in the quiet lobby.

He walked over and stopped in front of her. "Can I help you? You look kind of lost."

To Cabot's horror, she felt her cheeks flush at the frank appraisal in the tall Navajo man's eyes. She'd been thinking how striking he was, with shoulder-length hair and wearing a business suit. It looked, well, exotic. Now she was blushing, for God's sake. She cursed her fair skin for the billionth time.

"Well, no, I'm not lost. Um...I'm waiting for the woman I think you're supposed to avoid. Jane Manyfarms? She...I'm the new doctor here and I guess I'm supposed to check in with her." She shrugged helplessly. "Dr. Schiller doesn't seem to be here."

"The Porsche must be yours."

"Uh, yes."

"Then you're Dr. Chase?" He looked her over openly. "Everybody thought you'd be a man."

How would he know that? "Cabot Chase." She hesitated and held out her hand.

Nicholas took it and held it firmly. "Nicholas Nakai. Well, Dr. Chase, it's nice to have you here. They need you. And you'll see me around a lot. I'm running for Congress. I hope you'll vote for me." He smiled.

Cabot tugged her hand free. "Congress? Oh. Well, if I'm still here. I mean, well, actually I don't know what I mean. I've been in Arizona about an hour. I haven't given voting much thought." Where in the world was this Jane Manyfarms?

"Plenty of time. The election isn't 'til November."

"I'm afraid I'm not very well-informed. About voting here, and issues..." Her voice trailed off. Did that sound snotty?

He laughed and said to the other man. "Well, we'll just have to work at getting our message across to her." He turned back to Cabot. "This is Pete Price. He'll help me see you get caught up on all the issues. If there's anything we've got a lot of, it's issues."

With a creak and a wheeze the elevator door opened. Nicholas flashed another smile as they stepped inside.

Cabot watched the door close, vaguely discomfited. Who in the world was Nicholas Nakai? Indian, obviously, Navajo most likely. And he was running for Congress? Well, anybody from Massachusetts has shaken hands with a raft of politicians.

He seemed to have the hang of it. Unconsciously she touched her hair.

A chubby Navajo woman dressed in a turquoise polyester pantsuit and with an unmistakable air of authority, bustled up to the front desk. "Annie, was that Nicholas and Pete I saw get on the elevator?"

"You betcha. They was sure goin' to see Chairman Wauneka, you know them, they do what they want around here."

Jane Manyfarms sighed. "You're right. Wasn't your fault, Annie. Anyhow, the Chairman's out of Intensive Care tomorrow unless those two give him another heart attack." She looked at Cabot. "You're the new doctor? Thought you'd be a man with that name."

Cabot wasn't sure if there was any response to this now frequent comment, so she waited.

"I'm Jane Manyfarms, the assistant administrator of the hospital. Come on down to my office. You just get in? We'll have to get you fixed up with a place to live. Show you around."

Resignation settled over Cabot like a fog. She followed.

ADMINISTRATION was stenciled on the opaque, pebble-glass door into the small, windowless office. Stacks of manila folders covered the desk and rickety, khaki-colored filing cabinets. The lush, salmon-colored paint that covered the walls with what she'd seen of the rest of the hospital had given way here to a vibrant turquoise, closely matching Jane Manyfarms's pantsuit. The effect was startling, Cabot thought, like being underwater in a well-chlorinated swimming pool. The administrator brushed a fly away and motioned Cabot to a chair across from her desk and went to filing cabinet to pull out a sheaf of papers.

"Dr. Schiller, he's the head of staff, but you'd know that.

He had to go over to Ganado, but he'll be back tonight. You'll see him in the morning. Think he wants you in ER."

Cabot was encouraged. She'd always liked Emergency Room work. It was high intensity, like surgery. Or, at least it was where she came from. Nothing she'd seen so far had even hinted at high-intensity anything.

Jane Manyfarms riffled through the papers, then laid them in front of Cabot.

"Just the usual employment stuff. You work for the government, you got a lot of forms to fill out. Even the Navajo government." She pushed a pen across the desk. "You finish up here, I'll show you around. You ready to start work?"

"Oh, yes. As soon as possible. Tomorrow." Tomorrow would be June 15th. Now she would have a date for her liberation. A year from tomorrow, on June 15th, she would pack up and leave for Boston. She wouldn't cheat, she wouldn't count the days of travel or take a vacation. She'd promised grandfather a year. He'd get a year, no less. No more.

She picked up the pen and began on the pile of forms.

After about a half an hour she stacked up what she had. "I'll have to finish these tonight. Some of the information is in papers in my luggage. Is that all right?"

"Oh, sure. Now. You got a place to stay?"

"No. I thought I'd find a hotel, then this weekend look for an apartment."

"You need furnished?"

"Yes." She was going to be as temporary as possible.

"Tribe's built some new places off the highway to Window Rock. Nice. The best around. I'll call out and see what they got. Maybe you could move right in."

Cabot vaguely remembered some structures that looked modern. "Well, thanks. I don't have very much. Some stuff in the car, and UPS will send a few things when I get an address."

Jane Manyfarms talked with someone on the phone, and after what seemed a very long social chat about some family celebration or other and an inquiry about a sick relative and something called a *hand trembler*, she made some notes, then chatted about someone called Ogden Crowhunter for some minutes before she hung up.

"He's got two for you to look at. Here." She handed the paper across the desk. "Just go back the way you came in and turn off on Ganado Road. Big tan stucco complex. Whispering Winds Apartments. Real nice. Go to the office and talk to Bobby Becenti."

"Thanks a lot. You're making it easy. Should I go right now?"

"No. Bobby won't be renting 'em to anybody else. C'mon. I'll show you around. Staff meeting's at nine in the morning. You can meet everybody we don't run into today and get your schedule then."

As they stood, Cabot said, "I met a young man right before you came into the lobby. Nicholas Nakai? He said he was running for Congress."

"Nicholas? Oh, yes. He'll win, too. I know it. I lose my patience with him, but he's real smart. Graduated from Arizona State Law School the top of his class seven years ago. Worked for a time in Phoenix for a law firm, but the last two years he's worked for the tribe."

"So he's new to politics?"

The administrator grinned. "Aren't we all? But the 1990 census gave Arizona a Sixth Congressional District. After the redistricting lines were drawn, a large part of it covers Indian land, not only Navajo, but Hopi, Apache, Pima. We think we got a real good chance to elect the first Navajo to Congress."

"You seem to know him very well."

The Navajo woman laughed. "Nicholas? He's my nephew."

Chapter Five

TÁÁ' NÁAZNILÍ ASHDLA'

May, 1852 The Chuska Mountains

"They're coming, they're coming..."

The piping voice floated from the trees into the camp, somnolent in the warm spring afternoon. Activity in the clearing paused as everyone turned eagerly to the boy's cries.

"They're coming, they're coming, I saw Uncle Chii, they're coming."

Kii, Daago's little brother skidded down the steep path into the cluster of summer hogans, his eyes dancing with the excitement of his news.

"I was out gathering firewood like you told me..." Kii hesitated briefly. He had abandoned his armload of wood. But then he chattered on, his little chest swelled with the importance of his message. The camp had been uneasy for days.

Daago and her mother Hezbah, kneeling in front of a large loom, worked on a large red, white and black blanket. They jumped up, their shuttles and skeins of woolen yarns tumbled forgotten to the ground.

"At last," Hezbah whispered, then hurried into action. "Kii, run to all the camps and tell the people to come here. Where is Chii now?"

"Near the lake. I took the shortcut. He'll be here very soon. He said the main party was close behind."

"Hurry then. We must make a big welcome." Hezbah stopped but didn't turn. "Kii?"

The little boy stopped, then danced backwards, anxious to get to his important errand.

"Did your Uncle Chii say that your father was all right?"

Kii stopped. "No. He didn't say." He looked worried now.

She rubbed her hands on her skirt. "Run along. Don't dawdle. People will want to know."

His face brightened and he turned and scampered off.

Almost before Kii had time to spread the news, the clearing of the Manases family camp began to fill with families eager to welcome their men and see what they had brought from the long campaign.

Despite the elation that swept the camp, the return was solemn. Eyes counted the line of weary men and horses as they filed into the clearing. When it was obvious that the party was complete, wails arose from the families of men who could not be counted. Of the twenty men who had left over two months ago, five were missing. There would be mourning rituals to be performed as well as the purifying ceremonies.

Of the spoils, there were thirty-six head of horses and seventeen Mexican women captives. The women huddled together on horseback, dirty and exhausted, their eyes sullen and frightened. Two were heavily pregnant—a bit of luck.

There would be additions to the clan shortly. The infants, from the moments of their births would be considered children of the families to whom their mothers were given. They would be Navajo.

Families greeted one another excitedly; babies born while the men were away were proudly exhibited to their fathers. Manases and Chii, along with the medicine man, Chezhin, went to the families of the men who had not returned to offer their condolences and prayers.

As soon as Hezbah heard the raiding party was almost home, she ordered a sheep to be slaughtered, and the smell of pinon smoke and roasting mutton began to fill the cool mountain air as the sun dropped below the wooded ridge that protected the camp.

After the men and the captives had been fed, families drifted to their own homes. A guard was set to watch the captives and the rejoicing camp slowly settled for the night. Campfires were banked and gradually even the voices began to die out.

The division of the captured bounty would take place in the morning. The women would be divided among the clan; the horses would belong to the clan as a whole.

In the night, too keyed up to sleep, Daago heard the familiar stirring from her mother and father's side of the hogan. She knew almost exactly the progress of her parents' lovemaking, from her mother's first sighs to the athletic grunts and thrashings at the end.

A one-room dwelling holds few secrets for its inhabitants, but Hezbah and Manases always copulated in the dark, and though the children could see faint heaving shapes under the blankets and furs, details were scarce. There was information to be gleaned from the herds of goats and sheep, and from the horses, so Daago assumed her mother and father's matings were as the rams and ewes or the stallions and mares. It looked clumsy but they seemed to like it as much as her mother and father. Daago was sure she would too, if she could only find a husband. It would be soon she hoped.

Chezhin had questioned her very closely these past weeks, to verify that she was a virgin. She was to carry the Sacred Rattlestick that represented the jeweled Arrow of the Sun in the neighboring clan's camp for the ritual of the Enemyway ceremonial that would be performed when the men returned from the campaign. Although virginity was not especially valued by the Navajo, Chezhin had told her that virgins were thought to carry stronger messages to the deities and the curing ceremony would carry more efficacious medicine if she had pure thoughts. Daago wasn't certain what that meant, but she was pretty sure that she'd best stop those thoughts that thrilled her, those things she did that felt so good.

She plumped up her fur rug and turned away from her parents, trying to shut out the groans and squeals that grew more urgent only twelve feet away. And Daago knew that because her father had been away, there would be another energetic coupling with her mother after he had rested. Maybe more. She hoped she would be asleep.

Daago heard a muffled giggle from Kii's fur. She reached over and swatted him.

The camp stirred early, an undercurrent of excitement hurried people along. Ordinary days were humdrum affairs that brought little change from the rhythms of the clan's pastoral life. Today would be different. Like public punishments, there was a fascination in viewing captives that verified one's own superiority.

This unhappy group was made to line up before the assembled Navajo families and for several hours the women of the clan walked the length of the line assessing the value of this captive, the strength of that one. In this matriarchal society it would be the women who chose who came into their households.

First choice of the captured women went to the families of the men who had been killed in the raid. Next, mothers of unmarried men chose, then Manases' wife Hezbah took a captive, and on down the line as the clan tried to share equitably in the spoils of the raid.

"Each family who received a captive, other than those who lost a warrior, will bring twelve sheep to me. They will be shared by those who did not benefit from the raid. Now, go, and prepare yourselves for the Enemyway Ceremony," said Manases. He turned and gestured to Chezhin, the *hataalii,* and together they went into his hogan to plan for the four-day ceremonial that would negate the evil spirits of the dead, both their clan's and the enemies they had killed in the raids. It must be done quickly. The *chindi,* the evil spirits, had certainly followed them home and must be chased away before they did harm.

A large sweat lodge was built, an upside down, bowl-like frame constructed of branches and covered with mud. Its interior was heated to scalding temperatures from water poured on stones the men had gathered and heated until they were red-hot. In front of the entrance to the lodge they solemnly stripped and each adult male tied a string around his foreskin before stepping inside. Chezhin dropped a blanket over the door and the prayer songs began. As the men sweated, the songs continued in cycles of four, eight, twelve, and so on, depending on the endurance of the sweaters.

As the husky rhythmical chants of the men echoed down the valley, the women went about the tasks of preparing food for the ceremony ahead. The neighboring clan of the Deeschiinii had been invited to help with the sacred ritual and the women of the Todachinii clan would perish from embarrassment if everything weren't just so for their nearest neighbors. The camp hummed and clattered with activity and a veil of blue smoke from the cooking fires floated up into the soft spring air. The new slaves were being absorbed into the tasks of their new families: cooking, dying wool, helping dress those who would be going to the Deeschiinii camp.

Daago showed Dolores, the captive girl they had been awarded, how to crush the root of the yucca cactus between two smooth stones to make a sudsy shampoo that gave black hair a soft luster. The two girls were close in age and smiled shyly at each other as they tried to become acquainted.

"*Yinishye Daago.*" The Navajo girl pointed to herself and smiled encouragingly. "*Yinishye Daago.*"

"*Me llamo Dolores,*" She smiled shyly. "*Yinishye Dolores.*"

Daago was delighted. The girl could speak Navajo!

Excitedly she pointed to her self, and stammered, "Me…me yahmo' Daago."

The two girls giggled, pleased with themselves.

As Daago, consumed with curiosity, pumped her with questions, Dolores became chatty. She was an intelligent girl and had evidently begun to pick up a rudimentary mastery of her captor's language on the long trek away from the *rancheria* where she had been taken.

"I was very afraid, but your men treated me very good. At the *rancheria* I was often beaten. I know I will be a slave and have to help your mother, and work in the fields. But I always had to work in the fields and in the household there."

"Where did you sleep?"

"With the other slaves in a shelter away from the house. But then I would be made to lie with the master more and more. I will have to lie with your father, too. That I understand."

Daago gulped. How would her mother like that! She would be very hurt.

"But your father is *muy guapo,*" Dolores went on. "He is strong-looking and kind. My other master, he was fat and cruel. I had one child. He was a boy and I miss him. But I will have more with your father. Life will go on." She sighed with resignation.

This new information was unwelcome. But Daago had overheard her father when the clan men decided to go campaigning. Manases had exhorted the men to father more children for the clan, even take two or more wives if necessary. At the time she hadn't considered that Manases would be part of that plan, but obviously he considered it his duty as well. She and Kii, as well as Hezbah, would have to get used to the idea of a larger family.

Until then it would be fun to have a slave she could order around. She showed Dolores how to untangle her hair with a brush made of porcupine quills, and sat back with satisfaction as the girl worked the quills through the heavy wet strands of hair that fell past Daago's buttocks.

Hezbah glanced over at the two girls and pursed her lips. "Daago! Go fetch water. Show the girl where to go. I will help you with your hair later."

What good is it to have a slave, Daago grumbled to herself, feeling sulky that her toilette had been interrupted. She showed Dolores where the large water jars were kept, and settling an olla on her shoulder, stalked off into the woods to the spring, leaving the Mexican girl to stumble after her with the unfamiliar burden.

By late afternoon the Todaschiinii clan was ready to go. The men were dressed in loincloths, fringed leggings and moccasins, with varieties of beaded and boned necklaces, breastplates, bracelets and earrings. Most had tied feathers in their hair.

The women wore their newest blanket dresses in vivid shades of reds and blues. Their necklaces were also of beads, bones and shells, their hair tied up in colorful yarns. A few of the more prosperous wore Mexican silver beads or earrings, some of which had been "acquired" on the campaign to the Mexican *rancherias*.

The horses had caught the excitement and snorted and pawed the ground restlessly as the party that would go to the neighboring clan began to mount up.

A special ceremonial drum was brought forth for the occasion and its insistent hollow throb sounded throughout the valley as the men and women gathered for the twelve mile ride to the Deeschiinii camp. Chezhin the medicine man led the group out of the clearing, careful to hold the Sacred Rattlestick, decorated with turkey and eagle feathers, deer hooves, herbs and colored wool yarns, in a perfectly upright position. He set the pace, a slow, dignified canter that the younger people had difficulty maintaining. It was all they could do to keep from galloping headlong to the Deeschiinii camp to see whom they would meet over the next four days.

Daago's teeth were chattering, though she tried to maintain some semblance of dignity. Everyone knew she had a special role and she tried to look worthy of Chezhin's choice of her to carry the stick back. She had named the horse that her father had given her at her coming-of-age *kinaalda* ceremony. His name was Niyol. Wind. And she was used to riding him just that way. The sedate pace puzzled him. He strained and tossed his head at the bridle, a typical woven rope with two half-hitches in the middle that tightened around his lower jaw.

Daago leaned forward and whispered in his ear. "Stop it, Niyol. If you embarrass me today I won't find anyone to marry and if I don't, I'll make father take you back and I'll get another horse."

She patted the sleek chestnut withers, knowing she'd die before she gave up Niyol. But her words settled the animal and he melted into his glorious, even canter, seeming to match his hoof beats to the haunting pot drum and the rhythmic verses of the holy songs.

Chapter Six

June 15, 1992 The Hospital

It was six o'clock at the end of a long day when Cabot pushed open the door to the hospital cafeteria. Maybe she'd just get something to eat there. The new apartment didn't have any cooking utensils yet, and no food. Right that minute shopping was the last thing she felt like. She looked over the steam tables at the unfamiliar stews and Mexican style foods, as well as the fried chicken and meatloaf indigenous to cafeterias. Her stomach flatly rejected each selection, so she ended up getting a cup of coffee and a molded red Jell-O fruit cocktail thing on a piece of soggy lettuce. She glanced around the room, looking for a table, not wanting to catch anyone's eye and have to join them. Everyone had been friendly and welcoming today, happy to have another hand, but now Cabot was too tired for socializing.

She was discouraged, too. Working in the Emergency Room here wasn't really emergency-type care. It was more like General Practice. The Emergency Room was the primary medical source in this area of the reservation. People came here for colds and earaches. There were a depressing number of children with diarrhea, due to poor sanitation and lack of knowledge about proper food temperatures. She would have to learn to deal with these things on a primitive basis. For instance, she learned that you told Navajo mothers to give their sick babies tea. That was because they had to boil the water for tea. Prescription directions included pictorial labels; i.e, the sun in three positions indicated the patient was to take that particular medication three times a day.

Neurosurgery seemed far, far away.

As Cabot sat down, she noticed the two men she'd seen in the lobby the day before. They were hunched over their coffee, engrossed in some papers. Election stuff probably, she thought. Apparently they worked closely with this tribal chairman who was upstairs on the fourth floor, recovering from a heart attack. She'd caught a glimpse of him yesterday when he was still in Intensive Care, a burly, vigorous-looking man, hardly looking seventy. Or even ill. He had a steady stream of visitors, much to Jane Manyfarms's chagrin.

Cabot let her mind drift. She was quite pleased with her apartment. It was brand new and though the furniture was definitely motel-class, it was also new, and the colors she could live with. She'd get a few things to cozy the place up—not much, of course. She didn't want to accumulate a lot of stuff. But, after all, it was going to be her home and there should be some kind of effort to make it as pleasant as possible. She regretted now her two good paintings had been put in storage. There was a small fireplace and the one still life would look very nice there.

Having a place so comfortable surprised her. What had she expected? She didn't really know. It was something her mind just slid over, thinking she'd have to put up with what was here. A hogan? The thought of herself living in one of those beetle-like dwellings made her mouth turn up at the corners.

"You look a lot happier than when I saw you yesterday."

Cabot looked up quickly, suddenly aware she'd been sitting here talking to herself. Had she said anything out loud? She sometimes did. Everybody teased her about it. Nicholas Nakai stood smiling down at her.

She bit her lip. "I was just thinking of something I should have brought with me." The other man, she noticed, was gone.

"Anything we can get for you. Jane's pretty resourceful. I am, too."

"No. I'm just decorating my apartment in my head."

"Bobby Becenti's places are real nice. You're happy with yours?"

"Oh, yes. I'll be very comfortable. I was thinking of things to put in it to make it mine. More like a home."

"You get along all right on your first day?"

"Fine. Everyone has been so nice. Very helpful."

"That's great." He hesitated, then smiled again. "I expect I'll see you around."

"Oh. I imagine. Yes."

She watched him walk away, people stopping him to have a word or two. He was always gracious, seeming to have all the time in the world for them. I guess you do that when you're running for office.

She wondered if she'd been rude not to ask him to sit down. But she hadn't wanted to. He made her feel uncomfortable, though she knew she shouldn't feel that way. He'd been courteous and helpful the two times they'd met. Maybe because everything was so new, so different than anything she'd ever experienced before. And hard for her to believe this was still the United States, even though most everyone spoke English. Only the very old didn't speak it. Today she'd heard very little Navajo spoken, an odd guttural language. It was just the sense of dislocation that would go away in a couple of days. Of course it would.

Cabot reviewed the day. She'd met the staff, of course. Besides Dr. Schiller, the Chief of Staff, there were two Navajo doctors, an Asian Indian, two Mexicans, and three other Anglos besides herself. The hospital had sixty beds. It certainly wasn't on the cutting edge of technology, but adequate for most of the care they were called upon to do. For really serious problems, there were major trauma care hospitals in Phoenix and Albuquerque. She understood they could get Air Evac out of Flagstaff pretty quickly if they needed it.

Today she'd treated a broken leg, a dislocated shoulder, six babies with diarrhea, a concussion, a truck accident with three broken ribs, several cuts, and four maternities, two admitted before delivery, two delivered in the ER. This, she was told, was not uncommon. The Navajo ladies always cut it close and they delivered in the ER as often as not, those who made it to the hospital at all.

The pace, she found, was not the breakneck run-run-run that she was used to. There was a more leisurely pace here, to put it mildly. It was the newness that had exhausted her, she told herself.

Unexpectedly a lump clogged her throat and her eyes stung. She put her forehead on her knuckles and swallowed the wave of despair at all her skills drifting away in this remote hospital on the edge of nowhere.

Chapter Seven

June 23, 1992 The Rez

The five men and one woman gazed thoughtfully at the big wall map of the state of Arizona pinned to the wall of the conference room in the tribal administrative building in Window Rock. Jim Shackleford, Nicholas's campaign manager, had outlined the sprawling Sixth Congressional District in red.

"It's sure impressive," Jim rumbled, his barrel chest straining the pink dress shirt he wore, "and it looks great on the map that you've got a helluva lot of Indian territory. But there's a lot of real estate there where there ain't that many bodies. The Indian vote in the district will only be about twenty six percent, tops. You'll have that sewed up, Nick, but you've got to get the vote out for it to count. So, you won't be able to take anything for granted."

He heaved himself out of the chrome and green fake leather chair and walked to the map. He picked up a green marking pen and began circling other areas of the map. "You've got small town conservatives here, here, and here. And here." He circled Flagstaff, Holbrook, Winslow, and Globe. "And you got a lot of Phoenix northeast Valley here. And God knows what they'll do this year. There's everything from the Pima Reservation to multimillion dollar spreads around the golf courses at the foot of the McDowell Mountains."

"That's a lot of territory to cover, ideological as well as the demographics and geography, but we knew that," Nicholas said.

"It is, it is. And it'll cost. But that doesn't mean it can't be done. There's a lot of plusses."

"Number one is there's no incumbent. At least Nicholas doesn't have to fight incumbency," said Shirley Kee, editor of the *Navajo Times*.

To have member of the working press in the room didn't strike anyone as unseemly. Shirley would naturally be a strong advocate for Nicholas and would be invaluable in promoting tribal voter registration.

"Neither do any of the other candidates," Pete Price said.

Pete had no official title in the campaign, but was a close friend and Nicholas trusted his opinions. That he was a medicine man was viewed as proper by his Indian constituents. An advisor for the traditional ways would be important to older Indians, many of whom felt their traditions and beliefs threatened. Nicholas's family was well thought of, but Nicholas had spent an awful lot of time in the white man's world. It was important that he remember the old ways, too. There were two other men in the room. Zhealy Tso would oversee the Indian tribes for the campaign.

It would be his job to get out the tribal vote, not only the Navajo, but the Apache, Hopi, and down near Phoenix, the

Salt River tribes, Pimas, Tohono O'odham, Maricopas, and other small tribal enclaves that fell within the new District Six.

The last man was Russell Wauneka, the Navajo chairman who had been discharged from the hospital only two days before. The others watched him surreptitiously for any sign of fatigue. Nicholas had tried to discourage him from coming to the meeting, promising to give him a full report, but the chairman was stubborn. This new district was a once-in-a-lifetime opportunity to give the Indians an effective voice in Congress, and Wauneka was determined that all possible resources be brought to bear on this campaign. He had hammered through the tribal council the notion to hire a professional from Phoenix to run the off-reservation side of the campaign. Russell Wauneka never hesitated to use the white man's expertise when it benefited his people. He convinced the council to open the tribal coffers to finance Nicholas's campaign.

"But you're right," Jim was saying. "The sheer size of the district and the different constituencies it covers means you're going to be traveling a lot, Nick, and we're going to have to get a lot of newspapers and TV and radio stations to carry your message. That means dough. The very fact that you've hired me means you're serious. So am I. You'll get your money's worth and then some. I like the odds. I won't waste your money."

"We know that. That's why you're here," said Nicholas

"You're an attractive candidate. Handsome. Smart fella from Arizona State Law. You practiced enough in Phoenix to know some people. Your views are sensible and moderate. Don't get carried away with the environment stuff and I doubt you'll scare anybody too much. That's very important for a minority. You get a little hot over Indian issues, but that's natural. People wouldn't expect anything else. All you got to do is be reasonable. Everybody's sick to death of the regular faces, and being an Indian is kind of *in.* And not only to the do-gooders and tree-huggers, but the designer water and cucumber martini crowd. A lot of people are *still* smarmy over that movie *Dances with Wolves.*"

Nicholas let out a whoop of laughter. "You've got to learn to be more candid, Jim."

Jim grinned. "You'll always know where I stand. I'm not real subtle most times." He took some pages from a folder. "Bill Kemper in my office has made up a financial. We'll do most of the fund-raising in Phoenix and the towns. Your people don't have a lot of discretionary income, but Zhealy here will get what he can. And if they've thrown a coupla bucks into the kitty, they'll likely vote come election day."

Zhealy Tso was a gaunt, wiry cattle rancher and sat on the Tribal Council. He spoke up. "They'll be as generous as they can be. This is a big thing to them."

"Right now Nick needs to be traveling and talking to people. Every day, every night. We worry about the advertising later. Now we work on the free stuff. Try to get the media to cover what you say in the morning editions, nightly news, and the drive times." Jim put a stubby thumb to his chest. "That's my job."

"I'm working on getting the word out to every sheep camp and cattle outfit in the remotest part of the Rez. Let 'em know that one of the *Dine* can go to *Washeendon* if they wish it," Zhealy Tso said, giving the name Washington its Navajo phonation.

"There'll be something on Nicholas in every issue of the *Navajo Times*," Shirley Kee promised. "I intend to keep everybody stirred up around here. Get people to write letters, Zhealy. Everybody likes to see his name in the papers, then show it around to his neighbors."

Zhealy Tso consulted a schedule. "You're going to ride in the Fourth of July Parade in Flagstaff, and I told 'em you'd be in a couple of events at the Pow Wow Rodeo. Just like old times. Take your pick of the events."

"Yeah, that'll be okay. How about doing team roping again this year, Pete?" Nicholas asked, turning to the medicine man.

"Sure, though I recollect we came up zip last year," Pete grinned.

Jim Shackleford looked from one to the other in amazement. "Do I understand. that my candidate is going to cowboy it up in a rodeo? My God, you could get killed."

The Navajos all laughed. "You don't understand politics on the Rez yet, Jim," Zhealy Tso said. "The rodeo is where it's at."

"Rodeo committees all over the reservation are loosely-knit quasi-political organizations. It's a kinda hard to explain. But anybody with political aspirations usually has some kind of role in the rodeo," Nicholas explained. "Until recently the Navajo didn't have many central forums for voicing problems, so these rodeo organizations became kind of sounding boards for other issues. It's more than a little difficult to understand if you haven't been brought up with it. But if you want to be somebody, you work with the rodeo. Compete if possible."

"I'd no idea rodeos were such a big part of your life up here," Jim said.

"Yeah. You can find one somewhere most every weekend. They can get a little wild. Not everybody's very good. Not what you probably have seen in Phoenix and Scottsdale. It's not exactly world-class rodeoin'." Nicholas chuckled. "Not quite unorganized mayhem, but it gets close sometimes."

"Uh, Nick? You any good at it?" Jim looked from Nicholas to Pete Price. "What I'm tryin' to say…I mean it wouldn't do to make a jackass of yourself, much less wind up with a broken neck."

The room rumbled with laughter.

"I'm fair, Jim. I'm fair. Used to be pretty good, but I'm not a crazy teenager anymore. You gotta be partly nuts to be real good. But I promise you I won't embarrass anybody."

Jim grinned. "Then I'll arrange a photographer. Be kind of colorful to have the next Congressman on a wildass bronc on the front page of the *Arizona Republic*."

Nicholas feigned horror. "Who said anything about a wildass bronc?"

"He's too big for the broncs," Pete Price explained to the newly worried campaign manager. "The big guys like him wrestle the steers."

"Oh great," Jim groaned.

"Hey, Pete. I haven't done that since I was nineteen!"

"Just tryin' to get you on the front page, Nicholas. Just tryin' to get you on the front page."

Chapter Eight

TÁÁ' NÁAZNILÍ' TSEEBII

May, 1852 The Chuska Mountains

The small, rushing river, icy from the winter's snowmelt, broke into the open, lush meadow dotted with spring wildflowers. The sun had warmed the grasses and the late afternoon air was sweet. The Todachiinii clan rode silently toward the crowd that waited in front of the large, specially-built ceremonial hogan. The Deeschiinii medicine man would receive the Sacred Rattlestick. Solemn, he stood in front of the hogan door, a frail, ancient man, his face seamed with his years, awesome in the weight of his wisdom.

When the Todachiiniis slowed and brought their horses up, the old shaman gestured for Chezhin to come inside. Chezhin dismounted and surrendered his roan horse to a small, waiting boy, obviously nervous at the importance of his job.

The medicine man passed through the door of the ceremonial hogan and Manases and the Deeschiinii headman followed. Chezhin advanced to the old Receiver and handed him the Stick. Receiver turned and handed it to his assistant, who laid it carefully on a basket, its head pointing to the north. The two *hataalis* examined the Stick with great care to make sure it had been properly prepared. They nodded to each other, indicating the Stick was acceptable to them. The assistant then removed the bits of colored yarn from the shaft and handed them out the door to several waiting women. The yarns would be distributed among the clans as the four men sang the proper holy songs, accompanied by the small, special pot drum that would not cease its punctuating beats for the entire four-day proceedings.

While the music pulsed from the hogan door, the Todachiiniis stayed mounted and the two clans looked each other over cautiously. Everyone tried to look tall and impressive. Prosperous. These gatherings were rare and not only a welcome social occasion, but a time to find mates for the unmarried young people. There was a lot of sizing-up to be done on both sides. These marriages made the clans allies against outside predation. It was important that choices be made carefully.

Chii, as a warrior and Manases's brother-in-law, held authority when the headman was otherwise occupied. His eyes swept over the clan, to frown in displeasure if one of the young Todachiiniis behaved restlessly or was slipshod in controlling his or her horse. Satisfied that the marriageable prospects of the clan behaved in front of the neighbors, he glanced at his sister.

Hezbah sat proudly on a red sorrel horse. Chii knew she was aware that as the wife of their clan's headman she was being scrutinized carefully by the Deeschiinii women. Her blanket dress was new, one she had only finished weaving in the past weeks leading up to the return of the men from the campaign. Her necklaces were interspersed with silver beads, a new decorative motif from Mexico, just beginning to filter up to the north. Manases, as well as the other men, had added to their wives' collections from the raids on the rancherias and the women had eagerly embellished the dresses they had woven in the raiding party's long absence. Yes, the Todachiinii all looked their best.

He carefully studied Daago, mounted on Niyol, off to his right. Chii was fully aware that his niece was a prize. He must make the proper arrangements for her marriage. Last year, even before they had gone raiding to the Mexican rancherias, he, Hezbah and Chezhin the medicine man had already gone over the complicated genealogies of the two clans. It was imperative that there be no accidental crossing of either Hezbah's and Manases's clans with the prospective ally's genealogies. It would be incestuous if a mistake were made, taboos violated, and offensive to the Holy Ones.

Daago didn't know that her Uncle Chii had been in contact with the Deeschiiniis, as had other uncles of the Todachiinii clan. As Hezbah's brother, Chii, in his traditional role as the a*vunculate,* would recommend his choice to Daago. Theoretically she could refuse his candidate, but her refusal would be unlikely. Romantic love was not unknown, but it seldom had anything to do with arranging a marriage.

Chii had selected two possible prospects and he went over their qualifications in his mind. The most appropriate was the assistant to the Receiver, a young apprentice whom the Deeschiinii prayed would be ready to take over the duties of shaman when the old man's time came. The young man had been given to the medicine man to train when he was five years old. He was now sixteen, hardly time enough to learn the thousands of chants, the complicated ceremonies and sand paintings, as well as the pharmacopoeia of the typical medicine man. His name was Chilhajin. He had been discouraged from marrying to devote his time to his studies, but now he had grown restless and wanted a bride. The clan couldn't avoid it any longer and needed a suitable girl from the Todachiinii people.

Then there was Jadi, but Chii knew that Chilhajin was the proper choice for his niece. He was already a leader; he was tall and strong and fine looking. A bout of smallpox as a child had left his face slightly scarred. Daago would probably be put off by that, Chii knew. She was lovely and she knew it, he thought. Proud, too. She might think that Chilhajin was not quite perfect enough for her, despite his impressive qualifications. She might get rebellious if she found someone more to her liking. The warrior Jadi in all likelihood. All the women made eyes at the warriors.

Chii smiled wryly to himself. More than one set of limpid dark eyes had followed warrior Chii, more than one caress of invitation had brushed him in various places, even though he was married. His wife got terribly jealous no matter how much he reassured her. He loved his wife and hardly ever let his loins get the better of him. He shifted on his horse. Hardly ever.

Chii went back to the problems presented by his niece.

Daago would probably want someone like Jadi, a strapping brave with several raids under his belt. Chii studied the young man. A good warrior, courageous but conceited. A pretty boy. All the young women would sigh over him. It wouldn't be a bad match, but Jadi just wasn't the best match for the Todachiinii clan. A medicine man and a headman's daughter would be a powerful union, strengthening each of their clans. Chii thought of his sister, Hezbah. Hezbah would expect him, naturally, to guide Daago. He wondered if he were up to the job of directing the life of his beautiful, willful niece like a dutiful uncle should. Truly, having a niece was sometimes a heavy burden. It was consolation to know that his wife's brother would have the *avunculate's* responsibility when his own little daughter came of age.

Chii's eyes went to the girl seated restlessly on Niyol a short distance away. He grunted, half amused. In the Navajo language Daago meant "springtime." Oh, sometimes she was mild and gentle, but hot summer was more like her. Perhaps they had all indulged her a little too much. They all knew that they could attract an important ally with her betrothal.

Daago sat as demurely as she could, but Niyol sensed her excitement and pawed at the ground. The girl quieted the animal then continued to sweep the throng of Deeschiinii people through the fringe of her eyelashes. She had spotted the warrior Jadi right away and turned her eyes again and again to the handsome young brave who leaned nonchalantly against a pinon tree, absently slapping a braided quirt against his well-muscled thigh. Their glances met several times and he had given her a dazzling smile that set her heart to racing. She shifted her weight, conscious of the warmth of the horse through the red and black saddle blanket.

The two headmen and Chezhin stepped outside the ceremonial hogan, followed by the Receiver. With the first part of the ceremony finished, the Todachiinii dismounted and led their horses to a large corral made of pinon branches. Deeschiinii children helped them feed and water the animals before everyone returned to sit in a large circle before the ceremonial hogan, the men in front, the women and children behind. The Deeschiinii women brought bowls of mutton stew and blankets filled with fragrant cornbread for their guests, then distributed food to their own people. The two clans, as was proper, did not socialize during this part of the proceedings.

While everyone was eating, the Receiver beckoned to Daago to come with him into the ceremonial Hogan. She swallowed hard and tried not to look nervous as she stood and followed him, conscious of all the eyes that followed her. As she stepped into the gloomy interior, lit only by a tiny fire in the center of the circular room, she saw the Receiver and his assistant bending over, preparing the Sacred Rattlestick. When the young man, Chilhajin turned and moved to her, she felt a small shock. She hadn't seen him before and he was terribly impressive with the authority of his office. Medicine men were always old, weren't they? As he came close, she noticed the pits and scars on his face and felt a thump of disappointment. She'd thought him handsome at first, in the flickering shadows of the dying fire. His black eyes were compelling and she looked quickly at the floor, afraid he would read her disappointment and be offended.

Chilhajin and the old man showed her the proper way to carry the Stick so its symbolism wouldn't be compromised.

"You will lead everyone to the dance circle. Be sure to keep the Stick upright," Chilhajin instructed, closing her fingers gently around the Stick. He stood very close to her and she could feel his warmth, smell his man-smell.

His voice was very deep and Daago found he made her nervous. She nodded, unsure of what to say.

"It would be polite to choose our headman first," he said, "though you don't have to if you don't want to."

Daago knew she had to be polite or face her mother. "Yes, I will."

Chilhajin's eyes danced in the firelight, "I am called Chilhajin. And it would be polite if then you asked me to dance." He didn't smile, but there was a tiny quiver at the corner of him mouth. "But you don't have to do that either. If you don't want to."

Daago's heart sank. She'd counted on asking the handsome warrior by the tree, but now she was already two dances behind all the other girls who would also be dying to ask him to dance. She swallowed and nodded. Her mother, and probably her Uncle Chii, as well as her father would kill her if she didn't do the proper thing.

Life was terribly unfair.

Her disappointment eased as they moved from the hogan and down the short trail to where the young men had built a huge fire of juniper and pinon that crackled as the drops of pitch burst in the intense heat. Down the path the brilliance and perfume of the fire filtered through the trees. It was intoxicating and a level of intensity and expectation began to build in the assembled clans.

The ceremonial drum throbbed a hollow, mournful tattoo, though Dago scarcely heard it she was so caught up in being the center of attention as she led the crowd, carefully holding the Sacred Rattlestick upright. She lifted her chin and tried to walk as gracefully as possible so that the warrior could see. Let him see how special she was, leading his clan's headman in the dance. She tossed her hair. Yes, let him see. It was probably good that she didn't dash right out and ask him to the dance circle. Let him wait.

Life was wonderful after all.

It was full night, with only a quarter moon to light the path toward the dance circle. The men began to chant the songs for this part of the ritual, chants that would continue for another hour or more before the dancing could begin.

Gathering in a solemn ring around the fire, the nearest faces bronzed by the flames, the crowd swayed to the rhythms, a slight shuffling of their feet whispering on the sandy soil as they repeated the ancient songs. Daago wondered if they would ever finish. It was getting harder and harder to hold the Stick so it wouldn't wobble. Then Chilhajin was beside her. Though he didn't look at her, he gently took the weight from her fingers into his own. He had noticed that her arms were tired.

The young medicine man is nice, she thought, then dismissed thoughts of him as she spied the warrior watching her from across the fire.

When it was time, Chilhajin eased the weight of the Stick back to her, nodded, and she moved across the circle to the headman of the Deeschiinii clan. She took his arm and led him to the center, and as the tempo of the songs increased, she danced around the tall man, dressed in heavily fringed deerskin pants and moccasins, much like her father's. This was the signal for the other girls to choose partners. Daago watched in dismay as her friend Hanabah coquettishly touched the warrior's arm and the two moved into the circle of dancers.

When she went to Chilhajin for the next dance, he took the Stick from her and gave it to the old medicine, then moved with her into the slow procession around the fire. When they passed Chii, her uncle smiled at her with encouragement and Daago knew then that this was the man they wanted her to marry.

She didn't want to. He was good-looking enough, but he had scars on his face. He wasn't nearly as handsome as the warrior, and besides, he made her nervous, being so serious and important. And here she had this ceremonial role and hadn't even had the chance to dance with the warrior and somebody else would steal him. Oh, she was sure of it. She had thought: *oh, let him wait, because I'm so important, then he'll see how special I am. Ha! Much he cares with all the girls falling all over him.*

Daago fumed silently.

She was hardly aware the dance was ending until Chilhajin closed her fingers around a piece of turquoise, as warm and smooth as a robin's egg. He touched her face in a swift, feathery gesture then went to the old man to relieve him of the Sacred Rattlestick.

Daago looked at the glowing blue stone in the palm of her hand. It was a fine dance gift, lavish compared to most. What would the warrior give her she wondered excitedly? She would make sure that for the next dance she would be close enough to get to him first.

The next morning the Todachiinii prepared to leave for the second site, where the rituals would continue. The women went to the river to wash themselves, then returned with water for the men. By noon, tobacco, food, beads, had been given to them by the Deeschiinii and they mounted their horses for the return trip. Daago was given the Sacred Rattlestick, and together with her father and Chezhin, they moved away from the camp, careful to follow the exact route that had brought them to their neighbors, who would now come to them in a special place that had been prepared halfway between the two camps.

Daago smiled at Jadi as they rode out and felt a delicious thrill when he waved to her. She passed close to Chilhajin and knew he had seen her exchange glances with Jadi. Well, that was too bad! Nothing had been decided positively whom she was to marry. And Jadi was fun. She danced with him twice last night, and though his dance gifts had only been bits of colored yarn, he was terribly exciting. He whispered things that gave her heat and chills at the same time. Grown-up things they would do. She would dance with him as many more times as she could tonight. She was sure he liked her better than Hanabah.

The camp broke early for the last day of the healing ceremony. The Todachiinii left to prepare for the coming of the Deeschiinii, to finish the last of the rituals at their hogans near Canyon de Chelly. Daago again rode out with the Rattlestick, though her duties were not on her mind. Last night was on her mind.

It had all been so wonderful until the last. She'd danced with Jadi so often at least six or seven times it was all such a whirl she couldn't be sure the heat the glow of the fire and the beating of the drum and the rhythm of the drum had...aroused her.

Daago took a deep breath and tried to slow her thoughts, wondering if she could salvage something.

Jadi had smiled and laughed with her and touched her waist. Toward the end of the dancing he pulled her away from the firelight and into the dark forest, as other couples were doing. He held her and kissed her and his hands rubbed her breasts, pinching her nipples through the woolen blanket dress, which had hurt and felt wonderful at the same time. His manhood had pushed aside his loincloth. He had lifted her skirt and his fingers had found her secret place, which had sent feeling and sensations through her that she'd not thought possible. He pulled her to the ground to lie with her, as other couples were doing, but she'd had to struggle up from under him and explain her duties. He had smiled, squeezed her fingers around his engorged manhood, then taken her back to the fire. She hadn't seen him since.

The Todachiinii camp was in a fever of activity. Cookfires had been going since before sunrise to prepare for the day's activities. Slaves were grinding corn for the bread and preparing the jugs of herbal mountain tea. The gifts were gathered on a blanket in the ceremonial hogan, to be thrown out of the smokehole later on and collected by the Deeschiinii.

Soon after the Sacred Rattle stick arrived, the visiting clan could be heard galloping up the trail with shouts and a few gunshots. A mock battle was fought with the host clan and repeated four times, symbolizing the battle of Changing Woman's twin sons, Monster Slayer and Child-of-the-Water, and the enemy monsters in the Story of Creation. The two clans chased each other around the ceremonial hogan four times, in ever widening circles, yelling fiercely. Then the Deeschiinii retired to a small camp a few hundred yards away where food was bought to them.

The Todachiinii men who had raided the Rio Grande rancherias assembled and stripped off their clothing. Beginning with Manases, Chezhin blackened the naked men with a mixture of ashes, sacred plants and sheep tallow. The medicine man and Chilhajin walked among the men, helping them with the ashes, to repel the evil spirits that had followed them from the raid.

The men drank a special potion and were then led to a place where the scalps taken in the raid had been placed. While the drum beat faster and faster, the medicine men threw ashes on the scalps and the Marine Raiders beat the scalps into the ground to exorcise the evil spirits. After the ritual was repeated four times, they turned eastward and chanted a prayer to the sun, afterward scooping the sun's rays into their mouths to bring health and good fortune.

The raiding men were then admonished to pray and concentrate on the rituals of the past days—to erase the thoughts of the raids from their minds, not to hunt or handle their weapons. For four days they would not wash off these ashes and must sleep apart from their wives. After this part of the ritual Chilhajin fastened a band with an eagle feather around each man' head. The remainder of the day was taken with chants and prayers until it was time again for the women to dance.

Daago was anxious to invite Jadi again, to see if he were angry with her for refusing to lie with him. But when the pairing off began he only had eyes for Hanabah, and after the first song, the two disappeared. Daago danced with Chilhajin several times, but she was sulky and rebuffed his attempts to be kind. At the end he put another turquoise in her hand, a twin of the first one he had given her. She brightened a little. The two would make dazzling earrings.

The next morning Manases and Daago, with the Sacred Rattlestick, rode out of the camp with the Deeschiinii. When they were a mile or so out from the camp, the old medicine man stopped the group.

"We will dismantle the Stick in this place."

Chilhajin spread a blanket on the ground and went to Daago. He reached and took the Sacred Rattlestick from her hands, holding them a little longer than necessary. He searched her face but her eyes were cast down. Somehow she blamed him for all her troubles with Jadi. Now Hanabah had lain with Jadi, she was sure of it the way the girl had acted—all dimply, smug and superior. Hanabah's uncle was probably already making arrangements for their marriage. And she, Daago the special one, would have to marry Chilhajin—a gloomy, serious, scarred, medicine man!

Chilhajin looked at the sulky Daago and sighed. He went to the old man and handed him the Stick, then began to pass a pouch of corn pollen to everyone in the group.

Each placed a pinch on his tongue and threw the remainder into the wind for the Holy Ones. He and the medicine man knelt, and with chants and prayers, dismantled the Rattlestick, sprinkled it with corn pollen and buried it.

When the last handful of dirt covered the Stick, Daago turned Niyol away and spurred him to a gallop. She knew her behavior bordered on sacrilegious, but she was utterly sick of the whole long ceremony. She was going to a little private place she knew and cry and cry.

Manases frowned after his daughter and tried to catch Chilhajin's eye. But the young man was staring unhappily down the trail as Daago, her midnight hair flying, disappeared around a bend in the pinon forest.

Annoyed, Manases moved to follow her, then thought better of it. Let Chii handle it. It was an Uncle's job, after all.

Chapter Nine

June 27, 1992,Fort Defiance, Arizona

Dear Grandfather,

I'll try to write more often, I promise. Just haven't been able to get myself sorted out enough up until now to give you a good reading of my impressions. This, I don't need to tell you, is so different from any of my Eastern life that I sometimes pinch myself to believe I'm even in the United States. I know. I know. A failing of us New Englanders to believe anything else exists west of what? Philadelphia?

My place is nice. Not fancy, but nothing is here. It's new, though, and if I'm honest, it's really a lot better than that dump I called home at med school. Surprisingly, I have a dishwasher and a microwave, and even a tiny fireplace. I'm moving up in the world, amenity-wise.

My days revolve around the hospital, naturally. The staff is a polyglot mix; Jacob Schiller is an old testy German who should retire, but he's Chief of Staff and I don't think anybody knows how to get rid of him. Latchi Singh is Chief of Surgery. He's an Asian Indian from New Delhi, I think. He trained in India, been working for the Public Health Service for twenty years or so. I think...I think he knows what he's doing. He's very witty and funny. There are two Mexican doctors, Eusebio Sanchez and Xavier Morales, who are even younger than me; two Navajos—Keith Singer and Tommy Tootsie(Isn't that a wonderful name!); and three Anglos, besides me—Bill Riordan, Jeff Minelli, and Robert Lenhart. They're all married, with children, and their wives are nice, but—oh, well, all right—dull. Jeff Minelli's wife is a district nurse who travels around to outlying clinics. She invited me to go along with her sometime. Maybe I will if I can get the time off.

The Riordans had a dinner party, or cookout I guess you'd call it, for me this past weekend. That's where I met everybody's wives and kids. I realized how nice my apartment is compared to the housing available for families. What neighborhoods there are, and there aren't many, look about 1940s vintage, probably built about the time the hospital was. The people who work in the government offices live in them, too. The houses are small and everything seems weedy and shabby. Horses and dogs wander around loose. I also saw a goat and a rooster. The children go to the Indian schools.

I think everybody is kind of wary of me, afraid I'm looking down my nose at everything, which I promise you I'm not. But I'm kind of strange to them, except for the Lenharts. They're from the East, too. New York. They're here for all the altruistic reasons that people go into the Peace Corps. I just wish they'd be a little more quiet about it. They're real big into "the white man's crimes." I'll pass. For whatever reasons the others are here, their lives are not easy.

The hospital is clean and freshly painted in a color trying to match the red sandstone exterior. It doesn't have all the fancy equipment I'm used to, so I'll have to go back to basics, which is making you smile, you sly rascal.

I mentioned I was in ER. Have to deal with the usual broken bones, cuts and concussions. What are disturbing are the suicides, or the attempteds, and the alcohol-related traumas. Young, seemingly healthy men and woman are in despair. Their lives shouldn't be that stressful, but they are. They tell me it's an identity problem. They're sent to school to learn to live with the dominant culture, then come back here and don't have jobs, have lost their ties to the Navajo life, but don't fit in the white world either. But some succeed very well. The Navajos on the staff for instance. Everybody worries about it.

Got a letter from Mother and Daddy. I expect you sent them my address. I gather they're thinking about coming up for a visit, which is fine. I have a guestroom. I assume they're sleeping indoors these days.

I'm getting used to the routine, now I'll have to find some diversion. There's really not much of anything to do besides work. There's one movie theater and the films don't run to the very stimulating—cop and car crashes, horror movies, space alien junk, etc. You can imagine. I can go to the supermarket, but they don't have some things I'm used to and a lot of things I'm not. I'll probably need for you to send CARE packages from time to time. It's summer vacation so there's not much going on at the high school in Window Rock, except some politicking. Arizona gets another member of Congress as a result of the 1990 census, and the new district encompasses the northeastern quadrant of the state for the most part, but some of it wanders down to Phoenix. I've seen a map of the state's Congressional Districts. Woohee! It seems everybody gets a piece of Phoenix, which is the 800-pound gorilla as far as the population goes. But I shouldn't get snooty, with the crazy quilt districting in old gerrymandered Mass., should I?

The congressional seat is being hotly contested, so there's been a fair amount of speechifying. The primary is in September. I met one of the candidates, a Navajo lawyer who seems smart enough. As you can imagine, everybody here hopes he wins.

I should probably check on my voting status. I've never missed an election before. I suppose I would be considered an Arizona resident since I earn my living here, if I don't count the generous checks my grandfather sends me. Many thanks, but you really don't have to, you know. My schooling cost you plenty. I can do quite well on my own now. I don't make much, but there's not much to spend money on here, except for the wonderful Navajo-made rugs and jewelry. I expect I'll come back with quite a collection. I already have a ketoh *very much like yours. Can you believe I bought it at a gas station before I ever hit the Rez? I got it from Marcus Yazzie, do you remember him? He does you. Said you got to be friends. Isn't that amazing that he's the first Navajo I met? He's very nice and told me to bring the Porsche in when it needs work. Said he's the best mechanic around. Is that true? Anyway, his son is a silversmith and made the* ketoh *I bought.*

Rodeos are a big thing here, so I'll probably go to one, which should be sort of interesting. I've never seen one before. Jane Manyfarms, the hospital administrator, told me there's a big celebration and Pow Wow (Wow! You'll never know how exotic that sounds to me!) in Flagstaff over the Fourth and that I should go. Maybe I will, if I'm not on call. I certainly don't have anything else to do. I'll be sure to take a bunch of pictures, if I go, and send them on to you.

I've been thinking about trying to find somebody to lease a horse from. The country is very beautiful, as you know, and it would be fun to go exploring. I'm reluctant to take the Porsche off the main roads and a horse seems just the ticket.

I haven't ridden much since my horse-showing days, so it'll take me awhile to get my horse muscles back in shape.

Do try to come for a visit next month. I miss you. Maybe you could see your ladylove again. What was her name? You never told me. I'll bet she remembers you, too and maybe you could make up for lost time and you could trade places with me. Teehee.

Hugs, Cabot

Cabot reread the last line and thought about redoing that page, but instead she signed her name and folded the pages. She wanted the letter to be fairly light-hearted. It wouldn't do to let her grandfather know how lonely and bored and completely out of place she felt, but she left the line in because she wanted him to know she'd rather be someplace else. Almost anywhere else, if the truth be told. If only, oh, if only she didn't feel she was completely wasting her time.

Chapter Ten

July 4, 1992 Flagstaff

As the Window Rock High School band high-stepped past her, Cabot smiled. The Ohio State fight song blasted out of the trumpets and tubas, just like a thousand other high school bands in a thousand other Fourth of July parades. Then the band passed, and the rich plummy beat of Indian drums gradually superseded the fervent brass. Cabot turned to see a contingent of gorgeously costumed riders approach, billowing snowy feathered headdresses, swinging fringe and brilliant beading, members of the Sioux Nation the announcer said. Other tribes came by, the colors of their costumes dazzling in the bright morning sun.

Grandfather would love this, Cabot thought. She couldn't take pictures fast enough. Then the Navajo men and women appeared, led by Tribal Chairman Russell Wauneka. All the plumes and eagle feathers gave way to the brilliant velvets and satins the Navajo loved, and silver and more silver—set with turquoise and other semi-precious stones, in buttons, sewn into skirts and shirts, along collars, pant seams and hems, inlaid into saddles and bridles and boots. Silver swung from ears, around necks, and banded wrists and biceps. It winked and glittered and jingled over the clop clop rhythm of hooves on the warm asphalt of the street.

Cabot lowered her camera to watch, just as Nicholas Nakai, in a deep blue velvet shirt and heavy silver necklace, looked down at her and smiled a greeting. His saddle was heavily silvered and his black horse shone and reflected the blue of the sky. Cabot felt a small lurch somewhere around her pancreas.

A gust of a breeze blew a curly strand of hair into her eyes. Distractedly she pushed it away and Nicholas was past her. The announcer was introducing him as the future first Congressman from the new Sixth Congressional District. The crowd clapped and roared its approval, calling out as Nicholas waved and spun the black horse, obviously showing off and having a good time at it.

Cabot stared unseeing at the passing spectacle for a few seconds, then shook her head and raised the camera again. Miss White Mountain Apache was passing on a float, with her court. A pretty, dimpled dumpling of a girl, she waved at Cabot's camera, then passed as another fringed and beaded dancing group whirled by to insistent drums

Marching bands with their school banners and American flags flying, mounted posses, pompom girls, Pueblo Indian ladies balancing huge pots on their heads, more smiling queens and their nubile courts, dancing groups from a myriad of tribes, all swirled in a joyous mix of cultures. Cabot was enchanted. She loved parades, but Massachusetts never had anything to rival this yeasty celebration. Fourth of July festivities tended more to costumed redcoats with stalwart, musket toting pioneers in pursuit. So far there hadn't been a bloodied, bandaged Spirit of '76, fifing and drumming, in the whole procession.

The parade finally petered out as much as ended and Cabot milled around with the crowd, not certain what she was going to do next. Driving to Flagstaff had been an on-again, off-again spur-of-the-moment thing. The long holiday weekend stretched ahead and her aloneness finally pushed her to go. She was to be on duty Saturday, the next day, but the Fourth itself was free and she really didn't want to go to another cookout with the staff and their families. She still felt like an outsider among all the children and the housewifely talk, and the barbecues ran to flies, smoke, barking dogs, and squabbling, crying children.

She walked comfortably in the crowd, glad to be where it was noisy and congested for a change. The Pow Wow was at the fairgrounds, and the rodeo would be there. Cabot moved out of the crowd and looked at her watch. The rodeo didn't start for an hour and a half. She'd sort of half-decided to stay for it, but with nothing to do for that long, her aloneness suddenly became oppressive and she decided she'd find her car and go back to Fort Defiance. Maybe they needed a hand at the hospital, being a holiday and all.

A well-used pickup rumbled up to the curb where she stood.

"Hey, Cabot. You goin' over to the fairgrounds?"

Cabot looked up to see Jane Manyfarms, along with another Indian man and woman and a flatbed full of various sizes of dark-eyed children.

"Hi, Jane. Well, I don't know. I was going to get my car, then make up my mind. About going to the rodeo, I mean."

"Ever been to one?"

"Well, no." Cabot wished she'd been more decisive. Wished she'd said she had something definite to do.

Jane Manyfarms beamed through the open window. "Never seen a rodeo! Well, you just come along with us. We'll educate you. Otherwise you'd never guess what was going on."

"I..." Cabot looked in dismay at the loaded truck. There was obviously no room in the front cab. Not unless she was supposed to sit on the Indian man's lap.

Jane Manyfarms gave a sweeping gesture. "You just climb on up in back." She craned her neck out the window toward the bed of the truck. "You kids move over and let the lady in back there. And you be good, you understand?"

Oh, God, what am I going to do, Cabot thought, her mind racing in horror at the thought of riding in back of a dusty pickup truck absolutely stuffed with children.

Jane Manyfarms smiled benevolently.

Cabot moved toward the back of the truck. My God, I'm going to have to do this. I am doing it.

Clumsily she put her foot up on a flat surface that seemed to be the top of the bumper. She swung up and over the tailgate and stood uncertainly as ten pairs of lustrous brown eyes gazed politely at her.

She smiled tentatively and lowered herself between a boy of about eleven or twelve and a little girl about five.

"Hi," she said. She cleared her throat. "Uh, I mean *Ya-at-eeh*. I'm Dr. Chase. It's very nice of you to let me ride with you."

There were ten shy, snowy smiles.

The pickup lunged into traffic, throwing Cabot against the side of the truck. The children had all shifted naturally with the motion and continued to do so as Jane Manyfarms darted in and out of the heavy stream of traffic, mostly pickups, that were headed for the Pow Wow at the Coconino County Fairgrounds. Since many of the trucks were old the exhaust fumes were overpowering.

Jane Manyfarms, Cabot decided, could go head to head with any Andretti or Unser, as she bounced and clutched the side of the truck. They came to a large field overhung with a pall of heavy dust as what seemed like a million pickup trucks converged for the Pow Wow Rodeo.

When the truck had settled into a parking place, the ten children tumbled over the sides of the truck and melted into the crowd. Cabot watched them in surprise, then turned to Jane Manyfarms.

"Will they be all right?"

Jane grinned. "Oh, sure. Too many people around here know who they are. Relatives all over the place. They'll stay out of trouble or somebody'll be around to give 'em hell and a whack."

She indicated the man and woman who had been in the truck with her.

"This is my sister, Agnes Nakai and her husband Horseman Nakai."

Cabot smiled and wondered if they were Nicholas Nakai's parents. She was beginning to realize that Navajo families were as likely to call an aunt the mother of a child as his actual mother. A cousin might be announced as "my brother" or "my sister." Relationships were often blurred in the closeness of the extended family. It was rather sweet, really. She had not, to put it mildly, had an extended family. There was her grandfather, and on rare occasions, a mother and father.

"I think I've met your son," Cabot ventured.

Agnes Nakai's face lit up. "Nicholas? Yes, probably. He gets around. Learning how to be a politician." She laughed.

Cabot smiled. "Well, I think he's pretty much got the hang of it." She noted that, in the sun, Agnes had a reddish cast to her hair. And light, hazel eyes. Odd for a Navajo.

"Agnes is the principal of the high school over at Chinle," Jane said. "Horseman here is a rancher." Horseman Nakai ducked his head shyly at Cabot. She had seen the Navajo shake hands with each other, warmly, but she didn't know what the etiquette was. She remembered holding out her hand to Nicholas Nakai when she'd met him, and he had taken it readily enough. Held on to it rather a long time, actually. She must remember to ask Jane Manyfarms what was proper.

So far, Jane was the only Navajo she felt she knew well enough to ask about things like that. She had told Cabot, for instance, that an Indian considered it rude to look directly at someone, so Cabot shouldn't think her patients weren't paying attention to her directions. They were just being polite.

The rodeo stands were jammed and they'd barely squeezed into the second row bleacher seats, when, with a fanfare, the opening ceremonies began. All of the rodeo officials, some wildly-dressed clowns, a rodeo queen and her court, the contestants, and a flag team trotted around the ring in a chaotic mishmash of color and dust.

Jane explained the roles of the various riders.

"Those two are the pickup men. They're in charge of ring safety. They'll pull a cowboy out of trouble. You'll see later. The clowns aren't just there to be funny. They can distract a dangerous bull, for instance. The queen and the other two girls help with the stock. They have to ride real good, not just look real good."

Cabot looked at the three pretty Indian girls, all carrying waving flags. The queen had the American flag. They looked like they'd been born in the saddle. Probably had, just about.

The flag was raised at one end of the arena and a tinny rendition of the Star Spangled Banner squawked over the public address system. Cabot was surprised that many people sang. She was discovering that, though the Indians complained constantly and often bitterly about the government in Washington, they were, in reality, very patriotic. The government and the country were not the same thing in the Indian mind.

At the close of the anthem the announcer solemnly announced the recital of the "Cowboys' Prayer."

"Before our contestants begin the day's labor, knowing what they do is dangerous, it is traditional that we ask a blessing."

The crowd grew quiet and Cabot dutifully bowed her head, peeping around her curiously, then caught up in the simple, unsophisticated words, using rodeo metaphor, asking that "God guide us in the arena of life," and to give help " in living our lives in such a manner that when we make that inevitable ride to the country up there...that You, as our last Judge, will tell us that our entry fees are paid."

At the close of the prayer, the ring cleared and the queen raced around the ring at a flat-out gallop, the large American flag streaming behind her.

Cabot thought, here you are, the sophisticated easterner, and this sentimental stuff is really very moving. Amazing! Cabot, are you becoming a westerner?

"You go anywhere, Canada even, rodeos are pretty much the same," Jane explained. "Soon as the queen runs out of the ring, the action'll start."

Cabot watched bronc riders and calf roping, clowns doing slapstick routines; she listened to really dreadful jokes by the announcer who relied heavily on animal excrement and barnyard humor. The crowd knew it was awful and groaned loudly and often, but laughed at every joke.

"Now you'll see some pretty work," Jane said eagerly. "Nicholas and Pete are comin' up in team roping. They been working together since Nicholas was a kid. These next teams of cowboys are a real pleasure to watch. Always my favorite event."

Cabot felt her excitement. "Tell me what to watch for, Jane."

"Well now, the premise is real simple. Two cowboys come tearin' out from the chutes in hot pursuit of a steer. One cowboy is the header, who throws his rope around the steer's horns, then turns the animal so the second roper, the heeler, can lasso him by the hind legs. With both ropes looped around the saddle horns, the riders face the steer, backing their horses, with both ropes tightened. Okay, now watch these two."

The bell rang and it was just as Jane had described. The steer was released and the two mounted cowboys burst from the gate.

"They work against a clock," Jane went on. "The maneuvers originated in ranch work, when a steer had to be brought down for branding. That's pretty much what it looks like in real life."

"Why, this is wonderful! And the horses are marvelous," exclaimed Cabot. "They know exactly what to do."

"You bet. Working cattle's in their genes, but it still takes a lot of practice. Look. Here come Nicholas and Pete."

The chute clanged open and the steer sprang into the ring, with the two riders flat out in pursuit. In a process that took only a few seconds, it all moved so quickly Cabot hardly had the action sorted out before it was over, with the steer on the ground and the two riders poised, with the horses carefully backing to keep the ropes perfectly taut.

"They're very good," Cabot said. She was thinking that Nicholas Nakai, right this minute, would make a fabulous picture, but whether he looked like a Congressman was something else again. The Navajo cowboys wore their long hair clubbed, in a fashion called a *chongo*, as well as the requisite Levi's and western shirts. Would that play in

Washington, she wondered? Or make a campaign poster? He'd lost his hat. They all did. Picking it up out of the sawdust of the ring afterward seemed to be a part of the routine. He and Pete collected their ropes and loped casually out of the ring while the queen and the other girls hurried the huffy steer through another gate.

The loudspeaker announced their time as good enough for fifth place in the team-roping event.

"Nicholas and Pete good? Yeah," Jane said, grinning broadly. She turned back to the ring. "Oh, shit."

Cabot glanced quickly at Jane Manyfarms. The Indians had taken the white man's Anglo-Saxonisms with enthusiasm, and Jane was no exception. But this time her tone was truly exasperated.

"Now what is that crazy Nicholas doing down there going to wrestle a steer. Everybody's told him we got too much riding on him to be getting his ass kicked in doing some fool thing like that. He's not a kid any more."

"Oh, Jane, you know he doesn't have any sense sometimes," Agnes said. "But he's done this enough. He'll be fine."

Her voice was calm, but Cabot noticed a small frown line between her dark brows. Horseman Nakai grinned at Cabot and winked.

She looked down at the gate where the action would begin. They watched several of the contests: A big steer hurtled out of the gate, two mounted horsemen in pursuit. One was the *hazer*, who merely rode to keep the steer going in a straight line while the other raced with the steer, then took a flying leap, grabbing its horns and flipping it to the ground with all four of its hooves pointing in the same direction—at which time a buzzer sounded, stopping the timer. Since all of this involved overturning an irritated eight hundred-pound steer going thirty miles an hour, the event involved rather sizable and powerful men.

Then Nicholas was in the chute. Cabot noticed that his hazer was the tribal chairman, Russell Wauneka.

"My God, would you look at that. Russell's out there. And him only a few weeks out of Intensive Care," Jane moaned.

"Now, Jane. He just has to ride a few yards. He no more would stay out of the rodeo than miss a squaw dance," Horseman Nakai chuckled.

With a clang the gates opened and the steer hurtled out into the arena, the two riders tearing after him. In a flash, Nicholas launched himself over the galloping steer and with a heave and a spray of sawdust, the big beast was on his side, panting and struggling. The crowd roared, for the time was excellent. The announcer called out 5.5 seconds. Nicholas and Russell could very well win the event.

But when he stood up, Cabot narrowed her eyes. Nicholas's arm hung loosely, at an unnatural angle.

She rose, assessing what could be wrong.

Jane and Agnes looked at her uneasily as she watched Nicholas lean and pick his black cowboy hat out of the dust and stroll nonchalantly to the fence.

"He's dislocated his shoulder," Cabot said.

Jane spun around and stared at Nicholas, who, instead of swinging himself up onto the fence surrounding the ring, walked to a gate before he disappeared.

She jumped up, turning to Cabot. "Come on!"

As they squeezed through the crowded bleachers, Jane was griping. "They only have an ambulance here, with a coupla no-account medics who don't know their ass from third base."

Except for the girl barrel racers, in back of the chutes at

a rodeo was still pretty much a man's world, and disapproving glances were thrown their way as Jane marched Cabot through the milling cowboys and horses.

They found Nicholas with Pete Price and Russell Wauneka talking to one of the two medics assigned to the ambulance. The medic was gently probing Nicholas's shoulder.

"Just a minute there. I got a doctor here. Step aside."

Jane bustled into the group, pulling Cabot at her side.

"I don't know, ma'am. I'm supposed to take anybody hurt into Flagstaff Hospital if it looks serious. This looks serious."

Nicholas looked up and grinned at Cabot. "Oh, it isn't serious. Think I just knocked my shoulder out."

Cabot noticed a sheen of perspiration on his face despite his casual smile. A dislocated shoulder hurt like hell, no matter how stiff upper lip Nicholas Nakai wanted to play it.

She stepped up, glancing at the medic. "It's all right. I really am a doctor, and it would be much better if we deal with this before it begins to swell." She turned to Nicholas and ran her hands around his shoulder. "Yes, that's what you've done. Let's take the shirt off. I'll be careful. I know it hurts."

Just once, as she unbuttoned Nicholas's shirt, her doctor's persona slipped a little, when her fingers felt his heart beating under the warm skin of his chest. He smelled of horse and sweat. She felt his breath stir her hair and her fingers faltered. Only slightly. She was sure he hadn't noticed. Gently she eased the shirt off and heard the combined gasps of the surrounding people. A dislocation was always grotesque, always a shock to see the human body so distorted.

She positioned his arm carefully at his side.

"There will be an especially sharp pain right before it

goes into place." She looked up in sympathy, noting his eyes were not much above her own.

"I'll be fine. Glad you're here to do this."

Cabot braced herself and cupped one hand under his elbow. Sweat broke out on her forehead as she applied pressure. She repositioned her feet and renewed the pressure. *Damn.* She gritted her teeth. *Get in there you sonofagun.*

A groan escaped from Nicholas. A small pop and the big joint sprang back into place.

Relief surged through Cabot as she saw Nicholas's sudden smile.

Cabot swallowed her exultation. Repositioning a dislocation was one of medicine's pleasures. The relief is dramatic to the patient and his esteem for his physician soars, even though it is a matter of some simple mechanics, leverage and a little muscle.

"Why, it's fine now," Nicholas said, moving his arm carefully.

"Well, it isn't, quite. It'll begin to hurt. It feels good now because it was so painful before. Let these medics give you some ice and a couple of aspirin. And you should keep it as immobile as possible for the next week or so." She turned to the medic, who had watched in fascination. "Have you got a sling in the van?"

"Oh. Yeah. Sure thing. And ice and aspirin. Coming up." He hopped into the back of the ambulance.

Jane was helping Nicholas into his shirt. "Dumb jackass, scaring us all. Acting like some airhead teenager. You're damn lucky it wasn't more serious. Who in the hell you think you are, going out there doing that? Huh? I got your mother up there in the stands scared to death."

Nicholas winked at Cabot over his aunt's head. "Yes, Auntie Jane."

Cabot bit back a smile and took the sling from the medic, quickly tying up Nicholas's arm. "Take the aspirin as long as it hurts, but remember it's important not to stress the shoulder for awhile." She gave his arm a pat. "Stop in and see me at the hospital if it starts to bother you."

He looked at her carefully, a small quiver at the corner of his mouth. "Why, yes doctor. I'll remember to do that. I surely will."

Chapter Eleven

July 7, 1992 Fort Defiance

Cabot was sure Nicholas would come to see her at the hospital, though she knew there was no real medical reason for him to. His shoulder would hurt for a few days and if he was reasonably careful it would stay in place. She found she was rehearsing what she might say, faced with touching that glossy bronze shoulder, feeling those assessing eyes on her again. Funny. Nicholas's eyes were dark, like his father's, and his hair was a true black. She thought about Agnes Nakai's reddish hair and lighter goldish eyes and wondered if Nicholas had white blood in his ancestry. But his features were Navajo enough, the high cheekbones, rather slanted eyes.

But he hadn't come, and then she was confronted with her disappointment.

I just don't have enough to keep me occupied, she scolded herself. Imagining things that aren't there. You were so sure, you idiot, that Nicholas Nakai was interested in you and you were all busy trying to find a way to back him off, and he isn't interested at all. What's gotten into you Cabot Chase? You don't want to be involved with an Indian man a continent away from the center of your future. That would be absolutely insane! He's just a male. Intriguing because he's good-looking and Indian. Deep down you wonder how is he different? That's all. Your hormones have been neglected and they're antsy.

She tried to think of Larimer.

Cabot had her pictures from the parade developed and found herself turning again and again to the shot of Nicholas as he smiled down at her, burnished skin, glittering silver, and black stallion. Angry at herself, she stuffed the pictures into an envelope and sent them off to her grandfather.

So much for Big Chief Nicholas Nakai.

The next day she went to Jane Manyfarms's office.

"Jane? Got a minute?"

"Sure. Got something to show you anyway."

"Oh?"

Jane grinned and shoved a newspaper across the desk. "*Arizona Republic*. The state's big paper. Was in Monday's edition."

A color photo on the front page of Nicholas flying over the steer's back at the rodeo. Underneath was the caption: "*Future congressman cutting out the bull?*"

Jane was chortling and Cabot glanced down the page at the accompanying article. "Sixth Congressional District candidate Nicholas Nakai on a campaign swing through North Scottsdale and the Pima-Maricopa Indian Community, met with voters..."

Cabot felt a small surge of something like elation. He hadn't come because he'd been away. She brushed the feeling away, as unwelcome as a persistent fly.

"Oh, great picture. Nicholas is campaigning down in Phoenix?"

"Yeah, he's been down there all week. That's where he's got to make an impression." Jane was still smiling down at the news photo. "That's where he'll win or lose."

"Oh. I...I wonder how his arm is...shoulder, I mean."

"I expect it's all right. You said yourself it was a pretty straightforward dislocation. He's young. And strong. He probably didn't pay it much mind."

"Well, yes. That's what worried me. Men tend to think they're being sissies if they don't ignore injuries."

"Which makes it a good thing they're stronger than they are smart."

Cabot laughed. "I think you're a feminist, Jane."

"Not feminist. Navajo. Navajo women already got power. Now. What'd you want to see me about?"

"Do you know somebody who would lease me a horse? Or make some kind of arrangement. I'd love to do a little exploring, off the main roads. I have time I'm not using. I need something to do, to be frank, and I like to ride. I'd want a pretty good horse. I'm not inexperienced."

Jane Manyfarms looked at Cabot thoughtfully for several seconds. "We don't keep you busy enough, huh?"

"Oh, Jane, that isn't it. You know that." She waved a hand around vaguely. "There's a lot to see here. It's all so different from the country I'm from. Now that I'm settled, I'd like to explore a little."

Jane sat back and crossed her hands over her stomach. "You got a boyfriend back east?"

Cabot was startled. "Why...um...sort of."

"You miss him?"

"Jane, I..." Cabot felt her cheeks flush.

"So I guess you're a little lonesome. We got to get you to socialize. I tell you what. There's a squaw dance this weekend over to Canyon de Chelly. You're not on duty. I'll pick you up."

Cabot shifted uneasily. "What's a squaw dance?

Jane laughed. "You'll see when you get there."

"Well...I..."

"Don't argue. I'll pick you up Saturday."

Cabot couldn't think of an excuse not to go. How could she have? There wasn't anything to do. "All right. What should I wear?" she asked nervously, not sure what she was getting into.

"Oh, nothing fancy."

Slightly dazed at this turn of events, she stood to go.

Jane added, "And I can think of maybe ten people who'd love to let you feed one of their horses. I'll check around. I'll have somebody by Saturday."

Cabot walked down the lobster-colored hallway, shaking her head.

I guess she's everybody's bossy auntie, and I do what she tells me, just like everybody else. My God, I never even let my own mother tell me what to do. Now I'm going to a...what? A squaw dance? You're going native, old girl.

Cabot hooked the heavy concha belt around her waist and looked in the mirror. Several weeks ago she'd taken her car in for an oil change to Marcus Yazzie and he'd shown her the worked silver and turquoise belt of silver discs set with turquoise. She bought it on the spot and felt only a little guilty about spending the money grandfather kept sending her. He insisted that he was giving her a hardship bonus, but she mostly just put it in the bank. When she was doing her surgical residency at Johns Hopkins she'd be trying to make ends meet in Baltimore. She'd need her savings.

Cabot hadn't worn the concha belt yet. Now, for the

squaw dance she tried it with a denim riding skirt and a pair of delicately beaded moccasins that she hadn't worn yet either. She hoped she was dressed sort of like everybody else. This was her first Navajo social event and she'd be conspicuous enough.

She heard Jane Manyfarms's truck horn, slipped on her silver ketoh and gave herself one more anxious glance in the mirror.

Again there were nearly a dozen children in the bed of the truck, but this time Cabot got to ride in the cab.

"Thought you might like to be outa the wind." Jane grinned. "It's about an hour drive. Be a real luxury to have only two of us up front. Usually have two or three passengers as well as the crowd in the back."

"Oh. I hope you didn't throw anybody out just for me. Really, Jane, I wouldn't have minded the back," she lied.

"Nah. Everybody's got a ride who's goin'."

"Are some of the kids yours, Jane?"

"Two oldest boys are. One of the girls. The rest are, oh, cousins."

"I didn't realize you were married."

"I'm not, now. Been divorced two, three times."

"You're not sure?"

"Three times. Divorce isn't a very complicated business with us. Used to be a woman got fed up, she'd just put her husband's saddle outside their hogan. He'd know to go back to his mother's hogan. Nowadays, you just send 'em packing."

"Sounds sensible." Cabot was coming to admire many of the Navajo's pragmatic ways of dealing with their lives.

"It was the drinking mostly. Just happened to get three men couldn't handle it. Too many can't. The Indian disease. It isn't just the men either. It's a big problem."

"I know. I see it at the hospital."

The two women rode in silence. It was a soft, summer evening, the sun still low in the sky, tinting low-lying clouds into streaks and plumes of oranges and crimsons.

"I'll miss these sunsets," Cabot sighed.

"You going somewhere? You just got here last month."

"No, no, of course not. I was just thinking out loud. I don't know what I meant. Now, tell me about a squaw dance," she said, wanting to change the subject.

"It's part of a curing ceremony, actually, an Enemyway sing. Lefty Curlyhair was feeling poorly and had a hand trembler in to diagnose his problem. Hand tremblers are women—well, usually—don't have to be. They have special powers to diagnose sickness. We use crystal gazers, too. Well, the hand trembler told Lefty he needed an Enemyway curing ceremony. Like as not he had a bad experience with an Anglo that left him feelin' bad. We call these curing ceremonies *sings,* and the medicine men who do the sings are *hataalis*, or singers. Anyway, it's a three-day ceremony and the last night there's a squaw dance. It's real social. Be a lot of people there. And if you've never seen Canyon de Chelly...well, it's real pretty.

Real pretty was an understatement, Cabot discovered. The entrance to the canyon was at Chinle, and when they arrived, amid a crowd of pickups and horses, the canyon was becoming shadowy, with the last rosy reflections of the sun tinting the soaring sandstone cliffs shades of rose and lavender, deep blue and black. The sheer faces of the eight hundred-foot walls rose from a wide, sandy floor dissected by a smallish river lined with trees.

"Those trees are cottonwoods. Those are Russian olives.

Didn't grow here 'til the Civilian Conservation Corps planted 'em in the 1930s. Kinda crowdin' the native cottonwoods now. Another government screw-up," Jane said.

The scent of piñon fires and cooking meat mingled with the truck exhausts and smells of horses and livestock. Jane's truck bounced and churned its way through the sandy surface, going with the traffic, until they saw a large group ahead. Cabot thought it looked like a large cookout.

As they walked to the center of the activity Cabot wiggled her toes inside the moccasins. They were perfect for walking in the sandy soil. She began to feel a bit Indian. It crossed her mind that Larimer would disapprove. The thought made her smile.

Many of the women were in the jewel-tone, velvet blouses and pleated satin skirts that the Navajo women favored, though Cabot hadn't seen them much in town. The unisex, ubiquitous jeans, T-shirts, and athletic shoes had taken over for everyday wear. But tonight the colorful dress was everywhere. Many of the men also wore the bright velvet shirts with their jeans and cowboy boots. And there was no such thing as too much silver jewelry. Men and women alike wore whatever they could find room for on their costumes, much like the dress at the Fourth of July celebrations: Concha belts, squash blossom necklaces, heavy necklaces of more contemporary design, earrings on men and women both, buttons on blouses and shirts, marching up and down pant legs and skirts, and on moccasins. There were wrist and arm bracelets and several rings per hand.

Cabot decided her next purchase would be a necklace, and maybe some earrings, too. Then she smiled to herself. Where had this new passion for jewelry come from? She had the pearls her grandfather had given her when she graduated from high school, and her grandmother's diamond engagement ring stashed in a safety deposit box. That was it. She'd never really cared for jewelry one way or another, but, this finely worked silver with its warm blue stones enchanted her.

Jane Manyfarms moved them to the outer edge of the circle. A drum was pounding insistently as a group chanted sacred songs. A man emerged from what Jane explained was a ceremonial hogan. He was naked and his skin had been darkened with some kind of ash mixture.

"That's Lefty Curlyhair, the patient," Jane said. "According to the legend, the Monster Slayer, one of the sons of Changing Woman, was blackened so that the monster *Yeitso* couldn't see him. All of the curing ceremonies tell the story of one of the legends of the *Dine*."

They watched as the patient moved to a spot where a symbolic "scalp" was placed and with a jabbing motion of a crow's bill that he carried, he symbolically killed the enemy who had been causing him problems.

The drum rose to a dramatic crescendo, then subsided to a low, insistent beat that would continue until the dancing began, when a livelier beat would take over.

It grew dark and over the edge of the cliff a full moon rose, washing the canyon with silver. Some distance from the activities, teenage boys were building a large fire that would be the center for the dancing later. Cabot and Jane moved among the cook fires, sampling lamb stew, fry bread, beans, and cornbread. The lamb stew was kind of a uniform beige, the meat in a broth of onions and hominy. Cabot had thought it unappetizing looking, but in actuality it was quite good.

She began to feel more at ease. Everyone was unfailingly polite, and even though she was the only Anglo there, no one acted as if it were at all unusual that Jane had brought her. Jane knew everybody and Cabot began to feel she'd been introduced to at least a thousand people, though it was probably closer to a hundred. People she had treated at the hospital came and spoke to her. Marcus Yazzie brought his silversmith son, Emerson, over to meet her and was pleased to see her wearing his pieces. Emerson's children were the ones Cabot had met when she'd first driven into Marcus Yazzie's service station her first day in Arizona. Though Navajo words swirled around her, in her presence the Indians spoke only English.

For the past half-hour Cabot noticed that Jane Manyfarms seemed to be looking for someone, watching out for someone.

"C'mon. Got somebody who wants to meet you."

"Me?" *Who in the world?*

Jane laughed. "My mother wants to meet you."

They made their way through the crowd to a woman who had just dismounted from a black and white paint horse. She was small, dressed in a purple sateen skirt and emerald velvet blouse. Her silver jewelry winked in the reflection of the many small cookfires. She handed the horse over to one of the boys who had been in the back of Jane's truck—probably one of her sons, Cabot thought, then turned to meet Jane's mother.

The woman smiled when she saw Jane. "I didn't mean to be so late, but I had a sick calf."

Jane pulled Cabot over to the woman. "This is Dr. Chase, Mother. Cabot, meet my mother, Laura Begay."

Laura Begay took the hand Cabot held out in both of her own and smiled warmly, looking up at Cabot with large, tilted up eyes.

"I've been wanting to meet you. I knew your grandfather very well."

Cabot caught her breath, and the woman laughed. "We were great friends. I worked at the hospital then. I was a nurse there when he came on the staff."

Cabot regained her composure. She had halfway imagined what her grandfather's lady looked like, wondering if she would every find out who she was. Now, out of the blue, here she stood. Cabot smiled, delighted with the small thrill of this revelation about her grandfather that she'd imagined since she was a little girl. She found her voice. "He loved this part of the country. That's partly why I'm here."

Cabot studied the older woman. She was still beautiful, her skin barely wrinkled, though there were gray streaks in her hair. No wonder her grandfather had been smitten. Laura Begay must have been quite something to a young Boston doctor just out of medical school.

"And how is your grandfather? Well, I hope."

"He's fine. He'll be coming to visit next month. I'll write and tell him I met you."

"I'd like to see him again," Laura Begay said. "Will you tell him that?"

"I expect he'd like to see you, too. He's got such fond memories of the time he spent here." Cabot tried to keep her words neutral. She wasn't sure at all whether Cabot W.W. wanted to meet his former love. Maybe too much time had passed.

"I knew he'd married and had a son. Now I meet his granddaughter. That's nice."

Cabot chose her words carefully. She wanted Laura Begay to know that her grandfather was a widower. "He's talked often about coming out. Ever since my grandmother died he's promised himself, but you know how things get put off."

"Oh, yes. Yes, I do." She patted Cabot's arm. "I'm glad we met. Now I have people I have to see."

Cabot watched Laura Begay move off through the crowd.

Jane Manyfarms watched her mother go, too. "Well, I'll be damned," she said. "So she knew your grandfather. She never told me that. Wondered why she was interested when she heard your name."

"You knew my grandfather worked at the Fort Defiance Hospital."

"Well, yes. And sure she would have known him. She was a nurse there, right after World War II. Eventually she had the job I got now. She retired six years ago and lives here in the canyon. Keeps some livestock and sheep. A few horses. Treats the Navajo families in the canyon. Tells them when to come to the hospital. They trust her to tell them what to do. Back in some of the remote canyons around here the families can be real traditional. Don't want to have anything to do with the whites, and that includes their medicine. Don't mean to make you feel bad, but that's the way it is."

"You haven't hurt my feelings, Jane. Tell me. Is your father living?" asked Cabot.

"No. He died some years back."

Cabot, what are you thinking, you sly wretch. That if grandfather could come out and meet his old flame, maybe that obsession of his would be put to rest and you could go back east where you belong. You are thoroughly rotten to the core. A deal's a deal. Don't even think such devious thoughts. Don't even think such things. But wouldn't it be wonderful anyway?

There must have been some imperceptible change in the incessant beating of the drums that signaled the crowd to move toward the big fire that threw long, flickering shadows on the looming canyon walls.

As they neared the fire, a monotonous chant began. A group of young men sat around a large drum of leather stretched over a round base. The beat was made with a stick, about a yard long, with a soft round tip about the size of a softball, probably leather as well. The big drum made a thump that resounded in Cabot's stomach, and the song they sang was heavily rhythmic, but seemed tuneless and strange to her ears. Jane translated the words to the chants for her. There was a lot of repetition, and they seemed quite poetic and reverent, but she found it difficult to respond to the almost falsetto tones of the singers.

After a long series of songs, couples began to move into the big circle around the fire.

"Women get the men to dance. She goes to the man she wants and hooks her fingers in his belt. He's got to dance. When the song is over, if he wants to get away, he's got to give her a gift. Money or something. If she doesn't want to dance with him anymore and he wants to, she's got to steal something that belongs to him. Then he pays her to get it back and then she can leave," Jane explained.

Cabot nodded, caught up in the rhythms of the drums and rattles, the firelight glowing on the dark faces and jewel-toned velvet shirts. The dance was more a simple hesitation step that took the dancers around the fire.

"Go on. You got to go get somebody to dance. Can't just stand around all night," Jane urged.

"Me?" Cabot laughed nervously. "Oh, I couldn't possibly. I wouldn't know the first thing to do. Really, I'll just watch."

Jane's expression was determined. "Now, how hard does that look?"

She took a firm grip on Cabot's arm and propelled her around the edge of the crowd to a group of men gathered around the singers.

"Here's one you know."

"But..."

She poked Cabot's fingers in the back of the man's belt.

Cabot wished she could drop through the earth. The man turned. It was Nicholas Nakai.

His smile was surprised and pleased. "Well, hello. Hi, Auntie Jane. Heard you were here."

Cabot slipped her hand free and began to back away. "I'm sure you two want to chat. I'll just walk around and talk to people."

Jane caught her sleeve, then rehooked Cabot's fingers in Nicholas's belt. He took her hand, winked at his aunt and moved with Cabot into the circle of dancers.

Cabot's mind was having a hard time wrapping around the entire scenario. *This is bordering on surreal. What in the world am I doing here? Dancing around a fire in the middle of a canyon, in the moonlight, with an Indian man!*

Nicholas's hand rested lightly on her waist, his other hand had crossed over her and picked up hers.

"You're supposed to hook your thumb over my belt in the back." He grinned. "Otherwise, you're doing fine."

Cabot felt the dance step was similar to the step a bridesmaid makes coming down the aisle. Jane was right when she said 'how hard is that?'"

She ventured a glance at Nicholas. "I...um...didn't recognize you with your hair cut." She realized she sounded disappointed.

"You don't like it?" His face fell, teasing.

"Oh, no. I mean, it looks very nice. Very..."

"...upstanding citizen running for Congress maybe?" He cocked his head, amused.

Suddenly she relaxed and smiled. Again, she noticed his eyes were only a little above her own. "Yes, very." It was all right. The strangeness was wearing off.

"I've been down in the city campaigning. Protective coloration. Can't have long hair and earrings when I'm looking for votes in Scottsdale. Got to look civilized. Not scare anybody."

"Long hair doesn't scare anybody anymore."

"On me it would scare some people."

"Jane told me you were downstate. She showed me your picture in the Phoenix paper."

"I'm not sure that's how I want the voters to think of me," he chuckled.

"How's your shoulder? Bother you?"

"It did a little, at first. It's fine now." He smiled, catching her eyes. "I finally had an excuse to come in to see the beautiful lady doctor, then I had to go to work. I was terribly disappointed."

Cabot looked down. He wanted her to say she was disappointed, too. It...it would just not be a good thing to do. She knew that with a white man she would have flirted and been extravagant at how crestfallen she had been.

But her discomfiture passed as they continued the dance. Nicholas Nakai spoke easily, making little jokes that made her laugh. When the chant ended, Cabot thought that would be the end of it. But Nicholas walked her to the edge of the fire circle and continued their conversation.

She tilted her head, questioningly. "I thought you were supposed to pay me for dancing with me, so you could leave," she teased.

"Well, that's how it works sometimes. How much do you think I ought to give you?"

"Oh. Well, uh, I don't know. Maybe fifty cents?"

He whooped with laughter, the firelight dancing in his eyes.

"Well, I don't know these things. Is that too much?" She frowned.

"How about a hundred dollars?"

"A hundred dollars? That's ridiculous. That's way too much."

"Well, it's not too much, but since I don't have a hundred dollars, I guess you're stuck with me for the rest of the evening."

Cabot opened her mouth, but she didn't know what to say. The drumbeat began again and Nicholas pulled her back into the circle of dancers.

"Jane said I have to steal your hat or something," she said. "Do you have a hat?"

"'Fraid not."

She eyed the heavy squash blossom necklace he was wearing. "That looks like a possibility."

Nicholas looked at her carefully, then pulled her out of the circle of dancers. He slipped the necklace over his head and put it in her hands. She felt the weight of the warm silver and rubbed her thumbs over the fine inlaid turquoise stones. She felt a little breathless when she raised her arms and settled the necklace back around his shoulders. She knew her cheeks were flaming, but of course the heat from the fire would make them do that.

"I...it's all right. I'm having a good time. Maybe you can pay me later."

He grinned. "It's a deal. Later." He touched her shoulder. "Let's take a walk. I want to show you something."

The air away from the fire was fresh and felt cool on her face. The soft sand made a whisper under her moccasins as she walked beside Nicholas. She was relieved that he didn't pick up her hand. They simply walked, side by side, letting their eyes become accustomed to the silvery wash of moonlight, bright enough to cast their shadows ahead of them.

"Where are we going?"

"You'll see. It's not far."

Nicholas had been chatty and funny as they danced around the fire. Now he was quiet, a comfortable quiet. Cabot picked up his mood. The canyon seemed full of a strange magic. Actually, Jane had told her, it was a very holy place and figured in many of the Navajo myths.

Cabot followed as Nicholas turned to a sheer wall. He took her elbow and guided her around a chain link fence.

"Canyon de Chelly is a national monument. We call it *Tseyi,* which means 'within the rocks. The valley belongs to the Navajo, the ruins the government. They fence them off because people deface them. They've had to do a lot of restoration. It's an ongoing thing. The bricks are made of the canyon's red sandstone, which is soft, so erosion is a problem as well."

Cabot followed as he began to ascend the cliff, using small hand and footholds.

"Just follow me, it's not difficult. Are you nervous about heights?"

"No. I'll be fine. I'll follow you."

It was not a climb of more than twenty feet off the valley floor when they reached the ledge. The light from the moon picked out a small, ancient ruin.

"It's Anasazi. The Ancient Ones lived here approximately a thousand years ago. No one's exactly sure why they left. Drought. Marauding tribes. But they were the ancestors of the Pueblo tribes. This dwelling is a small one. Maybe five families lived here." He indicated a flat stone. "Sit down." He lowered himself beside her and looked around. "I love to come up here, especially on a night like this."

The valley looked ghostly and calm. The sound of the distant drum echoed softly against the walls.

"Should we be here?" she whispered.

His teeth flashed. "No."

Nicholas remained quiet and Cabot knew he wanted her to feel the mystery of the place. Bright moonlight drenched the soft sandstone, creating dark shadows in the rooms and in the stillness of the ruin Cabot began to feel the presence of the ancient families who had descended these walls daily to their farms and orchards on the valley floor. She closed her eyes and, with the pulsing drumbeat in the background, could imagine voices and children's laughter. She opened her eyes and glanced over at Nicholas and saw he was smiling at her reverie.

After awhile, he stood and pulled her up. Wordlessly they retraced the footholds down the cliff face. Nicholas went first. At the bottom he reached up swung her away from the last handholds and set her down gently, his hands lingering only a moment at her waist and when she turned he was already moving away.

They walked along the riverbed and the sound of the drum diminished and the splash of the water and the rustle of the cottonwoods took over.

"I think I'm lost," Cabot said.

"I know this place like the back of my hand, night or day. I was born here. It was my playground."

"Thank you for the ruin."

"I thought you'd like it." After a while he said, "Tell me something."

"If I can," she said.

"Why are you named for your grandfather?"

"It's my middle name, really. I chose to use it because...because it makes me seem, well, more masculine I guess. I want to be a surgeon. Women aren't very common in the surgical fields. I thought Cabot sounded more, well, authoritative."

Nicholas gave a short laugh. "Masculine. Masculine? You? That's really funny."

"It isn't," she said defensively.

He stopped her with his hand. "Okay. Cabot is more authoritative than what? What really is your name?"

She hesitated. "Lily."

He raised his hand and touched her hair. "I like it. It suits you. You look like a Lily."

Cabot held her breath.

His gaze was penetrating and he finally spoke. "Tell me, Lily Cabot Chase. Why are you here? I don't think you want to be."

"It's too long a story."

She felt herself tense under his scrutiny, wanting to edge away. His eyes swept her face, then his hand moved up and he watched his finger curl around a lock of her hair at her shoulder.

"Do you know something?" he asked.

She cleared her throat. "What?"

"Whenever I step toward you, or reach out to you, you step back. No, that's not exactly it. You...shy away."

"Oh, I don't."

Abruptly he moved closer. She jumped back. Her heel caught a gopher hole and she slipped to her bottom, her eyes startled and wide, her mouth open.

Nicholas squatted down, his elbows on his knees, grinning. "I rest my case. Close your mouth."

She bit her lip.

The light from the moon made his eyes glitter. "Are you afraid of me, Lily Cabot Chase?"

Her voice sounded hoarse in her ears. "Why, that's absurd. Of course not."

He held out his hand and pulled her to her feet.

She looked into the eyes that slanted so much like his grandmother's.

They stood, not touching, except for the fingers he wound through the curls along her shoulder.

He spoke almost absently. "I have a horse. She's red. Real pretty. But she's spooky. I've got to take her by whatever scares her a dozen times. Maybe more, before she settles down."

"Is this a parable?" she asked dryly.

There was a pause before he answered. "Maybe." His eyes held hers until she looked away.

From a copse perhaps twenty feet away, over the whispers of the river and the cottonwoods, there began to come sounds of lovemaking reaching a heated peak.

Nicholas clenched his fingers in her hair, then laughed shortly. "C'mon. We'd better get back before we step on somebody."

Chapter Twelve

July, 1992

Cabot drove along paved road until she passed the Good Shepherd Mission, when the Porsche bounced onto graded dirt. The surface had been oiled recently, so the dust rising as Cabot sped along was minimal. Jane Manyfarms had told her she would see the stables from the road about a mile past the mission. Jane had found a horse for her to lease last night at the squaw dance and Cabot was eager to try the animal.

When she pulled into the yard, she looked around with approval. The horse barn wasn't fancy, but it was clean, and the horses that happened to be out in their runs looked well fed and cared for. The family residence was a mobile home, much like the ones she had seen from the road ever since she had arrived on the reservation. There was a traditional ceremonial hogan to the rear of that.

Cabot parked the Porsche and got out to look around. Jane had told her to do that; someone would come out by and by. One just didn't march up and knock on the door etiquette-wise. It had something to do with evil spirits getting fooled into thinking you didn't really want to see anyone on the premises, and then they would go away.

Cabot glanced around, feeling a bit strange. She didn't see anything that looked like an evil spirit, but she waited like Jane had told her and hoped the rancher would come out sooner rather than later. She walked along the stalls, wondering which horse was the one she was supposed to try.

After about ten minutes an Indian man came out of the mobile home.

Relieved, Cabot walked forward. "Hello. I'm Dr. Chase. Are you Clah Chischillige?" Cabot hoped she was pronouncing it right. She found it difficult to get her mouth around some of the Navajo names.

The man nodded. "Jane Manyfarms says you want to lease a horse." He turned without another word and walked along the stalls.

Cabot followed. "Yes. I'll pay for feed, shoeing and vet bills, but I want the horse just for me. I'm never sure when I can come, so I want him free all the time. Is that all right?"

"I understand that. You pay by the week. Up front."

"Yes, that's fine. Did Jane Manyfarms mention I wanted a good, spirited horse?"

"She said that. I'll watch you ride first."

Cabot was slightly taken aback. Well, that was only fair. The man didn't want some novice hotrod ruining a good animal.

He unlatched a stall and disappeared, then came out leading a pretty chestnut mare. He led her down to a shed that served as a tack room and held the halter rope out to Cabot.

When he brought out the bulky western saddle Cabot realized she would have to learn how to tack the horse up. She was used to the small English saddle.

She watched carefully as Clah Chischillige readied the horse.

"Okay. Get on."

The Indian hooked his thumbs over his belt and stepped back to watch.

Cabot put her foot in the big stirrup and swung herself up. The mare danced a few steps.

"I've never ridden a western saddle before. Give me a chance to get the feel of it."

"That's fine. Just ride up and down the road there," he said.

The mare did her little dance again, but Cabot settled her and trotted down the road. They went up and down in front of Clah Chischillige a few times, then Cabot eased the horse into a lope. Her face lit up. The horse's gait was sublime. She could ride for hours like this.

The next time they passed the Indian, he said, "Gallop."

Cabot and the mare thundered down the road then pulled up and trotted back to Clah Chischillige.

"She's lovely. What do you think? May I take her?"

"Okay. If you want to go out now, you can pay me."

Cabot dismounted and led the horse over to her car and got out her checkbook.

"Check's fine, but after this I'd like cash. Thirty dollars a week feed and bedding, use of the saddle and bridle. I give you the farrier's and vet's bills."

"That's fine. I'll give you cash today if that's what you prefer." She dug into her billfold. "What's the mare's name?"

"Niyol. Means *wind* in Navajo." Clah Chischillige pulled out a worn, slim billfold and carefully inserted the thirty dollars, turned and started back to the house, then turned. "Mare's a little skitty. Just so's you'll know."

Cabot grinned. Aren't we both, she thought. She was still rankling a little from Nicholas's words the night before. Like he'd have to ride her a few times before she tamed down. Well, he hadn't exactly said that. But the implication was there. It sounded just a little too hairy-chested. Except Indians didn't have hairy chests.

Cabot shook the pesky thoughts of Nicholas from her head. "C'mon, Niyol, sweetie. Let's see if you live up to your name."

Chapter Thirteen

July 10, 1992
Marblehead, Massachusetts

Dear Lily,

It's always a joy to hear from you, but I must confess that your latest letter was especially heart lifting. I'm speaking, of course, of your meeting with Laura and that she expressed a wish to see me again. I had thought, over the years, that I would like to contact her. And that wasn't only after your grandmother's death. I know I don't tell you anything that you don't already know, or at least guess. My life with Arista was not unhappy, but our relationship was not a warm one. This was probably as much my fault as hers. I don't know. It doesn't matter anymore. However, it was not by accident that we only had the one child.

But Laura and I belonged, I thought, to another world, far in the past. Your news that she wants to see me has surprised old longings.

Contrary to what you believe, it was not I who ended our affair. Laura, and she was probably right, sent me away. I have no notion if things have changed measurably, but forty years ago our liaison was shocking to a lot of people, not only whites. She was wise enough to know that I wasn't really strong enough to weather such approbation. For whatever it's worth, I hate it that she was probably right.

But time changes things and at this point in my life I feel I would like to see her, to see if perhaps there isn't something we could add to each other's lives. Something else I don't know. Maybe she just wants to take a look at me and chuckle in relief that she had the good sense to turn me away.

Nevertheless, the thought of seeing her again has made me feel like a schoolboy. I feel like doing cartwheels, but refrain from doing so because of arthritic knees and a creaky shoulder. But other than the wear and tear of years, I'm fit enough. Perhaps I might make her heart beat faster still.

As you might have guessed by now, I'm moving up the date of my visit. If it's not convenient for you, I can stay at the motel there. I'm afraid I'm too impatient to get to Arizona to wait. Will arrive Friday the 25th. I've got a flight into Gallup and will rent a car there.

I'm greatly amused at your story of finding your patient sitting in the middle of a sand painting on the floor of his hospital room while a full-scale curing ceremony progressed around him. Things have changed so much for the better since I was on the staff there.

We treat a specific ailment, or organ. The hataalii treat the person as a whole. He uses a system of symbols that the patient knows and relates to. The curing ceremonies are long and monotonous and the chants so repetitive the patient has a response that creates an inner stimulus taking him to a higher plane, perhaps, which releases powerful healing elements, an interaction of the psyche with the physical.

Modern medicine has come to realize the immense importance of their own healing practices to the native populations. We can cure diseases and mend bodies, but if the soul thinks the body is sick, it's sick. And it works two ways. I understand the medicine men are now happy to work in tandem with clinical medicine. They have a lot to learn from each other. I like to think I was a little ahead of my time on this.

I'm glad you found such a compatible horse to do your exploring. It's incredible country and probably the best way to see it is from the back of a horse. Maybe while I'm there we can go out together. Laura and I used to roam around quite a bit. I'd like to show you some places that were special to us. I do worry a little about you being out in remote places by yourself. If you should fall or get into trouble, it could be dangerous. I know, I know. I can just hear you say..." when was the last time I fell off a horse?" Nevertheless, always take water with you. I'm bringing you one of the newest cellular phones that one of my MIT friends presented to me. I've not much need for it and I hope you'll take with you on your explorations. I'm not sure whether it will be operational where you are, but you can try. It will make me feel better about you, in any case.

Do you want me to bring your English saddle? You were still making up your mind when we talked.

I called Benjamin and Mariella. They still mean to come over to see you, but keep putting it off, which just about sums up their attitude toward life. I wish I could have sired a more dependable parent for you.

I look forward to seeing you, as you know, and as for Laura, I hope there is some time left for us. That she sought you out gives me encouragement.

Lovingly,
C.W.W. Chase

Chapter Fourteen

TÁÁ' NÁAZNILÍ' DÅ Å'TS' ÁADAH

June, 1852

Daago's chin rested on her knees as she stared absently at the toes of her moccasins while the sheep watered at the small, spring-fed pool. Her mind played over the events of the last few weeks. How changed her life was since the Enemyway ceremony and squaw dance. Now she was going to be a married woman, she would have her own hogan, her own cookfire, pots, and blankets. She would have her own small flock of sheep. She would find out what all the grunting and thrashing under the blankets was all about. She would have babies soon. That would be fun, having babies to play with.

She knew her girlhood was gone when she started bleeding and had her *kinaalda* last autumn, before the snows came. A girl's first menses was an important milestone in a woman's life and the Navajo treated the occasion with great solemnity. The ceremony stressed her role as a woman, celebrated her femininity with joy as well reverence, and that day she had glowed with pride at her specialness to the tribe. But after that day she hadn't felt much different until now. Now, somehow, she felt grown-up, but alone. Already she felt herself distancing from her family, but unable to place herself yet with a husband. Chilhajin. Daago had seen him several times these past weeks when the two families met to discuss the bride price and dowry, but they hadn't been alone together, more because of Daago's unwillingness than any proscription against their meeting. He had bought her small gifts, but seemed resigned to her petulance. The last time he brought her a black and white shepherd puppy and she had finally rewarded him with a smile.

Daago was bored. She wished she had brought the puppy today. She reached down into her moccasin and pulled out a small silver dagger. It had belonged to Dolores, her family's captured slave. When Daago found it, against Dolores' protestations, she had taken it for herself. She made Dolores tell her where she had gotten and the girl finally confessed she had stolen it from her former mistress. The blade was highly polished silver, the handle a twining vine. Daago loved the smoothness of the blade and the curves and curls on the hilt. Somehow the knife made her feel better, stronger, more independent. Older.

She twinkled the mirror-like blade in the sun, then held it up to her face. The blade was too narrow to get an overall picture, but if she held it crosswise, she could get a fair reflection of her eyes. She blinked her eyelashes at the image and studied the lustrous brown irises that gazed back at her. Pleased, Daago slipped the dagger back into the shank of her moccasin, stretched out on her stomach and leaned her face over the dark clear water.

Clouds shimmered on the surface of the pool. Daago tried to get a good look at her face, tilting her head this way and that, even getting close enough that the ends of her hair slid off her shoulders and fanned out over the water. But it was no good. The sheep stirred the surface as they drank and her image fragments blurred. Impatiently she rolled over on her back and let her eyes follow the great woolly, cumulous clouds that floated in the intense blue sky.

She was going to marry Chilhajin in a week's time. Her entreaties had fallen on deaf ears. Uncle Chii had not been impressed with the warrior Jadi at the Enemyway ceremony and had gone on to serious negotiations with Chilhajin's family. Now Hanabah was going to get Jadi for a husband and she was going to have to take Chilhajin. She tried to cheer herself with thoughts of the pale deerskin wedding dress that her mother and aunts were now busy beading. One good thing. Her wedding ceremony would be the first of all the marriages arranged at the Enemyway, her bride price was by far the highest: ten horses, twenty sheep and twelve blankets. It would be an important occasion for both clans. Preparations had been going on these past weeks to make sure there was plenty of food and a campsite for the wedding guests.

One aspect of the whole thing didn't bear too much thinking about. She would have to leave her family. Normally her husband would come to live with her people. He and Daago would build a hogan near her mother. But Chilhajin was too important to the Deeschiinii clan as their next medicine man to allow him and his bride to leave.

In some way this break with tradition frightened Daago almost to the point of panic. She had never been away from her village for long, and then always in the company of her family. Her friends all questioned her with wide eyes, awed that she would be embarking on such a frightening adventure.

Their respectful comments made her brave, at least on the outside. She would toss her head and say, of course she wasn't afraid. She would be able to do as she wanted, not have to obey her mother all the time. It would be wonderful, she'd say. And her future husband was a very important man, so important his clan couldn't spare him. So she would be important, too.

Her friends were very impressed.

Even better, she found out that Chilhajin went raiding, too, and was an exceptional hunter. So he was a warrior and his shoulders were every bit as wide as Jadi's. Maybe his face wasn't as scarred as she thought.

On the other hand, Daago worried to herself, what if the Deeschiinii women weren't nice to her? Maybe Chilhajin's mother would be harder on her than her own mother. Not let her be as independent as she wanted to be. Uncle Chii had insisted that her hogan would be as near to her mother's camp as possible. But after the ceremony, would everything happen as promised? She fought down her uneasiness. Her hogan was being built now, and Uncle Chii had told her he was satisfied.

A chickadee called out, breaking the soft silence. The shepherd dog whined and Daago sat up. She looked over at the quietly cropping flock. They weren't straying, content in the torpor of the afternoon.

"Be quiet, Yazhi. *Perro, silencia.*" The shepherd whimpered and reluctantly lay down with his head on his paws.

Daago used the Spanish word for dog. She and Dolores had been teaching each other their languages. She missed Dolores today. Ordinarily she came to help tend the sheep, but today Hezbah had needed the girl to help with the washing and carding of the wool. The men had taken all the bales on hand to the trading post at Two Gray Hills to barter for things they would need for the wedding ceremonies coming up and now a new backlog of wool for weaving had to be stockpiled.

Daago lay back and studied the clouds again. Perhaps there would be an evening shower. There were dark clouds forming over the mountain peaks to the north and showed an occasional spark of lightning. But these mountain storms were very localized and one could never tell. Her eyelids drooped.

A low growl rumbled in the dog's throat. He stood quickly, his hackles rising, then began barking wildly, then a strangled yip and he stopped as quickly as he'd begun. Roused, Daago raised on an elbow to see what had excited him. There was a soft scuffle behind her, then a hard, rough hand clamped like a vise over her mouth as her hair was twisted painfully. She caught sight of the black and white dog. He was thrashing spasmodically, blood spurting from the gash in his neck. Daago struggled and tried to scream against the crushing hand, but her voice died in her throat. She kicked and strained against other hands and arms that held her. She was spun off her feet and one arm twisted behind her back. Desperately she fought, but the pain in her arm sent a wave of nausea through her.

"Break 'er arm and I'll cut yer balls off."

Then she saw the white man. He was dirty, and his grinning mouth showed stumps of rotting teeth through a stained, matted scag of beard.

"Feisty little squaw, ain't she, Hardbelly?"

The man holding her grunted and answered in Ute. Terror swept over Daago. She was being taken by a white man and one of the vicious Ute tribe! Those Utes that preyed on the other tribes and collaborated with the terrible white men to enrich themselves. Her mind rushed to all the times her mother had told her and her brother to be good children or the vicious Utes would get them.

The dagger! Escape! A burst of adrenaline gave Daago the strength to wrest her head from the punishing grasp as she forced a small scream.

She didn't see the fist that struck her, but a wave of shocking pain, first red, then black spread through her head as her neck snapped back and the feeling left her legs.

It was dusk when a sliver of awareness seeped into the black in her head. Her dress was wet and a soft rain splashed on her cheek and arms. The feel and smell of the horse registered on her consciousness. The left side of her face was lying on the animal's neck. Her weight shifted forward. They were going down an incline. As her awareness slowly widened, Daago stirred. She was tied. She pulled at her wrists. They were bound around the neck of the horse, her legs astride were roped painfully at the ankles. She couldn't move. Daago fought down the hysteria that welled in her throat, replacing it with a hot rage that spread though her body. How dare they! How dare they steal the daughter of Manases, only days before her wedding. The terror struggled with the anger, but she fought it down, along with the tears that stung her eyes. She remembered the haunted women brought into the camp by her clan's raiding party: dirty, quaking, weeping. She had felt contempt for the cowardly ones; should she not feel contempt for herself if she allowed herself to be taken into slavery cowering and wailing? But what could she do? She had no idea where she was, where she was being taken, she couldn't move, and was guarded as well.

Fighting for control, she knew what she must do if she had any chance of saving herself. She must watch and wait. She must have patience and guile, watch and wait. Above all watch. And first she must get some kind of directional bearings. The pain in her wrists and ankles must be ignored. How long had it been since they took her?

Daago opened her eyes carefully. Ahead she could see the back of the big Ute, his hair parted into two pigtails that hung over the front of his bare shoulders, bronze and slick with rain. He carried a heavy rifle across his back, much like the one Manases had. Her heart sank even lower. The rain had made the skies dark, but it must be nearing evening. She could hear the ugly white man in back of her, wheezing and muttering to himself.

When the ground leveled out, the white man called out something to the Indian and they stopped. From the gesturing of the two men Daago thought perhaps they were getting ready to make camp for the night by the tiny stream that she could see meandering though the rocks. It was getting dark and they apparently felt no constraints about stopping. Why weren't they worried about pursuit? Surely her family missed her when she didn't bring the sheep home in the late afternoon and her father and Uncle Chii would have organized a search party.

Then she remembered the men wouldn't be back from the trading post until tomorrow. The women in the camp could only wait and then it would be too late.

The white man came over to Daago and she quickly closed her eyes so he wouldn't see she was awake. He grasped her hair and shook her head roughly, then turned to the Ute. "You goddam savage. You went and hit her too hard. How'm I goin' to sell her if she's out cold?"

He brought his face close to hers and she felt her stomach lurch at his foul breath and the stink of his clothes. A tear escaped from her lashes and, dismayed, she felt it trickle down her cheek.

"Well, now. Hee hee. Lookie here."

Daago opened her eyes and stared at him defiantly.

He grinned and wiped his nose on his stained buckskin sleeve. “We’re stoppin’ here to water the horses and take a leak. We’d make a whole lot better time if you was to ride straight up. It’ll be night soon. You be a good little girlie and we’ll untie you so you can ride proper. You understand?”

Daago hadn’t the dimmest idea what he was saying to her so she continued to glare at him. But he began to untie the tight leather cords around her wrists and she pulled herself upright. He untied her ankles and sharp points rushed up her legs as he yanked her from the saddle blanket. Her knees buckled when she hit the ground and she gasped with the pain as blood rushed to her extremities. The man called something to the Ute and then went to the stream and filled a leather canteen.

He stood over her, the canteen thrust in her face. “Drink this and I’ll take you over to that cedar bush for a piss. Don’t try to run on me, girlie. Yer worth a lot of money to me.”

Daago turned her face away. His calloused hands grasped her chin and jerked her head around and jammed the canteen against her mouth. “Drink, you squaw bitch.”

Reluctantly Daago opened her mouth and let the water trickle down her throat. The water had a peculiar musty taste, but she was desperately thirsty. The man let her drink what she needed, hating herself for her weakness. But pride wasn’t going to help her if she got weak from hunger or thirst. She must, must take what they gave her.

The white man pulled her to her feet and shoved her toward a clump of cedar shrubs. With gestures he made her understand that she was to relieve herself. He turned and left her to go collect the horses that had drunk their fill from the stream.

Daago squatted and lifted her damp skirt as carefully as

she could. She was terribly embarrassed. She emptied her bladder then started to rise, but was roughly pushed to her knees and elbows, her dress yanked over her buttocks. The Ute, grunting in anticipation began to mount her. Daago screamed as she felt his bulbous organ thrusting against her. She struggled and he pushed her face in the dirt as he probed to enter her. A sharp gunshot exploded in her ears and the Ute's weight collapsed on her, knocking the wind from her lungs. She strained to free herself from under the crushing body as a dark, spreading pool of blood formed in the wet, reddish earth by her face.

"You friggin' savage!"

Finally wiggling free from under the weight of the heavy Ute, Daago scrambled to her feet to see the white man, his face contorted with fury. "I'll shoot your friggin' balls off! You think Don Fernando'll buy another squaw from me he gets a dose of the clap?" He kicked at the inert Ute.

Daago tugged her dress down and stared at the Indian. He was dead, surely. Blood spread everywhere and he didn't move, his body twisted in an awkward angle.

Finally the white man turned the Ute over with his foot. The erection that had pushed at Daago poked obscenely at the sky, its mechanism of release frozen in death.

"Huh, dead, I guess. Well, good riddance." He kicked at the Indian's scrotum, still venting his anger. "That's a sorry lookin' sword now, ain't it, you red bugger. Maybe you find somepin' to poke it at in hell." He cackled wildly at his ugly witticism.

He turned to Daago, who stared at him with wild, terrified eyes. "Git over there. Git yer ass on that horse. And remember you ain't goin' nowhere but what I say." He pushed her over to the sorrel horse she'd been tied to and gestured for her to mount.

Daago was very frightened. The man had shot the Ute like some kind of animal. She was grateful that he'd gotten the Ute off her before he'd penetrated her, but the white was quick to anger. She felt sure he wouldn't shoot her if she did what he wanted, but she knew now she must be cunning, strong. Meekly she threw herself over the horse's back and scrambled to a sitting position. Even though she didn't understand his language, he made it clear what he wanted her to do.

He seemed to be satisfied that she wasn't going to give him any trouble, so the white man collected the Ute's horse, then swung onto his own mount and motioned for her to go down the trail ahead of him.

Chapter Fifteen

June 1852, Fort Defiance

"Not too arduous a journey I hope, captain."

Major Electus Backus, commander of the remote new outpost known as Fort Defiance, sized up his latest medical officer. Hard to tell how they would react, these doctors, to the harsh conditions, and the danger. He'd lost three in the last six months. One dead of cholera, two simply disappeared. Discipline was shaky in the Ninth Military District of the Army of the West. It was too easy to desert and head for the goldfields in California if the heat and dust, snakes and scorpions, lack of women and water weighed too heavily. Or the Indians got more rapacious than usual. It was hard to tell what brought a man west, and what it would take to hold him here.

"Do sit down, captain." The major motioned to a wooden chair. "I fervently hope you're more militarily inclined than our last medical officer. We sorely need you. It's one thing to deal with insect bites, the agues and the runs, but when we began chastising the damned Indians in earnest, there will be more urgent problems. Arrow wounds and the occasional scalping are bad enough, but the savages are getting more guns every day and learning how to use them."

The new doctor sank gratefully into the high-backed chair and ran his fingers through his unruly red curls. He suppressed an urge to wince as his buttocks hit the hard seat. It had been a tedious journey. He was not yet accustomed to long days in the saddle and his bum was sore.

"All in all, my journey was uneventful. Rather pleasant, in fact quite interesting. I've not been in this part of the country before." he replied easily, not wanting to admit fatigue on his first meeting with his superior. "I came by rail as far as St. Louis, where I was assigned a mount, then to a company headed for Ft. Fauntleroy. I came the rest of the way alone. Not far."

The major grunted. "Shouldn't travel alone in this country. The Navajo can't be trusted. We've made treaty after treaty, but they break them when it suits them, which is almost always. They're duplicitous rabble."

"Ah. We recognize the Indians as political units capable of binding treaties, but without any rights to the land where they live. A paradox, no?" It crossed Captain Nathaniel Cabot's mind that he had overstepped. He wasn't quite acclimated to the army yet, though his position was rather outside the usual military hierarchy. The Cabots of Boston were wont to voicing their opinions and it irritated him that this was frowned upon in the military. He decided to test the waters. He knew they desperately needed him here and would probably put up with a little insubordination, as they called it.

"Captain Cabot, I assure you these are treaties only to

remain at peace. There is no delineation of territorial boundaries," the major said primly.

"A big difference assuredly." The doctor grinned. "I understand the Navajo are quite scattered and have developed a taste for our horses."

"We make better livestock suppliers than allies, it seems. They're inveterate thieves. They raid the rancherias, too, and other tribes, of course." Major Backus shoved some papers in disgust. "Anybody who has anything they want. It's out of control. In four years, the Navajo under their chief Manuelito have stolen eight hundred thousand to a million sheep and cattle, some twenty-five thousand horses and mules in the New Mexico Territory.

"That many, eh?" Nathaniel gazed thoughtfully at the motes dancing in a shaft of dazzling sunlight. His eastern eyes were still unaccustomed to the brightness of this sun-baked land. He turned to the major. "I don't suppose it helped that we killed Manuelito's father-in-law after the Bear Treaty conference," he said dryly.

Major Backus looked uncomfortable. "Oh, you heard about that, did you? Unfortunate incident. An inexperienced recruit thought the old man was escaping."

Nathaniel raised an eyebrow but made no further comment. He was here to make his fortune. Policy should be outside his interest. Really no point in tweaking the major. The man's job was not an easy one.

Four years ago the United States had seized the territory of New Mexico. Now these lands had to be pacified, then settled. Fortunes would be made and Nathaniel Cabot planned to be in on the making. In medical school, he had had no intention of sitting in a dull office in Boston treating old dowagers for the vapors. Upon graduation, over the protests of his father, he'd taken a commission and headed west. He would serve out his commission and get rich doing it. At the end of his three years he would get very rich. Let others go chasing after gold in California. Nathaniel Cabot would chase land. Out here there were miles and miles of it practically for the taking. Some Indians would have to be cleared out, but that was the charge of the Army of the West and its loyal Army Surgeon, Captain Nathaniel Walker Cabot.

He brought himself back to the subject at hand. "What's the strength of Ft. Defiance?"

"We're four companies of horse, one of artillery, and two of infantry. There are roughly four thousand Navajo, with a thousand warriors under arms, and I'm not just talking about bows and arrows. They're getting firearms. Steal them when they can, trade for them when they can't. We're in the heart of Navajo country, which they resent, of course. Think it's their ancestral home or some such rot. In reality they're just nomadic savages." The major slammed the flat of his hand on the desktop with finality. "Thieving, perfidious, treacherous...well, you'll see soon enough."

Nathaniel studied the irate man. Under a strain, no doubt, he thought. His orders were difficult and the country was harsh. "I'd like to have someone show me the hospital," he said.

"The corporal outside will show you your quarters and take you around. As for the hospital, infirmary, you'll want to set it up. We've got a sort of dispensary," he sighed, "but your predecessor took most of the supplies with him when he decamped for the goldfields." The major's face registered his disgust.

"I was issued supplies. And I ordered more to be sent from St. Louis when the next shipment arrives from Chicago. With luck I'll make it until they get here. Good day, sir. I'd best get to my job." He rose and turned to go.

"Oh, captain?"

The tall young man turned. "Yes? I mean, yes sir?"

"We don't have a lot to do here. But the Mexican rancher downriver invites the officers over for dinner and cards occasionally. The whisky's good and there's a lot of it. He sets a right decent table and the wine isn't bad. Beggars can't be choosers here."

He snorted, his smile crooked. "And he's an inept poker player, though luckily for us, he doesn't think so."

Captain Cabot grinned. "Why that's just fine. I'd be pleased to join you the next time you go."

"Tomorrow night, as a matter of fact. Why I brought it up. Don Fernando and Dona Eugenia have extended a kind invitation to the officers of Ft. Defiance." He winked. "Bring money. The man likes to wager." He picked up a paper on his desk, blew the dust off, then added, "Oh, another thing you'd best know. His wife is very beautiful, also flirtatious. Might be good to remember that Don Fernando is also very jealous. These Mexicans are quick to take offense."

Captain Cabot grinned. "I'll remember that, sir. Good of you to mention it."

Nathaniel Cabot stepped out onto the porch of the commandant's office. The Major's aide came to his side—a southern boy with rosy cheeks damp from the early summer heat.

"The officer's quarters are gettin' finished up. They're right nice, suh. I expect you can move your kit right in." He gestured toward a series of adobe buildings across a dusty rectangular plaza centered around a flagpole flying the thirty-three starred American flag as well as the green and yellow regimental flag. The boy pointed across the expanse, busy with the activities of the fort. "The men are bivouacked in tents over along the river. The blacksmith's shed and the corral are over yonder, where you see the supply wagons. The horse barns will be over there, too. Right now the horses are corralled near that copse of trees. The pasture's just beyond where the river cuts into the canyon."

Cabot found it nearly impossible to make out the corporal's directions. The entire camp was in a fever of building. Indian laborers were busily turning the adobe bricks while soldiers framed in windows and doors of the earthen buildings and sealed them with mud.

"The men's quarters will be along the side yard over there. In back of the men's quarters is the makeshift laundry, and the latrines are aways back from that. You'll be expected to get your own laundress, suh. Ind'n woman. Most like."

"And how do I go about hiring an Indian laundress, corporal?"

"Oh, you don't need to hire one, suh. You buy one. They're pretty cheap, considerin' we don't have much to spend our pay on here. Two hundred dollars, maybe a little more, should get you one. Dependin' how pretty she is. The children, well, they're cheaper, but you'll be wantin' a woman, suh, if you know what I mean."

Cabot was astounded. "A slave you mean!"

"Well, if you want to call it that, suh. You northerners have more trouble with that than we do in the south."

"I see." He frowned. This was incredible. "And where, corporal, do I buy this…woman?"

"Oh, there are men. Pretty unsavory types, I must say, who come through here from time to time. Haven't had any for awhile, so we're probably due. They seem to know when we have need. They grab the women when they're out tendin' their flocks and herds. But the Ind'ns expect it. They're out stealin' and maraudin', too. It's a way of life for them. They don't even come lookin' for them, most times. And usually our men treat their women pretty well. And their lives are probably easier here than back with their people." The corporal turned and gestured. "Your infirmary, suh, is right over there. There's a small kitchen out back and a storage shed in back of that. You've already got a patient with a bellyache waitin'."

"Thank you, corporal." Cabot recognized a change of subject when he heard one. Now what the devil was he going to do about this buying a woman laundress business? His New England sense of propriety balked at the whole idea of buying a human being, regardless of how the southerners felt about slavery.

As they walked through the turmoil of construction over to the hospital, Cabot looked around the fort, surprised at its seemingly vulnerable position. "Somehow I pictured something different," he said, sweeping an arm around at the rocky heights surrounding the area. There seemed to be nothing to deter any kind of Indian assault. "Where are the fortifications? This is as open as any New England village. What happens in the event of an attack?

"Well, suh, as I understand, an attack isn't expected."

"You don't look like you believe a word of that, corporal."

"Not my place to say, suh. The site was chose for the water and the pasturage. We're just here to keep the Ind'n in check, civilize them and the like. They'll never be all the way human, but we can teach them to farm better and maybe believe in the Lord and the Good Book. They'll learn they can't slow down progress."

"Oh, definitely not." Progress. That's what had brought Captain Nathaniel Cabot west and would make him a rich man. "Now, corporal, let's go take a look at that patient."

Chapter Sixteen

TÁÁ' NÁAZNILÍ HASTÁ' ÁADAH

June, 1852

After a week of descending mountains and canyons, then down a small, shallow river, Daago and the white man rode into a large compound made up of white stucco buildings. Daago had never seen structures like these. Were these like what her father described as the rancherias where they had gone raiding? Her heart began to pound, knowing that this was their destination and she would find out what her captor was going to do with her.

A small boy took their horses and a young man came to lead them to one of the buildings. They looked like Dolores, so they must be Mexican, Daago thought. They spoke her language, but so quickly she could only pick out a few words and they made no sense in the rush of impressions filling her head. As they neared a low building, Daago faltered and the white man shoved her in the back. She stumbled, but caught herself and followed the young man.

She had never seen an encampment like this. Everything seemed enormous. It was mid-afternoon and the sun was bright and hot off the white walls. She blinked her eyes from the glare. There were vines and cultivated trees of beautiful flowers and a pool, with a large stone thing with water splashing out of it. The young man indicated a doorway. Daago hesitated, then with her head held high, she stepped through it, fear curling through her stomach. The room was cool, softly lit by sunlight that filtered through some kind of sticks that covered the window.

As her eyes adjusted to the shadowy room a swarthy man sitting behind a table rose when they entered. "Ah, Señor Moran. You've brought a beauty this time. Don Fernando will be pleased."

Moran swiped his nose across his sleeve and grinned. "An unspoiled one. A bargain at a thousand," he crowed, his bloodshot eyes glittering.

"Pesos, of course."

Moran turned and spat. "Dollars."

The Mexican eyed him with distaste. "Oh, come, señor. You jest."

"You said yerself she's a beauty. And she ain't been used. A thousand."

"Don Fernando has never paid anything close to that."

"Look at 'er." He jerked Daago closer.

The Mexican gazed impassively, tapping a quill pen on the tabletop. "Three hundred."

"Eight."

"Let's see her.

Without warning, Moran's hands were on Daago's shoulders and her dress was ripped downward. Stunned she tried to cover herself with her hands, but the white man pulled them behind her.

Daago closed her eyes in humiliation, fighting the tears that stung her yes.

The Mexican looked her over noncommittally, then motioned the white man to turn her around. He strolled out from behind the table and continued to study the frightened girl. "A virgin is she?" He turned Daago toward him. He tipped up her chin and rubbed the small cleft with his thumb, then dropped his hand to pinch her nipples between his thumb and forefinger.

Daago swallowed the sob that filled her throat.

Abruptly the Mexican's fingers went between her legs and probed into her secret place.

She gasped in disbelief at this painful invasion, but Moran's grip dug into her arms and he snarled something in her ear. He shoved a knee between her thighs to spread them further apart.

The Mexican's fingers lingered, then left her and went to his lips. "*Es verdad.* It is true." He smiled lasciviously and licked his fingers, then turned back to his table. He pulled a small, woven cord. A bell chimed in the distance. He pulled open a drawer and brought out a stack of American money. "Six hundred." He laid out the bills one by one.

Moran snatched them up, counted them again.

"Stop by the kitchen on the way out, Moran. The cook will give you something." He made no attempt to hide the contempt on his face.

A plump, dark woman appeared and the Mexican waved at Daago. "Take her away, Clemencia. Clean her up. Don Fernando will want her tonight. She has not been used. Tell her what is expected. "

The woman's eyes were sympathetic as she wrapped a blanket around Daago.

"Always know when we've got a new slave, eh, Clemencia? You always have the blanket ready, no?"

The woman didn't raise her eyes as she led Daago to the door. *"Si, señor."*

"Wait." He pointed to Daago's dress on the floor. "Get rid of that."

The Mexican woman took Daago across the wide courtyard and down a small alley to a long, low building similar in style to the rest of the complex. They entered a large room that appeared to be living quarters. Here was a door that led to a ramada where nearly a dozen women were busy at various tasks. Daago was startled to see two Navajo women, their looms set up under a tree, busily at work on the typical red, white, black and gray blankets of the tribe. Other women were making baskets and at one end, where there were firing ovens, others turned pottery wheels.

Clemencia called in Spanish to the two Navajo women. "Come, you two, here is another of your kind. Come, make her understand what will be expected of her. She is innocent and knows nothing. Clean her up as you have been taught. Dress her in a blouse and skirt. Show her how to do up the buttons."

Daago was able to understand little of what the woman said. She must try to understand more of the Spanish. She regretted that she had not worked harder at it with Dolores.

"Tell her Don Fernando will want her tonight. Tell her what to do. The don does not like weeping."

Clemencia left Daago with the two women. She let herself cry quietly as they led her into a room where water came from a hole in the ceiling. They unwrapped her blanket and pulled off her moccasins. When they found the silver dagger they became frightened and wanted to hide it.

Daago stopped her tears and struggled to regain her composure. "Don't you dare take it. I will keep it in my moccasin always. No one will blame you, but I don't intend to stay in this place. Now, show me what you do. Tell me what I need to know."

One of the women said to Daago, "I have been here three years. I was taken near Toodhiilii. We are not treated badly here. You would be very foolish to try to escape. We don't have to work in the fields, but spend our days weaving blankets and things for the household. The Pueblo women make the pottery, the Hopi and Apache the baskets."

"That's all you do?" asked Daago, astonished that their work wasn't more arduous.

"That and have babies," giggled the other. "But once you're pregnant. The master leaves you alone and takes someone else. We're both pregnant now. You will be soon, too. Don Fernando has strong seed."

Daago's heart plummeted. Today would have been her wedding day, and tonight she would be expected to lie with, not her new husband, but her new master. How cruel the Holy Ones were being to her. Punishing her for being difficult about Chilhajin, she knew. How she wished he were here now to rescue her, take her away from this place, to her wedding and her own hogan.

"How many children do you have?" she asked tremulously.

"I have two," one answered.

"I have three. But I have been here longer."

"All the children are raised together, but we get to see our own for a while in the evenings. While they are small. After they're six, they start training for household work, or we begin teaching them weaving, pottery and basket making. The boys of the Navajo and Apache mothers are taken to work with the horses and cattle."

The two women activated the crude shower and washed Daago's hair with some substance that smelled of flowers and made a froth of suds. After she was dressed in the Spanish skirt and blouse, she was taken outside where cook fires were being started to prepare the evening meal.

"We're allowed to cook our own food that is familiar to us. Don Fernando is generous that way. We get our provisions from the kitchen. After he gets us with child, we can wear our own blanket dresses. When we are taken to him at night, we are dressed like you are now."

The other interrupted. "But it isn't always at night. Don Fernando needs a woman at some of the oddest times."

"Why don't you try to escape? How can you bear to be slaves?"

"Life is not hard here. When you get used to it, it's pleasant not to have to work in the fields and herd the sheep. We don't have to fetch water, or firewood. We can play with our children when they are young. All we do is for the weaving. Washing the wool, dying, carding and spinning. We can design our own blankets, though Dona Eugenia wants something different from time to time. New colors. Of course we're watched. But how would we get back to our people? We're far away and have no horses. They would follow us and catch us. Then we would be beaten. You will find that after awhile you won't mind having an easier life."

"Except for having to lie with Don Fernando. He can hurt you if you don't do what he wants. We all pray to get with child."

They have grown spoiled, thought Daago with contempt. Never. She would never give up until the day she was back with Hezbah and Manases and Kii. And Chilhajin.

It surprised her that she had a pang of longing for Chilhajin. His quiet assurance and strength pulled her more than she could explain. She could hardly remember Jadi's handsome face and lusting eyes.

I've changed this past week, she thought. Have I become a woman? I am certainly no longer a child.

Daago looked around at the roomful of women. The women who had no man but this Don Fernando. *I promise myself this. I will be wife to Chilhajin. I will. I will do whatever I have to do to be free of this poisonous place, whatever I have to do to get back to my own people and my wedding. I will smile. I will open my legs, and I will kill if I have to, but I will find my way back.*

Then she thought, what if Chilhajin marries someone else while I am gone?

But she knew that he would not.

Chapter Seventeen

June 15, 1852, Fort Defiance

My Dear William,

As much as I deplore the thought of you making the journey to this back of the beyond, I wish you could experience this place where your older brother will be spending his next days. It's a raw place, still in the process of being built, though my quarters are finished and commodious enough. I have a bed, a chest, a chair and a kerosene lamp, so you see I have all I need. Meals are in common with the other officers. I daresay you would find the food very plain, but there is plenty enough and it will sustain me. I have made headway in setting up my hospital, though the Army calls it an infirmary. Considering I have only been here a day, I am quite pleased with my progress. My predecessor absconded with most of the supplies, but I was able to bring enough from St. Louis to stock my pharmacy.

The country is arid and harsh, with few trees except along the river. A pitiless glare from the constant sun will take some getting used to and it is very hot for a New Englander accustomed to cooler climes, though I understand the winters can be quite severe.

The fort lies on flat ground. It is virtually unprotected, but I am assured no attacks are expected. We will have to chastise the Navajo and Apache, for they are very prone to raiding and stealing, but they don't attack frontally, or so I am told. I suspect this is an optimistic appraisal for they seem very fierce.

I was somewhat shaken to learn Indian women serve the men as laundresses, but in actuality they are slaves, purchased from disreputable men who have stolen them from their flocks and they are forbidden to leave. I assure you I will not fall into this arrangement, however, though some of the women are quite comely.

This evening takes me to a neighboring rancheria, guest of Don Fernando and Eugenia Chavez. It will be my first experience with Mexicans. I shall try to remember everything I see to share with you.

The mail packet is leaving so I will close. Send my affections to Mother and Father. I pray that his disappointment in me and the manner in which I chose to pursue my fortune will ease in time.

I miss you all, but truly think I can find my place here. My regards to Kitty. I am sorry I will miss your wedding. You must write and tell me all.

Your loving brother, Nathaniel Cabot

Chapter Eighteen

June, 1852

"We are resigned now, of course, we Mexican families. It has been two years that the New Mexico Territory has been part of the United States. But it is you Americans now, *Capitan,* who must protect us from the Indian tribes. These Navajo and Apache."

Dona Eugenia smiled prettily at Captain Nathaniel Cabot, who was seated at her left at the long, formal dining table. A dozen tall yellowish wax candles in elaborate worked silver holders illuminated the table and guests. She leaned forward and touched his arm flirtatiously, exposing plump, ivory breasts that strained at the white lace bodice of her gown. In the soft, wavering candlelight a delicate gold cross winked piously in the lush valley.

"They steal our servants, our sheep, our cattle. I even fear for my own safety," she breathed. "It is a relief to have the American army nearby." She allowed tapered fingers to linger on his sleeve a shade too long.

Nathaniel Cabot spoke to the tantalizing breasts and raised his wineglass to his lips, letting his tongue delicately lick the rim before he drank. "We will be vigilant, *señora.* We would never allow anything to happen to such a lovely neighbor. You make our time here worthwhile. Very, very worthwhile."

The silken breasts heaved. "You are a doctor, no? Perhaps the army could spare you to treat me. My husband would be so grateful. I have such terrible headaches. And sometimes a sharp pain here." Her fingers delicately stroked her cleavage. "Would your duties allow you to get away from the fort and come to the hacienda soon and…" She reached over and delicately ran a finger over his hand… "examine me? Find out why I ache so?" Even white teeth caught her full bottom lip and she sighed with long suffering.

Nathaniel's mind raced. *I expect Don Fernando is why your head hurts, my dear. I've heard about his stable of concubines. As for your "sharp pain", I would guess that's not where you hurt. I think your "ache" is much lower down. My God, the dona is certainly tempting. She's making sure of that. Those glorious breasts are setting my jaws on edge. I would like to do a very thorough examination of Dona Eugenia with my teeth and my tongue. Extremely thorough.* There was a heated stirring in his lower abdomen.

He smiled over the rim of his wineglass. Yes, she could be gotten into bed with little trouble, no doubt about it, and she wants to make sure I know that. Would it be worth chancing the wrath of Don Fernando? He felt another pang in his loins. He hadn't had a woman since St. Louis. He glanced down the table at his host, who raised his glass with a small smile, his black eyes glittering with awareness at his wife's flirtation.

Nathaniel's loins calmed. For the time being he would be immune to the señora's charms. For the time being. Breasts like those had a way of changing things, particularly if they were the only ones around for miles and miles. Snowy white ones anyway. Very white...silken...with plump dark nipples...

Nathaniel blanked the irresistible picture from his mind with difficulty. The ache in his jaws faded slowly. Reluctantly he turned his attention to the excellent river trout.

Dona Eugenia spoke softly to a servant in her lisping Castilian Spanish, and the table was cleared for the next course. The wine glasses were changed and filled. The meat course was served, a roasted venison with wild asparagus. Conversation quickened again. Dona Eugenia politely turned to the gentleman on her right, a neighboring rancher, and engaged him in a small flurry of gossip before she turned again to Nathaniel.

...Don Fernando had brought his bride from Spain and surrounded her with all the trappings of an aristocratic *hildago*. She had borne him four children, three boys and a girl in four years time, and then he had turned his tastes to earthier pleasures. For several years, entrepreneurs had known that a pretty Indian girl fetched a good price at Don Fernando's rancheria.

The don told himself he was simply breeding a better class of servant and ranch hand. He now had twenty children by the Indian women, the oldest a twelve-year-old Navajo half-breed who was beginning to make himself useful in the stables. Some of the girls were learning to weave and make pots already and there were two under the tutelage of the cook and three more being trained by the housekeeper.

He treated the women well when they came and once they relaxed he found they had few inhibitions. Sometimes he got a little rough at the height of his passion, but they knew better than to complain. Clemencia took care of any injuries. It was rare to find a virgin, though, and his heart began to race at the thought of the lovely creature whom the despicable Moran brought in today. Ysidro, his foreman, had testified to her purity, amazed that Moran and that Ute savage he usually had with him had the self control to stay off her. Eugenia would, of course, be difficult for a few weeks, then would go back to her languor and her headaches.

Dona Eugenia rose to take her guests to a small salon, six officers from the fort, the foreman Ysidro and his wife, and the neighboring rancher and his wife. Don Fernando watched Eugenia carefully as she gaily tucked her hand through Captain Cabot's arm. She had begun taunting him with the officers of the new fort, but he had told her if she were unfaithful, he would kill her as well as her lover.

Was she more interested than usual in this handsome redhaired American captain? He would bear watching. Perhaps the Indian girl could wait for tomorrow night while he serviced his spouse. Maybe he would go to Eugenia after the officers had gone. Perhaps he would take the longer whip to remind her to keep her charms only for him, not the United States Army. Don Fernando found the prospect stimulating. He weighed the charms of the Navajo girl against the exhilaration of disciplining his wife....

The salon had a dozen or so small, gilded, red velvet chairs. The dona indicated where Nathaniel was to sit. "Fernando always wants me to sing for our guests. I will sing my songs directly to you Captain Cabot. Do you understand Spanish?" The dona's eyes glowed over the lacy edge of a delicate silk and ebony fan.

Nathaniel bowed graciously, knowing the best plan would be to stay away from the lady as far as possible. The woman's invitation was unmistakable, her perfume intoxicating, her husband jealous. Her watchful Mexican husband. Unfortunately not a fortuitous combination for a liaison with the dona. He would think a little on that score. Maybe the don was away from the *rancheria* from time to time.

"I'm flattered, *señora*. I've had too little of the civilizing benefits of a lovely lady of late. And I'm afraid I speak only a very little of your language."

"It is of no importance." She swept her lashes up at him. "The best Spanish is spoken with the eyes."

Dona Eugenia arranged herself artfully on a brocade stool, fanning the white lace dress around her black silk slippers. A servant stepped forward and handed her a mother-of-pearl inlaid guitar. She tested several strings, then began to strum softly, saying dreamily, "All the ladies in Madrid were learning the guitar before I left. I understand it is still quite fashionable."

The liquid notes filled the room. Nathaniel had never heard guitar music before, or seen a woman play anything else but a piano, as far as that went. He found himself growing agitated by the passionate flamenco songs his hostess was singing directly to him. Damn it was hot in this room! He shifted uncomfortably in his gilded velvet chair.

Nathaniel felt a distinct relief when the musicale ended and the company moved to the game room where the poker game had been set up. The women left the men to their brandy, cigars and cards, Dona Eugenia taking special care to invite the doctor captain to come visit her.

Her husband watched her go.

Nathaniel drank two glasses of cognac too fast. The attentions of the *señora* had been distracting, rousing appetites better left suppressed. He began to concentrate on the poker hand that was being dealt. He had learned the game in medical school and found he was very good at it. More to the point, he was lucky. He moved a blue chip to the center of the table and sucked in on the very excellent cigar that a servant held a flame to.

A fragrant blue haze settled over the room as the game progressed. As the major said, Don Fernando bet heavily, but he was a poor card player, impatient and impulsive. Nathaniel on the other hand was having phenomenal luck. His winnings began to pile up on the polished marquetry of the game table. He began to back off his betting, feeling it impolite to take advantage of his host. But the don began to push him. When Nathaniel won another big pot, the young doctor laughed and pushed his chair from the table.

"You're making me a rich man tonight, Don Fernando. A very gracious host. I can't impose on your cordiality any longer. I have never had such a run of luck."

"Ah! Surely you aren't thinking of leaving so early?" The Mexican smiled, his eyes half-closed.

"It's not all that early, sir, and the ride back to the fort takes at least an hour."

Two of the officers had already left, unwilling to match the larger bets. The foreman had departed after a few hands, along with the neighboring rancher and the two wives. The games were only to take the Americans' money after all. Now, the only players left were Nathaniel, Major Backus, an infantry captain and a cavalry lieutenant. There was a general stirring around the table to leave. Glasses were emptied, debts were settled.

Don Fernando downed a cognac. "You've won a lot of money from me tonight, Captain Cabot."

Nathaniel laughed uneasily. "Yes, sir, I have. You've been a generous host. More than generous. I'll doubtless not be so lucky again."

The Mexican's expression was bland. "Would you like to wager that you won't be so lucky on the next hand?" He turned to a servant boy and whispered something.

Nathaniel's smile faded. What was the man driving at? He stood. "Another time. It's late and tomorrow begins early for me."

"One more hand. Straight poker. Just the two of us." The black eyes probed.

"No, really." Nathaniel was beginning to be annoyed. Why was the man so insistent? Was he goading him because his wife had been so openly flirtatious?

The don raised an eyebrow. "You won't give me one more chance to recoup my losses?"

The major was intrigued. "Go on, Nate. It won't take long for one hand, winner take all."

"I'm afraid I can't afford to lose that much," Nathaniel said, then forced a laugh. "And if I won there's nothing to spend that much money on."

"I'll make it interesting for you." The don's voice was silken. "I bought a young Indian woman today. Navajo. She's innocent. A beauty. I'll wager her, even up."

Nathaniel's head was woolly from the late hour and too much cognac. "I really don't think…"

"Go on, Nate,"

"Don't be a stick in the mud."

"Come on, Nate," the others urged. "You haven't gotten yourself a laundress yet. Maybe now you'll win one. Save you the purchase price."

"Give the don a chance."

The idea was catching on and the air began to crackle with anticipation at the sexuality of wagering a woman.

With much ribald teasing, the other officers sat the protesting Nathaniel back down in his chair.

"Don't be a spoilsport, Nate," the major said.

"Let's take a squaw back with us, eh," the infantry captain chuckled.

Nathaniel was still protesting when Clemencia brought Daago into the room.

"Ah, here is the girl. She's worth a chance, don't you think?" asked Don Fernando, his voice smooth and challenging.

Nathaniel stared at the girl as the room grew quiet. She was tall and slim, with blue black hair that hung past her buttocks. Her plump bottom lip trembled slightly, but her eyes were defiant. She had been clothed in a white, lace-trimmed linen nightdress that, made for smaller Mexican women ended five inches above her ankles. She still wore her moccasins.

Don Fernando licked his lips, then shrugged. "Take her gown off. The *Capitan* Cabot should see what he's wagering for."

Clemencia moved to untie a ribbon at the throat of the white gown.

"No!" Nathaniel half rose from his chair. "No. Don't. It…it isn't necessary. I can see that she's quite pretty."

"Oh, come on, Cabot. The girl's only Indian. Let's have a look."

"I said no. If she's to be mine to win or lose, let her be," Nathaniel said evenly. "Can't you see she's frightened?"

Clemencia moved back.

Nathaniel ran his hands through his hair in agitation, wishing he could somehow get out of this ludicrous situation.

Don Fernando's voice cut into his desperation. "Major, would you do us the favor of cutting the cards?"

An uneasy silence hung over the room. Although the men truly believed in varying degrees that the Indians were savages of an inferior race, the presence of this proud and beautiful girl as a stake in a poker game was proving unnerving.

The swish of the cards being shuffled drew all eyes to the major's hands. Savoring the moment's attention, the major dealt the cards slowly. One by one, five cards fell face down in front of Nathaniel Cabot and Don Fernando.

When the cards were dealt, the major said, his voice heavy with the drama of the occasion, "You may place your bets, gentlemen."

Nathaniel moved his stack of chips, over two thousand dollars, to the center of the table. Four month's salary, he thought, with a sinking heart. The Mexican gestured impatiently at Daago.

"Don Fernando, as player to the left of the dealer, you should uncover your hand first," the major said.

The man smiled slightly and turned over the first card.

The ace of diamonds.

Don Fernando's mouth quivered at the corner.

Nathaniel frowned. *Why the hell did I stay? Gotten myself into this. I could lose almost four months salary, plus some odd winnings, or wind up with the pot and an Indian girl I don't want. Don't lie to yourself. I didn't, but I do want her now. I want her very much, but devil take it, I can't own someone, regardless of what the southerner said. Even an Indian woman. I'll keep on hiring my laundry out to that enlisted man's woman. That's fine with me. Let the others have their Indian concubines. There are prostitutes in Santa Fe if my needs get too burdensome."*

The major cleared his throat.

Reluctantly Nathaniel turned over his first card. The three of spades. Not a very auspicious beginning, he thought.

Don Fernando turned over the ten of diamonds.

Nathaniel the nine of clubs.

Major Backus coughed. The lieutenant lit a fresh cigar. His hand shook slightly as he held the flame to it.

The Mexican fingered his card before he turned it. The jack of diamonds. He leaned back in satisfaction.

He could have a royal flush, Nathaniel thought. I wonder if I've been set up. He turned over the four of clubs.

Don Fernando toyed with his card, then flipped it over. The ace of hearts.

The lieutenant stood, then sat down.

Nathaniel turned over the three of diamonds. A pair of threes. The six spots swam in his eyes. The odds against the only chance left to him were enormous.

Don Fernando's face was impassive except for a small twitch in his left eye. His well-manicured hand hovered over his cards, then turned over the ten of spades. "Two pair, Captain Cabot." His mouth turned up at a corner.

Nathaniel looked at this last card lying face down on the table, trying to suppress the fires the *señora* had lit earlier and rekindled with this dark and defiant Indian beauty, making him hope with each card that he'd won her. He felt her eyes on him and glanced up. Her gaze fell again to the floor. Then he knew she was aware of what was going on—that in this gambling game, she was the prize.

He felt a small muscle jerk in his right hand. He turned the last card.

A three of hearts.

A wave of triumph welled in his chest. Three of a kind. He'd won.

A silence filled the room. The Major wheezed.

"I will write a title to her." Don Fernando smiled tightly, his finger tapping his losing cards in agitation.

Then the others rose in congratulation. "Good luck, there, Nate."

"A bit of suspense there, old man."

"Thought you were a goner, there, Nate."

"The pot and the girl, too. I know which I'd rather have, you lucky dog."

Nathaniel stood awkwardly. He didn't quite know what to do next. He'd won this Indian girl, but now. Now? What the devil was he going to do with her?

Don Fernando turned to Clemencia. "Get her a blanket. The night is sharp."

"Come on, Nate," said the major. "Pocket your winnings and come on. The girl will ride with you. Let's get going. It's late."

The other officers made to go, polishing off any brandy that remained in glasses. Stubbing out cigars, thanking the don, expressing eagerness to enjoy his hospitality again.

Nathaniel felt clumsy. He motioned for the girl to go outside and began to stuff his winnings into every available pocket. The don watched him impassively, then sent the servant to fetch a paper and pen. When the man returned, Fernando scribbled impatiently and flipped a title to Daago across the table.

"It has been an interesting evening, don't you think, captain?" He tossed down the remainder of his cognac. "I must thank you for diverting my wife. She misses Madrid. Spain. Life is slow in this part of the country and we must find out own entertainment. And Eugenia would be angry with me if I was remiss in asking you and the other officers to dine with us again very soon."

"That would be my pleasure, sir." Nathaniel bowed. His mind raced, *I'll never set foot in this place if my life depends on it. It probably does considering the open invitation in Eugenia's eyes. And the fact that I've won the don's newest virgin.* Aloud he said, "You're very kind, sir. Please convey my gratitude for the evening to your charming wife. You set a fine table and the music was quite engaging."

"I will tell her, most certainly. And of course I must congratulate you on your skill at cards."

"It was luck, I'm afraid, Don Fernando, sir. You've been very kind and I thank you." He folded the title to Daago and slipped it into his jacket. A dubious title, to be sure. The man had paid some brigand for kidnapping her. Title indeed! What a farce.

But what did that make him? He wanted her for the same reason as the don.

When the men had left the gaming room, Don Fernando stubbed out his cigar sourly. He had been too hasty in wishing to challenge the captain. The girl was truly a prize. *I let the American captain make me lose my composure. Eugenia provoked me. She will pay for this.*

He stood and swept his losing cards from the table.

The Americans' horses were brought and saddled by sleepy stable boys and tied to the hitching rail. The boys glanced surreptitiously at the Indian girl whom they knew their master had bought that very day.

Nathaniel stood a minute, making a decision. "Carry my saddle, will you, lieutenant? The girl and I will just use the saddle blanket. It will be more comfortable for her."

He unbuckled the cinch and slid the heavy military saddle off his horse's back.

The lieutenant adjusted the unwieldy bulk across his horse's withers. The horse bucked in protest at the unexpected weight. "I don't know, captain. It's an awkward load." The horse snorted his displeasure at the burden and danced sideways.

"Yes, and it can't be helped. You're the ones who wanted to take the girl back and she's got to ride. Give me a leg up, will you, Major?" Nathaniel swung onto the horse's back. "And give me a hand with the girl, if you will. She will have to ride astride."

"With pleasure, Captain Cabot." The major grinned.

When Nathaniel mounted, he reached an arm down to Daago. She raised her eyes, hesitated, then put her hands up. Major Backus lifted her by her waist then gave her a boost, his hands lingering on her round buttocks. She settled in front of Nathaniel, her head down, taking a handful of the horse's mane as they moved off.

Clemencia ran from the hacienda, a red and black Navajo blanket in her hands. Nathaniel pulled his horse up and took the blanket from the Mexican servant. *"Gracias, señora."*

Clemencia smiled encouragingly at the girl. *"Adios, Daago. Buena suerte."*

Daago said nothing, her eyes on the horse's withers.

So that's her name, thought Nathaniel. A strange, alien name.

Awkwardly he arranged the wool blanket around Daago's shoulders. She slowly raised a hand and pulled it closed. Nathaniel looked at the bowed head in front of him. *How in God's name am I going to communicate with this girl?*

The four horses moved out of the courtyard and into a trot as they hit the trail back to Fort Defiance.

The chilly night air cleared Nathaniel's head of the cognac and cigar smoke, but a sense of unreality still hung over his situation. He'd won this Indian girl. The idea was preposterous. And why had Don Fernando wagered her? He'd been unlucky all evening. Did he really feel his luck would change? Did he want Nathaniel to win her so he would stay away from his wife? Actually that was probably a very good tactic. Nathaniel had been toying with the idea of sampling the charms the dona was openly tantalizing him with. Now he had other charms to savor, if he chose to. Would he not take the girl?

Nathaniel shook his head. He'd never know what the don's motives were. He stopped his reflections and let himself enjoy the sensations of the black, fragrant hair blowing across his face, and the rhythmic motion of the horse as it rocked the girl's buttocks between his thighs, the white, embroidered gown pulled enticingly up over her long legs. She rode with her back erect, moving easily with the horse, her hand resting lightly in the horse's mane. He wished she needed to hold on to him, but he'd been told that the Navajo were natural horsemen and the girl appeared to be no exception. She rides as if she were in a rocking chair, he thought. Was she really a virgin?

Nathaniel had not had much experience with virgins. There had been the Irish servant girl in their household when he was fifteen. He'd been a virgin himself and he remembered the girl bled, had cried a lot and he'd been terrified someone would hear. She hadn't seemed to like it much either. Then there'd been the hot-eyed daughter of the parson. She had pulled him into a hurried kissing and coupling behind the organ in the choir loft of her father's church. Her virginity had been something it appeared she wanted to lose as quickly as possible. She'd squealed when he pushed in, but then thrust and groaned with abandon. After he'd ejaculated, she'd wiggled out from under him, flipped her pantaloons up, her skirt down, brushed away some dust and scurried out from behind the big instrument without looking back. He'd done up his flies and scuttled away before somebody saw him. It had hit him later how much he'd liked it.

Not much to go on, but he'd learned a lot since then. Not from any virgins, however.

So Nate Cabot, you've decided you'll have her. Well, why not?

He felt acutely the motion of the horse between his legs.

Chapter Nineteen

TÁÁ'NÁAZNILÍ' NÁHAST'EITS' ÁADAH

June, 1852

It was kind of Clemencia to give her the Navajo blanket, Daago thought. The red, white and black blanket and her moccasins were all she had to remind her of her former life. That and the little dagger. When the Navajo women had found it as they helped her bathe, how frightened they had become. But she spoke to them sharply, determined to keep it. She had worried that the women were so cowed that they would reveal her secret, but they hadn't, and now she had a weapon. Would she get a chance to use it? When the time came would she have the courage to use it, she wondered? The vows she made to escape and get back to her family and her wedding with Chilhajin? Were they only empty promises to herself? She had been taught how to slaughter and butcher a sheep. Would it be like that? To kill a man?

Daago shuddered, as much with despair as for the chilly night air.

She thought of the Indian women at the *rancheria* and sat up straighter. She must have courage or she deserved not to be the daughter of Manases, but to be a slave, weaving blankets for someone else, a breeder for whoever wanted to mount her. Never to have a husband or children that she could keep for her own, never to see her people again.

Her thoughts turned to the strange events that led to her present situation. When Clemencia had come to get her and taken her to the room where the men were gathered, she was frightened and confused. In the small room where they had put her after she had been bathed and dressed, she waited with trepidation to be taken to Don Fernando. The Navajo women had explained to her what he would do with her and what she must do. She had been ill with dread. The man had come earlier in the evening to assess his purchase, turning her face this way and that, rubbing her hair between his fingers. His lecherous eyes ran over her eagerly, but he had not had her undressed. She recoiled at the thought of this man with lewd eyes and wet mouth touching her, but the women warned her to acquiesce to his attentions. He had a quick temper and little patience with a reluctant woman. Or a tearful one.

In the room where the men were, the heavy smoke made her dizzy. And all of them, too, looked at her with lust. At first she feared that she would be made to lie with all of them. They were going to take off her pretty white dress and she willed herself not to cry, to let them take away her pride. Then this tall man with the flaming hair had stopped Clemencia when she began to untie the ribbons. She felt gratitude toward him, remembering the rough fingers of the foreman this afternoon as the dirty white man held her hands behind her and forced her legs open.

Then slowly she realized the men were gambling and began to understand why she was there. Both the men and the women of the tribe loved to gamble and had animated games in which all kinds of things changed hands with much laughing and high spirits. She tried to remember if anyone had ever wagered a slave, but she didn't think so. It would not have been seemly.

Daago had tried to follow the game being played, but it meant nothing. She did feel the crackle of suspense in the air and her heart had pounded at the thought of what the outcome might be for her. Then suddenly the game was over and the men had been boisterous in congratulating the man with the flaming hair. So he had won her.

She had the courage to look once into his eyes. They were a strange color—a yellowish green. Once, last summer, she had come face to face with a mountain lion when she was out with the sheep. The cat's eyes were that color. She had thrown rocks at the animal again and again before it finally, reluctantly retreated. She had never forgotten those eyes and how frightened she had been. More than she was now. Now that she was free of the *rancheria*, she could reflect on her situation. After all, she had been taken seven days ago and nothing very terrible had happened to her yet. She had been struck hard once, by the Ute, and painfully humiliated by the Mexican foreman. But she'd been fed, clothed, and she still had her dagger. Would she lie with this man. Yes, she felt sure. His strange eyes were not predatory, like the mountain lion's. Or the Don Fernando. He was kind and he touched her politely.

A sure determination filled her. She didn't know exactly how, but she would escape. She had been given a reprieve from the Mexican don. The Spirits had helped her and now it was up to her. Ever since she had gotten over her original panic, she had observed. She knew now that they were going northwest. She would be going closer to her home. Away from the *rancheria* and its guards she would have a better chance of getting free. She must be ready for the first opportunity.

A few lights shone ahead, signaling their arrival at Fort Defiance. The four officers passed the sentry and rode down to the corral where the horses were being kept until the stables were finished. The men stripped the horses and shouldered their tack before sending the horses through the gate to join the quiet herd.

Daago's eyes darted around quickly, committing everything she saw to memory. If she escaped she would need a horse. It would be easy to take one from the corral if there were no lookouts.

But there was. He emerged from the shadows and spoke to the officers.

"Have any luck at Don Fernando's, sirs?" he called out.

"A good evening, corporal," said the major. "The captain here has won himself a squaw."

"A squaw! I'm damned," the sentry guffawed. He leered appreciatively at Daago.

Nathaniel ignored him and retrieved his saddle from the lieutenant, then motioned for Daago to follow him. They walked across an expanse lit by the three-quarter moon. Daago noted that there were few bushes, low grass, and no trees. An occasional light shone from a window here and there in the fort itself, adobe buildings similar to the hacienda, except they weren't white.

When the four men reached the plaza, they separated, good naturedly wishing Nathaniel a good night's rest.

"Sick call's always crowded Monday mornings, captain. I know you'll be wanting to get to the infirmary early, so you'd best turn in right away." He chortled at his joke and slapped Nathaniel's shoulder.

"Now I do envy you, sir. She's easily the prettiest squaw in the camp." The lieutenant looked longingly at Daago, then strode off to his quarters.

Nathaniel smiled uncomfortably and pushed open the door to a room at the end of the long building and stood back for Daago to enter. She hesitated, then stepped into the dark room. He followed and she could hear him stow his saddle. It startled her when the room filled with a soft light. He had started a fire in one of those strange, clear pots she had seen at the hacienda. He put it down on a big wooden box and turned to her. His red-gold lashes caught the light and she held her breath. Would it be now?

He cleared his throat. "My name is Nathaniel Cabot," he said, pointing to himself. She had heard them call him Kaapt'n Kaab't, so she knew that was his name.

Her heart was loud in her ears as she swallowed. She had to be docile for this cat-eyed man with the beautiful hair. But of all these strange white men, he was the most courteous, the least frightening.

"Me llamo Daago," she said softly. She remembered Dolores had told her the Spanish word for her name. *"Primavera,"* she added.

His reddish brows shot up. "You speak Spanish?"

"Pequito. Yo hablo pequito."

"Why this is wonderful. Are you saying Daago means springtime in Navajo? Uh, *perfecto*. At least I'm not totally in the dark about what to say to you. *Ven*. Come." He motioned for her to go to the small bed. She stepped warily over to it. She understood from the hacienda that this is where one slept, not on skins or blankets on the ground. How did a person not fall off?

"Let's see. *Sientate*. Sit. Sit down." He patted the bed and sat down.

Daago gingerly lowered herself to the edge of the bed. He moved over and took her hands. She recoiled at his touch and pressed her back against the wall.

Nathaniel turned away from her abruptly and put his head in his hands. "Dear God, I can't do this." His anguish made his voice tremble as he cried in despair, "I've never had to take a woman against her will. This girl is afraid of me." Then he laughed bitterly. "A fine gift from Don Fernando. I want her but I'm not dishonest enough to take her. My slave. What a joke."

Daago watched the red-haired man, puzzled at his unhappiness. She'd thought he would take her right away. She was going to be brave because she needed his desire.

He looked up. "Look, Daago. I'm not going to hurt you. I'm…I'm going to get you back to your people. This has all been a mistake."

His words puzzled her and she watched him rake his fingers through his hair in seeming frustration. "My God, you're beautiful, looking at me with those great dark eyes."

He started in surprise when she put out her hand, hesitated and touched his hair. He sat very still as she tentatively wound a finger around a curl.

"So you've not seen red hair before, eh?" He cleared is throat. "And you think it's pretty do you? Well, I can tell you I've been teased about it all my life." He touched his hair. "*Lindo?*"

"*Lindo.*" She smiled shyly.

He slowly reached out and rubbed his knuckles on her cheek.

She stiffened and dropped her hand from his hair, but didn't pull away.

"*Linda.* You are very *linda.*" He ran his fingers over her face.

Daago sat very still. *Is he going to lie with me now?*

Nathaniel reached down and took her hands again. "We'll sit here for awhile. Get used to each other a bit. I don't quite know the protocol here, but I don't want you to be afraid of me. You'll sleep here tonight. Tomorrow I'll make some kind of arrangements to send you to your home. And you don't know a damn word I'm saying..."

I don't understand. I don't understand. What does he say?

He began to speak again. "I'll tell you my life story. That's what I'll do. You won't understand, but it wouldn't be much more exciting if you did."

She tilted her head to one side, trying to stem her impatience. The soft lantern light cast shadows on his face. She could feel a pulse racing at her throat.

"Well, where to begin. At the beginning I should say. I was born in Boston, Massachusetts a long way from here. On February first, 1831. That makes me twenty-five years old. I'd guess you're maybe twelve? Thirteen? Still...still a girl."

Daago saw the man frown and falter over something he'd said.

He cleared his throat and went on. "My father was a doctor, as were my two grandfathers, one great grandfather, and on back." He laughed shortly. "Runs in the family. Well, I had a very proper upbringing and went to all the right schools, and when the time came I went to Harvard Medical School as was expected. Also expected, I would go into private practice with my father and spend the rest of my life treating the society ladies and gentlemen of Boston. I would make a fair amount of money at it, marry a proper Boston girl and have proper children who would also go to Harvard Medical School. If they were boys, that is. The girls would be accomplished ladies who would marry young men who had gone to Harvard Medical School. Are you beginning to see a pattern here?"

He brought his hand up and rubbed a thumb over her lower lip. "Your lips are like ripe cherries, did you know that?" He stopped. "I'm losing my train of thought here. Uh, let's see. Yes, and all the while this marrying and such was going on, there would be exciting things happening on the frontiers of this enormous, rich, and empty country. Thrilling things that they don't even dream of in Boston. Only I didn't want to be a dreamer. I also didn't want to be a doctor in Boston. My father, as you can imagine, was furious. Said he had no intention of financing such irresponsible, foolhardy schemes as I had in mind. I hardly had any funds of my own, so when I went looking for a way to underwrite my journey west, I found that the army desperately needed doctors in the New Mexico Territory."

Nathaniel hesitated, then moved to put an arm around Daago's shoulders.

She felt a flicker of relief and gazed back at Nathaniel placidly. *I must get him to lie with me. The dirty man said hardly anything, but this man talks and talks. I must entice him. I must be seductive. Then, when he is lost to himself, I will kill him.* She made herself relax.

Nathaniel was quiet a moment and continued. "I made arrangements, took my commission promising to complete three years of duty. I took the railway to St. Louis. I imagine you've never seen a railway train." He raised her hand and delicately rubbed her fingertips over his mouth.

"St. Louis is in the state of Missouri." He coughed. His voice was getting hoarse.

I must be more seductive. I have no experience. What must I do? Then she remembered Hannabah, and how she flirted with the men. How she'd enticed Jadi. *I will be as Hannabah.*

"I attached myself to a unit heading west. That's how I

came to be here. At Fort Defiance. That's where you are. Did you know that?"

Daago leaned against him and looked up with Hannabah eyes.

Oh, don't look at me like that. I'm weak. So weak. Just a moment. I'll stop in just a moment, he thought, as he touched a finger under her chin and lifted her face. "And by the craziest sequence of events, you and I..." Her eyes, black in the lantern light, gazed back at him.

Mesmerized, he slowly lowered his mouth to hers. She caught her breath but didn't pull away. When he brought her closer, she put her arms around his neck and arched into his arms.

He would mount her soon, but this was not unpleasant. Hurry, hurry. I need the night.

She ran her fingers through the flaming curls, amazed at how they wound around her fingers. She thought of the things that Jadi had done at the Enemyway ceremony. What had she ever seen in Jadi? He was handsome, but had been rough and clumsy, only thinking of himself. This strange white man was gentle with her. It was sad, what she had to do. She dropped her hand to his trousers to caress him.

"No!" He covered his face. "I can't do it. I can't have a slave. I can't have you. You're not much more than a child. What am I thinking?"

Anxious that her enticements had gone awry, she hurriedly put her arms around his neck again and made her smile inviting, as she had seen Hannabah do.

Nathaniel groaned and crushed her mouth to his.

Daago did not resist his kisses, relieved that his reluctance had passed.

Nathaniel hurriedly pulled off his clothes. His erection glistened in the lantern light, springing from the coppery pelt of his pubis. Daago was fascinated by the tight red curls and the sight of the stiffened, circumcised penis. But there was no doubt what he wanted.

She put her fingers around him as Jadi had showed her. He shuddered when she touched him, then lifted her nightgown over her head. Hurriedly she slipped down to the floor on her elbows and knees, arching her back in presentation, smiling at him over her shoulder. This was how the rams and ewes and the horses and mares mated. Let it be now she thought desperately, while there is enough night to get away.

Nathaniel stared at the rosy buttocks. "No, not like that," he cried. "Stay with me then."

He swept her off the floor and onto the bed. Daago was confused, but when he opened her legs and knelt between them, she realized he would mount her from the front. Did her mother and father do that under the furs?

He leaned to suckle her breasts. Then she felt his penis press against her. He pushed steadily but surely, until her body yielded with a sharp pain that made her gasp. She struggled but Nathaniel wouldn't release her. He moved slowly with in her, relentlessly, whispering, "The pain is over now little one, don't stop, don't stop me now."

The pain abated, but the sharp stab had sobered her enough to focus for a moment. He had wrapped her legs around his waist, but her feet were still in her moccasins. Nathaniel's thrusts were becoming more urgent and with relief she knew it wouldn't be long before the final, noisy outburst like her father made.

Her heart thundered in her chest as her hand reached and slipped the dagger from her moccasin. Something exploded in her and when Nathaniel shouted above her, she drove the dagger up into his ribs again and again, willing her fingers to be strong enough to propel the blade deep enough.

Nathaniel made a strangled cry and slumped down, his weight pushing her flat against the bad, her legs flung wide under his collapse.

Daago lay there, triumphant and horrified at what she'd done. She felt unable to move under Nathaniel's weight as his life gushed over her breasts and stomach.

Then the Navajo fear of death, with its dangerous spirits, overcame her paralysis. She struggled out from under Nathaniel and tried to calm her racing thoughts. She listened carefully. Had his cry aroused anyone's suspicions?

She stood in the lamplight, swallowing the spasms of nausea that rose from her stomach at the sight and the hot metallic smell of the sticky red blood on her breasts and belly. She picked up the white nightgown and scrubbed at herself frantically, then looked at the bloodstained gown. What would she cover herself with? She threw the gown on the floor with disgust.

Nathaniel's uniform lay in a heap by the bed. Her head whirled with indecision. Then she knew she would have to wear his clothes. A dead man's clothes. Oh. Surely his ghost would follow her and wreak a terrible revenge. Daago fought down her panic because she had no choice. If she reached her home, Chezhin would purify her with all the proper rituals. Thus was she able to fight down her growing hysteria. Grimly she picked up the uniform.

But she must hurry, hurry, flee the angry spirits that would try to catch her.

The buttons on the coat and breeches gave her difficulty. Her fingers fumbled with their unfamiliarity. She found Nathaniel's soft, broad-brimmed campaign hat and twisted her long hair under the crown. Hanging over the back of the one chair was a small firearm on a belt. Daago picked it up gingerly. Her father had a Springfield rifle, and he'd shown her how it worked once when she'd been curious. A Colt .45 felt heavy in her hand. Should she take it?

She decided she would. She wrapped the belted holster around her waist, fumbled with the buckle, but at last figured out the fastening. In her concentration her fingers had stopped shaking and her breathing was slowing. She stepped to the bed with determination and picked up the bloody gown. She put it under the blanket and pulled the wool blanket up over Nathaniel's body so it would look as if he were sleeping.

She prayed the evil spirits had not come yet to infect her. She found the small dagger in the bed clothes and wiped it clean before placing it back in her moccasin, then took a larger, military knife from Nathaniel's dresser, slipping it from his sheath to run her finger along its blade. Yes, it felt very sharp. How to know what she would need on her journey?

The Navajo blanket lay on the floor where it had fallen when Nathaniel pulled her close. Should she take it or would it be an encumbrance? With its bright red, black and white pattern, would it be easily seen? With regret she decided to leave it and prayed the uniform would be warm enough as she got into the mountains.

Daago stepped carefully from the room onto the raised, covered walkway. The fort was silent. The sentry she had seen when they had arrived seemed to be nowhere in sight.

The moon was much lower, but still bright as it illuminated the field across which Daago must cross to the corral. This relieved her. All Navajo feared the dark, with its swarms of ghosts and evil spirits. She darted off the walkway and scurried to the nearest clump of small scrub, crouching as low as she could until she felt she hadn't been observed, then creeping across the expanse in this manner, stopping at whatever scraggly vegetation she could find. She circled around the back of the corral and waited. The smell of the horses rose strong in her nostrils and gave her a sense of purpose.

Where was the lookout?

The gate was to her left now and she moved silently in the shadows. A horse nickered and blew, sensing her presence. She froze. There were some restless stirrings in the herd, then quiet. Crickets sang down by the river. A night owl hooted.

Daago reached the gate and slowly lifted the latch. It squeaked lightly and she stood stock still.

"Halt there, sir," the voice said politely.

Daago didn't move. She heard the steps approaching and reached to grip the heavy military knife.

"Would you be wantin' a mount, sir?"

When the sentry came close she whirled and struck upward. She could see his wide eyes and stunned face in the moonlight. A young face she noted with a clutch in her stomach. The boy crumpled with a groan.

Daago threw the latch and opened the gate wide. Her glance flew over the horses and in a flash she chose a big black animal that looked strong and fast. Quickly she led him by the forelock over to the fence, and with one foot on the railing, threw herself on the horse's broad back. It would be better to have some kind of bridle, she thought, but she could ride him with just her legs to guide him if she had to. She would be a poor Navajo if she could not.

There didn't seem to be any kind of alarm yet, so she trotted the horse softly until she was at the mouth of the canyon that led upriver. She had no idea where it led, but it went north and that's the way she had to go.

She moved the horse to a gallop along the river's rocky bank, glancing up at the sky. There were about two more hours of darkness. At first light they would find the sentry right away. Perhaps it would be a while before they found Kaab't.

That's when they would know she was the one who had murdered the two men. And they would come for her.

Daago felt a pang of regret. Kaab't had been nice and he had been gentle. Then she set her mouth. There was a long way to go and she would probably be caught and they would kill her. She must not think about what she had had to do. It had been necessary and that should fill her thoughts and strengthen her resolve. If she could do what she had done, she could do anything.

She slowed the horse and moved him into the stream. The moon had slipped below the rim of the canyon and it was very dark. She would have to move carefully, letting the horse find his footing as the gently flowing water carried away their trail.

Chapter Twenty

TÁÁ'NÁAZNILÍ' NAADÍÍN

June, 1852: The Canyon

The black horse had been a good choice; nimble and intelligent, he knew Daago's mind almost before she did herself. Before dawn she had made herself stop and improvise a bridle. Quickly cutting strips from Nathaniel's jacket she fashioned a typical Indian bridle, a simple loop and two and a half hitches under the horse's chin, which gave her more maneuverability and stability on the rocky, uneven streambed.

She followed the flowing water to cover their tracks as long as it was dark, running the horse when she could, taking a chance on the slippery rocks, anxious to put herself as far as possible from the fort before daybreak. When the sky began to lighten, she stopped the horse and dismounted.

"We must drink, Blackhorse. Drink. I have nothing to carry water and we'll be climbing now. I'll keep you as long as I can, but soon it will be too steep and I can make better time without you." She found it reassured her to speak aloud.

The fort would be coming awake by now and they had probably found the sentry. She was afraid, but by now she had learned to make her fear an abstraction, pushed to a still place, out of the realm of emotion. She had decisions to make and terror would cloud her judgment. She set her mind to the fact that she was free and going toward home. Fear was a luxury to dull the senses and weaken determination.

She had killed. She could do whatever was necessary. That was what she had to hold to, that she was strong. She had courage. She was the daughter of Manases.

Daago drank from the stream until she felt uncomfortable, not knowing when she would find water again. When she relieved herself, her urine stung the small tear of her lost virginity. She pushed the sensation away and led the horse to a flat-topped rock to mount.

The sun crept over the top of the cliff and its light began working its way down the canyon wall, washing the scrubby blackbush and cracked, rocky surfaces in mauves and pinks. Daago began searching for a likely route to begin her climb. She had no idea what she would find if and when she got to the top of the canyon. This was rough country, seamed with endless red sandstone and shale canyons and washes. She would be very lucky to find her way out.

The canyon continued to go north, however, and if only she could keep her bearings, it would lead eventually to the Chuska Mountains. There might be other Navajo camps along the way. She would have to be careful, though dressed as she was in the uniform of a soldier. What might another Navajo think? Would they welcome her? Give her a proper blanket dress? Or would they kill her. She was desperate to get rid of Kaab't's clothes. They were awkward and uncomfortable, and there were undoubtedly evil spirits lurking in them.

Homecoming must fill her thoughts. How happy they would all be. If she didn't panic and kept to the north, the mountains would be there. Daago's sense of the larger world was limited, but if only she could get to the mountains she knew she would find her family.

A likely route opened to her left. She and the black horse began to climb the rocky incline and were soon out of the cottonwoods and willows of the streambed. The vegetation got scrubbier and thinner as they gained altitude.

They reached the point that Daago dreaded. She would have to abandon the black horse. She would move faster on foot and be able to hide more easily if she were pursued. But she had attached her hopes to the horse when she had taken him and found it hard to let him go.

It must be done quickly and calmly. She halted and slid to the ground, slipping off the makeshift bridle. She turned the horse to face down the trail they had climbed and smacked his sleek hindquarters sharply.

"Go, Blackhorse. Go. I don't need you anymore."

The horse looked at her curiously over his shoulder and turned around to nuzzle her shoulder.

"Go on. Go back to your other horse friends." She turned him down the trail again. There was a large lump in her throat. Maybe he was a Spanish horse.

"Vaya!"

The horse looked back then stepped daintily down the rough path and gradually eased into a slow trot.

Daago watched him for a few seconds, then turned to scan the rocky cliff face. She had never felt so lonely. She had sent away her only friend.

She began to climb in earnest.

It was late afternoon as she worked her way through the boulders and small passes along the face of the cliff when she heard the shouts of the search party drifting up from a distance.

Perhaps they had found Blackhorse.

The canyon magnified voices, she knew that, but it was still difficult not to panic. She must be very careful when they got closer not to be seen. There were plenty of places to hide and she had been careful not to leave an obvious trail. An Indian would be able to track her, but if there were only white soldiers, perhaps she would be all right. She had found a tiny trickle of water coming from the rocks about an hour ago, and some edible plants that she'd made herself eat, although she hadn't been hungry.

It would be dark at the bottom of the canyon in about an hour and the search party would make camp until morning. She would go as long as she could before she had to rest. She was achingly tired.

Daago sensed dawn before the sky had even begun to lighten, a momentary pause in the silent velvet darkness, before the morning birds awakened. The moon had set and the stars had moved. She scrambled from the small declivity she had curled in to sleep. Her stomach cramped from hunger and she was very thirsty, but she was afraid not to hurry away. Last evening she hadn't heard the soldier's voices for an hour before she couldn't take another step forward and had collapsed into her small shelter.

She felt stiff and awkward at first, but her muscles smoothed as she inched her way in the faint light.

About midmorning she heard the voices again. They were closer, but still on the floor of the canyon. They hadn't decided to climb. Or perhaps they were only the mounted contingent and she was pursued by other men on foot, on the cliffs. She must be watchful and not be taken by surprise, though thus far the soldiers had not moved stealthily.

About noon the horsemen were directly below her and she knew she would have to stay hidden until they either moved ahead or turned back. She crouched behind a big formation of round rocks, her ears straining to match any sounds with what she imagined the soldiers were doing.

Their voices began to diminish. She was now behind them. She would try to maintain that position, but still stay hidden in case they turned to come back. Now there was nothing to do but go forward as cautiously as she knew how, but moving ever northward. Toward home.

At nightfall she knew she would have to descend to the canyon floor again. She desperately needed water and the vegetation at this elevation was too sparse to find anything to eat.

But that must wait for a little while. Her body ached with weariness, her hands were scratched, her knees skinned through the now torn blue uniform breeches. Worse, her moccasins were worn into tatters. Daago curled her body in the shelter of two boulders and was instantly asleep.

A full moon rose over the lip of the canyon. The light made her open her eyes. It was about midnight. She felt only a little refreshed but her thirst drove her. The going was slow down the steep cliff face and her moccasins gave her feet little protection now.

It was nearly an hour before she could hear the cricket song and the liquid rush of the stream. But there were also, not far ahead, the smoky fires and voices of the search party.

The ancient Navajo fear of the dark was the lesser danger to her now. Worse, food would have to be postponed until morning light. She could drink, but light was necessary to identify edible plants. Maybe, if the stream weren't too shallow, there would be fish. Daago had eaten fish rarely, her people preferring lamb or mutton, but one would be welcome now, even raw.

She slipped soundlessly to the bank of the stream and drank eagerly. A nearby thicket would provide excellent cover. There were about two more hours of darkness before the canyon floor would be light enough. Would the soldiers be going toward her when they broke camp. Or away? It was a precarious position, but it couldn't be avoided. She dozed and tried to rest, but her heart raced and kept her uneasily awake. The shadows and night sounds activated her imagination and fingers of panic stabbed her again and again. She huddled fearfully, imagining a witchwolf, or the Coyote Trickster of Navajo legend, a mischief maker with sometimes animal form, sometimes human, who might give her away. The harsh cry of a hunting nighthawk startled her and she found it almost impossible to stay hidden in the copse and not flee to the safety of the heights.

Imperceptible at first, a pale light began to fill the canyon. The first sounds of the soldiers breaking camp joined the birdsong.

Daago furtively searched the vegetation. There were a few edible berries and several handfuls of wild carrots. Her eyes scanned the water, hoping to see the silver flash of a fish, but there was nothing. Her meager meal would have to be enough. To search longer was too risky.

The crackle of branches made her freeze. Someone was coming. Daago shrank into her thicket, sure the pounding of her heart was loud enough to be heard. She eased the Colt .45 into her hands, pointing it with clumsy unfamiliarity at the nearing presence. It wouldn't do. She'd be wiser to use the big military knife. A gunshot would bring them all. Her hands trembling, she slipped the gun back into its holster.

A soldier moved into her line of vision. He looked only half-awake, scratching and muttering to himself. He stopped and let his eyes drift around the stream, the bushes, the trees. His glance swept over Daago and her breath stopped in her throat.

He unbuttoned his breeches and urinated against a tree. Then he squatted.

Daago had been taught that elimination was private. She turned away, embarrassed that she had observed the man in an intimate moment.

The soldier wiped himself with a handful of grass, farted, then stood. Daago thought it would take him forever to get his breeches fastened up, but at last the man shuffled off.

Shaking with relief she put the knife away and, quiet as a shadow, began her climb back up the cliff face.

Again she worked her way northward, praying the search party would turn back to camp soon. Expending this much energy, Daago needed something more substantial than some roots and berries. Each day she had become more exhausted.

By noon, sounds of the search party had faded away, but her senses were becoming blurred. Had they gone ahead? Or turned back? When had she heard them last?

Sounds would deceive her—a birdcall, an insect hum, the rustle of a small animal disturbing the loose scree. Then quiet. Her footsteps were becoming less sure. She stumbled on, every uphill step a terrible effort.

Daago tripped over a small, sharp rock. She grabbed at an outcropping ledge to catch herself. There was the most agonizing pain she had ever imagined in her life. Through bleary eyes she saw the beautiful diamondback curl away.

Now she knew she would never see her family again, never marry Chilhajin, never hold her own children.

There were the small marks of the snakebite on the fleshy

part of her hand. Already it was swelling. It was torture. Waves of pain shot up her arm.

Daago staggered toward the shelter of the rock ledge. She knelt, careful to keep her hand low, below the level of her heart. She pulled the small dagger from her ragged moccasin and slashed a strip of cloth from the uniform jacket and clumsily made a tourniquet above the bite. Next she cut a quarter inch deep incision connecting the two fang marks. She gently squeezed the honey-colored venom from the wounds. Blood began to flow freely. Hope flared and she continued to apply pressure, trying desperately to cleanse her body of the deadly poison.

First her arm grew numb, then her breathing labored. Her vision began to blur as she fought the nausea that threatened to choke her. A paralysis crept over her and slowly she slumped to the ground.

Chapter Twenty-One

TÁÁ' NÁAZNILI NAADIIN DÓÓ B'AA LÁÁ' ÍÍ

June, 1852

He saw it again, in the corner of his eye. The soldier's color. Was it a soldier lying in ambush? The blue didn't move and Chilhajin readied his rifle and advanced slowly. The trail was precipitous and the spotted horse had to be urged to continue. Half of Chilhajin's mind told him he was foolish to investigate this blue, the other half shouted at him to go forward, that this was what he sought.

And then he saw the black hair spilling over the rocky ground, the bloody arm, the ragged, dirty blue uniform. And the moccasins. He slipped off the spotted horse and ran to Daago. He knew in seconds what had happened and what he had to do. Chilhajin knelt beside the unconscious girl.

He had brought his healing herbs, antitoxins, decoctions, balms and theraputants—the *materia medica* of the Indian medicine man. Swiftly he opened the pouch he carried over his shoulder and chose what he needed. With hands made sure from years of practice, he made a poultice of the crushed bulbs of the white-flowered mountain death camas and wrapped Daago's limp, horrible swollen hand. He built a small fire and roasted more of the bulbs, then when they had cooled enough, he held them warm over Daago's wounds.

Later he made a tea from the dried flowers of the yarrow plant, to fight infection and strengthen immune response. Holding Daago in his arms as he let the liquid trickle into her mouth. He continued the camas poultices into the night, then held Daago close, giving her the heat from his body as he softly chanted prayers to restore her to harmony with the universe. He sang old childhood lullabies that she would know as he rocked her. Toward morning the faint racing pulse strengthened and slowed.

In midmorning of the following day, he heard the commotion of the soldiers in the canyon. Had they turned back from their mission? They would be below them soon. Before Chilhajin had found Daago he had tracked the party for two days, not knowing exactly why, but that they had something to do with her.

Tense, he held Daago close, his hand over her mouth, afraid she might waken and cry out. But she remained quiet and burrowed against him.

The soldiers passed below the overhanging ledge where Chilhajin waited. His rifle lay ready beside him. He had tethered the spotted horse above where they huddled and he held his breath when the horse nickered softly at the nearness of other animals.

But the soldiers, apparently anxious to get back to the fort, were noisy. They splashed down the stream and gradually their sounds faded.

By the next day Chilhajin discontinued the camas poultices and applied a salve of heart-leafed arnica to fight infection. He made a tonic of dried valerian, pleased when Daago swallowed a bit of the anti-convulsive. She was not comatose, but continued to be mildly delirious. At times he thought she would recognize him, but her glazed eyes would close.

That evening she slept normally, her heartbeat steady and stronger. He held her close still, letting himself sleep for short periods.

When the skies began to lighten, Chilhajin went to fetch the spotted horse. Daago would be well enough to travel now. They must leave this canyon as quickly as possible. He had left her for only short periods to care for the horse and now led the animal down the slope where she lay, still sleeping.

The rocks dislodged by the horse's descent wakened her. She sat up slowly as Chilhajin came around the stone ledge leading the spotted horse.

He saw her and stopped, suddenly afraid. She hadn't wanted him. Would she still not want him? The tall young man felt a constriction in his throat, felt his eyes fill with emotion.

She looked up at him and smiled shyly. "You have cared for me. How did you know where I was?"

His heart soared. "I will always know where you are."

Chapter Twenty-Two

July, 1992: Fort Defiance

Wearily Cabot saddled Niyol and pulled herself heavily into the saddle as the first laser-like rays of the sun glinted over the Chuska Mountains. It had been a long and discouraging night. She had just gone on duty at four o'clock yesterday afternoon when they'd brought a young man into the ER. He was a welder at the Navajo Forest Industries plant north of Fort Defiance. A piece of heavy equipment had fallen on him, crushing his chest. His blood pressure had dropped dangerously low and he was in refractory shock. He was quickly put in the trauma room and the staff worked feverishly to save the young man's life and to stabilize him enough to Air Evac him to a hospital in Phoenix. Midnight, when she was supposed to go off duty, came and went, but she hardly noticed, not even considering abandoning the fight.

Cabot had worked in other Emergency Rooms—great hospitals in the east. She wasn't unaccustomed to cruel injury and death. But this man she knew. It had only been three weeks before that she had delivered his new son and had seen his face glow with pride when she went to tell him. ER personnel don't often get to know their patients. They either treat them and discharge them, or admit them to the hospital where they pass from their jurisdiction. And this had always suited Cabot just fine.

The Fort Defiance Hospital was small, however. And not always busy. She had begun to go up to the other floors to check on the progress of some of her patients. They seemed to appreciate it, liked having her remember what ailed them and to hear her reassurances. Many of them were fearful of being in the hospital, with the Navajo uneasiness that people had died there and evil spirits lurked about. She found her red hair fascinated them. Hair has great power to the Navajo and they must have figured the tall lady doctor with the curly red mane would surely have strong medicine.

This young family had delighted Cabot in its joy of the infant and she went up to the nursery each of the three days the mother and baby were there to admire his downy black head. For some reason she found Navajo babies and children particularly winsome, a feeling she had not often had with the children of her own race.

At the squaw dance, the young man and his wife had brought their baby over for her to see. And now the proud father was dead. Cabot had been the one to tell his wide-eyed wife at the end of the long desperate night. Exhausted, Cabot had gone home, but the Indian girl's grief-torn face came to her over and over. So she had come out to take Niyol for a ride, hoping the fresh air and the peace of the morning would lighten her heart.

Gradually the sun climbed in a cloudless blue—a typical summer morning sky in the high desert country. Dark green juniper and mesquite ranged for miles, casting shadows against the dun-colored soil, interspersed with stretches of lemony chamisa, the goldenrod-like shrub just coming into full flower, its dense masses scenting the early air with a heavy, aromatic sweetness. The melodious trill of sage sparrows followed the flicks of their white-edged tails as they darted after the day's emerging insects. Cabot set Niyol into a long, easy lope that soon put the stable far behind.

Once, she came upon a Navajo shepherd boy and a flock of about thirty sheep. It always amazed her to see these children, some not more than six or seven, with the sole responsibility of a large, woolly flock. She stopped to speak to him, but the boy was shy and Cabot realized that he was looking uneasily at her red hair.

She had set her sights for a low escarpment of brick-colored sandstone, but as the sun crept higher in the sky, it didn't seem to get much closer. Cabot had begun to realize that the vast, empty landscape in clear, dry air made judging distances difficult. But her mood gradually eased, cleared by the immense dome of sapphire sky and endless horizons. Also, she was getting hungry. She turned Niyol in an arc and headed back home.

The clicking rattle only registered on her consciousness before she was jerked forward and sideways in the saddle, then helplessly tried to regain her balance on the panicked horse. Niyol skittered again and Cabot was thrown clear. She hit the dry ground hard, her left wrist and ankle taking the force of her fall. She jumped up, wincing as her ankle took her weight. The diamondback was curling away in the brush, as startled by the encounter as she.

Niyol, however, was off at a full gallop, the clops of her hooves growing fainter in a cloud of dust.

"Oh, dammit, dammit, dammit! You silly red beast!"

Cabot cried. "Look what you've done. What am I supposed to do now? It'll take me at least five hours to walk back to the stable."

Cabot brushed the dirt from her jeans, cursing herself for her stupidity. Her cellular phone was clipped very carefully to the saddle, now disappearing in a dust cloud. Along with her water bottle.

"God, Chase. You're a real wilderness kid. Did it never occur to you, you jerk, that the phone and water should be on your belt, not on the horse?"

Fuming in frustration at her carelessness, she squared her shoulders and started to walk. One thing was fortunate, at least. She could just follow the horse's tracks. The perfidious little bitch was undoubtedly halfway back to the barn by now.

She'd gone no more than a few steps before she realized her ankle really hurt. She hobbled over to a boulder and sat down. It wasn't likely more than a sprain, but it made walking uncomfortable, and she had a long walk ahead. It would help if she could wrap it. She picked up her foot and, wincing, tugged off the cowboy boot and sock. She didn't have anything except what she had on. Her denim shirt had an ample hem. She pulled it out of her jeans and took it off. It would tear easily enough once she got it started, but she wished she had a knife as well as her phone and her water.

A sharp rock might do it and she limped gingerly around her boulder, picking up and discarding stone possibilities until she found one with an edge sharp enough to penetrate the denim cloth.

The makeshift bandage accomplished, Cabot yanked and pulled her sock and boot back on and tentatively tried a few steps. It was much better. And after all, there were Navajo families and flocks all over these hills. She'd surely run across someone with a pickup who would run her back to the stable.

They were unfailingly generous about helping when they could. Their lives were sometimes precarious and they all understood that they themselves might be the needy party the next time. She tried not to think that the only Navajo she'd seen in three hours had been the little shepherd boy.

"Stop whining, Chase, and walk. This is as good as it's likely to get." She trudged on.

It was nearly noon. She was due to go on duty again at four. If she wasn't there she'd be missed. Jane Manyfarms might guess that she'd taken the horse out. Maybe. Would Clah Chischillige be at the stable when Niyol showed up? He often wasn't until later in the day.

Cabot's ankle began to hurt a lot and she tried to put as little weight as possible on it. She fashioned a makeshift cane out of some brushwood, but it wasn't thick enough to be much support. She was beginning to be achingly tired. She had gotten up at seven the morning before, and had eaten nothing since before she'd gone on duty yesterday afternoon. She felt another pang as she remembered the long, torturous effort to save the Navajo welder. Billy Thompson. That was—or had been—his name. At least her predicament was taking her mind off of the tragedy of Billy Thompson for awhile.

Cabot needed to rest for a few minutes. She saw a likely rock ahead and limped toward it. Her ankle throbbed even with her weight off it. Her wrist hurt, too. She looked at her watch. It was nearly two o'clock. She hadn't made a lot of progress on the bum ankle. She wished she could curl up under a bush and sleep for just a little while. But the thoughts of the rattlesnake squelched any ideas of a nap. The sun was very bright and hot and she was beginning to feel lightheaded. She shook her head to clear it and rose to go.

After a few steps, it dawned on Cabot that her situation was beginning to be serious. Her ankle was swelling under the makeshift wrap, the dry air made dehydration a real threat. And she was so very tired.

Her eyes swam in the shimmering sun and she began to experience the odd mirages that looked like distant water.

Something caught her eye and she blinked her eyes to make sure. There seemed to be a dust cloud slightly off to her left. It was a little too far away to tell for sure, but it must be a horse and rider. "Oh, please," she whispered. "Let it be."

Cabot shouted and waved her arms, then realized she was much too far away to be heard. She scrambled up on the big rock and waved her arms. Was she wrong or did the dust cloud seem closer? She wished she had a red flag or something bright to wave. Well, her shirt wasn't very bright, but it might do if it didn't totally blend into the blue sky.

She unbuttoned her shirt for the second time that day and waved it frantically over her head.

Yes, she was definitely sure. The figure was heading her way. She could actually see it was a mounted rider. She crouched down on the rock in relief, her head on her knees. She put her shirt back on and slid off the rock. Should she wait here, or start to walk? She stepped forward, then groaned, and sat back down to wait. She was hot, tired, hungry, hurting, dirty, and miserable and hoped the Indian would hurry up. She needed to get back and clean up before she went on duty.

Cabot narrowed her eyes, hoping to sharpen the image of the rider.

What on earth! It couldn't be. It was. It was Nicholas Nakai. What was he doing out here? She rubbed her hands over her face and ran her hands through her hair. God, she looked an absolute fright, and here he was, coming at a fast lope on the big black stallion. Cabot stood up and waited, feeling awfully silly, like anyone does who has fallen off his mount. Her ankle throbbed. She sat again.

Nicholas pulled up the big horse.

"Hi," she said.

He squinted down, looking her over carefully. "You all right?"

"Uh, pretty much. I've sprained my ankle a little. What are you doing here?"

"Looking for you." He threw his leg over the red and black saddle blanket and jumped down. He unhooked a water bottle from his belt and handed it to her.

She hadn't wanted to admit how thirsty she'd become in the dry air and drank the tepid water gratefully.

"C'mon, I'll give you a leg up. I imagine you're anxious to get back."

"How did you know I was lost?" She was truly puzzled. This was just too bizarre.

"Clah Chischillige called me over at my office in Window Rock. Here."

He held his locked fingers down and Cabot put her foot into the cup and felt herself sail upward and over onto the horse.

"But how did you know where to look?"

"I'm Navajo." He looked up at her and grinned.

"Oh, that. Right. You probably learned to track at your Daddy's knee."

Nicholas threw himself over the horse's broad back and scrambled up behind her, reaching around to take the reins from her hands.

She heard him chuckle.

"I track about as good as you do. I'm a lawyer. Big deduction that you were probably in the same direction as the horse came in. And I came across a kid out with his sheep who told me he'd seen you."

She felt his thighs shift and the big horse broke into a trot. "But why would Clah Chischillige call you when Niyol came in?"

"She's my mare."

Cabot heard her voice squeak as she tried to turn around on the horse's back. "She's yours?"

"Yeah. Actually I'd have let you ride her for nothing, but Clah needs the money."

How had she wound up with Nicholas Nakai's horse? "Why am I sensing a conspiracy of some sort?"

"Oh, it's not so sinister. Jane asked me if I had a horse you could ride and I kind of liked the way you and the horse sorta look alike."

"You really think I look like a horse."

"Calm down. Your hair is the same color and all, you've got to admit."

Cabot didn't answer. What could she say? It was.

"Actually, I started to tell you at the squaw dance, but you got kinda ticked off when I said you reminded me of my red mare."

"That wasn't why I was ticked off," she grumbled.

"Whatever. I just took the mare over to the Chischillige place the next morning and told him not to tell you that he wasn't the owner. I was afraid you'd get all bent out of shape and not take her. She was starting to get fat. I really need somebody to work her while I'm off convincing the voters how terrific I am."

"Well, she's skittish all right, which is why I was in the fix I was in. But I can't blame her. My mind was on something else. She heard a rattlesnake. It kind of spooked me, too. But come to think of it, you mentioned that about me," she said dryly.

"Oh, here." He reached around and put the cell phone in

her hand. "It's a great idea. Too bad it was tied to the horse. If you go out, I wish you'd put it on your belt. I might not always be available. This time I just happened to be back from making speeches in Holbrook and Page."

"This time? I really don't need you standing by for rescue service, you know. I can't remember the last time I fell off a horse. I was careless. I know that." Cabot shifted her shoulders. "Would you mind if I took those field glasses? They're poking me in the back."

"No, of course not. Sorry." He slipped them over her head.

Curiously she picked them up and looked around the landscape. They were very powerful glasses. A slow realization grew.

"Did I get my shirt back on in time?"

Nicholas cleared his throat. "Uh...not quite."

There was no answer for that. It certainly wasn't his fault. But she felt her cheeks get hot anyway.

They rode in silence a few minutes before Nicholas asked conversationally. "You were out awfully early Clah told me. You go out every morning?"

She was grateful he'd changed the subject. "No. It was, well, it was just to kind of clear my head. We'd been up all night trying to save Billy Thompson." A lump rose in her throat as the terrible night came to her again.

"I heard about it."

"We...we didn't."

"I know." He patted her shoulder.

"A major trauma center might have, but we could never stabilize him enough for Air Evac to get him to Phoenix. There are things this hospital just doesn't have."

The discouragement washed over her again and she stopped talking.

"And so we lost another good man." His voice was pained. "There's so much of so many things we don't have. I've wanted to change that for a long time."

They rode in silence. The energy surge she'd gotten when Nicholas found her suddenly faded. She felt like she'd been dropped over a cliff. *My blood sugar is low because I haven't eaten,* she thought. *I'll eat something as soon as I get to the hospital. That'll fix me up.*

Dots swam in front of her eyes and Cabot shook her head trying to clear the fog that had come out of nowhere. Moments later she realized she'd drifted briefly off to sleep. Had her eyes closed? She didn't remember. She sat up straight and made herself think of anything else but how tired she was. The brilliant afternoon sun danced off the desert floor and the bright yellow chamisa. The rhythm of the horse's trot was hypnotic and despite her struggle to keep her eyes open, they kept closing.

"You were up all night. It's okay if you want to go to sleep. Just lean back against me. I won't let you fall."

But she was already going under. She collapsed against him, her hands limp on the withers of the horse. She barely felt his arms go around her.

"I'm not really asleep," she muttered. "Just have to close my eyes for a few seconds. Be fine then."

"It's okay. I'm not going anywhere."

Nicholas smiled and settled her against his chest, with her head tucked in the hollow of his neck

He'd been casual enough with her when he'd found her, but in reality it had been real lucky. She had ridden Niyol in pretty much a straight line, headed maybe to the ridge of

Quartz Canyon. He'd counted on that—that she was too unfamiliar with the area to veer much to the right or left. But she could have. He'd alerted the tribal police that they might have to do a Search and Rescue.

The little shepherd boy seeing her had been lucky, too.

Then, he spotted her. She stood on a rock and waved her shirt, but it was actually her hair that caught his eye first as he scanned the endless brush with his glasses. It was a bright blaze in the sun against the green and dun-colored landscape. Not that he hadn't enjoyed the picture of her waving the shirt.

Without thinking Nicholas dropped his face into her hair and drew a deep breath. The light flowery scent of the red tangle that brushed his face was just how he thought it would be. Having a warm horse and a warm bottom rocking between his legs was making it damned difficult. Her breasts rested on his arms. He smiled to himself. What the hey. Might as well enjoy it.

She woke up slowly, aware of a change in motion. Then she sat up quickly. She was in her own car, speeding along the road to Fort Defiance.

"What are you doing?" she said, feeling groggy and bewildered.

"I'm running you by the hospital so they can take a look at your ankle. Then I thought I'd take you somewhere and get you something to eat. Your stomach has been making terrible noises." He grinned, the wind tossing his black hair. "But the real reason is that I wanted to drive this car. Wanted to since I saw it the first time, when you just got here. Figured with you out cold this might be my only chance."

"But I have to go home. I'm on duty at four. What time is

it?" She looked anxiously at her watch. "Oh, it's past four," she wailed. "And I have to change my clothes. I'm a mess."

"I used your phone and called the hospital. They said no problem, they'd get somebody else. Didn't think you'd better be on that ankle until they'd X-rayed it."

Cabot slouched in her seat and crossed her arms. "Somewhere I seemed to have lost control," she muttered crossly.

"Just because I've taken a busy day out of the office to ride maybe twenty miles to rescue a grouchy redhead doesn't mean I have the right to make a few suggestions, right?" he said pleasantly.

They rode in silence.

Cabot felt her mouth twitch and she pressed her lips together. But it was no use. It was funny and she was behaving badly.

"I'm sorry. I'm tired and cross. I really am grateful. I'd probably still be stumbling along if you hadn't come. And I apologize for falling asleep on you."

"I kinda enjoyed it," he said.

She narrowed her eyes. "What do you mean by that?"

"Well, I didn't have to worry about saying something that would tick you off, for one thing."

"Are you saying I'm bitchy?"

"Sorta. Testy would be a nicer word."

"I said I was sorry."

"That's right. You did. Apology accepted." He smiled. "I really don't want you mad at me."

Cabot let that pass. "Tell me. How did you get me off that horse and into the car? I'm not real little."

"I'll say."

She made a face. "Be careful how you say that."

"Well, I guess I'm not used to throwing six-foot girls around."

"I'm not a girl."

"Six foot doctors."

"That's better."

"You know, it was sure awkward. Ever seen anybody wrestle a big old ram to shear 'im? When he doesn't want to be sheared?"

Cabot opened her mouth to retort, but nothing came out. Then she began to laugh. "No, I can't say I have."

"Well, if I hadn't had experience doing that, I'd never have gotten you into the car."

"Why in the world didn't you just wake me up?"

"Why didn't I wake her up, she says? I've never heard anybody grouse and grumble like that and not be awake. You kept telling me to go to hell."

"I didn't! You're making that up."

"Nope."

"Oh. Well. I'm awfully sorry. I don't usually say that," she said. "Unless I'm real mad."

"Funny. You were so nice and snuggled right up when you were asleep."

Cabot glanced at him, but he kept his eyes on the road. "For future reference, there're no words in Navajo for I'm sorry."

"Really? How do you apologize for something?

"We don't. You just kind of make it up to the person. To restore the harmony. We're big on harmony."

Cabot studied the sharp profile. "I guess I'll have to make something up, then. What shall I do to make you feel harmonious?"

He grinned over at her. "I'll try to think of something."

* * *

He slid into the booth across from her at the local Burger King.

"Not a whole lot of places to eat out here. This do?"

"Oh, yes. It's fine."

They'd just come from the hospital where Tommy Tootsie, the young Navajo doctor, had X-rayed her ankle and confirmed that it was only a sprain. He'd wrapped it and said to see how it felt tomorrow before she decided to come in. The rotation was changing anyway, so he'd just exchanged shifts with her. But they could manage all right without her unless things got busy.

"There's a pretty good salad bar," Nicholas said.

"No. I want a double cheeseburger, french fries, and a chocolate milkshake."

He raised an eyebrow. "That stuff'll kill you. I'll go to the salad bar."

"Now I'm surprised."

"I have to eat so much junk out campaigning, I try to be careful. I should make a record of that for my mother. She wouldn't believe it."

Cabot absently watched Nicholas cross the restaurant. It was the dinner hour and the restaurant was crowded. He knew people, of course, and stopped to speak to many of them. He had an effect on those he spoke to, she saw. They obviously admired him, and felt flattered that he noticed them. He never seemed to hurry, but in fact moved rather quickly. And well, she thought. There was grace and sureness to his movement. He had the high cheekbones and slightly slanted eyes of his race. Was that what gave his gaze such intensity, she wondered? When he looked directly into your eyes, you found it very hard to look away. Most Navajos did not do this. It is considered impolite, and Cabot noticed he didn't do it with his own people. But with whites, his gaze was direct, a learned behavior from his exposure to the Anglo culture, she supposed. When he was a lawyer in Phoenix he'd had to suppress those cultural differences.

She admitted that, after a while, when she was with him, it was sometimes easy to forget he was Indian.

He watched her polish off the last of her french fries. "You eat like a cat," he said. "A very hungry cat. I expect you to lick your paws any minute."

"First a red horse, then an old ram, now a cat," she said. "I'm a veritable zoo."

"I'm a country boy. I think in terms like that. Your eyes, if you didn't know, are the color of a mountain lion's." His chin was in his hand and he leaned on an elbow studying her.

"Don't do that. You make me nervous. I notice when you're with your own people, you don't do that."

"No." He didn't look away.

"How did you learn to act differently? It must have been difficult."

"I don't know. It came slowly. I've been educated by Anglos. Went to mission schools. My last two years in high school, I got a scholarship to a private boys school in Phoenix, taught by Jesuits. The scholarship guys were kinda outsiders. Observers. Oh, I had friends. I was good at football and track. That gets you accepted. Some of the kids I hung around with were rich kids and I watched and learned how they did things.

"The family I stayed with was great—always including me, making me feel like a son. I still see them whenever I'm in Phoenix. They invite me a lot, for holidays and things. Anyway, then I went to University of Arizona and onto law school at Arizona State. By the time I graduated, I hardly felt a hitch when I went from one culture to another. The tribe wanted me to specialize in tax law, always with the idea that

I'd be in politics eventually. And that was an important part of it, that I be comfortable in the Anglo world and that Anglos would be comfortable with me."

"Your tribe has always had those plans for you?"

"Pretty much. We'll see how that all works out in the primary. If I win that, then we'll see how comfortable everybody is sending a Navajo to Washington. The tribe's invested a lot of money in Nicholas Nakai. I hope to justify it."

The focus of his eyes had drifted away from her and to somewhere inside himself. For a moment he didn't seem to know she was there. Then he came back. "Now, you'd better go home. You've got dark circles under your eyes and I'm keeping you up."

"I'll take you back out to the stable to pick up your truck. And your horse." she said.

"No. I'll just walk over to the gas station. Somebody there'll run me back."

He opened her car door and stood while she turned the ignition.

She looked up, not sure what to say. So the Navajo were funny about thank you's. "You were...I'll thank you anyway for what you did today. And for dinner."

"I like being with you Dr. Lily Cabot Chase." The flashing neon from the restaurant made his face go from shadow to red light to green to shadow and again she felt the compelling eyes on her face.

"You always call me all that. Just Cabot would be fine."

"Then goodnight, Cabot."

She smiled into the dark eyes. "Goodnight, Nicholas."

He watched her drive away. Cabot. What strange coincidence had sent this Cabot here to disturb his days and nights. Her name was so like his own secret war name, given to him by his grandfather. His grandmother had given him the name Nicholas, but his grandfather had given him his real name, Kaab't, after one of the great 19th century Navajo chiefs who had negotiated his people out of the hateful Bosque Redondo in New Mexico and back to their beloved Dinetah.

It was a powerful name in his clan. Powerful enough to take him to Washington, he was sure of it.

Chapter Twenty-Three

August, 1992, Near Red Lake

A hard wind blew steadily, making the American flags flap flap flap over the graves in the Navajo Nation Veteran's Cemetery. Cabot William Walker Chase walked slowly among the burial mounds with their plain white stones. The graves were set among the natural grass and saltbush landscape, some lovingly tended and festooned with bright American flags and plastic flowers, some marked with tattered, faded and forgotten Stars and Stripes. It was a wild and beautiful place, a final rest for the young men who had dreamed of Dinetah in the alien places where they had fallen.

He'd never been here. It hadn't existed when he'd come to work at the hospital after the war. He'd spotted the memorial on the road from Fort Defiance to Red Lake and Canyon de Chelly. The sign announced that the cemetery had been dedicated in 1988. Would Nicholas Begay be here? He passed through rows of the dead from the Persian Gulf, Korea,

Vietnam, and eventually found himself in the area of veterans from World War II. There were a lot of them, but he finally found the gravestone marked Nicholas Begay. The flag that waved over it was bright and fresh. Someone had kept watch over it. Laura?

Cabot William Walker Chase was on his way to see the woman they had both loved. What would the ending of the story be? He crouched down and awkwardly patted the scrub-covered mound, then rose stiffly and stood with his head bowed, the wind ruffling his rusty silver hair.

"She was as much yours as she ever was mine, Nick," he said softly.

The melancholy Cabot Chase felt at the cemetery lifted as he neared Red Lake, tinted such by the iron oxides in the surrounding soil. Ah, it was good to be back. He breathed deeply and gazed with pleasure at the water's rosy surface rippling in the stiff breeze. In a little while he'd see Laura again. He'd written her as soon as he'd gotten Lily's letter and she had answered, apologizing that she didn't have a telephone, but would come to meet him in Chinle. It would be good to see him after so long. They could explore Canyon de Chelly again, as they had done years ago. Would he like that?

Would he! He'd rummaged around for his old cowboy boots, afraid that Arista might have thrown them away; but they turned up in an old trunk with his faded Levi's and denim shirts. The Levi's didn't fit anymore. God, had his belly ever been that flat?

He bought more Levi's and had the maid wash them a dozen times so he wouldn't look like a total greenhorn. She'd told him he could now buy real fancy, expensive jeans as faded and shabby as he wanted. He told her he'd be embarrassed to show up in anything like that. He wavered as he packed and wished they had faded a bit more. And frayed.

There was little traffic on the two-lane road. Most of the tourists to Canyon de Chelly would be coming up from Ganado. He felt he had the huge expanse of high desert, mountains, and sky all to himself. To come from the crowded, hectic cities of the east and find oneself in this empty *amplitude* was overpowering. Cabot let the vistas sweep through him, acclimating himself, reducing himself.

He thought of Lily. Had he done the right thing making her come here? She seemed softer somehow. Less edgy. Even as a little girl, in her exasperation with her aimless parents, she had grown impatient with human frailty. She was bright and ambitious, but he feared her desire to go into medicine was based on its intellectual challenge more than a desire to heal the sick. As much a way of saying to her parents: See what you could have done with your lives? Now I will make up for your silliness. Your selfishness.

Did he have any right to interfere? He hadn't had much success in raising a son. Was he any wiser raising a granddaughter?

Or had he wanted to happen what had indeed happened? Lily had met Laura and Laura wanted to see him. Why had he not had the courage to come himself? Alone.

He passed through Tsaile with its ultramodern community college campus. Signs announced he was near the rim of Canyon de Chelly and his pulse picked up.

Signs directing tourists to the scenic overlooks appeared. Then suddenly he was in Chinle. He had expected the town to be more settled, and it was, but it still wasn't much.

Cattle grazed along the road into town. One contented beast was lying halfway on the blacktop, chewing her cud, oblivious to the cars and trucks that veered around her. There was a fair amount of traffic here. Canyon de Chelly was a favorite of tourists and it was the middle of summer, the time of Winnebagos and families giving their children a taste of the variety in their sprawling country.

There was a new Visitor's Center he noted. A couple of motels, one a brand new and very nice Holiday Inn. A modern high school. A tribal chapter house. But it was still weedy and rural.

He drove through a wooded campground and through the trees was the entrance to the canyon. He followed several four-wheel drive excursion trucks full of tourists, then pulled off before he reached the mouth of the gorge—his rental car would be no match for its floor of shifty sands. Laura would meet him here.

He got out and stood uncertainly, then wiped his palms along the sides of his Levi's.

Christ, I'm seventy and feel sixteen, he thought. *It's a good thing my heart's okay or I'd think I was fibrillating.*

"Ya-at-eeh, Cabot."

He whirled and there she was, smiling at him from the back of a black and white paint horse.

"Laura."

"I was watching for you up on the road, but I missed you."

She was leading a glossy bay, dark brown with a black mane and tail. With a quick movement she dismounted as he moved to her, his hands extended.

"My God, Laura. You look like a girl."

She laughed, a sound that made time drop away so quickly he caught his breath.

"Oh, I can't believe that, but the years have been lucky for me." She tilted her head and her eyes swept over him. "You're as handsome as ever. And very distinguished."

He grinned. "Which means I sure don't look like a boy."

"No. But I didn't come to meet a boy."

They stood, smiling at each other, letting the years fall away.

"I've never seen you dressed as a Navajo."

She looked down at her blue velvet blouse and rust satin skirt.

"No. I wanted no part of that for a long time. Now, I find I feel at home this way. I am home. I live here now, in a hogan in one of the small canyons off the river. I thought I'd try it after I left the hospital. For a while. Then I kept staying longer and longer. Now I leave only in the coldest months, when the snow gets too deep to drive back and forth." She indicated the horses. "I thought I'd bring the horses in. I've brought a picnic." She laughed. "I'll see how much of the place you remember."

"Laura, that's a great idea. C'mon. What are we waiting for? We've got a lot of catching up to do."

He leaned and cupped his fingers for her foot. She was as light as a feather as she mounted in one fluid motion.

He looked at her wryly as he took the reins of the bay horse. "I'm not as agile as I used to be." But he made a fairly good show of mounting, which pleased him. He wanted to look as young as he felt with her.

As they moved into the canyon, he said, "Now, if I remember correctly, the first ruins are up a little way on the left."

After their first burst of words, they rode quietly, settling in to the idea that they had a bridge of forty years to cross and there was no hurry about it.

Cabot was intensely conscious of the small woman who rode beside him. He studied her as well he could without seeming to, relieved that she didn't seem alien to him at all.

He had worried that their lives, passed so differently, would erase the closeness they had once felt. Even her clothing hadn't startled him and he suspected she dressed in the traditional Navajo costume to somehow test his feeling. The fact that he had dreamed about her for so long, carried the memory of her so close to him, that to find her so little changed had astonished him. He felt his nervousness ease, to be replaced by a joy so intense he felt like shouting to the thousand foot walls that he had come back.

As before, the canyon dwarfed them. A thousand feet above, Permian sedimentary rock was exposed on the crest. Stands of dark juniper trees clung, tiny from this depth. Below the rim, the rocky cross-bedding was on a grandiose scale—steep, swooping laminae with wind-eroded pits and potholes. For over the six million years of its weathering, when it rained, small ponds formed in the potholes and tiny plant and animal organisms lived out their life cycles. Living and dying, they deposited weak, metabolic acids that remained after their little pools had dried, gradually weakening the calcium carbonate cement that held the Shinarump sandstone together. Great slabs and sheets gradually fell away from the weakened wall rock, deepening recesses where the ancient Anasazi built their living quarters seven hundred to a thousand years ago.

Laura smiled at him. "You didn't forget." She halted the paint horse and pointed up the cliff face to an ancient ruin. Cabot pulled up beside her.

"How could I ever forget?" How indeed, he thought. He'd made love to her several times in the shelter of its ancient walls.

"I wish we could have our picnic up there, but it's off-limits now. The ruins are too fragile and only government restorers go up there now."

Cabot stared at the ruins and he struggled with the words before he spoke.

"This place is part of me. I haven't had a very happy life, Laura. I've regretted leaving a thousand times."

"You would have been more unhappy had you stayed. I was always a more romantic figure in your life than a practical one."

"You're probably right. You generally were."

"You were such an idealist, Cabot. Your feelings that you somehow owed something to Nicholas. You didn't, you know. War is never fair. I saw it so many times. You go mad trying to figure out why some were spared and others not."

"I know we both saw things in the war that we wished we hadn't. We survived. Nicholas didn't. And I came here to somehow repay that." A mirthless laugh sounded in his throat. "And then I'd have times I'd be consumed with guilt that I'd fallen in love with you."

"I loved Nicholas. And then I loved you. One had nothing to do with the other." She smiled. "I named one grandson Nicholas, did I tell you?"

"No."

"Yes. I delivered him here in this canyon. And I named him. My husband gave him his war name, but I called him Nicholas. Navajo men call their war name their real name, but to me, Nicholas is his real name. You'll like him."

"Even now? A war name?"

"They're really names of power. Names with strong medicine to help a young man be successful. That used to mean war, but now it means other things. Only a very few people ever know or it weakens its power. I, for instance, don't know what Nicholas's war name is." She laughed. "Do you think we're hopelessly primitive?"

"Of course not. I'm thinking my son could have done with a war name."

"Oh?"

"He's a disappointment to me, but perhaps he isn't to himself." Cabot snorted. "Well, that's the first time I've ever thought of it that way. You've begun to influence me already."

"Your son disappoints you? Were you happy with your wife?"

"We got along, for the most part. But it wasn't a...warm marriage." He turned and looked directly at Laura. "And what of you, Laura? Have you been happy? Your name is Begay now?"

"Yes. Two years after you left I married Franklin Begay, Nathaniel's brother. He was a good man, gentle and kind. He died ten years ago of kidney disease. I have two wonderful daughters and a dozen grandchildren. I've delivered most of them. That's a fine thing, to deliver your grandchildren."

"It must be. I have only the one. Lily. Though," he smiled wryly, "for some reason she prefers to be called by her middle name, Cabot. Thinks Lily is wimpy, as she calls it. Maybe it's similar to having a war name to her, using a man's name. Maybe that's it."

"That's quite possible."

"We're very close, she and I."

"She's like you. In looks anyway. Very tall. And she has your eyes and such red, beautiful hair."

"Mine's not very red anymore." He chuckled.

Her eyes rested on him for a moment. "Why is she here, Cabot?"

"A little coercion on my part. I'm not exactly sure anymore of my reasons. Now that I'm here with you, I see that was part of it. She didn't want to come, but I think she's better for it. She may even begin to agree with me."

"She's a strong girl."

"Oh, God. Don't let her hear you call her a girl. That's not done these days."

"I forget." Her voice took on a teasing edge. "Your Anglo women haven't had the power we Navajo women have always had. Young females now are so touchy. Indian girls are becoming so acculturated that they're forgetting they always had most of what they think they want now."

He reached over and took her hand as it rested on the horn of her saddle. "You're damned right about one thing. A man doesn't stand a chance around a Navajo woman."

Laura laughed and squeezed his hand. "Damn right. Now, how do you feel about a little race to the end of the canyon? Then we'll have our picnic."

"You're on. Just say when." Cabot's horse immediately sensed the tension in his legs and danced impatiently.

"Now!"

But he was no match for Laura on a horse. He never had been.

Laura's picnic was an assortment of pates, cheeses, French bread, and a bottle of wine. It was the same as she had done for their first picnic, things she'd come to love when she'd been in France during the war.

"So I went into Flagstaff and tried to remember what we'd had. It was all easier to find than it was in the 50's. Did I come close?"

"You're wonderful. I'd forgotten all about it. Yes, I'm sure it's right. It tastes right."

"I'm dead set against alcohol on the reservation, but I told my conscience to shut up, just this once." She held up a clear plastic cup with a ruby-colored wine. "I'd make a toast, but I don't know what to say. Except I'm glad you're here, Cabot. It's been too long for both of us, I think."

"I'm glad I'm here, too. I've spent a lot of years without you Laura. I'd like to be part of your life again, for as little or as much as you want."

After their picnic, they meandered with the horses through the ancient canyon, stopping to examine petroglyphs incised in the shiny *desert varnish*—dark, manganese and iron oxide deposits to contrast with the pale peach sandstone beneath. Earlier artists had carved these powerful images of antelope, horses, and men for whatever reasons of piety or luck, or to satisfy an artistic impulse. The canyon was a holy place in the Navajo religion, and some of the most traditional of the tribe's members still lived in its hundreds of tributaries.

When the sun dropped below the tree-lined rim, Laura said, "I made a reservation for you at the new Holiday Inn you passed on the way in. It's beautiful and we're all very proud of it. The rooms are comfortable and they have a good restaurant. I think you'll like it."

He hadn't wanted to think about the day ending. "Oh. Fine. Thanks very much. I appreciate that."

She looked at him carefully, her dark eyes catching the rosy glow of the sky.

"Or, we could go back to my hogan. I can cook some lamb stew, perhaps."

Cabot tried to keep his voice steady, but despite himself, it broke slightly when he answered. "I'd like that, Laura. Very much. Very, very much."

"The bed won't be as comfortable as the Holiday Inn." She smiled.

"I don't think I'll notice."

Chapter Twenty-Four

August 18, 1992

So Grandfather had left three days ago and she hadn't heard from him yet. Cabot pulled out of the parking lot at the hospital and hummed a series of random notes. She really was pleased for him. He'd always been a lonely figure to her, courteous and solicitous of her imperious grandmother Arista, kind and protective of her, his only grandchild. She knew he mourned for the son he couldn't reach, which made her disgusted with her father. Her beautiful, quirky mother just drifted after her feckless husband, and Cabot was a little more forgiving of her airy passivity. As long as she could remember, they were off on some radical cause or another—either that or some gauzy religion. Their passions were wide, but not deep. One day they'd be manning some barricade or being dragged off some picket line to jail, then it would be off to a commune, or some guru with the solution to their existence. There was acid and pot, uppers, downers. Now it was New Wave touchy-feely crystals, mantras, etcetera. No wonder her grandfather despaired and had taken her in and given her the only stability she'd ever had.

When she was twelve and at her most romantic, she imagined a tragic love affair for her grandfather, and when in later years she found it was true, she wondered why he hadn't just gone after his Indian woman and taken her back to Boston with him. What was wrong with people! If you wanted something, go after it. Think of all his wasted years. She, by God, had mapped out her life and that was the way it was going to be and she would *make* it be that way.

She would marry Larimer and get that out of the way, then get on with her career.

Oh, eek! Had she really said that to herself? Get marrying Larimer out of the way? It had just popped into her head, revealing and unbidden. But maybe she shouldn't analyze it too much, really, one always had some doubts about big steps, after all, and she had so many good reasons to say yes to Larimer.

Good, solid reasons.

She would think about Grandfather. That made her feel wonderful. She'd had a halfway part in getting him back with his love and it looked like things were going just the way she'd hoped. Maybe she'd get out of here sooner than she thought. *Oh, don't say that, Cabot. Things are much better than I thought they'd be, and I'm making a real contribution here. There's so much need. It's a less-stress-interlude, that's what it is, before I have to get back to studying the medical hard stuff again.*

A thought intruded. Grandfather was seventy years old, although he didn't look it. He'd been gone three days. She hoped they didn't overdo.

Cabot pulled into the parking area of her apartment,

noting absently that there was a crowd milling about a curious tent-like structure in the field next to the building. She got out of her car and started into her apartment.

She stopped.

She turned.

It was a yurt. In the meadow. She was sure it was a Mongolian yurt, and it was in her meadow. There was a hint of incense in the air.

Oh, for God's sake. It was Mother and Daddy. They'd pitched a tent. A yurt! Outside her apartment building.

Cabot marched over to the curved, felt-covered Himalayan structure. In front there was a brazier over a bed of hot coals with a kettle boiling.

"Mother?"

She heard a little flurry and jingle inside the tent.

"Mother? Daddy?" She sniffed the air and pushed open the tent flap. "Mother? Are you smoking pot in there?"

A wisp of incense wafted out the door. That sandalwood tang had always been a dead giveaway.

"Come in, Lily darling. No. Of course not. We gave that up, didn't we, Benjamin. We're not polluting our bodies any more."

"I'm delighted to hear it," Cabot said dryly.

"Aren't you going to say hello, Lily? Would you like a cup of tea? Lapsang Souchong? I think the water's ready."

Cabot wrinkled her nose. "It is, but no thanks. You know I think that tea tastes like rancid yak butter."

Her mother lounged on a pile of batik-covered cushions. Her father sat cross-legged in some kind of yoga position. He seemed reluctant to come back to the business at hand, but finally ended whatever was occupying his thoughts and rose to welcome his daughter.

"Lily." He held his arms out. "We didn't bother to call

that we were coming. We had the yurt, and if it was inconvenient for you, we'd just stay out here."

He embraced Cabot, who patted his back weakly. It was hopeless. They were children.

"It's all right. But I don't know that you can stay here. The…tent and all. This is Navajo reservation land. I don't know what they allow."

"Oh, we've never had any trouble with Native American peoples," her mother said blithely. "They never mind our yurt. After all, it isn't much different than a hogan."

"You can move inside. Grandfather is visiting and has some things in the extra bedroom, but he's gone for a time and I'm not sure when he'll be back."

As if on cue, she heard her grandfather call.

"Lily? Is that you? Are you in there? Is that you, Benjamin and Mariella?"

Cabot ducked out through the tent flap. "Yes, it is, Grandfather. They've stopped for a visit. Hello Laura." She raked her fingers through her hair. "It's nice to see you again." She checked her grandfather anxiously, but he exuded well-being. He was holding hands with Laura Begay. "I was just telling Mother and Daddy I could put them up in the apartment."

"Dr. Chase?" It was Bobby Becenti, the apartment manager.

Cabot spun. "Oh, yes, Bobby." He was looking over her shoulder.

She turned back. Her parents were ducking out of the yurt's opening. Her mother was dressed in a silky lavender sari with a red dot in the middle of her forehead. On various spots of her costume, spangles glinted and tinkled and each arm carried a load of gold bangles.

Her father wore some kind of sarong and Birkenstocks, his red curly hair was pulled back in a ponytail and an explosive cinnamon beard mingled with the mat of curls on his chest. He still had the ring in his nose she noted with dismay, and another winked from a bushy eyebrow. There was a tattoo of some kind of winged creature on his belly.

The crowd of Indian children tittered.

Cabot gulped. "These are my parents, Bobby. Is it all right if they stay here?" She gestured helplessly at the yurt. "My grandfather's staying with me right now," she looked imploringly at her grandfather, "and I don't think I have...I mean I don't have another bedroom."

"Oh, c'mon, Bobby. Be a sport. They're not going to bother anybody."

Cabot froze. Something formed a knot in her throat and she felt hot spots on her cheeks. Then she turned slowly toward the voice, wishing with all her being that it couldn't be so. Nicholas stood, surveying the scene with interest.

"Um...hi, Nicholas." She wished her voice weren't so high and squeaky in her ears. "What are you doing here?"

"Just checking to see that your ankle got better. Hi, Grandmother." He waved to Laura, then eyed Cabot's parents with friendly curiosity.

"Um, Daddy and Mother, this is Nicholas Nakai." She waved her hand weakly. "Mariella and Ben Chase. And that's my grandfather, Cabot Chase." She looked from her parents to her grandfather and added hopefully, "Laura is Nicholas's grandmother."

"I'm real happy to meet you." Nicholas said, thrusting out his hand to Benjamin, then Cabot W.W. "Sir. Seems to be more than one Cabot Chase."

Her grandfather laughed. "She's Lily to all of us."

Bobby Becenti stepped in, looking worried the situation had gotten away from him. He looked uncomfortable. "Well, I don't know." He sniffed at the pungent sandalwood suspiciously. "What's that funny smell?"

No one was paying any attention.

"Father?" Benjamin was staring at his father, still holding hands with Laura.

"Hello, Ben. This is Laura. Time you met her."

"Why Father, this is wonderful!" Ben exclaimed, stepping forward to enfold the small, startled woman to his rufous chest.

The crowd of spectators was growing, and the whirl of voices was making Cabot's head spin. She sagged with horror and resignation when a gleaming black limousine pulled into the parking lot and the driver jumped out smartly to open the door for Larimer Madison.

Scowling, Larimer strode toward the milling scene, his nose wrinkling at the sandalwood and the motley crowd assembled around the exotic yurt.

Cabot ran to him. "Larimer. What are you doing here? Why didn't you tell me you were coming? Please, please go away. I mean, please. Just for a little while. I have things to sort out. I can't talk now." She tried fruitlessly to turn him around.

"Why, of course I won't go away. Just tell me what needs to be done here. I've come all the way from Boston to see you, Cabot." He looked with disapproval at the sari-clad woman advancing on him, her face a wreath of smiles.

"You must be the banker." She smiled brightly, jingling, holding out a gracious, be-ringed hand.

Cabot croaked, "Larimer, this is my mother, Mariella Chase. Larimer Madison."

"Your mother? I can't believe this." Larimer looked stunned. "I...uh...how do you do?" He edged away.

Mariella drew the gauzy sari around herself haughtily. "I prefer the Indian, Lily. The sex will be better, believe me."

Cabot wished she could faint, be unconscious somehow. "Mother!" She could only imagine the shades of red that flamed her face.

"Hello. I'm Nicholas Nakai." He was holding out his hand to Larimer, who took it like a sleepwalker, then jumped back as if he'd been electrocuted.

Nicholas beamed.

Cabot wanted to choke him. She pushed Larimer hard toward the limousine.

"Larimer, please. I'm asking you. Do this for me. I promise it will all be all right. Just give me half an hour," she begged. At last she had tugged him over to the car.

"Who in the hell is that Indian?' he muttered. "What's he got to do with you?" he said suspiciously.

"Nothing. Nothing. He just lives here. It's a reservation, Larimer. Please. Go." She put his arm into the fascinated driver's hand and shoved. "Go."

He reluctantly climbed into the car, only to bump his head when Nicholas asked pleasantly, "Will seven o'clock give you enough time, Lily? I'll pick you up for dinner at 7:30 if that would be better."

Cabot's mouth dropped as she looked from Nicholas to Larimer, whose outraged face now glared furiously behind the tinted window of the limousine. Cabot motioned frantically to the driver and finally the car moved away from the parking lot.

She spun on Nicholas. "What did you say that for?" she demanded. "We're...we didn't have a dinner...date. Now, look what you've done."

"I don't know what came over me," he said, his face a study in mock amazement.

Cabot stormed back to the crowd, who were now in varying opinions that the yurt was violating no tribal ordinances. People were starting to wander curiously around the yurt, assessing its wool felt fabric, earnestly discussing its fire-proofness and general soundness. A couple of small children peeked through the door flap, then disappeared inside.

Nicholas wandered over. “C’mon, Bobby. It’s a field. Nobody’s bothering anything.”

“It’s the fire hazard, Nicholas.” Bobby said.

A tribal police cruiser pulled up and a large sergeant heaved out of the driver’s seat.

“Oh, my God,” moaned Cabot. “This is the worst day of my life.”

Nicholas pulled the sergeant aside, and after a few minutes of dickering, came back to Cabot.

“It’s just that they had trouble with...uh...hippies awhile back, so they don’t allow camping except in designated areas. I told him your parents would just use the tent for sleeping, and they wouldn’t light any more fires. He said they could stay out here for three days.”

“I promise you, they’ll be gone tomorrow,” Cabot said morosely.

“Why? They seem very nice. Aren’t you glad to see them?”

“I...I...well, yes. I guess I am. Yes.” To her surprise, she really was. “I am.”

“I’m glad to see you. You’re still limping.”

“A little. Look. I really have to sort this all out.”

“Can I pick you up at seven o’clock?”

“Nicholas, I can’t. Really.”

“Who is he?”

She was going to ask who he meant, but she knew very well who he meant. “He’s a friend. From Boston.”

“I guess you didn’t know he was coming.”

“No.”

“Will he stay with you?”

Nicholas was smiling, except his eyes weren’t. They were flat and opaque.

"I...no...I don't think so," she said. Her heart was thumping, making her breathless. "I mean, my parents are…or rather grandfather is…at least he was until..." Then it hit her. Nicholas Nakai was jealous! "Look, Larimer isn't staying with me. I don't even *know* how long he'll be here."

"Can I pick you up tomorrow night, then, at seven?"

"Nicholas, can't it be another time?" She gestured helplessly.

He reached up and brushed her shoulder. "Sure. Really, I came by to say goodbye for a week or so. I'll be down in Phoenix. Just didn't want you to think I'd forgotten you."

"Oh." She felt her disappointment somewhere in her stomach.

"Can I call you when I get back?"

"Well, of course. You've called me before."

"Not the same thing. That was just to ask you how your ankle was. This time I want to ask you to have dinner with me."

"Well, we've had dinner before, after all."

"That isn't the same thing either."

"Oh, well. Yes. The answer is yes. Call me as soon as you get back."

His white teeth flashed. "Good."

She watched him go, then sighed and turned back to her family.

"I don't know why you're acting the way you are, Larimer. I've described my parents to you in great detail many times. Now you're acting like I've tried to put something over on you. I told you they were unconventional."

Cabot had gotten him up to her apartment while the limo

driver waited outside. He had looked around, disdainfully poking at her collection of Indian pots and rugs.

He turned back to her. "Unconventional is putting it mildly, Cabot." He sniffed. "They will look frightfully out of place at our wedding. Our friends will not understand."

"But look, you're really jumping ahead. I haven't said I'd marry you. I'd made no promises."

"Well, it's time you did. This whole charade has gone quite far enough."

"Are you trying to bully me?" Cabot's voice had taken on a dangerous edge.

"No, no. Of course not. But you must agree. I can't tell you how horrified I am at the conditions here. It's far worse than I imagined. Good God! It looks like a Third World country up here. And that hospital! Appalling! Why, you've been exposed to the finest medical institutions in the east. In the world! And you're giving...wasting…as in throwing away...an entire year of your life. It's criminal what your grandfather has made you do, absolutely crim...

"That's enough, Larimer."

"Cabot, you know I only have your best interests at heart."

She sighed. "I know that. But this isn't a waste. I know I thought so in the beginning. But, it's been very rewarding. I'm truly needed here. I never saw how important that was."

He threw up his hands in disgust. "And there are no amenities here. Zero. What do you do for intellectual stimulation? I saw one movie theater. Do you know what was playing there? Do you? Do you? One of those ghastly detective films that consist of nothing but car crashes, gore, and four letter words. I checked. I got out and looked. That trash and more monster/slasher/vampire crap. The same sort of thing will be playing there next week, and the week after. There aren't any restaurants. None. Pizza and fried chicken and hamburger joints. One of each. Everywhere you look there are Indians."

"That's very common on an Indian reservation," she said dryly. "Did you look at the mountains, and the sky? It's really very beautiful here."

"By God it looks like the *moon!* A more desolate landscape would be hard to find," he exploded. "Really, Cabot." He ran his fingers through his silver hair in frustration. "I don't know what's come over you."

"There was more of the same," Cabot said to her grandfather. "So he stormed away, telling me to call him when I came to my senses." She sighed. "I think I have come to my senses, and Larimer is a casualty. I guess I really never did want to marry him. I certainly kept putting off making a decision."

"I'm relieved. He's too old for you. Young people should marry young people."

She smiled. "And older people should marry older people?"

He laughed. "Touche´. But no. Laura and I won't marry. But we can be close. She doesn't want to go back east. I can't blame her for that. But I can come out here whenever I want. Stay as long as I want. I imagine I'll spend a lot of time with her." He leaned back in the chair and stretched out his legs, crossing his arms behind his head. "God, I'm happy. I don't deserve to be so happy."

"Yes, you do. She's lovely. I can see why you carried the torch for all those years."

"I don't want you to feel I was disloyal to your grandmother."

"Oh, Grandfather, don't. I lived with her, too." Cabot

felt a thickness in her throat. "To her I was an annoyance, my parents thought of me only sometimes. If it hadn't been for you, it would have been terrible for me."

"You'll find love, Lily. That's why I'm glad you've put Larimer behind you. Young people need passion. Larimer is many fine things, but he is not a passionate man. Though I doubt he'll give you up so easily. Larimer Madison doesn't like to lose."

She smiled slightly and watched her fingers play with a button on her skirt. "Well, we'll see."

There was a brief silence.

"What do you feel about Laura's grandson?" her grandfather asked.

Her head snapped up, and she unconsciously tucked a strand of curly hair behind her ear. "What?"

"Nicholas. He likes you."

She cleared her throat. "Oh, well. We've met a couple of times." Cabot got out of her chair and walked over to absently rearrange a small collection of Indian pots on a table. "I fixed his shoulder at the Flagstaff Rodeo on the Fourth. Did Laura tell you about that? He dislocated it wrestling a steer, I think that's what you call it. The event, not the shoulder. And then, well, he came to get me out on the desert when my— His horse threw me. A rattlesnake scared her and I sprained my ankle." She shrugged. "That's all."

"He came out and got you and it was his horse."

"Oh, it's too complicated. It turned out that the horse Jane Manyfarms, you remember, the hospital administrator, who is Laura's daughter, actually. Anyway, the horse she arranged for me belonged to Nicholas, although I didn't know it at the time." She took a deep breath.

"I see."

"Well, no. You don't see. Look, you're just in a romantic

frame of mind." She smiled nervously. "That seems like a tidy equation to you just now. You're in a glow about Laura and you think I...it would be...if Nicholas. Well...it isn't."

"Isn't what?" Cabot W.W. grinned.

"Isn't a *thing,*" she said hotly. "He's much too busy running for Congress, and, after all, I'm only going to be here until next June."

He passed a hand over his face to wipe away his smile. "You're probably right. Blame it on my euphoric state. Now, do you suppose Mariella is finding enough macrobiotically sound junk at the supermarket to conjure up some kind of edible dinner?"

She realized she'd been holding her breath and let it out slowly, so he wouldn't notice, glad to have a change of subject that was making her terribly uncomfortable. "I'll fix you an enormous steak with french fries after they leave."

"Thank God."

She sat among the batik pillows with her mother, the inside of the yurt softly lit with a kerosene lantern. Cabot hoped they weren't violating the no-fire stipulation that Nicholas had negotiated with the tribal policeman.

There was a Red Sox game on television that her father and grandfather didn't want to miss, so she and her mother had come out here. She couldn't remember the last time she had been alone with her mother, but it was pleasant to sit here, letting her mother rattle on.

"...so we opened the shop. We have our regulars, then a lot of people come for the harmonic convergences, so we make a living. I have some clients for my astrology readings and I do Tarot cards, too."

Cabot wondered idly if her father's trust funds from his mother had gone up in incense smoke.

"We don't really work very hard and if we feel like going somewhere, we close up."

"What are convergences?" Cabot was feeling drowsy but hungry. Her mother's concoction of pinon nuts and brown rice hadn't been very filling. She had some ice cream in the freezer back in the apartment and some chocolate syrup. She knew her grandfather would want some, too.

"There are sacred spots in the world with incredible energy. Sedona is one. We gather on Airport Mesa, hundreds of us sometimes. Your father sets up the copper pyramid. People in the special places all over the world hum and chant at the same time. We cause an energy shift. We have the ability to influence reality for good impulses because of our sheer numbers. We'll initiate an era of peace and harmony."

Cabot smiled dreamily. "We could use it."

Chapter Twenty-Five

August 25, 1992

Cabot had the canvas board propped up against a stack of books, a so-so solution. She'd have to get an easel if she were going to keep at this. She put a brush between her teeth and looked critically at her painting. It was terrible. She hadn't painted since that oil class she'd taken in college her junior year, but she had so much time on her hands in the evenings when she wasn't at the hospital, she decided to try to capture some of the dramatic landscapes that were a constant presence in the life here.

She'd found some basic supplies at a Wal-Mart in Gallup and had thought she'd first paint from snapshots she'd taken, then maybe take a few things along on her rides with Niyol, after she'd practiced a bit.

She squinted down at the canvas and compared it to her photograph.

"I stink," she said with disgust, but took her brush out of

her mouth and dabbed it in the pie plate she was using for a palette. She bent over the landscape and tried to tone down a delicate shading of burnt umber. She was trying to invoke the gradations of color on the cliffs at Canyon de Chelly and found her lack of skill frustrating. It had been so beautiful, she had been sure it would also be easy to duplicate.

The apartment was still except for an occasional snort of exasperation from Cabot. When her doorbell rang, it startled her. Callers were rare and it was after ten o'clock. It was probably Bobby Becenti about something or another. She wiped her hands on her makeshift smock, an old green surgical gown, and went to the door.

"Hi. I saw your light on, so I took a chance you were still up." Nicholas stood on the landing, his thumbs hooked over his silver belt buckle.

"Well, hi." She hesitated, conscious of her paint-smeared gown and her general dishevelment. "C'mon in."

He stepped inside and looked around curiously.

"Don't look over there! I mean…well…I'm trying to make a painting and it's so awful I don't want anybody to see it."

He smiled. "Okay. I won't. I really just wanted to see if maybe you'd like to go for a walk."

She looked at him quickly. He sounded different. Tired.

"Well, sure. Yes. I'd like that. I'm certainly not getting anywhere with my masterpiece. You'll have to wait, though. I've got to clean this stuff off my hands."

"Take your time."

Cabot went to the table and quickly turned her painting so he wouldn't see it, then looked at him sheepishly.

"I wasn't going to cheat," he said.

"Well, no. I know." She wiped her hands with turpentine and a rag.

Nicholas ambled around the living room, stopping to pick up one of her Indian pots or run his hands over one of her Navajo blankets she had thrown over the couch and several of the chairs.

She could see him through the pass-through as she washed the solvent from her hands in the kitchen sink. He seemed moody and depressed.

When she came into the living room he held up a pot.

"Looks like you're single-handedly trying to run up the economy of the reservation."

"I get to talking with the artists and then I can't resist. The things are made so beautifully. They...they're just so...satisfying." She ran her fingers through her hair. "It's hopeless. You'll just have to take me as I am. I'm too far gone. I wasn't expecting company."

"You're fine. Women worry too much. I know what you look like."

"Then, let's go."

They left the lights of the apartment buildings; it was very dark now, and they picked their way carefully along a gravel road leading to some isolated farms and hogans until their eyes became adjusted to the velvety, moonless night.

"That was one of the hardest things for me to get used to," she said. "The darkness. And the silence. Cities are full of diffused light, even at their gloomiest. And they're never quiet."

"I know." He gestured. "This wraps around you. It has a tangible feel to it. It's like...fur. I miss it when I'm gone."

"I've never seen stars like this. Makes me sorry I didn't study astronomy and know what they all are. That big bright one up there, for instance."

"There? That's Aldebaran. It's the brightest in the constellation Taurus. It's called Alpha Tauri. First magnitude star, big in navigation."

"I'm impressed."

"I'm showing off."

"Do you know that because you're Navajo?"

"Nah. I just like astronomy. As you say, you see the skies like this, you want to know. The older people, they know. Had to. They have Navajo names for everything. I only know some."

"Like, for instance...?

"Well, the Big Dipper is *Nahookos*. Orion is *Atse-ets-ozi*."

She groaned. "Here I was, going to have you teach me. I can handle *Nahookos*, but *Atse*...ah... Your language defeats me."

"I'm available for star walks and Navajo lessons whenever you say."

They walked without talking for perhaps a quarter of a mile. The night was cool and crickets sang from damp gullies along the sides of the road. The sweet smell of freshly mown alfalfa hung on the still, summer air.

"I'm not very talkative," he said. "Sorry. I take you for a walk, then I'm not sociable."

"That's okay. I feel that way sometimes. It's nice to be quiet."

"It seems like I've done nothing else but talk this past week. I've talked, made speeches, debated, done interviews, answered questions, and then some more questions."

"What you're doing isn't easy," she said.

"Lily, maybe it's too easy. Promises just roll off my tongue. I'm going to do this. I'm going to do that. Just watch me take Washington by storm. I'll get more jobs, job-training, day-care, protect the environment, balance the budget, clean up the cities, abolish crime, hatred, floods, famine, and pestilence." He raked his hands through his hair in frustration. "Hell, I don't know if I can do a fraction of what I promise. Whether I can do anything at all. Whether I wouldn't even make things worse."

"You're just tired," she said. "Even your voice is hoarse."

"I went before the editorial boards of the big Phoenix and Scottsdale papers. They're really state newspapers. It's so important that they write favorably about me. The part of the district in Maricopa County has a lot of votes—from Indian reservations to ritzy bedroom communities. I'll get the reservations, but it's the urban areas and the towns that I don't know if I'm getting across. They're looking at me carefully. The primary is in two weeks and I've got a heavy case of the doubts. Am I ready enough? Do I know enough? Are voters ready for a Navajo to represent them? Any Arizonan knows Nicholas Nakai is an Indian name. Will they trust me?"

"You're a lawyer. That's wonderful training. You're used to cross-examinations. I'm sure you were impressive. I know you were."

His teeth flashed in the dimness. "You really are cheering me up. And to think I didn't even know where I was going when I started out."

"Didn't you?"

There was a pause. "Well, maybe a little bit."

"Where do you live, Nicholas? Window Rock?"

"This side of. A couple of miles up the gravel road that runs by the high school. I built the place after I came back to the Rez. Nothing fancy. I had a couple of ideas, not that they're all that original. You've noticed that some of the new public buildings are eight-sided, like the hogan. I just built kind of a modern hogan."

"Did you build it yourself?"

"Some of it." He laughed. "I'm not especially handy. I needed a lot of help. Bobby Becenti's a genius at almost everything, so a lot of the work is thanks to him. It took us about two years."

After a minute they turned and started back. The lights

of the apartment buildings twinkled in the distance. Cabot was amazed they had come so far.

"What made you start painting?" he asked.

"Oh, I don't know. I'd done a little when I was younger. I was...let me see, what did my professor say? 'You are competent, Miss Chase. Painting should give you many hours of pleasure.' Which translates, I should never show my stuff to anybody."

"What are you working on?"

"Oh, just some studies of Canyon de Chelly. I wanted to see if I could capture some of the colors. It's just a pastime. I needed something to do. I'm not busy enough here."

"What do you really want to do, Cabot?"

"You called me Lily before."

"Did I? I didn't notice."

"I know." She took a deep breath. "What do I want to do? Well, I'm a doctor. That's what I want to do. But more than that I want to be a surgeon. Probably a neurosurgeon. I'm not exactly certain just yet. I'll need more years of study. What I'm doing here is kind of a detour."

"You said it was a long story."

She laughed. "It's still a long story. But when I leave here I'll go to Johns Hopkins in Baltimore for a three-year surgical residency. It's a fine hospital and I was lucky to be accepted."

"I don't like to think of you going away."

"Well, it's a long way off."

"Did your grandfather have anything to do with your coming here? I didn't know about him and Grandmother."

"I knew there was a Navajo woman that he'd been in love with for years. And then I met your grandmother at the squaw dance. She told me she would like to see him again. I saw why he'd never forgotten her. When I wrote, he couldn't get here fast enough."

"My Auntie Jane was real surprised. She always knows everything." He chuckled. "Or thinks she does. She didn't have a clue about that, though."

"What was your grandfather like, Nicholas?"

"I don't remember him very well. A good man. Quiet. He wasn't an educated man. My father only went through high school for that matter. It's only the women in my family who are the educated ones. And they were determined that I'd go to college." He laughed fondly. "The three of them—Mother, Auntie Jane, Grandmother, plus my sisters—yap, yap, yap. I wanted to be a cowboy but I didn't stand a chance."

"I can't remember wanting to be anything but a doctor. I'd drag down Grandfather's medical books and look at the gruesome pictures. I spent most of my growing up years with him. Mother and Daddy...well, I wasn't always a convenience." She shrugged, then said, "I haven't answered your question. Yes. I came because of Grandfather."

"And not real happy about it."

"It wasn't what I planned. No. I'd never been familiar with Indian life. It was totally alien to me. Oh, there are the Wampanoag in Massachusetts, around Mashpee and Plymouth. Some on Martha's Vineyard. But they seemed anachronisms to me. Every once in a while you'd read about some lawsuit or another they'd filed, claiming downtown Mashpee or something. But most of the time they were invisible to me. I know I sound very unenlightened to you. I'm sorry. I'm trying to explain how it was."

"You're being honest, that's all. I was kinda dragged kicking and screaming into the Anglo world. Change isn't easy."

"Grandfather wanted me to know a place he'd come to love. I'm not sorry I came anymore."

"I'm not either."

Cabot glanced at Nicholas from the corner of her eye, seeing the sharp nose and strong chin outlined faintly against the starry sky. What did he want of her? Here was a man in the middle of an intensely important political campaign. And yet he'd taken the time to find her, talk to her. And she found herself increasingly drawn to him. She could not see herself with an Indian man. And yet...

"Was the guy in the limo sorry you came out here?"

The voice was flat and noncommittal. Cabot remembered the look on Nicholas's face that chaotic day when Larimer had arrived unexpectedly.

She wasn't sure she wanted to talk about this.

"No," she said.

"And you wish I'd change the subject.

"Yes."

"All right. Let's see."

She didn't say anything, wondering what he would come up with.

"Your parents seem very nice. Not what I'd have expected, though."

She laughed. "You're being very polite."

"You aren't close to your parents?"

How to explain, she thought. "My mother and father have been, oh, something of a burden to me. But I felt a little differently this time. Who's to say a life is a success, I guess. They seem happy. They've not done a great deal of harm. I survived because I had my grandfather and now I don't need them. It's time I took them as they are. I was bitter for so long. Angry that they didn't put me first. It's a relief not to feel that anymore. I feel that I can now think of them with affection. It's nice."

They walked in silence. Then Cabot said, "It's funny I told you all that. I've never told anybody."

"I never told anybody things I said tonight. That makes us even."

When they reached her door, she hesitated, then asked, "Would you like some ice cream, or coffee?"

"No. Thanks. I've kept you up late enough. I shouldn't have stopped, but I needed...someone. For a little while. I hope you didn't mind."

"I didn't mind."

He reached up, then hesitated.

"You have paint on the tip of your nose."

"Oh, no. Why didn't you tell me?" She scrubbed with her fingers.

"It was cute. You looked like a little kid. You're always so damn beautiful you kind of scare me."

She felt her breath catch at the look on his face.

He finished his gesture and feather light, his fingers brushed her cheek. "Goodnight, Lily."

"'Night."

She watched him disappear down the walk before she turned to go inside. Star walks and language lessons. He hadn't even asked her to go to dinner like he said he would. But he said he had needed someone.

And he'd come to her.

Chapter Twenty-Six

September 2, 1992

The young football player looked so glum Cabot patted his shoulder. He'd broken his arm in a pre-season practice and from what little he said, she ascertained that the Fort Defiance High School's championship potential was greatly diminished by this catastrophe.

"It's a good, clean break, Brian. Maybe you won't be out the whole season. School doesn't start until next week. You might get in a game or two. You're young and in good shape. You'll heal fast."

"It still sucks," Brian said dispiritedly.

Cabot hid a smile. She still wasn't used to these kids. They straddled two worlds. In one, they were just like teenagers everywhere, watching Saturday Night Live and Jay Leno, using the same vocabulary, eating the same junk food. They had names like Brian and Kevin, Ashley and Michelle. And yet, she remembered this boy at the squaw dance, a singer chanting over the drum with the firelight flickering off his intense Indian face, a singer of ancient rituals in a Dallas Cowboys T-shirt and 501 jeans.

"Don't get the cast wet, whatever you do. You can put a plastic bag over it when you shower if you're careful. If you get it wet, you must come back. I'll want to X-ray it again in four weeks. If you have any trouble in between, be sure you come in."

"Sure."

As he left, Cabot called after him. "Brian?"

"Yeah?"

"Girls love to autograph casts and write crazy things."

"They do?" His face split in a wide smile. "Cool. Thanks."

Cabot brushed a loose strand of hair from her forehead and sighed. Brian was the last one. Time to go home.

She went down to the staff room and pulled off the white coat and put it in the laundry hamper, then got her sweater from her locker. Summer was over. The beginning of September marked the onset of autumn in the high country.

Outside she ran into Keith Singer and Eusebio Sanchez, two of the staff doctors.

"Hi, Cabot. Just leaving?" Keith asked. "We're just talking about Nicholas Nakai getting the *Arizona Republic's* endorsement. Great, huh?"

"It really is," she answered. "Jane's been on cloud nine all day. She ran up to the shopping center to buy all the papers but there weren't any left."

It was marvelous, she thought, as she drove home. Nicholas had been discouraged the night they'd gone walking. He must feel vindicated. Encouraged now. It was an incredibly important endorsement. The *Republic* was the state's big morning newspaper and carried a lot of weight.

When she got home, she spread the paper on her dinette

table to the op-ed page and read the lead editorial again. He had obviously made a good impression on the editorial board, the meeting he had fretted about with her. The column closed with the recommendation that he be the choice in the primary next Tuesday.

Cabot sat back and smiled. She wished she could tell him how pleased she felt. She supposed his campaign had moved downstate since it was less than a week before the primary election.

It might be fun to leave a note at his house so he would find it when he came back. She was the only one who knew how worried he'd been.

She wondered if she could find his house. Along the road that ran by the high school, that's what he'd said.

Impulsively she jumped up and tugged her sweater on. Why not? It wasn't quite dark. If she couldn't find the house, she'd just come home.

The sky was still rosy in the west as she turned onto the gravel road. He'd said a mile, or was it two? The Porsche began to shimmy as the road got rougher.

"Now I know what a corduroy road is. And I was never, never going to drive on any unpaved roads," she muttered. "What was it Marcus Yazzie had said at the gas station? You drive on the Rez, you'll be driving hard. Truer words..."

She passed a couple of pre-fab houses, then drove a mile without seeing any kind of habitation. Then, almost hidden behind a large grouping of boulders, she saw what must be it. His truck was parked to one side, but there were no lights on.

There was more gravel road up to his house, which was situated so the front door faced east, the traditional Navajo arrangement of their hogans, to greet the rising sun. There was no landscaping, but Cabot was used to that by now. Navajo dwellings sat in the natural grasses, shrubs, and wildflowers, with no cultivated lawns or gardens other than truck gardens or small cornfields. There was a three-horse barn in the back and Cabot could see the big black stallion and another spotted horse with their noses snuffling in their feed bins. He must have somebody come to feed them when he was away.

She'd just stick the note in the door. She pulled the Porsche in front of the house, but when she started up the path, the door opened.

"Cabot." He was smiling broadly. "Hello. I thought I heard a car pull in. This is a nice surprise. C'mon in." His hair was rumpled and she wondered if he'd been sleeping.

Her heart sank. She hadn't wanted to see him, only let him know she was pleased for him. "I thought you were away. I only wanted to leave you a note. No, really. I won't come in. You're busy."

"Not that busy."

He came down to meet her and took her elbow. She reluctantly allowed herself to be led.

"I saw the *Republic* this morning, with the editorial endorsement. I just wanted you to know I was happy for you."

He plucked the note from her fingers.

"Oh, don't read it. I'll feel silly." She reached to take the note back, but he slipped it in his shirt pocket.

"Then I'll read it later." He held the door open for her and she stepped inside. "I'd really like you to see my house."

The only illumination in the large room was from a reading light on his desk and the screen of the computer terminal. Nicholas flipped a switch that turned on a couple of lamps, and the room sprang to life.

As he had told her, the house was octagonal, and except for what was apparently a small bedroom off to one side, there was only this one big room, perhaps forty feet in diameter. There was a kitchen and eating area on one side, an office on another, and a living area on another with three glass floor-to-ceiling windows that looked out over the prairie and toward the Chuska Mountains, now fading in the last light of a blushing sunset. In the center, where the hogan would have a fire, or stove, was a round fireplace, with a suspended copper vent over it. Most of the wall-space was bookshelves, with a few pots and baskets on display, but the rest filled with books. There were Navajo rugs on the floor and the designs were repeated on the couch and chairs.

"This is really charming, Nicholas."

"One of my sisters decorated it. Annie works for a design studio in Flagstaff."

Cabot continued looking around, picking up a basket here, a woven throw there, other pieces of Navajo craftwork. "You mentioned once you had sisters. Tell me about them."

"I've got four. Only one's on the Rez. Another teaches biology at ASU. Another is an artist in Albuquerque."

Cabot walked over to a painting of Canyon de Chelly. "This must be hers. It's what I was trying to capture the other night when you came."

She smiled at the pride in his voice. "Yeah, it is."

"I'd like to meet them. Really, Nicholas, you have an amazing family."

"You'll meet them if you're coming over to the high school Tuesday night to watch the election returns come in. The tribe's going to set up some TV sets in the gym, and the high school kids are hanging up balloons and crepe paper to celebrate Nicholas Nakai winning the primary." He grinned. "It's all planned, so I've got to win."

"Why, I'd love to come. And I know you will." She glanced over at the humming computer. "I really am interrupting you. I'll just run along."

"No, don't. Not yet. Just let me finish one thing. Have

you had dinner? I picked up some ribs in Holbrook. Great stuff. I always stop when I'm there. There's plenty for two."

"I really...well, no...but..." She clearly had no alternative. After all, she'd shown up at his door at dinnertime. "Actually, I'm starved."

"Terrific. Then you'll stay. We never did have our dinner date, so this will make up for it. Just look around the place while I finish up. Then I'll make us a salad."

"I could do that. Unless you'd rather."

"You're on. Stuff's in the refrigerator. Knives are there on the counter, there's a bowl in the cupboard on the right. There's a tomato patch out by the barn if you feel like picking some. I'll put the light on for you."

"You delegated all that pretty fast. I seemed to have happened along at an opportune moment."

"You sure did." He grinned. "I'm not a very good cook."

Whatever Nicholas was working on took longer than a few minutes. By the time he'd turned off the computer and printer, Cabot had harvested three plump tomatoes, made the salad, put the ribs in the oven, and set the table. She looked at the table critically, then rummaged in the cupboards to find a bowl, then went outside to pick a bunch of the small sunflowers that grew in profusion around the house.

He came over to the table. "That looks nice. Did I have all this stuff?" he said in amazement.

"Yes, you did. You're entertaining equipment is kind of Spartan, but you did have two of everything." She laughed. "Most everything. We can use paper towels as napkins. More practical with ribs anyway."

"Wait a minute."

He disappeared into the bedroom and came back with a handful of utility candles. "Power goes out a lot here. Keep a bunch of these around." He set four on the table and when they were lit, the little table glowed in the big, darkened room.

In contrast to the night they had gone walking, Nicholas was in high spirits. He made her laugh with funny stories of his campaign odyssey and when dinner came to an end, she was surprised that it was past nine o'clock.

"I think I've got some cookies in that jar. I don't know how fresh they are."

"No, I'm fine. The ribs were fabulous. Now, will you tell me if I've got barbecue sauce on my nose. Or anywhere else, for that matter. I feel like I need a bath."

"Nothing I can see. I can look a little closer."

"Not necessary." She stood up. "Let's wash these, then I do have to go."

"I'll wash, you dry. You can put all this stuff back where you found it. I don't know where it goes. Annie must have bought it all," he grinned, "so I'd be prepared to entertain beautiful women."

Cabot hoped she didn't blush. "Well, now you know."

"Yes. So you'll have to come back."

She brushed back a stray lock of hair. "I'd like that."

There was a hint of autumn in the crisp night air. Cold weather came early to the high country and before long the Navajos would be moving from their summer hogans, bringing their flocks into the protected valleys.

Nicholas draped his arm casually across her shoulders.

"Are you going to be warm enough? I can round up a jacket for you."

"No. I'm fine. I can turn on the heater if I get cold."

"I'm glad you stayed."

"So am I. It was fun. I really thought you'd be away so close to the election."

"I almost was, but decided since I was in Holbrook, I'd run on home and go back in the morning. I get tired of motels."

"After you win the primary, there'll be two more months or so of it all. Will you hate it?"

"A little."

They reached her car and he turned her toward him. "But it will help if I can come back and see you."

"I'm always here." Impulsively she leaned up and kissed his cheek. "Good luck Tuesday. I'll try to vote for you twice. It's an old Massachusetts custom."

She moved back and started to get into her car, but he held her. His hands moved up to frame her face and he let his thumbs stroke her cheekbones before he bent to kiss her. Softly at first. Then more than that.

When he pulled back, her eyes fluttered open. When had she closed them? There was a draft of air between them, cool, where it had been warm.

His voice was rough. "Be careful driving home."

She had to find her voice. "Yes, I'll be careful."

Inside, he unfolded her note.

Dear Nicholas,

I'm thrilled about the Republic *endorsement. All your worrying was for nothing. I told you you'd be impressive. Any time you need cheering up, we'll go for a walk and you can teach me stars.(And maybe some Navajo?) You'll win Tuesday. I'm absolutely never wrong about these things.*

Cabot

He walked over to his desk and propped the note against his computer. He sat and studied the note, his legs stretched out, his hands behind his head.

It was lighthearted, just a friendly note. Or was it?

It also said she had been thinking about him, was happy for him, had confidence in him, and wanted to see him again. Stars and Navajo? That was sweet. Not bad for a few little words.

And what did he know about her? There was the strange coincidence of their names, though she chose to be called Cabot, he always thought of her as Lily. She had a couple of off-beat parents, had been hurt by their rejection of her, was intensely ambitious, had a supportive and probably rich grandfather, who, for some reason made her come out to a world totally alien to her, probably having to do with his grandmother.

He'd been attracted to her from the beginning. Just because he was a man and she was a beautiful woman? Maybe. Then she challenged him because he wanted to make that wariness in her eyes disappear? To be replaced with what he saw moments ago when he'd kissed her. When her eyes had opened, a little dazed and unfocussed, they told him what he wanted to know. Lily Cabot Chase saw him now as a man, not an Indian. Now that he'd proved that, he could put her into perspective. He had no time for emotional entanglement when there was so much at stake.

Yeah, right.

But perspective wasn't what he wanted now. He wanted her. Not the beautiful white doctor, but the woman whose mouth had trembled under his for a few moments.

Chapter Twenty-Seven

September 8, 1992

The high school gym was beginning to get noisy. In an explosion of pride, the students had decorated with abandon. American flags hung everywhere. Red, white and blue crepe paper streamers fanned out in the rafters and around the basketball nets. Matching balloons floated above everything that didn't move and some things that did. The high school band, mostly in tune and blaring energetically, drowned out the cheerleaders who were trying to get a N-A-K-A-I chant going, but the crowd milled about, too disorganized for cheers. Since the polls had closed only an hour before, election returns came over the television sets sporadically. So far the exit polls showed no clear trends in the state.

"We'll start picking up some hard information in about a half an hour," Jim Shackleford said. The campaign chairman gazed around at the lively crowd. "No lack of enthusiasm here, Nick. Hope they all voted today."

"Zhealy Tso had trucks going all day. He would have registered the sheep if he could have, and anybody who registered voted. He's a pretty persuasive guy."

Nicholas watched a group of tribal singers move a large drum into the gym. "They've got all the bases covered—Sousa and the spirit world." He laughed. "I wish the rest of the district loved me as much."

Shirley Kee, the editor of the Navajo Times, strolled by. "I've got my headlines all set for tomorrow's edition. 'NAKAI IN LANDSLIDE.' Goddamn it's noisy in here." She made a *V* sign and moved off, a cameraman in tow.

The medicine man, Pete Price, arrived with Tribal Chairman, Russell Wauneka and his entourage.

Nicholas watched the growing crowd. Many of the government workers came in, as well as tribal members from more outlying areas. This was a big event in their lives. He wished he could watch the returns come in privately, but that was an impossibility. If he lost, he would have to do it in public. Another black cloud of doubt had assailed him off and on during the day and he shook off the feeling with difficulty.

Cheers went up at several TV sets.

"Some national returns coming in. It's still a little early for us," Jim said.

Pete Price called over, "Saw Father Valeriano today. He said a Mass this morning for you." Then he chuckled. "Sometimes I wish we had prayers for election outcomes. Got to let our Christian brothers do that for us."

Nicholas grinned. "You don't think you could come up with something?"

"Well, I sang a few songs this morning." He chuckled. "Informally."

Nicholas saw Cabot come in with a group from the hospital. She smiled and waved, but didn't come over.

Pete Price gazed at her, his face thoughtful. "Funny thing about the woman doctor's grandfather and your grandmother. I was a young man when he worked here at the hospital. You think I would have known." He shrugged. "But I was busy with my studies."

Nicholas sensed that Pete did not approve. That mixing of Indian and white further undermined the Navajo traditions. On more than one occasion Pete had tried to convince Nicholas that he needed to find a Navajo wife. It would make a statement to his people and the Anglos that he would make a strong Indian presence in Washington.

"It's a funny world," he said noncommittally.

Jim Shackleford checked his watch. "Let's go have a look."

The blond anchorwoman from the Phoenix station was reporting.

"Maricopa County precincts are beginning to come in. First, that race for the new Sixth Congressional District. Nicholas Nakai, the Navajo lawyer from Fort Defiance, is making an unexpectedly strong showing with early returns in from Maricopa County, he's running behind, but the metropolitan area was going to be his weakest spot. With 26 precincts reporting, he's getting about 36% of the vote against 46% for John Compton. This one will be a late call. Nakai's stronghold is in the rural north, and those precincts will be slow in getting to Election Central here at KPNX. In the race for District Three..."

Nicholas, Jim, Pete, and Russell Wauneka moved around the gym to sets tuned into different stations, but the message was the same

"This is good news. If we can stay about that percentage, we're in good shape," Jim said. "If you drop below 32% in Maricopa County, we'll start worrying. It wouldn't be good, but maybe we'll make it up somewhere else. It's a funny year. People are restless. Hard to figure."

Within an hour the northern precincts started coming in, very strongly for Nicholas. His percentages dropped slightly in Maricopa County, but he was winning comfortably in Flagstaff, Winslow, and Holbrook, as well as the reservation precincts.

Jim Shackleford was rubbing his hands together. "It's lookin' pretty good. If we can hold these numbers. I'm disappointed in Casa Grande. It's rural. Thought we'd be doing better there."

"Is it time to start cheering, Nicholas?" Jane Manyfarms came up to slide an arm around his waist.

"Not yet, Auntie Jane. Is mother here?"

"She will be. She was going to bring in your grandmother, but it looked like it was going to storm and Mother didn't want to get stuck driving in the canyon. She said she'd listen on the radio and knows you'll win. You seen your sisters yet?"

"I've talked to Natalie and Hattie. Susan's classes just started at ASU last week and she was too swamped to come up. She said she'd come when I won in November," he said.

"Annie just got here. I introduced her to Cabot. Understand she was out to your house." She winked. "Liked it a lot she told Annie."

"Now what was that look for, Auntie Jane? It was just a friendly call."

"What look, Nicholas? Can't imagine what you're talking about."

Cheers went up at several television sets.

"That must be good news. Let's go see."

He'd spotted Cabot's hair, bright in the sea of dark heads. Hands patted and tugged at him excitedly as he moved through the crowd toward her as she stood absorbed in the figures marching across the screen.

"I guess something good happened," he said in her ear.

She turned, smiling. "You've pulled nearly even in Maricopa County. You're going to win, Nicholas."

"I'm afraid to start celebrating," he said.

The pager at her waist sounded and her face fell. "Oh, darn. That'll be the hospital. I'm on from midnight 'til eight this week, but I told them to call and I'd come in early if they needed help with the celebrators."

"I hope you don't have to leave." He touched her shoulder.

"I'll just run out to the car to my phone. It might be nothing."

Nicholas caught a high school boy's arm. "Show Dr. Chase where there's a phone she can use."

"Sure. There's one right outside the gym door."

She called the hospital ER. It was Tommy Tootsie who had paged her. "We got a call from Marcus Yazzie, Cabot. He's up at Canyon de Chelly. His granddaughter is real sick and his son refuses to bring her into the hospital. He wonders if you would come. The father's one of these Vietnam vets, bitter, turned his back totally on whites. Wants to go it alone in his little corner of the Rez, and that includes medical care. But Marcus put the screws in, I understand, and Emerson will let you look at his little girl. Her name is Asun."

"I know Emerson Yazzie...and Asun. I didn't realize he felt so strongly. Did Marcus have any ideas about what's wrong?"

"From his description of her symptoms, I'd say it's a strong possibility it's diphtheria. It crops up here and again on the Rez, especially in the remotest parts. Cabot, I've put together a bundle with antibiotics, an antitoxin, and a tracheostomy tube. Some other stuff I thought you might need. Vaccine for the rest of the family in case you can persuade Emerson to allow it. There's a medicine man working on her now, but the little girl is sinking. I figure you can be there within an hour and a half, two hours by the time you get to the hogan. It's back aways."

"Tommy," Cabot groaned. "How on earth will I find it? I've only been in the canyon a couple of times. It's pitch black out there. I don't have a four-wheel drive. Can't we get Air Evac in there?"

"I'm trying, Cabot. They'll stand by, but Emerson will only let you see her unless you can persuade him otherwise. He's got the say-so."

She felt like screaming. Time was precious.

"Cabot," Tommy said, "Jane Manyfarms will take you. I know she will and I know she's there at the gym..."

"I'll be there as soon as I can. Have the stuff at the door."

Cabot turned and ran into the crowded gym, searching frantically for Jane Manyfarms.

Nicholas touched her arm. "What is it?"

"Marcus Yazzie's granddaughter is very sick, probably diphtheria. Her father will only let me look at her. I've got to find Jane to take me out to their place in the canyon. Please, Nicholas, have you seen her?"

"Let's go." He took her arm and hurried her through the door.

"Oh, Nicholas, you can't leave. What about the returns?"

"If I win or lose, it won't change anything if I'm here or not."

At Chinle, Cabot turned to Nicholas. "We won't be able to get Air Evac on the cell phone once we get into the canyon. How long will it take them to get to Emerson's from Flagstaff?"

"If they leave right away, forty five minutes."

"Nicholas, I'm going to go out on a limb and call Tommy at the hospital and have them come in for her. It will take me about a half-hour to treat the little girl. But I'm afraid it's essential that she be hospitalized. I'll just have to convince Emerson."

"We can build signal fires. Have Tommy tell them when they get to Chinle to fly northwest up the main canyon. After they enter the canyon at Chinle, they'll see the fires in under ten minutes, off to their left."

Rain had begun to spatter the windshield as Nicholas pulled into the Yazzie camp. Inside, the hogan was stifling, lit by a kerosene lantern and what light there was from an oil drum stove. The stoves were common twenty years earlier, but seldom found in the more modern dwellings. The haze from the fumigant the medicine man had burned added to the suffocating air.

The little girl lay on the floor of the hogan in the middle of a sand painting and various sand prayer sticks mounted by the medicine man.

Marcus Yazzie had greeted Cabot and Nicholas with relief and brought them to the little girl's side.

The medicine man, scowling and aloof, moved away. Cabot glanced at him, guessing his professional reputation had been sullied by this intrusion of the white doctor. It would have been better to have an ally, but she couldn't worry about his feelings now. Clearly, the little girl was in grave condition.

Marcus Yazzie's son Emerson stood at the back of the hogan, his face stubborn, as if reluctant to admit his lateness in allowing a doctor to see his daughter might cause her death.

The stricken mother stood with the girl's brother and sister clasped to her skirt. The boy sucked his thumb and looked at Cabot with large, anxious eyes.

Cabot knelt beside the gasping little girl and felt the faint, fluttery pulse, the badly swollen glands in her neck. She opened the child's mouth, and directing a flashlight beam on the telltale milky membrane covering the tonsils and palate.

"Do you need more light?" Nicholas asked. "I've got a propane lantern in the truck."

"Good. Get it," Cabot said. She turned to the father. "Emerson, Ason must have hospital care. I can help her now, but she can't stay here. Tommy Tootsie is sending Air Evac. You were in Vietnam. You'll know how large an area the helicopter will need to land. You'll need to build signal fires. They'll be here in about half and hour. Go do it now."

She watched Emerson Yazzie struggle within himself, then nod and leave the hogan. Marcus looked at Cabot gratefully, then followed his son. There was a close rumble of thunder and a hard spatter of rain on the roof of the hogan. Lightning flashed, about three miles away. Cabot prayed the worst of the storm would hold off until the chopper got Ason Yazzie out of the remote canyon.

Tommy Tootsie at the hospital had assembled the medications just as she would need them, and within minutes she had administered penicillin and the antitoxin that would begin to cleanse the destructive toxins from the girl's blood. Cabot glanced around the hogan. She would have to do the tracheostomy and the conditions were septic and primitive. *Damn these people. Diphtheria was completely preventable and because of some willful hostility to white men's vaccines, this little girl was dangerously close to dying.*

She looked at the stove. There was a kettle on a grate at the top.

She spoke to the mother. "Linda? Do you understand English well enough to follow my directions?"

The woman nodded.

"Your daughter needs a tube in her throat to breathe. The air in your hogan will have to be kept moist. Damp. I want you to keep a pot of water boiling. Do it now."

Nicholas came back with the propane lamp, its bluish light casting an eerie glow in the dingy hogan.

"Nicholas, I'll have to do a tracheostomy. The child is having too much difficulty breathing. Tommy sent everything I'll need. It's not complicated, but it would help, since it's awkward on the floor, if you could hold the light for me."

"Just tell me what to do," he said.

Cabot wiped her hands with disinfectant towels and pulled on surgical gloves. She then assembled what she would need close to the child's chest and had Nicholas move the lamp as close as she dared.

A bright flash. Moments later, thunder boomed. The storm was closing in.

She took a deep breath but felt remarkably calm. She had only done a few of these procedures, but as she told Nicholas, it was not difficult.

She swabbed the little girl's neck and injected a local anesthetic. She waited a moment, not as long as she would have wished, but time was crucial. She touched the area where she would insert the tube with a needle and the girl didn't recoil. She then made a small incision in the skin overlying the trachea, between the Adam's apple and the collarbone and gently pulled the muscles apart.

The light wobbled.

She glanced up and frowned. "Are you all right, Nicholas?"

His face was tight and covered with a fine sheen of

perspiration. His voice shook slightly as he answered. "Sorry. I'm okay. Don't worry about me."

Cabot stitched the edges of the larynx to the skin and inserted the tracheostomy tube, fitted gauze around the opening and attached the foam-covered circle around the child's neck. By the time the Air Evac helicopter set down in the sandy canyon floor between three signal fires, Ason Yazzie was breathing more easily and her pulse, though faint, was regular.

Rain beat with a steady tattoo on the brush and mud roof of the hogan, with alternate thunder and lightning.

It had been decided that Emerson Yazzie would accompany Ason into the hospital in Flagstaff. When Cabot watched the grim veteran climb aboard she wondered what terrible memories the helicopter would raise, memories that had made him want to withdraw from the world and might cost him his daughter.

As the chopper lifted off, the rain that had been falling turned into an opaque curtain of silver glistening streaks in the light of the signal fires. There was a bright flash of lightning and the following crack of thunder sounded almost immediately. Cabot watched with relief as the helicopter's winking red lights disappeared over the edge of the canyon wall.

"We should finish up here and get started back. If it keeps up this hard, the sand is going to get real shifty," Nicholas said.

"I want to vaccinate the rest of the family and check them over. I promise it won't take long, then we can go. You should be back at the gym celebrating."

"You're sure I won, aren't you?"

"I've always been sure." She laughed. God, it was good to laugh after the last tense hours.

Marcus Yazzie held the little boy and then his sister while Cabot gave them a DPT shot. Before they left he spoke to her, his voice shaking with emotion.

"Emerson, he's not a bad father. He has his reasons. Maybe this will change some of the ways he feels."

Cabot patted his shoulder, then she and Nicholas hurried out into the downpour.

Chapter Twenty-Eight

September 8, 1992

The truck's headlights didn't illuminate much but slashing rain. Cabot glanced over at Nicholas as he peered over the steering wheel into the silvery deluge that swamped the windshield wipers. "Get a little shaky at the sight of blood, do you?"

"Dear God, to think you want to do that for a living. I thought I might lose it there for a minute."

The wipers struggled against the onslaught of water thrown up from the hood, as well as the cascade from the sky. The truck skidded, then caught, and continued to plow through the wet sand.

The headlights would pick out a boulder. Cabot could see a tree flash by, a rock formation loom out of the pelting rain. She wondered that Nicholas knew where he was, but as he'd told her, he was born here and knew the canyon like the back of his hand. It was almost one in the morning. She wondered if the gym had closed up, the election-watch over, the celebrants gone home to bed. Nicholas seemed remarkably unconcerned that he'd missed his victory party. They had been unable to get anything on the radio from the canyon bottom, but they'd called Jim Shackleford at his motel from a lonely phone booth at one of the canyon's tourist stops. The campaign chairman was elated, but grumpy that his candidate had disappeared right as he was going to be declared the winner.

"Everybody wondered where in the hell you'd gone. At first we were pissed off, but you know, it'll make a great story, rushing the doctor to the sick little girl. The press will love it."

"Don't use it, Jim." Nicholas said. "No mention of the little girl to the press. I mean it."

"Are you crazy? You'll be a hero. Get serious."

"Pay attention, Jim. I said, don't use it. And I'm real serious."

After they'd broken the connection, Cabot said, "That was unselfish of you."

He was quiet until they'd gotten back in the truck to continue to the mouth of the canyon. Then he said, "That wasn't for me, or even Ason, but Emerson doesn't need that kind of attention. I don't know what he carries from Vietnam, but it's pretty heavy. I'll stay as far away from this as I can get so the press doesn't attach me to it in any way." The rear end skidded and Nicholas shifted down. "Of all the things I've had to get used to in this campaigning business, it's the lack of privacy. The constant attention. Jim's always on to the small thing that might catch the interest of the press. I can't blame him. I realize I'm colorful to them. My family is real colorful. If I win I'll be making some kind of history. My family, they signed on. They're not real shy anyway. Well, maybe my father. But I don't want other people to have their lives interfered with. Especially someone as fragile as Emerson Yazzie."

The truck was beginning to labor in spots, but Nicholas drove with the skill of long experience maneuvering on the unstable canyon floor.

"Water table is pretty close to the surface down here, so it doesn't take much for it to get soupy," he remarked, shifting to an even lower gear during a particularly sloppy patch. "Chinle Wash is up ahead and it'll be running pretty good. We get through that and we're home free. Have you home in an hour." The dash-lights lit his face, his sharp features somber, preoccupied with keeping the truck moving forward.

"You can drop me at the hospital. I'm still on duty, remember?"

"That seems hundred years ago," he said distractedly, swerving to avoid a large boulder that loomed up in the headlights.

She wiped a clear spot on the windshield that had begun to steam up, and peered into the curtain of rain.

Suddenly he jerked the steering wheel, sending the truck up a small, steep incline. The wheels spun uselessly and with a lurch, Cabot felt the truck settle.

"Shit, I was afraid of that."

"What is it?" Cabot asked as Nicholas opened the truck door and stood to look out over the hood.

It became obvious with the roar of the water coming from the Chinle Wash ahead. In the headlight beams she saw a small tree hurtle by, ripped out by the rushing torrent of water, fed by hundreds of tiny trickles and streams swollen by the rain that tumbled down the precipitous walls of the great canyon and all its tributaries.

"I take it there isn't another way around," Cabot said.

He lowered himself back in the cab, wiping his streaming

face. "No. We're stuck here until morning, at least. It depends if the rain stops sometime soon. It's too dangerous to cross, even with four-wheel drive. Even if we didn't get swept away, no telling what might be washing down."

"Like that tree," she said as a good sized sapling hurtled past the headlights.

"Like that tree. I'm really sorry, Cabot. You won't be making it back to the hospital tonight."

"Why should you apologize? You shouldn't even be here. You should be celebrating with your family at the gym. It's me who's sorry you got into this."

"Okay. That's settled. We're both sorry," he said. "And I don't even believe in 'sorry.' But, we can't stay here. If it keeps on raining the wash will rise even more. There's a hogan up through those trees. There are trees over there, believe me. The ground's quite a bit higher. We'll be all right there."

"Does somebody live there?"

"No, it's a ceremonial hogan for the Quincy Tahome family. There should be some wood for a fire. That's probably all we can hope for. Nothing to eat in case you're hungry."

"I was thinking I was starved," she said ruefully. She opened the door, but didn't push it open. "Well, what are we waiting for? You've convinced me I've got to get even wetter than I already am."

"There's a flashlight in the glove compartment. And some matches. Get 'em, will you? And anything else that looks promising. I'll get the propane lantern going. Just follow me."

He jumped from the truck and in a minute Cabot saw the lantern glow and move off into the black rain and the invisible trees. She hesitated, then jumped from the truck, gasping as the cold rain hit her face and sent an icy stream down the front of her sweater. Within seconds she was drenched and water had seeped over the tops of her loafers. She slipped and staggered after the propane lantern, clutching the flashlight and matches, her handbag over her shoulder. She had also found a dog-eared, half-bag of Oreo cookies in the glove compartment.

Nicholas waited at the top of the rise. "Yeah, this is the path. You doing all right?"

"Marvelous," she said, her teeth starting to chatter. It was a cold rain and the temperature had dropped into the low forties.

He took her elbow. "It goes up again here. Watch your step."

Cabot slipped off a rock and stumbled, but he pulled her upright.

"Nicholas, watch the cookies. They'll turn to mush if they get wet."

"Oh, my God. Were they in the glove compartment? They must be three months old."

"You don't want 'em, I do," she chattered, scrambling up a step-like rise.

There was a brief flash and a boom of thunder, but it wasn't as close. Cabot hoped the storm was abating, but she knew another might be following right behind.

"The door will be to the right."

They felt their way around the wood and mud-plaster walls to the opening on the east side of the hogan. Nicholas pushed aside the rickety wooden door that scraped along the packed, earthen floor. The propane lantern threw its cold light against the gasoline drum stove and a stack of sheepskins and another of Navajo blankets. The vent of the stove fitted into the ceiling but rainwater trickled down the pipe, making a small puddle on the floor. The room smelled damp with a musky essence of lanolin from the sheep hides.

Nicholas sniffed. "Whoo! Perfume of old ram."

"Uh...you don't think there are any...creatures in here,

do you?" Cabot stood uncertainly, ready to bolt out the door if anything lunged at her.

"Don't see anything." He moved the light around, illuminating a small stack of wood behind the stove. "I'll get a fire going. I know you're cold."

"Aren't you?" she asked, hugging herself to keep from shaking.

"We learn not to pay any attention to it." He set the lamp on the floor and knelt to open the stove door, crudely cut in the side of the drum.

He peered inside. "These metal gasoline drums were common in the old-style hogans. It covers a firepit and that galvanized pipe vents the fire through the center of what used to be the smoke hole."

Cabot crouched down beside him and watched as he skillfully put the fire together. She handed him the matches and clenched her chattering teeth. Her hair and clothes were wet and clung to her like ice, but if he could ignore the cold, she could at least try.

The fire caught and they both stared at the tiny flame, watching as it slowly grew bigger and began to spread. Faintly at first, then more strongly, Cabot could feel the fire throw off warmth. She scooted closer and held her hands out to the open door. But the heat was only marginal and she was shivering badly.

"I'm sorry, but ignoring the cold wasn't part of my upbringing."

"I hate to be the one to bring this up," Nicholas said, "but you're going to have to get out of those wet clothes. There are plenty of blankets over there. You can wrap up. Go do it." She glanced at him. "I won't look."

"Oh, I'm all right, really." But the last word ended in a shudder she tried hard to swallow.

He looked at her closely, then shrugged. "Suit yourself."

Reluctantly she stood up. "You're right. I'm freezing to death."

She moved over to the pile of blankets and looked down at them skeptically. Gingerly she lifted a corner. "Uh, Nicholas. Would you kind of just shake them out? Please. I'm not very outdoorsy. About spiders and snakes...and things."

He laughed and came over. "You can cut somebody's gut open without a second thought, then get hyper about a little bug. Amazing."

"I'm not hopeless, you know. When Mother and Daddy were going through their candle-making-in-the-woods stage, I did learn a few things." She watched him go through the blankets, pointing it out whenever he missed one. "I can cook lots of things in a skillet over an open fire, for one thing." She pointed. "You skipped that one. Biscuits, even bake a cake. I'd show you, but unfortunately we don't have anything to cook."

He handed her several blankets and took two for himself. "Here." Then he went to the stack of sheepskins. He pulled several off the pile and arranged them on the floor by the stove. He sat down, facing away from Cabot and occupied himself pulling off his wet boots, denim shirt, and jacket. He wrapped the blankets around his shoulders.

Cabot looked over at him, then stepped out of her skirt, pulled off her loafers and stockings and tucked a blanket around her waist. She then yanked her soggy sweater over her head. She hesitated, then slipped off her wet bra and wound another blanket around herself, sarong-style, and another around her shoulders. There were several pegs at intervals on the log walls, so she hung up her sweater and skirt. Her skin still felt like ice, but the blankets were beginning to feel warm. A little scratchy and musty. Sheepy. But comforting. Her shakes were gradually subsiding. She thought a minute, then wrapped a blanket around her hair, blotting it as dry as she could.

She went to kneel on a sheepskin by the fire and dug around in her bag for the small brush she carried. Nicholas gazed at the stove, chinks and cracks throwing a soft glow on his bronze, preoccupied face.

Cabot began the struggle to untangle the wet mess of her hair, hundreds of red corkscrews, curling unrestrained from the dousing they'd gotten in the run to the hogan.

Squatting on his heels he watched her without seeming to, making small patterns in the dirt floor with a stick of kindling. He would make love to her tonight. He knew that. But right now he was content to just look, see her work at the coppery tangles, separating them with her brush and her fingers, loving the total preoccupation of a woman when she fiddled with her hair.

It was beginning to dry and catch the light. Once she looked up and the lynx-colored eyes rested on him briefly, but then she went back to herself.

The waiting was hard. He wondered how it would begin. There would be a gesture, or a sigh, or a glance. And then he could hold her, kiss her, push the blanket off her shoulder. It would happen. The series of events that led here could not be disregarded. This woman who had come from nowhere was before him, her hair a cascade of fire around her face and shoulders. He remembered its fragrance when she rode in front of him the day he'd found her in the desert. The thought made him move restlessly and she looked over. But this time he met her gaze and held it.

The fire readjusted itself inside the stove and flared,

illuminating her face briefly before the wood settled again. She dropped her eyes and her fingers played with her brush. He didn't look away. She knew now, he thought, if she didn't before.

Slowly she began on her hair again. Her breathing was rapid and he knew her heart was pounding as hard as his own.

The rain lessened its drumbeat on the roof and the galvanized pipe vent. The smell of the pinon wood scented the hogan, a drop of resin made a small explosion.

Into the silence he said, "I'd like to do that."

The golden eyes looked to him again, and he saw them change and darken. She looked down, then back.

"All right."

In a fluid movement he stood and moved behind her and knelt. She handed him the brush over her shoulder.

He began at the crown, separating the damp curls, watching them wind around his fingers. He moved slowly, wanting her used to the idea of him touching her. When the outer layer began to dry and crackle with electricity, he lifted the hair from her neck and ran his fingers through it.

"Nicholas?" It was a whisper.

"Yes?"

"Kiss me."

He pushed the blanket away from her shoulders and turned her to him.

She sighed softly, sliding her arms around his neck searching for his kiss, her lips parted, her breath shallow and fast. He pulled apart the sarong and closed his arms around her hard, wanting her, now, not content to wait. His kiss was urgent as he thrust his tongue between her lips and explored her teeth and the inside of her mouth.

She sank down on the sheepskins and pulled him over her. Impatiently he flung the blankets aside and moved down her body to the triangle of red curls that had haunted his days and nights. She watched him through the veil of her lashes when he rose to his knees, then jerked down the zipper of his jeans to spring free. Then he was in her thrusting deep and slow. He shuddered with the effort to control the fever pitch that drove him, holding to this storm of sensations. Her breath came in gasps in the quiet hogan. His heart thundered in his ears then exploded.

He could feel his heaviness on her and rolled to one side, carefully keeping her legs around him still, both lost to all but one another. Her finger traced over the features of his face, around his eyes, his nose, around his cheekbones, tracing his mouth and chin.

His finger circled her nipple, pale and rosy, not the rich chocolate of a Navajo woman, but pink as a flower.

After a while, she sighed. "Let's do all that again."

"Lily, Lily. I'll never get enough of you."

Later, as they lay locked together, he felt her squirm beneath him. He tipped up her chin. "I don't want to leave you, but I'm too heavy."

"Yes. I'm sorry. I don't want you to go."

He rolled off her and pulled her close, her head against her shoulder. "Are you warm enough?"

She smiled. "Yes. I am now." She raised herself on an elbow and looked down at him. "This was always going to happen, wasn't it?"

"Yes."

She resettled herself, running her fingers over his chest, down to his navel, touching his genitals, now softly nestled in a wiry brush.

"I thought you wouldn't be circumcised," she murmured.

He grunted, amused. "Mother wasn't sure, Grandmother insisted. So, I understand, did Aunt Jane. Maybe Grandmother admired the way your grandfather looked. Who knows? But they apparently thought it was the modern thing to do. I caught a lot of hell when I was around Indian boys." He tipped her face up and grinned. "Now, tell me. When did you begin thinking about my equipment?"

She caught her breath and blushed. "I...well...I mean, I didn't know. Most of the men I treat at the hospital aren't."

"And so Dr. Chase sat around every night and dreamed about Nicholas Nakai and wondered about his penis."

"I didn't," she said hotly.

"Ever?"

"Well, when you kissed me that night, I, um, sort of guess…maybe I did. Sort of."

He was relentless. "And is Dr. Chase disappointed?"

She wrapped her arms around him and buried her face in his chest. "Stop teasing me. Or I won't let you make love to me again."

He grinned. "Oh?"

A faint gray light showed in the chinks and cracks of the hogan, and there was a small insistent birdcall. The room was chilly, the fire nearly died out in the gas drum stove. Cabot awakened slowly. She pulled the blanket tighter around her shoulders and looked at Nicholas. He'd thrown the blanket aside and lay with his arm flung over his head. He slept with such concentration, she thought. A frisson of desire passed through her as her eyes swept over him and she thought of all that had happened in the night.

Carefully she moved over and straddled him. He groaned and she felt his body stir under her. "Don't wake up. Just let me make love to you," she whispered.

She watched the expressions on his face as his sensations changed, loving the feeling that she was doing this to him.

Nicholas had held himself in a kind of half-sleep, wrapped in its voluptuous vulnerability.

"I never woke up quite that way before," he murmured into her shoulder.

"Did you like it?'

He whooped and flipped her under him. "It's got a lot to recommend it, even if your nose was cold." He bent and kissed her. "We've got to get up and see if the truck is still there."

"Mmmm. I suppose so," she said, her voice muffled in his chest, not moving. "I'll think about it if you'll get me an Oreo."

He sprang from their bed of sheepskins and Navajo blankets.

She watched him pull on his boots and jeans as she wolfed down the chocolate cookies, sitting cross-legged amid the red, black, and white blankets, her hair a profusion of unruly spirals that fell over her breasts and shoulders.

She licked the chocolate crumbs off her fingers. "Are your clothes dry?"

"Not even close. And they're full of sand. It's not a real pleasant feeling."

He sat on the floor and pulled on his boots, then stood and hooked his silver and turquoise buckle. He moved to the door and pulled it open, but turned and looked at her for a long moment.

"My God, you are beautiful," he said. "Lily."

Cabot left the warm blankets without enthusiasm and dressed in her damp clothes with distaste. When she stepped outside, the sun was coming up over the cliff walls and the air was cold and clear. A silver frosting covered grasses along the still rushing wash.

Through the trees she saw the truck. It had moved downstream a short way, but Marcus Yazzie was winching it out of the now shallow, fast-running water with his tow truck. She saw Nicholas approach him and the two men fell into a discussion, gesturing where to pull the truck.

Cabot turned back to the hogan and began folding their blankets and stacking the sheepskins, trying to remember exactly how they'd been arranged. When that had been done, there was little evidence they'd been there. Against the wall was a small bucket and shovel, so she cleaned the ashes from the stove. In the daylight she could see details that were not so evident last night. Hanging on the walls were objects that seemed ceremonial in nature. There were a couple of small drums, some baskets, and some gourd rattles. A feathered stick.

It was a strange, alien place. If it weren't for the tenderness between her legs, it would have been difficult to imagine that the past hours had happened.

She pushed the door open and stepped out, carefully pulling it closed before she walked down the path to the running stream, now abating with the rain four hours past. She was a little embarrassed meeting Marcus Yazzie. With the way she looked there wasn't much doubt about how they'd passed the time in the hogan.

With Marcus Yazzie's help they were able to get across the swollen wash. He followed them out of the canyon, and though they were nearly stuck again, Nicholas kept a roll of chain link fencing in the truck, which he put under the tires to break free of the shifty wet sand.

When they got to Cabot's apartment, it was nearly nine o'clock.

"I'd just about be coming home from the hospital. I can't believe the whole night happened."

He grinned. “You’d better believe it.”

“Come in. I’ll fix something to eat.”

But when they got inside her door, Nicholas pulled her to him. “Breakfast can wait. I haven’t made love to you for over two hours.

“I won’t be able to walk,” she breathed, startled at the searing flash of desire that flashed through her.

“I have to be away for the next few days. I don’t want you to forget me,” he muttered.

“Can we take a shower?” She was finding it hard to talk with his kisses covering her face. “I smell like a smoky old sheep...and—

“Shhh. To a Navajo that’s sexy as hell.”

Chapter Twenty-Nine

September 10, 1992

She missed him. Every time she thought about the night in the canyon she got breathless. All her reservations about a relationship with a Navajo man were swept away with the realization that Nicholas Nakai had touched emotions and sensations she didn't know she had. It was a terrible letdown to have him gone. She opened the *Navajo Times* and spread it out on the kitchen table. He'd had to leave to go down to Phoenix. She'd have to get used to reading about him and occasionally seeing him on television.

NAKAI WINS BIG, the headline shouted in two-inch letters. That was slightly overstating the case, but understandable under the circumstances. The whole reservation was bursting with pride. Shirley Kee knew her readership.

Cabot had met Shirley Kee, the editor, and had nearly

laughed out loud. The crusty editor of the *Boston Globe* was a friend of her grandfather's and if he ever had a clone it was this feisty Navajo woman on a remote reservation a continent away. The paper was a weekly, but Shirley Kee was as serious as any editor of a big city daily.

Cabot glanced over the *Times*, then turned to the *Arizona Republic*. There was front page article about Nicholas's race and profiles of the two candidates for District Six in the general election. She was curious to know about the man whom Nicholas would be running against.

Marvin Willoughby was a well-financed Washington bureaucrat who had moved to the state only two years ago. He had run in the primary with the theme that he was a Capital insider who knew how to get things done. Nicholas had told her that Willoughby's primary opponent hadn't hit it hard enough that the man looked suspiciously like he had searched for a state with a newly-drawn district in which to run. He had no ties to Arizona, and he wouldn't have to face an incumbent. The fact that he had moved three times during the redrawing process made it obvious that he had made sure his residence fell within the new district.

Cabot looked at the man's picture. It was a bland face, and considering the bothersome details about his residency, Cabot wondered how he could have won the primary. But he had a lot of money, his signs were everywhere and he'd spent heavily on television spots. Could Nicholas compete with that?

The tribe didn't have that much money to spend, and funds from other sources were hard to come by. Her grandfather had offered to raise some money, admitting contributions to an unknown candidate in an obscure district in a distant western state would have little but marginal interest, if any, to contributors in Massachusetts. But he'd gotten promises of donations from some of his friends and he had made a sizable one himself.

Grandfather was coming next week to spend a few days with Laura—a last idyll in Canyon de Chelly before she moved up to the plateau for the winter. Cabot wondered just how much she wanted to tell him about herself and Nicholas. How much did Laura know, for that matter? She was sure Marcus wouldn't gossip about her and Nicholas spending the night in the hogan in the canyon, but it was probably common knowledge. It was absolutely eerie how information flew like wildfire on the reservation.

The telephone rang.

"I knew you'd just be getting back from the hospital and I took a chance you hadn't gone to bed."

She couldn't stop smiling. "No. Not yet. I stopped and got the newspapers. Shirley Kee has you elected president."

He chuckled. "Shirley Kee loves me. Now all I have to do is get everybody else to."

Cabot's heart skipped a beat. Was it just a casual remark? About love?

She said quickly, "Everybody will know you're wonderful by November. I was just reading about Marvin Willoughby. He looks like a creep. I really don't like his looks. Why he's nothing but a carpetbagger."

"He'll be tough to beat. He's got a hard-core constituency in his party and a pot of money. He'll try to make me look like the worst amateur, like he did with his primary opponent. And there'll be people who wouldn't vote for a Navajo. Ever. Period. The fact that I've not had much government experience is a weak spot. It'll be hard to live down. He'll keep hammering on it."

They were quiet a moment.

"I hate not being able to see you," she said.

"I know. It's hard to concentrate when all I want to do is think about you."

"I keep staring out windows and bumping into things. When will you be back?"

"Probably not for two weeks it looks like now. Maybe I can break away when we swing through Globe and Winslow. We're getting the mobile headquarters organized. It's a real nice motor home. Your grandfather's money bought us that. What a generous thing to do. They're painting my name on it now. We've got to hit all the shopping centers over the district on weekends. Gotta shake as many hands and kiss as many babies as I can until November. Jim Shackleford regrets that I have to take the time to eat and sleep."

"I've asked Jacob Schiller and the chief of surgery if I can help out in the O.R. Maybe even do some surgery myself if things get busy. I'll be at the hospital a lot. If I'm not home, or out with Niyol, that's where I'll be."

"Hey, that's great. Not my line, as you well know, but good for you."

"Come when you can."

"Don't worry. I'll find you."

Cabot sat in the office off the Emergency Room. It was getting close to two in the morning and there hadn't been any emergencies since a maternity at midnight. Tommy Tootsie sat at another desk, dozing over a report, and his occasional drifting snore was making Cabot feel sleepy. When she heard the outside door open, she rose quickly and headed to the admitting desk.

Nicholas stood talking to the desk nurse.

"Nicholas. Hi. I had no idea you'd be getting in tonight,"

Cabot said. It had been over a week since she'd been with him in the canyon. The jolt she felt when she saw him made her pulse race.

"We got into Holbrook about midnight with the motor home. Want to open up first thing in the morning at the Walmart shopping center, so I'm here for just a little while."

Cabot turned to the desk nurse.

"I'll take a break now, Wilma. Just give me a beep if you need me. Tommy's back there about nine-tenths asleep. Tell him I've gone up with Nicholas to check on little Ella Etcitty."

"Take your time. Nothin' happenin' around here," Wilma said.

They walked to the elevator. "I hope you don't mind. I told her I'd come see her in the night. Dr. Schiller let me take out her tonsils. My first honest-to-god-me-in-charge surgery," she grinned.

In the elevator he leaned back against the wall, both hands behind him, his eyes dark and intense.

"You don't know how much I want to kiss you right now," he said. "After you see your little girl, find a dark corner somewhere."

She felt her nipples tighten. "Yes."

They stood over the bed in the softly lit room and Cabot brushed the glossy black hair from the child's forehead and re-tucked the blanket under her chin. Ella Etcitty's eyes fluttered open and she smiled. "I've been waiting for you, Dr. Chase. I knew you'd come. They give me ice cream whenever I want it. Isn't that cool?"

"Wow. That's terrific. It's the best thing in the world to get your throat better." Cabot patted the little girl's cheek. "Now, go to sleep. I'll see you tomorrow."

In the silent hallway Cabot took Nicholas' hand and after a few steps pulled him abruptly into an empty patient room. She pulled the door closed and turned into his arms.

His kiss was hard and urgent as he ran his hands up and down her back, kneading her shoulders, her waist, her buttocks. She returned the demanding kisses, and when he spun her over to one of the beds, she fell across it, pulling him over her.

She yanked up her skirt and opened her legs, pulling him hard against her.

"Lily, Lily, how I want you."

His fingers unbuttoned her shirt and shoved her bra up. She gasped and moved against him, stifling the sound that rose in her throat. When his hand moved between her legs, she whispered, "Tear them, just tear my stockings." She reached for the zipper to his pants and freed him as his fingers tore the fragile barrier of her stockings. She fell back and he drove deeply as she matched his thrusts. She stifled her cries as she felt him buck and shudder.

He fell on her breasts, panting. "I promised myself I wouldn't do this, throw you on the nearest bed," he muttered in her neck. "But God, I needed this."

She stroked his damp forehead, her heart still hammering in her chest. "Yes. I needed it, too. I didn't realize how much."

Reluctantly she let her legs slide to the floor.

"I better let you get put back together. Someone might come. Though a minute ago I wouldn't have cared if the whole staff trooped in here," he said.

He stood and pulled her up, helping to adjust her skirt and button her shirt.

Cabot smoothed the bed. They'd hardly disturbed it.

With a last soft kiss, they opened the door and walked back down the silent corridor.

Chapter Thirty

September 24, 1992

The church hall was crowded and Cabot had trouble finding a seat. Tonight was the first of three televised debates that Nicholas would have with his opponent, Marvin Willoughby, and he had asked her to be there if she could get away from the hospital. Latchi Singh and Bill Riordan volunteered to take Emergency Room duties so that Cabot and the other doctors could go to Flagstaff and give Nicholas moral support. Jane Manyfarms offered Cabot a ride, but she made up an excuse. She wanted to spend the night with Nicholas. She was longing to be with him, and she didn't know if his family guessed how far their relationship had gone. Or if they would approve if they did.

She looked around at the gathered spectators. It was a mostly white Flagstaff crowd, but there were also a number of Indian supporters, not all of them Navajo. Cabot was learning to tell the subtle physical differences between the

Hopi, Apache, and Navajo people. The district included those reservations, as well as the downstate Pima, Maricopa and Tohono O'Odham communities. The Apache and Navajo shared common Athabascan language roots, but any Native American would tell you he was as different from other tribes as he was from Anglos. The catchall *Indian* or *Native American* embraced an incredible diversity of societies that passionately wanted to preserve their uniqueness.

Against a wall she saw Pete Price and Russell Wauneka. There was no doubt there how they felt about her relationship with Nicholas. Pete Price looked at her impassively and turned away. Cabot unconsciously clasped her arms at her waist and rubbed the elbows of her suede jacket. These men disapproved of her being with Nicholas. Did Nicholas know how much? Would it matter to him?

The television lights were turned on, bathing the stage in bright light. There was a rustle of anticipation and excitement at watching the behind-the-scenes preparations for the broadcast. People were as much interested in the camera crew as they were the moderator when he came out to sit at a desk to the side of the stage. There were two lecterns for the candidates set up in front of a light gray curtain. Spotlights with reflectors came on, to eliminate shadows on the candidates' faces. There were some crackles, squees, and squawks as a technician adjusted the microphones.

The moderator made some opening remarks describing the evening's format as the two candidates came out, each to stand at his place. The format was simple. There would be ten questions that had been decided beforehand. Each man would answer each question, then the other would rebut. There would then be ten random questions from the audience, handled the same way. Each candidate would have a final five minutes summation.

Nicholas looked wonderful, she thought. He wore a navy blue suit and a red print silk tie. She noted his natural coloring was extremely photogenic on the monitor, whereas the other man's cheeks looked too artificially rosy in his sallow face. Cabot also knew that Nicholas's natural color offended some. His heritage wasn't an advantage. He would have to show that he would be a congressman for all of the people and not just an advocate for Native American issues and rights, that many thought were too extensive in the first place.

Cabot had not seen Nicholas speak in public before. She prayed he'd be good. She found her hands were damp, her throat dry, and she had large and restless butterflies in her stomach.

But Nicholas was good. Physically poised, he smiled easily, moved and gestured gracefully, not intimidated by the camera and the lights. Plus he was intellectually organized and articulate. His training as a lawyer showed. Cabot tried to be objective, knowing she would think him wonderful anyway, but she felt convinced after seeing him that he really was.

To Cabot, the other man seemed smug and patronizing, almost sneering that someone without his own Washington experience would dare to try for office. Though bland looking, he had a surprisingly deep and resonant voice and presented himself as a vigorous, hard-hitting speaker. As expected, he hit hard with Nicholas's lack of political experience. Many would be persuaded that he could tackle Washington as an insider who knew what buttons to push. Reluctantly Cabot had to conclude that, attractive as Nicholas appeared to her, this man was a formidable opponent. And one with a lot of cash.

Nicholas was the last to speak, chosen by drawing, when it came time for the five-minute summations.

"You've listened to the things I have to say tonight, and I'm sure you've concluded that I'm big on education, jobs, and the environment. And you can say, well, isn't everybody? I certainly hope so. They're intricately connected. With a well-educated workforce, jobs will stay and new ones will come to the state. As for the environment, it's our duty to protect the planet that nurtures us. Educating, and in other cases, re-educating and retraining, are a necessary given. But there are trade-offs that will have to be made in how the care of our air, water, and land will affect the abilities of people to feed and house themselves and their children. It will be a tightrope at the end of this century, and the 21st that lies just ahead of us, with danger of falling on one side to the detriment of the other.

"Sweeping generalizations cannot be made. It's going to be feel-our-way every step, carefully weighing the merits of each case that threatens the other. Thoughtful men and women can do this. Is water-hungry cotton a crop that should be grown in the desert? Does a golf course use too much water, when tourism brings enormous revenues to this state? Should we re-introduce wolves and then lose cattle to predation? Should we drain a precious wetland to house workers for a big new industrial plant that will employ hundreds, only to doom nesting eagles? If not, will those industries go to Nevada or Texas? These are hard questions, and we're running out of time to find the answers. It won't be easy, but it's a challenge I want from you.

"In closing I'd like to comment on my opponent's insistence that I'm not a Washington insider like he says he is. Now, I don't happen to think that that's a bad thing. However, that's up to you. I can't change that. But I would like to say I'm an Arizona insider. My family's been in this area for over five hundred years. I was born an hour or so up the road. I went to mission schools, and high school in Phoenix. I got my undergraduate degree in business from University of Arizona and my law degree from Arizona State University. I worked for one of the largest law firms in the state for seven years. I've roped cattle on my father's ranch, wrestled steers in rodeos all over the state. I've hiked Arizona's mountains, ridden horses over its canyons and its prairies. Its incomparable sunrises and sunsets are part of me. If you send me to Washington, and I hope you do, there won't be much that comes up that I won't know if it's good or not for the Sixth Congressional District of Arizona."

Nicholas grinned and stepped back from the microphone waving to the cheers and applause.

Cabot sat back in relief and wiped her hands on her skirt. Until she relaxed she hadn't realized she'd practically been holding her breath for the entire time Nicholas was speaking. She thought it was a beautiful speech. The audience seemed to love it, though she had to admit there was a natural constituency here. She hoped the television audience would love it too, and dismiss Marvin Willoughby as the carpetbagger he was.

The moderator was banging his gavel to settle the audience for the close of the program. Then the bright lights went off and the crew began to dismantle the complicated wiring.

Cabot wanted to go to Nicholas, but she held back, seeing him surrounded by his staff and family, and a horde of well wishers. And Pete Price and Russell Wauneka.

It was all right. He would come to her later.

She opened the motel room door. He rattled with paper bags of food.

"Big Macs and french fries," he announced. "Thought you might be hungry. You usually are."

"Are you insinuating," she rushed to take some of the bags, "that my appetite isn't ladylike?"

He tossed the bags on the bed and grinned. "I know your appetite isn't ladylike."

She made a face at him while she rummaged through a bag and found several french fries. "Where's your salad?"

"There are times," he said solemnly, "when only a Big Mac is equal to the occasion."

He was clearly elated at how the evening had gone.

She fed him a french fry, wiped her hands in a flurry of paper napkins, and undid his proper red regimental tie. Then she began on the buttons of his politically correct white shirt. Slowly, between catsup and mustard foils, Big Macs, they undressed, licking greasy fingers, then other things, before settling into a sensual copulation among the wrappers and clam boxes on the king-size bed.

They lay curled against each other, relishing the feeling that they had this great big bed for the entire night, a luxury they'd never had and didn't know when they'd have again.

They stroked each other and dozed. He began to stir and she caressed him gently. He groaned and stretched, beginning to pulse and twitch under her hand.

"You know," she said drowsily, "the first time we made love, I thought you would want to do it from behind. I saw a movie once and that was what the Indians did. It was very sexy."

There was silence. When Nicholas spoke, his voice was tight. "Doggie-style, you mean?"

"Well, yes. Is that what you call it, too?"

"No. That's what you whites call it. Us Indians picked up the term."

He rose on an elbow over her.

"Nicholas, I didn't mean..."

"I'm still different to you, aren't I? The Indian. I'm not simply a man. Am I the savage fucking the white lady?" His eyes were dangerous in the light that seeped through the window from the parking lot.

"I'm sorry I said anything. I was just sort of thinking out loud." Her voice quivered. "I didn't mean to offend you. I would never…"

He gripped her shoulder. "Maybe you'd like that. A little fantasy about the big Indian on the warpath stopping off at the cabin to rape the daughter of the white settler."

"Stop it." She was alarmed at the look on his face. "You're insulting."

"A quick fuck before I go after the scalps."

Cabot glared at him, but he dropped his head and mashed her mouth against his, jamming his tongue down her throat as he squeezed her breasts and pinched her nipples. A protest rose in her throat, but the fire between her legs took over and she returned his angry kisses, throwing herself against the rigid penis that stabbed at her stomach.

Suddenly she felt herself whirled off the bed and spun face down on the floor. His knee forced her legs apart roughly and he rammed himself into her to the hilt, coming up sharply against her cervix.

She yelped in surprise, but he held her pinioned, his breath rasping in her ear as he threw himself into a pounding piston rhythm. What had begun as a sharp hurt became mixed with elemental, primal sensations, as his plunging penis battered her womb and sent a series of almost unbearable orgasms tearing through her. They arced, one into the other as he rode her, his chest and thighs slick with sweat, sliding relentlessly back and forth along her back and hips. Her throat sobbed but not with tears. She rose on her arms and threw herself back to meet him thrust for thrust, on and on, animal grunts curling up from her chest. Then he reared and with a strangled shout, shuddered and gushed into her.

They were still, panting raggedly for a moment, then he rolled off her onto his back, his forearms over his eyes. She stayed on her hands and knees, then dropped her cheek to the rough shaggy carpeting, her breath coming in dry whimpers, slowly softening as reality intruded.

His voice was glum. "I wish you hadn't enjoyed that so much."

She was over him like a cat, arms on either side of his shoulders, her voice quivering with outrage. "*I* enjoyed it! *You loved it!* You're accusing me of thinking you're different from me. What about *you*? Don't tell me it doesn't thrill you to make love to me because I'm white. What's wrong with being aroused because we're different from one another? You're the most exciting man I've ever met that's why I've fallen in love with you and if you think..."

His hands grabbed her upper arms in a vise-like grip and he flattened her breasts against his chest.

"...and if you think..." she fumed and began again.

"That last part," he said, his voice guttural. "Go over that last part again."

Her heart was pounding in her anger and she had to remember what she had said. "It's why...it's why..." She finished in a whisper. "I've fallen in love with you."

She was crushed against him, her breath pushed out in a sharp whoosh.

"That's what I thought you said." His voice was muffled in the curve of her neck.

Chapter Thirty-One

September 25, 1992

"Dammit, Nicholas," Pete Price was saying, "the woman doctor has got to go." He and Russell Wauneka were meeting with Nicholas, Zhealy Tso, and Jim Shackleford the morning after the Flagstaff broadcast. "Russell and I prayed you'd eventually come to your senses, but now it's reached the point that it's got to stop. You're endangering the campaign. What the hell were you doing to her last night? The desk got three complaints."

"None of your goddam business, Pete," Nicholas said evenly.

Russell Wauneka spoke. "Fortunately the night clerk is Navajo and will keep his mouth shut, but it could have gone the other way. The press would get real excited to find out you were shacked up in a motel room with a white woman, fucking her brains out. You don't think Marvin Willoughby wouldn't give his campaign budget to get that going around.

Scare all those white women that an over-sexed Indian is on the loose."

"Oh, come on, Russell and Pete. You're over-reacting. Nick's a bachelor. The lady isn't married, I understand," Jim said.

Jim Shackleford was having trouble keeping a straight face. He'd seen the redhead in question. With tits and legs like that there wouldn't be a male in the district that wouldn't love to throw her into bed. He'd heard the commotion last night and it'd given him such a hard-on he'd had to jack off to get some sleep. You had to hand it to Nick.

As for being an oversexed Indian to frighten the white women, he not only wanted women to think that Nick was sexy, he counted on it. He was a handsome dude and it had never been his experience in all his years in politics that a gorgeous girlfriend ever hurt a bachelor candidate. Now a married man, that was different. You could run into trouble there these days. But a good shot of testosterone in a candidate was a plus. Another plus. She was a gorgeous doctor working on the reservation...a real East coast altruistic woman. The canapé and chardonnay crowd will love it. These three old guys might screw things up if they insisted on this big Indian thing.

"We could overlook this whole thing if you'd been discreet, but you haven't."

Zhealy Tso was clearly miserable about saying anything, but Pete Price nudged him. "Uh...everybody in Canyon de Chelly knows you screwed all night in the Tahome ceremonial hogan. That offended some people. You been to her apartment. You had relations on a hospital bed a week or so ago when she was on duty there. Now last night. I guess you got to end it with the woman, Nicholas. She's threatening the campaign."

"I hadn't realized the depth of interest in my romantic

life," Nicholas said dryly. "Obviously I haven't been as discreet as I thought I was. For that I apologize. Discussion closed."

"You should have a Navajo wife," Pete insisted. "We've been through this, even before the woman doctor came. You're sending the wrong signals to the *Dine* with your affair with this woman. Karen Daghalani is back from Los Angeles. You should start showing an interest. She's a beautiful woman, intelligent and educated. She would make a good impression in Washington."

"The *Dine* would like that," Zhealy added.

"Karen's a nice girl," Nicholas shrugged. "Bobby Becenti thinks so, too. Why would I want to piss him off? He's loved her since they were kids. Look, just stay out of it, Pete. You too, Russell. Zhealy."

"Maybe you could escort your lady doctor to social events in Phoenix. Take this Karen Daghalani around when you're up here. The whites admire your white girlfriend, the Indians admire your Navajo girlfriend." Jim suggested.

"Jesus, you're cynical," Nicholas said.

"Just thinking out loud, Nick. Just thinking out loud."

"You're cynical out loud. Chill out. I said the discussion is closed. Period."

Thinking out loud, that's what Cabot had said last night that had started that whole crazy episode on the floor. They both had rug burns on their knees and elbows.

"Let's get on with scheduling the motor home," Nicholas said. "We've got six more weeks until the election. Do you think we'd get enough District Six voters to make it worth setting up one weekend at the State Fair?"

"I think we'd do better sticking with the shopping centers," Jim said. "But we'll set up the booth with literature. I got some good-looking young people to staff it."

"About the Polaroids with prospective voters and me. How do you think that's gone over?" Nicholas ignored the glum Navajo men.

"It's a winner," Jim said. "Folks show them to their neighbors, put 'em up on their refrigerators. Since Bill Kemper got the distributor to donate his expired film, it's been a real cost-effective promotion. He can't sell the stuff, but the film's still good."

The meeting went on to other things until it was time to leave for another shopping center. As they broke up, Russell motioned for Pete and Zhealy to stay behind.

The three men watched Nicholas and Jim drive away in the big blue and white motor home emblazoned with *Nicholas Nakai for Congress* in blue foot-high letters.

Russell turned to the medicine man. "That didn't go well, Pete."

"No. I handled it wrong. Got him mad. We'll have to back off him for a time, but it's only six weeks until the election. At least he'll be more careful about sleeping with the woman."

"I think we'd better go talk to Karen Daghalani. Don't let on to her what our thinking is. Just have her around when Nicholas makes a speech or anything. Get Shirley Kee to take some pictures of them together for the *Times*. Get her to have something in every week until the election. Put Karen to work on the campaign so it looks natural that she's around." Russell said.

"Worth a try," Zhealy said. "Doubt Nicholas will be fooled."

"The woman doctor is well-liked, Pete. She's made a good impression since she's been here. Maybe Shackleford is right. Maybe we're over-reacting to this situation," Zhealy said.

"We don't want the first Navajo Congressman to have a white wife, Zhealy," Pete said, his face stern with determination.

"Pete's right, Zhealy. There's too much at stake."

"I guess you're right," Zhealy said.

"I think it would be good to have a talk with the woman doctor." Pete's face was determined.

"Nicholas won't like that," Zhealy said.

"I don't know, Pete." Russell said.

"The elders have to step in sometimes, Russell and Zhealy. You know that. Young people get sidetracked. Got their brains between their legs."

Chapter Thirty-Two

October 1, 1992

"Will you be back this weekend? I'm absolutely worthless. All I do is think about you. People are starting to look at me funny."

Cabot was sitting cross-legged on her bed, the phone tucked under her chin, a copy of the *Navajo Times* opened out across the black, white, red and gray geometric Navajo blanket she used as a bedspread.

Nicholas sounded pleased. "I don't think I can get back, much as I want to. The debate in Casa Grande is next week and we've got to move around to generate some interest. I did the poorest in the primary there. We kind of took it for granted because there are a lot of Tohono O'Odham people down that way. It's farming country and we thought they'd be for me. But they weren't. They're worried that I think cotton's a bad crop for the desert. I question it, but there are things going for it, too. There are maybe better alternatives, but they need to be talked about. Anyway, we'll have to work harder."

"I've been reading about you in the *Times*." Cabot turned back to the front page. "Who's the beautiful girl cuddling up to you?"

"What girl? What are you talking about?"

"It's right there on the front page. Big picture of you and some mayor with Pete Price and Russell. And, let's see..." Cabot looked at the caption. "Karen Daghalani."

"Oh. That must have been in Tuba City a couple of days ago. Karen's an old friend just back from L.A. We went to mission schools together, then U of A. Russell's got her working on the campaign."

"Ah, yes. I see. An assistant in charge of candidate adoration."

"Oh, come on, Cabot. She was standing next to me. What's the matter? You jealous?"

"Yes. She's standing very, very close. And I'm far, far away."

There was a moment's silence.

"I'm glad you're jealous," he said. "If you were here right now I'd show you how much you don't have to be. I love you, Cabot. I miss you. I miss holding you. When this election is over, let's go somewhere for a few days and shut the world out."

"Oh, can we, Nicholas?" Then she thought about it. "Even if you win? I'd love it if we could, but I won't let myself be disappointed if we don't. You'll be terribly busy and you know it."

Her doorbell rang.

"Darn. Somebody's at the door. Can you wait a sec?"

"I'd better go. I'll try to call again tomorrow. Will you be there about this time?"

"Yes, I'll be here. I'll hurry home."

Cabot opened the door. Pete Price and Russell Wauneka stood outside.

"Yes? Can I help you?"

"*Ya-at-eeh*, Dr. Chase. I am Russell Wauneka and this is Peter Price."

"*Ya-at-eeh*. Yes, I know who you are." She was puzzled and uneasy.

"May we come in, please?"

"Oh, yes. I'm sorry. Do come in." She stood aside and the two men filed into her living room. "Please sit down."

They settled, Russell in her big armchair, Pete on the couch. They sat stiffly, formally.

She looked at the two silent men.

"May I get you some coffee?" She had learned that offering coffee was a big thing with the Navajo.

Russell answered. "Yes, coffee would be good."

Cabot hurried to the kitchen and busied herself with the preparations. She put a cup of water in the microwave, got out the cups and measured coffee grounds.

Whatever did they want? Was it about her and Nicholas? The thought made her heart pound.

Thank God she didn't have to wait for a coffeepot to brew. She found some cookies and saw her hands shake when she arranged them on a plate, wondering if the second cup would ever boil.

When she returned to the living room the two men were just as she had left them. They each took a coffee and one cookie.

Cabot sat down on a small side chair and smoothed her hands over her skirt. She would just have to wait for them to come to the reason for their visit. There was no way you could rush a Navajo. He would get to his business when, at some subtle point, he decided he was ready.

Cabot looked from one to the other, but their faces told her nothing. The cups tinked in the oppressive stillness of the room.

Finally, Russell cleared his throat. "Dr. Chase. You have become a friend of Nicholas Nakai, one of our people."

"Yes." Oh, God, she was right. What did they want?

"As you know, he is running for the United States Congress. It is very important to the Navajo that he should win."

"Yes, I know that."

"It is not so important to you that he should win."

"What? I don't know what you mean. I desperately want him to win. I understand how..."

Pete Price interrupted, rare for a Navajo. "What the chairman means is, you are here only temporarily. I think you are scheduled to leave your duties here next June?"

"Yes, that's true."

"You will have had your Navajo lover, and then you will go back to your world. Will you care about Nicholas then?"

Cabot stood abruptly. "I don't know what you're talking about. But it isn't your business, about Nicholas and me."

"What we're talking about, Dr. Chase, is this. If Nicholas wins this election, he needs to go to Washington as an Indian presence. And, yes, it is very much our business. The tribe is not happy that he has a white mistress. We want him to go to Washington with a Navajo wife."

She hated it that he had called her Nicholas's mistress, but could she really argue with the word? It was a little old-fashioned, but accurate enough in its meaning.

"But surely that's up to Nicholas." Her voice had turned cool, but she could feel the beginning of panic.

"Not entirely. The tribe has a lot invested in Nicholas. We have groomed him. I think that is the proper word use.

We have given him special direction since he was in high school to do important things. Today we are, of course, trying to groom all of our children, but when he was a boy, with the resources at hand, we could only look to our very brightest."

"Nicholas knows your expectations of him. He has every intention of fulfilling them," she said.

"Oh, yes. At least he remembered them until he met you. Now he is distracted. He is distracted at the most crucial time of this campaign. The outcome could be very close. He cannot afford to have his people desert him now."

The silence in the room roared in her ears.

"We want you to go away, Dr. Chase," Pete Price said.

"It would be good if you would do that," Russell agreed, obviously trying to soften the medicine man's abruptness. "Of course, if you choose not to, there is nothing we can do."

She was in the middle of the Navajo reservation, working at a Navajo hospital with Navajo patients. There was probably a great deal they could do if they so chose, she thought.

"Does Nicholas know you were coming here?" But she knew he didn't. How could he have spoken to her as he did a few moments ago if he knew? Then she remembered the tiny hesitation when she mentioned Karen Daghalani. She was the Navajo woman they had chosen for him. And he knew it.

"No, of course not," Russell replied.

She tried to keep the desperation from her voice. "I love him."

"Then it will be easy for you to do the right thing."

After they had gone, Cabot sat, numb and empty. She was battling something she didn't truly understand. Western minds were so strongly individualistic. One felt the strongest responsibility to oneself. These people's belief centered around the welfare of the group. The individual was less important than the benefits to the whole. How powerful was that instinct in Nicholas? He was strongly acculturated, had indeed been especially singled out to be. But for the benefit of the tribe.

And yet...and yet. Hadn't the things the two men had said insinuated themselves into her own thoughts? In the small hours of the night?

Cabot had no idea what to do. Her mind spun off in a thousand directions, unwilling to face not having Nicholas in her life, now, when it had become of overpowering importance to her.

There was defiance on one hand, or capitulation to the two men who had confronted her, and only confusion in between the two extremes. She had no one to confide in, no one who could look at this situation dispassionately. What she meant, she admitted to herself, was that she wanted someone to tell her what she should do because she had no idea.

She thought about her grandfather. He had always been her closest confidante. Her only one, if truth be told. But he was somewhere with Laura and she had no idea where. But under the circumstances, would he know any more what to do than she? What she really needed was a woman's advice. Jane? No. That would never do. She would say what Pete and Russell had said.

When she thought more about it, it seemed obvious. She would go to her mother. Her mother had liked Nicholas. Her mother had been a rebel for the man she loved.

Was she hoping that her mother would tell her to be a rebel?

It was Thursday. She was on duty tomorrow, then she had two consecutive days off. She could be in Sedona before dark if she left the hospital right after work on Friday.

Chapter Thirty-Three

October, 1992

The setting sun had turned the majestic red rocks of Sedona to flames and streaked the sky with vermilion and lavender, but Cabot was scarcely aware of the tumultuous beauty of the sky and the sandstone formations that brooded over the town.

She found the small, shingled house set back on a side street that the pony-tailed filling station attendant had described. His crystal earring swung and sparkled in his excitement at finding out Cabot was Mariella's daughter. Mariella was his astrologer.

Casa Capricorn. The sign was newly painted, but the house itself had a faintly seedy look about it. A bed of frost-nipped geraniums had been left to droop disconsolately by the sagging front step. It appeared that the front of the house, perhaps the living and dining room, were given over to some kind of retail enterprise. There were lights showing inside and a hand-lettered sign hung crookedly in the front door declaring the shop OPEN. Cabot pushed the door as a small attached bell jingled musically. A faintly musty odor was overlaid with the pungent scent of sandalwood. She heard her mother call from in back of a curtain of green and amber beads.

"Be out in a minute. Look around. Help yourself."

"It's me, Mother," Cabot answered.

She glanced around at the overrun cases and shelves—a dusty hodgepodge of health foods, crystals, rocks, horoscope-related books, T-shirts and posters imprinted with New Age aphorisms, as well as an array of incense, candles, teas, ouija boards, and tarot cards. There were other objects that Cabot couldn't have put a name to, perhaps dealing with the arcane and occult, or maybe the drug culture.

Mariella materialized in a haze of gold-embroidered pink silk and a tinkle of gold spangles.

"Lily. What a delightful surprise. You're just in time for dinner."

And in fact something in the back smelled rather good. Ricey, but good. If she were hungry, which she wasn't.

Cabot smiled. "You don't look the least bit surprised to see me, Mother."

"Well, I was rather expecting you. My horoscope was very definite for today. Someone related to me would come. That doesn't give me very many possibilities."

Mariella led Cabot into the back of the house where there was a small, cluttered living room/dining room area, and a kitchen. She motioned for Cabot to sit at the table, a round affair covered with a red and blue tie-dyed silk shawl edged with long fringe. Mariella sat opposite her. Cabot got the fleeting feeling that, if her mother gave consultations, this was probably where she did it.

"You needed to talk to someone," Mariella said.

"Well, yes. Is it a bad time? You said you were getting ready for dinner."

"Oh, no." Mariella crossed her arms on the table and smiled shyly. "I've thought so many times it would be nice to have you come and need to talk to me. But, well, we've never done that sort of thing, have we?"

"No. We haven't had that sort of relationship."

"I'm sorry for that."

"So am I," Cabot said, meaning it for the first time.

"I suppose it's a problem with a man. It usually is."

"Nicholas Nakai. You met him."

"The handsome Navajo. A beautiful man. Are you lovers?"

"Yes. Well, now I don't know. The tribal elders have told me to go away."

Then Cabot went back to the beginning. How she'd fought her attraction to Nicholas at first, uneasy about a relationship with a Navajo man. His campaign for Congress and the expectations of the tribe for one of its brightest sons.

"And what about you?" her mother asked. "You were going back east anyway, for your surgical residency. Would you give up all your plans for this man?"

"I don't know. We never got far enough to discuss any future." Cabot stared at the swirling red and blue dyes on the tabletop. "All I can think of now is that I don't want to go away, never see him again. I'm in love with him. I don't want to give him up because they told me I have to. You can see that, can't you?"

"Yes, I can see that. Does he know you've been told to leave?"

"No."

Mariella seemed lost in thought for a few moments. Then she said, "What if this man loses his election? Does he plan to stay, in that case, on the reservation? What of you then? Would you stay, too? Continue to work in the reservation hospital?"

"I suppose. I'm really needed there," Cabot answered reluctantly.

"And what about your ambitions to go into neurosurgery? You couldn't do that there. I didn't think anything would ever side-track that."

"Maybe that's not so important."

Mariella played with a long, gold spangle in her ear. Cabot was conscious of something simmering on the small stove. She noticed a gray tiger cat for the first time, watching her with smoky, half-closed eyes from atop a carved teak cabinet.

"You must do as the tribal elders say. Go away," Mariella said. "Let Nicholas find his Navajo wife."

Cabot was stunned. She hadn't expected her mother to say those words at all. Her mother was going to tell her to stay, love Nicholas, tell the world to go to hell. That's why she had come here.

"Mother, I love him," she cried in anguish.

Mariella's eyes rested on her daughter, then drew inward across the years. "Thirty two years ago I was going to be the finest architect in the country," she said softly. "I was going to build buildings that people marveled at. I wanted the world to be amazed at what I could design, the brilliant things I could think of. Then I met your father. He's a fine-looking man now. You should have seen him then, with his fiery red curls and those yellow-green cat's eyes. He was bright gold to me...he was *shining*." Her mother caught her breath. "Well, you know. You look at yourself in the mirror every day. Except your hair is a little darker, not as goldish red," She smiled at Cabot. "Mixed a little with mine, I expect.

"Anyway, I forgot every ambition I ever had. Your father

dropped out of Harvard after some mix-up at a sit-in. He'd set fire to the dean's desk. There was a big stink. I followed him." Her mother's voice dropped. "After that, I always followed. Into every blind alley, drug escape, group sex, commune, guru, rainbow. And now I'm a silly, middle-aged woman with a red dot on my forehead when I remember to put it there. I float around in filmy saris in a cloud of sandalwood, in a ridiculous little shop that sells worthless things to ridiculous people.

"The only bright spot was you. My stern, determined, brilliant little girl was going to do glorious things. Take a look at me, Lily. A good long look, before you let a handsome man dictate what you do with your dreams."

Cabot got up and walked around to her mother's back and cradled the dark head against her stomach, smoothing the fine, silky hair with her fingers as the tears streamed down her cheeks and her heart ached for her mother's despair.

There were steps on the back porch. Her father burst into the kitchen, his ruddy beard bristling from the dry cold air.

"Look who's come for a visit, Ben." Mariella's voice wavered only slightly. "I was just telling Lily I should cast her horoscope. I really haven't in ever such a long time, have I, Lily?"

Cabot wiped her cheeks and struggled to erase the tears from her voice. "Hi, Daddy. It's been a very long time, Mother. Yes. You must do that."

Chapter Thirty-Four

October 5, 1992

Jane Manyfarms slammed the flat of her hand down on the letter. "Goddam those two meddling old fools!"

She picked up the letter and read it again.

Dear Jane,

It is with deep regret that I have to resign my position with the Fort Defiance Hospital. I have written a formal letter to Dr. Schiller, but I expressly wanted you to know how much I have enjoyed working with you and being your friend. I will treasure my memories of the Navajo people and the time I have spent among you.

My reasons are personal. I am a serious person and I did not weigh them lightly against my undeniable obligations to you and the hospital. I will think often of your kindness to me.

Sincerely yours, Cabot Chase

The letter didn't mention the visit from Pete Price and Russell Wauneka, of course, but Jane knew they had gone to her apartment last Thursday. An upset Bobby Bescenti had called her when they left. Bobby knew that Pete and Russell were pushing Karen Daghalani at Nicholas. Karen had told him.

As Jane thought about it, she could probably give a fair approximation of the conversation between Cabot and the medicine man and tribal chairman. She knew of Pete's and Russell's disapproval of Nicholas's liaison with Cabot. It just so happened that she disagreed with them, as did Agnes, Nicholas's mother, and Laura, his grandmother. It wasn't only that they made a fine-looking couple, which wouldn't be lost in Washington. Cabot Chase and her grandfather had ties to the Eastern establishment. Russell and Pete didn't look far enough ahead. They dreamed of a Navajo Congressman. Laura Begay, her daughters and granddaughters, saw a future senator, and perhaps, who could know? An American president?

Not that any of this had been planned, but Cabot Chase had dropped out of the sky. There had to be a reason for such an illogical happening. It could not be disregarded. The girl's grandfather could have contacted Laura Begay any time over the years. Why just now did his granddaughter, and then he, appear? Pete Price didn't know everything.

Jane had called Cabot's apartment off and on all morning, then called Bobby Becenti. He kept a pretty good eye out around the apartment. He said Cabot had loaded a couple of suitcases in her car and driven away just after sunup.

Jane hung up and rubbed her eyes. "Probably headed back east," she fretted. "I got to get in touch with Nicholas down in Casa Grande. He's got that big debate tomorrow night. Goddam. He'll be upset when he needs a clear head." She pulled the telephone over. "You got to do it, Jane. He needs to be told about Russell and Pete. Cabot probably left him some kind of explanation, but he won't know what's behind it. Ah, shit. Wish I wasn't the one got to do it."

She dialed Jim Shackleford's number down in Phoenix. He'd know where to get a hold of Nicholas. She hoped he could think of something to do. Those two old goats had screwed up everything just when it had all been going so well.

Cabot left Albuquerque behind her, her heart a cold lump in her chest. She was doing the right thing, for both their sakes. She was positive. She'd left a letter for Nicholas explaining her reasons. That each of their careers would be hampered by their entanglement with each other. He needed to find a Navajo woman, like Karen Daghalani. His people wanted to see him with one of themselves, not a maverick white doctor who didn't entirely understand them. She had to get on with her studies. No matter how much she tried to see a way, her ambitions didn't fit his. She loved him. She was sure he loved her. But time would ease the hurt of parting. She hoped he understood. She was proud of him and knew he had a brilliant future in Washington.

The drive across the country was a depressing affair for her, heartsick and physically sick. A flu-like bug pursued her and a huge gray and rainy cyclonic system covered the center of the country and followed her unrelievedly to the east.

The sun broke through finally when she crossed into Massachusetts, to meet a blaze of autumn leaves, brilliant against a crystalline blue sky.

The traffic seemed almost overwhelming to her and she'd lost the knack for maneuvering around the chaotic rotaries, setting off cacophonies of horns a half a dozen times. But by nightfall she was at the coast.

She drove to the house on Marblehead, wanting nothing more than to curl up in bed and lick her wounds.

Her grandfather's houseman opened the door. "Dr. Chase. I was getting worried."

"Oh, for heaven's sake, Jeffrey," she said tartly, "You've known me since I was a child. Call me Cabot—or Lily, if you can't get used to that."

The old man grinned. "Let me get your things from the car, Miss Lily. Imelda's left a casserole to warm up if you were hungry."

"Tell her thank you, but I'm just exhausted. Could I have some tea in my room? A piece of toast, maybe. I'm going to take a hot bath and go to bed."

"I'll see to it. You just go on up." He turned before he went down to the car. "A Mister Nakai called several times. The messages are on the pier table there."

Cabot swallowed hard. "Yes. Thank you." Of course he would call. What did she think? That he would accept her letter without some further explanation?

"I told the gentleman that you were expected today. Your grandfather called also and I told him I had spoken with you. He would like you to call him as soon as possible. He told me to tell you he would be staying at your apartment in Fort Defiance."

Cabot nodded.

"The Mr. Nakai. He, uh, seemed rather exercised. " The houseman, seeing her dismay, turned and hurried down the broad front steps of the house to her car.

Cabot glanced at the messages from Nicholas. They all said the same thing: "Call me, please." "Cabot, you've got to call me. Please." "Cabot, you can't leave me like this." And more.

Her hand closed hard around the messages and she stuffed them in her pocket.

When she got to her room, Cabot took off her clothes and put on a fleecy terry robe. While her bath was running, she nibbled without appetite on the toast that Jeffrey had brought, but her stomach didn't want it.

She put it down carefully in the silver bowl and tucked the linen cozy around it with elaborate care. She squared her shoulders and walked over to the big cheval mirror in the corner of the bedroom. Slowly she untied the sash of the robe and slipped it off her shoulders. She stared for a long time at her reflection. The realization had crept over her two days ago. She hadn't had the flu at all.

She was pregnant.

She slipped her hands under her breasts. Already they seemed fuller, their nipples darkening. There was no longer any mistake about the tenderness that made her jump whenever something brushed against them.

When had it happened? Probably the very first time, in the hogan in Canyon de Chelly. She started on the pill the next day, not even considering the possibility she would conceive. How many Navajo girls had she explained the facts of life to? All it takes is once, dear, so be careful. Yeah. She'd said that about a hundred times. And the girls would nod and promise they would.

"Physician, heed thyself," she said ruefully. "Oh, Cabot....how could you have been so dumb. So irresponsible. What were you thinking of?"

But you weren't thinking. Just threw yourself into his arms. And you'd do it again.

Dispiritedly she crossed into the bathroom and turned off the water. She stepped into the pile of white bubbles and sank down heavily. What on earth was she going to do?

When Cabot had left her apartment in Fort Defiance, she had left everything but what she'd brought with her from Massachusetts. The brilliant rugs, the baskets and pots, the jewelry all stayed behind. She left a note for her grandfather to dispose of the things as he saw fit. Give the jewelry to Laura, if she wanted it. She wanted no reminders of her stay in Arizona. No souvenirs.

She rested her hands on her still-flat belly. The irony of it. She brought back with her the most unforgettable of mementos.

"My little Navajo souvenir," she said, swallowing a lump in her throat.

Chapter Thirty-Five

October 11, 1992

Cabot was in her grandfather's computer room. She had decided she would try to get into the Johns Hopkins residency program immediately. She would have seven months to work before the baby was due. She would simply have to make her plans as things happened. Whatever, she mustn't waste any more time and she needed to throw herself into something to ease her pain.

Jeffrey tapped politely at the door. "That Mr. Nakai who's been calling? He seems to be here. I assumed you would speak to him. I put him in the library."

Cabot stood, shocked. Numb. But of course she'd expected it, down deep. "Thank you Jeffrey. Yes, of course. I'll speak to him. Tell him I'll be right down."

She stood at the top of the long, curving staircase and ran her fingers through her hair nervously. She started down, wishing with all her being that she didn't have to face this meeting.

She took a long, shaky breath and stepped through the big, dark walnut doors that led into the library.

"Hello, Nicholas."

He turned from the long, mullioned windows and her heart constricted. Oh, God. How was she going to get through this?

His voice was tense, his eyes dark and angry.

"Cabot, would you kindly tell me what the hell is going on?" He was dressed in a dark suit and still wore a trenchcoat, spotted on the shoulders with rain, his hands jammed in his pockets. "I tell my girl I love her on the phone, and the next thing I know I get some half-assed letter telling me she's left and hopes I understand that she's gone off to do her own thing because I was in the way and again she hopes I'll understand and thank you very much."

"There were reasons," she said unhappily.

"Two old guys come to you and tell you to get lost. Yes, Jane told me. And you go? Just like that? You sure couldn't have loved me very much."

Here was an opening. She had to take it. "Nicholas, maybe I didn't." She winced inwardly at the pain that crossed his face. "I…I thought so once, but it wasn't enough."

"You know," his voice broke, "driving up that long driveway in the cab, I thought, Nakai, you've been in some pretty fancy places, but this is way out of my league. Is that it? I couldn't ever offer you anything close to this kind of life."

Her cheeks flushed in anger. "This has never had anything to do with anything."

"What is it then?" he pleaded. "I never would have stopped you from doing what you want to do. Being what you want to be."

"Not intentionally. I know that. And I wouldn't have

meant to harm your chance at being a special thing to your people. But we would have. Think about it Nicholas. The reservation is your home. It's strange to me. It's beautiful, but I'm out of place there. Some things I could never begin to understand. Your people would know that. They do know it."

"What's all this crap about 'my people.' You make me sound like some goddam Martian."

"In the beginning you were almost that strange to me. Then...then...I didn't think it would matter. But it does, Nicholas. I was always just...temporary help on the reservation."

"My God, I can't believe this is happening." He turned and paced in his frustration, then stopped directly in front of her. "I didn't seem all that strange to you when I was inside you. No, don't look away." His voice trembled. "How can you forget that? How can you forget how we were together?"

Somewhere she found the strength to look at him and make her voice cold. Make the tears stay hidden. "Please, Nicholas. My mind is made up. I just wish you'd go."

If he didn't go, she'd break apart.

But he did.

"Well, I had to fly across the country to hear it from you. Somehow I thought if you had to say it to me, you'd realize what a goddam stupid thing you're doing."

He stormed from the room and she heard the great front door open, then slam shut, setting the crystals in the big chandelier to ringing. There was a splintering tinkle as one dislodged and shattered on the black and white marble floor.

She went to the window, watched Nichols get into the taxi in the drive.

He had told the driver to wait.

Through the blur of her tears, the bright yellow cab disappeared into the misty rain and the riot of red and gold autumn leaves.

* * *

She heard from Johns Hopkins that she could begin on the 16th of November. She went to Baltimore and found an apartment and made arrangements to have her furniture moved from storage. She bought a washer and dryer. She stocked the new apartment with soaps, detergents, towels, and a hundred things to make the place her home. She walked the streets to familiarize herself with her new neighborhood. Arranged parking for the Porsche.

But then she went back to Marblehead, curled into the bed in her old childhood room. She walked the beach, turning her face to the cold raw wind trying to find some solace in physical misery. Once, she gave in and went to the library and found an *Arizona Republic*. The race for the 6th Congressional District was impossible to call. It would be extremely close. The *Republic* had endorsed Nicholas again for the general election. Other state papers had as well, but others had not.

It crossed her mind that he might lose. What if he lost by one vote? Her vote. As November 3rd approached, Cabot became obsessed with the idea that if she didn't vote, he would lose. She tried to tell herself that it was crazy new maternal hormones making her irrational, but by the Sunday before election Tuesday she was frantic. She tried to make arrangements to go to Arizona, finally finding a flight into Albuquerque the morning of Election Day that would allow her time to drive to Fort Defiance where she was registered to vote.

Chapter Thirty-Six

November 3, 1992

The polls would close at seven. It was six thirty when Cabot, with shaking hands, poked the little stylus into the computer card beside Nicholas's name. She pulled her ballot out, put it in its official folder and stepped around the little canvas curtain to hand it to the official, an old Navajo man solemn with this responsibility of citizenship. Nicholas was her only vote. She couldn't remember anyone else or anything else.

Cabot went to her apartment to pick up a few small things she had left behind. She had no intention of staying in Fort Defiance a moment longer than necessary. She had an early flight out of Albuquerque the next morning and had booked a room at an airport motel there. She had done what she could for Nicholas and now she was desperate to leave.

When she opened the door the smell of something chocolate baking wafted from the kitchen. Laura appeared around the counter, wiping her hands on a towel.

"Cabot, you gave me a start. What are you doing here? Have you come from Boston? I was just getting a couple of sheet cakes out of the oven to take over to the gym." Seeing Cabot hesitate, she said, "I hope you don't mind that your grandfather and I are staying here."

Cabot recovered from her surprise. "Oh, Laura, no. I told him to use it until the lease runs out. Keep it if you want to. I...I won't be using it again. I just came back to...to vote. Silly, but I got the strongest feeling that Nicholas might lose because of one vote. I couldn't stand that." She laughed self-consciously, thinking how dumb it sounded. To break off with Nicholas and then rush across the country to cast one little vote.

Laura looked at her with dark, sympathetic eyes. "I'm so sorry about you and Nicholas."

Cabot squared her shoulders. "Yes, well. It will be the best for both of us."

"I hope so, Cabot."

Laura's tone made Cabot drop her eyes. "But you don't think so. Are you angry with me?"

"Angry? Oh, my dear, no. We all do the best we can, make decisions as best we know how. I can understand your position. I was in the very same predicament myself once."

"And you sent grandfather away," Cabot's voice pleaded for understanding.

"Yes. And then I think I was right. He does, too."

"But you think I'm wrong, now, Laura."

"Yes. I do. It's a different time. I think you and Nicholas would have managed very well. But the decision isn't mine to make."

Cabot moved around the living room, stopping to touch a piece of pottery here, stroke a woolen rug there. Her fingers followed the design of a thunderbolt on a red and black blanket.

"Anything you want of this, please take, or give it away. It's not part of my life, now." Her voice shook and she cleared her throat to cover it. "My...the silver jewelry is in the top drawer of the bureau in the bedroom. I wish you'd take that. It's very beautiful, but it really wouldn't look right with what I wear back east."

Laura's eyes followed her around the room.

"That's very generous. You bought some lovely things. Emerson is a fine silversmith."

"Yes. He is." She plumped up a red and black pillow, then straightened. "Well, I'd best pack up those few things I forgot, then get going. They said there might be snow and I'd like to miss it if possible."

"I understand. Yes. That's a good idea."

The room was very quiet and Cabot felt Laura study her.

"Cabot? You're pregnant, aren't you?"

Cabot froze. How could Laura know? She only just knew herself several weeks ago.

Laura smiled, then spoke. "First, I'm a nurse, second I'm Navajo. The nurse thinks maybe. The Navajo thinks probably. Around the middle of May," she said gently. Cabot slumped into a chair and ran her fingers distractedly through her hair, not wanting to look at Laura.

Finally, she answered, the words barely audible. "Yes. I...the baby should be due around the middle of May."

"And you don't plan to tell Nicholas?"

"Oh, Laura. Not now. Not yet. I'm only just getting used to the idea. He's got so much to think about right now. Please don't tell him. Please. I will tell him, just not yet. Oh, promise me you won't say anything, Laura?"

Laura stood. "I'll leave you to your packing. I promised to bring these cakes over as soon as they were done. The returns are probably starting to come in and I want to be there."

"Laura? Out of all this, I'm happy about you and grandfather. It makes up…a little…for Nicholas and me."

Laura moved to Cabot and stroked her hair as she held her. "Yes. And now we're to be great grandparents." She smiled. "I wonder if the baby will have this glorious red hair that I fell in love with. Thirty years ago. How remarkable that would be."

Cabot turned away and buried her face in her hands.

She patted Cabot's shoulder. "Why don't you stop over to the gym and see how it all turns out. Everyone's there. They'd love to see you again."

"Oh, no. Really, I couldn't. Nicholas doesn't want to see me anyway. He's very angry. I can't blame him. I'd just ruin his celebration."

Laura smiled. "I think he's going to win, too."

Cabot found the few things she wanted, then stopped at the painting she'd struggled with of the ruins she and Nicholas had climbed to that first night at the squaw dance in Canyon de Chelly. It leaned against a wall and she reached down, thinking she would put it in the trash bin when she left.

She held the small canvas and her mind flew back to that night. Minutes passed as she stood, lost to the emotions that assailed her then. Impulsively she decided to take the painting with her. She wrapped it in newspaper and found a piece of string to tie around it.

When she had everything, she stood briefly at the door, glancing around the room one last time. She locked the door and walked briskly down the path, not looking back. There was a raw, gusty wind blowing, and the air smelled of snow. Small pinpoint flurries touched her cheeks.

At the small rental car she opened the trunk and laid the painting carefully down, along with the tote bag she'd brought. She raised her head to close the trunk and found herself looking straight into Nicholas's eyes. His anger was palpable and she caught her breath at the force with which it struck her.

"I think you'd better go inside, Cabot." His voice was ragged. "I need to talk to you."

"No, Nicholas. I was just leaving. I have to get back to Albuquerque."

She tried to step around him, but he caught her arm.

"I'm prepared to discuss this here in the street if I have to, but I think it would be better if we do it in private."

She started to protest, but thought better of it, considering the look on his face. With dread, she retraced her steps to the apartment.

Inside she moved over behind the big armchair and turned to face him, her hands gripping the back to keep them from shaking. He stared at her a moment before he spoke.

"I understand I'm to be a father," His voice was tight with controlled anger.

She couldn't look at him and dropped her eyes to her hands.

"Laura promised me she wouldn't tell you." Cabot had begun to tremble and she wrapped her arms around herself for support.

"Did she? I doubt it." He said sarcastically. "She must have thought it was kind of important for me to know."

"Nicholas," she begged. "I didn't want to tell you just yet. You have so many things to think about right now. I didn't want to make you feel...obligated. I didn't come running back here for that."

"Why did you come back?"

She didn't want to tell him. It sounded like such an empty

gesture. But in the end, she said, "I wanted to vote for you. I had to. All I could think of was what if you lost by one vote, and it would be my fault."

"How very generous. I'm just goddammed knocked over by that. Then you could tell our child sometime, 'See that man? He's your daddy. He doesn't know it, but he is. And see, he's a Congressman, and I voted for him.'"

"That's not fair."

"Oh? It's fair we want, is it?"

"Nicholas, I'm sorry I wasn't using anything that first time. I didn't say anything. I didn't even think about it."

"Oh, my, everything is your fault tonight, isn't it? Did you forget I fucked you?"

"Don't say that ugly word. It wasn't like that."

"Getting squeamish? Wasn't that all I ever was to you? A good fuck? A good *Navajo* fuck. You always got real juiced up because of that, didn't you?"

She felt the blood drain from her face. The words were like a physical blow and she recoiled. "Nicholas, don't say those things to me," she gasped. "It wasn't like that."

His shoulders sagged and his voice was low and hoarse. "No. No. It wasn't like that." His eyes filled with tears and he turned away to hide them. "That first night..." he faltered, then went on. "That first night, you gave me everything. You held nothing back. You never did. I hadn't expected that and you will never know what that meant to me."

She winced at the pain in his voice. "I'm sorry. I don't want you to be angry. Please."

He whirled on her savagely, "How else am I supposed to feel? I feel used. I loved you and you weren't even going to have the decency to tell me about our child." His words were thick with his tears.

"Nicholas, I was going to. Please try to understand," she begged. "This is so new. I haven't been thinking very clearly."

He strode around the chair and she jumped back.

"Oh, we're back to that, are we?" He seized her upper arms and pulled her back. "And how about now? Are you thinking clearly now?"

"No. Yes. I don't know." Her teeth were chattering.

"Then start, because this is what we're going to do. You're going to marry me, you're not having a bastard. And then after the baby is born, you can do whatever the hell you want. But the child is mine, too. And I won't ever allow you to forget it. Ever."

She squeezed her eyes shut and let the tears stream down her cheeks. His hands hurt her arms where he gripped them, and his words lashed over her misery.

"All right," she whispered. She could think of nothing else to do. She had no arguments for him. "Please let me go. You're hurting me."

But instead he pulled her roughly to him and crushed her mouth under his.

The touch of his kiss was a release so powerful, a relief that washed through her so completely that she fell against him, unable to support her own weight. She felt herself picked up and carried, felt the bed absorb her as he undressed her. She took him into herself when he came to her and it was not lovemaking, but a possession, each of the other. An outpouring of love and anguish and passion. They both wept, tears wrenched from the agony of the last days.

He held her cradled against his shoulder, his fingers toying with her hair.

"I think I missed this the most, the way your hair winds around my fingers." He brought a curl up to his mouth and pressed it to his lips. "You have very affectionate hair."

"Nicholas?" His chest was damp under her cheek. She pulled the sheet up so he wouldn't be cold. Then remembered that he never got cold.

"Yes?"

"What did you mean, about I could do whatever I wanted after the baby comes?"

"Forget everything I said tonight. I was half-crazy. I wanted to hurt you. I wanted to hurt you as bad as I was hurting." He tipped her face up. "Lily, don't ever leave me again. I couldn't survive that hell a second time."

"I was so wrong. I knew that in Boston. After you left. And then I was afraid if I came back, you'd think it was only because I was pregnant. I hated it that you'd think that."

"But you did come back." He smiled. "Did you really come back to vote for me?"

"Yes. And now I think, what if I hadn't run into Laura? What if you hadn't come when you did? A minute later and I would have been gone. And what if you'd been too angry to kiss me?"

He smiled down at her. "Always did just fall apart when I kissed you."

"I think when you kissed me the first time, at your house when I was leaving. Everything was just inevitable. Then I think, no...it was when you came to see me that night and we walked and you told me about the stars. Or was it the squaw dance, when I got a little mad that you thought I was like your horse? Or when you rescued me? Or when I fixed your shoulder at the rodeo? Then I think it all probably started the first time I saw you at the hospital when I'd just got here."

"Yeah. I guess I knew it, too."

"What will Russell and Pete say?"

"Well, for starters, Pete's going to marry us."

She raised up on an elbow, astonished. "He is?"

"Unless you don't want a Navajo wedding. I'll do anything you want."

A dreamy look crossed her face and she curled against

him. "I never thought about it, but yes, it would be lovely. Perfect. When should we do it?"

"I was thinking under the circumstances, right away."

"I don't know what to do. I've never even been to a Navajo wedding."

"You don't have to do anything. With the women in my family, you'll be married before you know what happened."

"I'm supposed to start Johns Hopkins on the 16th," she said, worried about what he'd say.

"No reason you can't. I don't know how this election is going, but why don't we just go ahead and get a place in Baltimore. If I don't win, I'll go with a law firm there, or Washington. We won't be apart."

"I already have a place. I've got it all ready to move into. Will it be hard to find a job?"

"For me? Nah. Not likely. Law firms salivate over Indians. It's very 'in' to be a Native American." He rumbled with amusement. "And with me they get a smart lawyer as well as an Indian. I'm a real find affirmative-action-wise."

"Nicholas? What about Karen Baghalani? Will she be angry with you?"

"Karen? She and Bobby Becenti got married last week. You still jealous?"

She snuggled against him. "Well, of course not, if she's not competition anymore."

"Cabot, you'll never have any reason to be jealous."

"You call me Cabot when you're talking to me and Lily when you're making love to me."

"I know you want to be called Cabot, but it's hard for me."

"Why hard?"

"It's my name, too."

"Your name?"

"Well, yes. At least it sounds like that. It's my war name

my father gave me when I was born. All Navajo boys have secret war names. They're strong medicine. Very few people are ever told what they are. That weakens their power. I think my father and Pete Price are the only ones who know mine. It's Kaab't." He spelled it the way he'd been told.

"Go on. This is amazing. I'm getting all kinds of vibes about this."

"Let's do some more vibes."

She swatted him. "Later."

"Okay, okay. He was my great, great, great grandfather—a famous headman in the 19th century. We never really had chiefs. Just lots of heads of clans. He was the oldest of seven children of a Daago and a medicine man, Chilhajiin. Kaab't was a great negotiator and got our reservation back. There's no mention in the history how he got his name. There're a couple of pictures of him in the museum in Window Rock." He took her chin. "Now you know how much I love you. I've given you my secret name. You have power over me now."

"What does Kaab't mean?" She was moved that he told her.

"Nothing. It isn't a Navajo word. No one knows where it came from."

"Maybe they spelled it wrong," she mused. "Maybe there was a Cabot way back in your family," she teased. "Except none of the men in my family ever went west of Philadelphia, I don't think, until my grandfather came out here. Too bad. Wouldn't it be fun if you were a Massachusetts Cabot." She giggled. "God, would the Cabots and the Chases be surprised. We'd be related." She tickled him. "Nicholas Nakai and his Cabot Chase squaw."

He grabbed her and rolled on top of her. "I think you need some more of those vibes now, squaw."

There was a sound of voices and the door to the apartment opened. The clamor got louder and then the bedroom began filling with a cheering, excited crowd. Jane Manyfarms was there, Marcus Yazzie, Nicholas's mother and father. The hospital staff. Jim Shackleford. Shirley Kee. A sea of faces. Laura. Nicholas's sisters.

Cabot yanked the covers under her chin, astonished at this intrusion.

"Get up, you two," her grandfather shouted. "Nicholas has won! Get dressed. There's celebration and you have to be there. It's pandemonium over there at the gym."

Cabot gasped, then, the sheet forgotten, threw her arms around Nicholas.

He hugged her, then began shaking hands that were thrust at him, making high fives, kissing his sisters. People shook her hand, too.

Cabot suddenly realized where she was—naked, in bed with a naked Nicholas, with a swarm of smiling people offering their congratulations and frankly admiring her breasts.

"Oh, my God! How embarrassing!" She dived under the covers. "Nicholas, tell them we'll be there in a minute." Her muffled voice brought another round of cheers. "Grandfather, go away!" she begged. "Please."

"We're going. Get dressed, my dear. We'll be waiting for you over at the gym."

Nicholas shook a few more hands, then urged the crowd out with promises that they'd hurry.

When the last well wisher had gone, he reached down and pulled her out.

"Oh, Nicholas. How will I ever look at people? I'm simply so humiliated, sitting right up here with both of us stark naked with my boobs hanging out in front of everybody. And it was obvious what we were doing. I simply can't go over there."

"Here I am, I've just won the election to the Congress of the United States of America and you're worried about what people will think about your tits. They'll think they're beautiful and I'm damn lucky is what they'll think. And what else would we be doing? We're in bed. You got to start thinking like a Navajo. It is no big deal."

"Jim Shackleford isn't a Navajo," she said glumly. "He loved it."

He laughed and grabbed her, then rolled on top of her.

She felt the laughter bubble up from her stomach. "Oh, Nicholas. I really am thrilled for you. For us. I just hope there wasn't a photographer in the crowd and we'll be plastered all over the morning papers."

He nuzzled her ear. "Now, to get back to where we were. How about a constituent having a quickie with her Congressman? All that burrowing around you were doing down there got me all stirred up again."

She ran her hands down his back, kissed his chest and purred, "You'll be a fine Congressman, being so thoughtful about putting your constituents needs first...and everything...oh."

Chapter Thirty-Seven

November 9, 1992

The nine women filled the living room of Cabot's apartment with their chatter. Cabot sat on a kitchen stool while Hattie Nakai, Nicholas's sister, wove strands of blue turquoise and white shell through her hair. They had already done Mariella, who had eagerly taken to Navajo dress and was now resplendent in the traditional velvet, albeit with much added fringe and beading, along with a turquoise mine of silver and turquoise jewelry.

"Your hair is fun to work with, Cabot, once you get the hang of it. It holds the beads better than straight hair." Hattie anchored a white shell. "I'd love to paint you sometime. Your hair's such a dynamite color and you've got great bones." The young woman held up a hand mirror for Cabot to see.

"I'll never be able to do this," Cabot said, admiring Hattie's handiwork. "I can't do hair. All I was ever able to do with my own was wash it and try to get a comb through it. I'd kill for your gorgeous straight hair."

Hattie laughed. "We always want what we don't have. C'mon. We're all dying to see you in the dress."

Cabot slid off the stool as Annie Nakai shook out the white deerskin dress that she'd worked night and day to sew and paint with an elaborate red, gray and black border. At first they'd tried to find a wedding dress to borrow, since time was so short, but Cabot was too tall, so Annie had volunteered to make it, along with matching leggings and moccasins. Natalie, the one sister who lived on the reservation, had worked the silver beading on those.

The fine leather was buttery soft, silky on the inside as it slipped over Cabot's head, down her body, and settled like a sigh around her shoulders. She shivered with the sensuality of it, skin against skin. The women had assured her with smiles that bras and panties weren't worn under Navajo wedding dresses.

Cabot laughed at that. It really was a sexy feeling without the undies. Nicholas would love it. "It's really a work of art, Annie and Natalie. How can I ever thank you? I don't know how you ever got it finished in time."

Annie smiled, pleased, her dark eyes flashing, so much like her brother's. "It's pretty good, I admit, though it's not strictly a Navajo dress. I did a lot of interpreting. Threw in some Apache and Zuni. I want to enter it in the big craft show at Santa Fe this summer, if that's okay with you."

"This'll go into the Smithsonian someday," Jane Manyfarms announced. "They always get wedding dresses from the Presidents' wives."

Cabot hugged her. The women had confidently vowed that Nicholas would be President someday, and she loved their dreams for him. But, why not, really? In twenty years, Nicholas would only be 52. Maybe in twenty years the country would be ready for a Native American president.

The women had also not concealed from her their reasons for so strongly supporting his relationship with her. She was white, beautiful, highly educated, polished. Her family had connections to an establishment that was closed to them. She would help Nicholas be noticed. They were a physically beautiful couple. The media would love them.

Cabot was taken aback by their candor, then pleased by it. They trusted her. They also made it clear that she was also extremely lucky herself, that the advantages to the union were not at all one-sided.

She began to wonder that Nicholas had turned out so well, so levelheaded, considering this coterie of adoring females that thought he was so extraordinary. She thought of her own childhood, where, with the exception of her grandfather's encouragement, her own self-worth had been manufactured, piecemeal, from a solitary, rock-hard core of determination. She had had to prove herself to herself a thousand times before she truly believed she could be whatever she wanted to be.

But it was all right now. She smiled at her mother, fussing over her along with the Navajo women. Somehow she never dreamed that her mother would be at her wedding, twittering and fluttering, like any other mother of the bride.

Had Cabot W.W. Chase any idea what he'd begun? She had found a rapprochement with her parents, a man she loved without reservation, a direction to her life, and the promise of a child. A lot had happened in half a year. It hadn't taken her an entire year to find the heart her grandfather had hoped she would find here. In truth, she'd found it rather quickly. She hoped that would pacify him, since she hadn't fulfilled his conditions. But then, it wasn't the timetable that had concerned him, she imagined. All in all, he had gotten a lot more than he'd bargained for.

Cabot put on all her silver and turquoise jewelry—the ketoh, the big squash blossom necklace, the concha belt, and several rings.

Agnes, Nicholas's mother, held out a pair of long silver earrings, set with an unusually deep blue turquoise. "These belonged to Horseman's mother, Nicholas's other grandmother. I thought you might like to wear them—something old, something borrowed, and something blue. Isn't that it?"

Cabot was delighted. "Yes. Yes it is, and these are perfect. What a lovely thought."

The group took her into the bedroom where there was a full-length mirror. Cabot stood for a long moment, gazing at herself dressed as a Navajo bride. The Indian woman stood reflected with her, smiling, pleased with their work.

"I like the way I look," she smiled back. "Not exactly Navajo, but not exactly 'not' either."

Cabot drove with Jane Manyfarms and Agnes in Jane's pickup to Nicholas's house where the wedding would be. The bride was customarily married in her mother's house, and they had seriously considered bringing the yurt over from Sedona, but eventually decided it would be too small. And Nicholas's house had already been blessed.

When Jane parked amid the various vehicles outside, Cabot's mouth suddenly became dry and she could scarcely make herself get out of the truck. When Jane and Agnes saw her stricken look, they each took one of her elbows and guided her up the path to the house.

"Only natural to get skittish. It's a big step. Once things get going, you'll be all right. Just remember to do what we told you. Nobody expects you to know everything." Jane chuckled. "Nobody expects you to know anything."

"I don't," Cabot croaked. "I can't remember a word you said."

Her father, resplendent in blue velvet and masses of silver, met her at the door and took her hand, which was now like ice. Inside, the big central fireplace was lit. Nicholas sat cross-legged on the northwest side, along with Pete Price, her grandfather, Russell Wauneka, and Horseman Nakai, Nicholas's father.

Cabot saw Nicholas catch his breath when he saw her, and she smiled nervously as her father seated her next to him. She glanced around at the crowd, some familiar faces, some not. An air of unreality swept over her. I'm not in a panic, she tried to tell herself. It's just that it's so strange. Her eyes flew to Nicholas. He winked. It was okay.

Jane handed Nicholas a basket of corn porridge and pointed to a specific place in the design made on the surface, to the door on the east side of the hogan-like house. Russell took a handful of white corn pollen and made a cross, then a circle around the rim to signify long life. He then took a handful of yellow corn pollen and did the same. White for male, yellow for female.

The headman then turned the design to Cabot and Nicholas. Pete Price held a bowl of water to them and they washed each other's hands. Nicholas's touch was a final reassurance to Cabot, his hands strong and gentle as he held her eyes with his own. He knew she had dreaded this meeting with Pete Price and Russell, but the men's faces were reverent, absorbed in the ritual of the ceremony. She could detect no animosity to her at all.

Nicholas had told her when Pete and Russell realized the inevitable, they accepted it calmly. What was done was done. Pete would marry them, with joy that Nicholas and Cabot would have a Navajo ceremony. Apparently, she thought, it was true.

Nicholas took a pinch of porridge from the bowl in front

of him, first from the circle to the east, then bits from the south, west, and north. Cabot followed the gesture each time. That was what the ritual meant—that she would follow him in all things. She glanced at Nicholas. The corners of his mouth twitched in a smile. She had complained loudly about that.

When they had done this, the basket was passed among the friends and relatives jammed into Nicholas's house. Marcus and Emerson Yazzie were there with their families, little Ason recovered and smiling. The hospital staff that wasn't on duty had all come, Karen and Bobby Becenti, Clah Chischillage who'd boarded Niyol. Laura, Agnes, and all the sisters and their families. Jim Shackleford and the election committee had come, along with photographers from *People* magazine and the *Arizona Republic,* whom Nicholas had warned to stay out of the way. Shirley Kee had her own staff photographer in tow. There were a lot of people that Cabot didn't know, but recognized as patients and relatives. Invitations were not sent to Navajo weddings. If one felt a connection to the couple, of any kind, one attended the happy occasion.

Emerson Yazzie scooped the last of the porridge from the basket and a cheer went up. That brought good luck. He ceremoniously presented the now-empty basket to Mariella, who accepted the honor with a great swishing of fringe and jingling silver and turquoise bangles. Cabot suppressed a smile. Her mother's words of the other night might never have been spoken. Mariella was once again her dreamy, theatrical, and now Navajo, self.

Then the speeches began. It seemed that everybody there had something, usually very long-winded, to say. The elders in particular found it necessary to outline an entire code of marriage behavior, a lot of it sexual behavior, necessary for a happy and fruitful marriage. Especially fruitful.

Cabot blushed furiously over and over at the carefully described specifics. She glanced edgily at Nicholas periodically, but he would grin at her, then assume a solemn and innocent expression. She was ready to kill him. He'd never even hinted at this outpouring of sexual direction. She figured that what she did with her mouth and her hands and her various orifices to please him was strictly her business and vice versa. The crowd, however, got a big bang out of it all, particularly watching her discomfiture and fiery cheeks.

Finally a drum began, and songs and chants of the Blessingway began to fill the hogan. Pete Price laid out the contents of his medicine bundle, the most important of which was the pouch that carried bits of soil from the four sacred mountains that marked the boundaries of Dinetah. There was a flint crystal and a bag of corn pollen, and two talking prayer sticks. A turquoise bead indicated the male stick, and a white shell indicated the female. The songs and sand paintings of the Blessingway ritual centered around the emergence of the Navajo into this world, Changing Woman, and fertility. It offered the Navajo assistance in every aspect of his life; identified him or her with the inner forms of earth itself and pointed to a long and joyous experience of living.

Nicholas translated the songs for her. Pete sang of the earth spirit, who was Changing Woman: Of the lovely earth and the spirit within, the strengths and thoughts of the earth. All that belonged to the earth, all that surrounded the earth, all the voices, all the sacred songs of the earth belonged to Changing Woman. And all was beautiful indeed.

After the chants and prayers of benediction, the crowd spilled outdoors and the feasting began. Roasting pits had been dug out of the frozen ground and had been cooking all day. The meat was being uncovered and served, along with corn, tortillas, and beans. The air was frosty but clear. A bright peach three-quarter moon rose over the Chuska Mountains and its light washed the high country meadow behind Nicholas's house where a great bonfire warmed the wedding guests.

As the night drifted toward morning, a sparkling frost coated the meadow's grass and turned the fields to silver.

Finally the guests began to drift away. The bride's and groom's families were the last to go, and Cabot hugged her mother when she whispered that she was awfully happy Cabot had not heeded her advice.

"I never did know the right things to say to you, Lily. Fortunately you knew to ignore me most of the time. But I told you the wrong thing for the right reasons this time. I'm happy you came back to Nicholas."

"It was just a different situation, Mother."

"Are you going to have a honeymoon?"

"Oh, sort of. We're going to spend a few days at the house on Marblehead. I'm going to walk Nicholas up and down the Atlantic, in a nor'easter, I hope. He thinks he never gets cold. He knows nothing about New England winters. Then we'll go down to Baltimore. He's got a lot of orientation programs in Washington for new Congressmen. There'll be some politicking to do for committee assignments. Then they'll assign him an office and he'll start putting a staff together. I'll be at the hospital, plus getting a room and things ready for the baby. We're both going to be terribly busy."

"Are you going to be all right, working so hard with the baby coming?"

"I feel marvelous. I've never had so much energy. I'd go crazy if I didn't have my residency to do. I'll work as long as I can, then we'll go from there. I'll probably stay home a month or so after the baby comes, then we'll have to find a nanny."

Her mother asked shyly, "You'll let me come from time to time, won't you, Lily? I'd like to try to be a better grandmother than I was a mother. And your father is bursting with pride at the thought of being a grandfather. Knows it will be a boy."

Cabot felt a lump in her throat as she kissed her mother. "Come whenever you like. Nicholas adores you both. He thinks you're very Indian."

Her mother looked so pleased Cabot kissed her again.

When they were finally alone, Cabot collapsed on the couch. "Navajo weddings are exhausting! I'll try not to sleep for a week."

He came over and held her. "I never had any idea I would get so choked up over everything. When you came across the room to me in that goddam gorgeous dress, I wanted to cry and I wanted to cry at everything after that."

"Well, there were some things I didn't want to cry at," she grumbled. "My God. Half that stuff they made speeches about was absolutely pornographic. You might have warned me."

"I forgot." He grinned.

"I'll bet. Just some speeches, you said. No wonder you're so sexy."

"I sort of liked it when Pete told you, you ought to put my..."

She flopped a big Navajo pillow on his head. "I've already done that, several times."

"Why, so you have. Perhaps you'd like to do it again." He nuzzled her breasts under the soft deerskin.

"Your sisters told me I couldn't wear anything under my wedding dress."

His voice was muffled. "I love my sisters."

"Promise you'll be careful with my wedding dress. It's going to be in the Smithsonian."

Chapter Thirty-Eight

November 12, 1992, Marblehead, Massachusetts

"It isn't that I'm not cold, Cabot. You miss the point. Of course it's cold. You just rise above it. Go to another plane of consciousness, I guess."

"So you're on another plane. I wish you'd come back down here with me." She gritted her teeth at the icy blast that went straight to her bones as they leaned into the wind that swept down the deserted beach as a choppy tide, already high with the full moon, foamed toward their feet. Leaden clouds discharged a misty sleet that stung their cheeks. She'd gotten her nor'easter, but Nicholas was unimpressed.

"You've got to understand when people spend a lot of their time outside in every kind of weather, by necessity, without really adequate heating inside, it's simply a matter of survival. Close to the fire it's hot. Away from the fire it's cold. Sometimes your face is roasting and your ass is freezing. When we were kids, we'd take long runs in the winter, a lot of times in snow. We didn't wear anything. It was to make us tough."

"You ran naked? Through the snow?"

"Sure. We all did it."

"Nicholas, the penis is very sensitive to frostbite."

"Oh, we had a kind of pouch for that. But only when it was *really* cold."

"Nevertheless. It's a wonder you didn't freeze yours off."

He grinned. "Under the circumstances, it doesn't appear that mine suffered any damage. There really is a lot to that business of mind over matter. The Navajo religion is full of it. Many of the most holy chantways are held in winter. They last all night for nine nights, and the nights are long. Man, are they long. The rituals are called *Yeibichais*. The *Yeis* are Holy People. The ceremonies are a total experience, and the cold is part of it. It's a powerful physical presence and it focuses you inward."

"Yes, I think I can see that."

"Western medicine treats a specific thing. You know that. We treat the whole person. It's a very complex system of healing."

"Yes, my grandfather said much the same thing. I think it was a good thing for me to learn about, be exposed to. I wasn't really out there long enough. Then I got tangled up with you and never thought about another thing."

"Well, now that's not all bad. Why don't we go back to the house and talk about it some more? Perhaps I can demonstrate that I didn't suffer unduly from frostbite damage to my anatomy."

"I think we can say your previous demonstrations have been convincing. I haven't been vertical more than a few hours since I married you."

"We're bonding."

"We're what?"

"Bonding. I read about it one of your grandfather's medical magazines. 'Frequent intercourse by the honeymoon couple is a necessary step in the marriage bonding process.'"

She stopped and looked at him skeptically. "You're making that up."

"I know. Sounds good, though, don't you think?"

"Terribly scientific. I'll race you back. I'm freezing."

"Think about what we're going to do. Some active bonding. That'll warm you up. As a matter of fact, I could take my jacket off, it's so balmy out here."

"Liar."

"We'll see who's a liar." He stopped and drew a line in the sand. "All right. Get set. Go!"

She was faster than he expected, but even so, he slowed slightly so she moved ahead. He admired the flying red hair and the lush buttocks as she sprinted through the hard, half frozen sand.

He'd been uneasy about coming to the big house on Marblehead. How was he, for instance, going to deal with a butler, for God's sake? Cabot insisted he was a houseman, and for some subtle reason, this was supposed to make a difference. But it didn't matter what you called servants, Jeffrey was a butler to him.

He was a nice gentleman, though, and Nicholas hadn't felt uncomfortable at all. The cook he rarely saw, the maid who did the cleaning ignored him and Nicholas understood that she racially disapproved of him. He saw some gardeners from a distance, mostly raking the mountains of red and gold maple and oak leaves that carpeted the grounds as winter approached. A lot of the kids he'd gone to high school with in Phoenix had had household and garden help, but nothing like a staff. Well, he'd be running into this in Washington. Good he'd had a chance to get some practice.

It had been an idyllic honeymoon, and now he was regretting a little that they would have to leave, as much as he was exhilarated at the thought of going to Washington. It was like he had arrived at the foot of the mountain. He was bursting to begin the climb but was fully aware of the hazards ahead.

Nicholas was down in the computer room working on resumes that he would need when he got to Washington. Cabot wandered up to the attic of the big house. She'd loved to explore it when she was growing up, with its old trunks, dusty antiques, armoires of old clothes from other eras, and stacks and stacks of books, moved up here as shelves downstairs overflowed. She liked the boxes of old letters best, from ages when people wrote to one another, long epistles that described their daily lives. A lot of the letters were just day-to-day stuff, but there were many love letters, too, and it was always wonderful to run across these, ardent words that ached with longing.

There were few letters about trips taken. Her ancestors didn't seem to move about much. Then, in eras where physical contact between lovers was only after marriage, there was much tedious correspondence about the ordinary minutiae of quiet lives. Cabot and Chase doctors stretched back into the misty past, graduates of Harvard Medical School after it opened, educated in England before that. Their correspondence was rarely lively. Cabot laughed to herself as she rummaged through another musty box. If she hadn't done the exciting thing of going west and marrying a Navajo, would her correspondence be any less stuffy?

She picked through a stack of small notes and invitations

to a William Cabot. There were several packets of letters and she untied the dusty rose ribbon that held one. She smiled. Letters from a lady friend. Her mind went back to the young woman as she followed the prim romance of William Cabot and Catherine Clement. Then there was a wedding invitation, and the correspondence tapered off dramatically. There were a couple of letters when William went down to New York to wrap up some sort of business after the marriage, but then that was all.

Cabot idly picked up another packet, absently hoping Nicholas was about through in the computer room.

The new batch was apparently from William's brother who had left home to join the army. Cabot began to get interested. Then letters that described this Nathaniel Cabot's arrangement to get to his new posting...Cabot turned the page...to Fort Defiance in the New Mexican Territories.

She let out a delighted shriek and jumped up, careful not to clutch the fragile letter in her hand while she tore down the attic steps two at a time.

"Nicholas! Nicholas! Guess what!"

Nicholas shot to the door of the computer room, then sagged against the jamb in relief when he saw that she was all right.

"My God, Cabot. You scared the hell out of me. I thought you'd fallen."

"No, no," she said impatiently. "I've found an ancestor who was in Fort Defiance. Listen."

Cabot read the letter with excitement, then dragged Nicholas up the stairs to go over the next few letters. Nathaniel Cabot described his trip west, then gave a detailed account of the fort, then under construction.

June 15, 1852

Dear William,

As much as I deplore the thought of you making the journey to this back of the beyond, I wish you could experience this place where your brother will be spending his next days. It's a raw place, still in the process of being built, though my quarters are finished and commodious enough. I have a bed, a chest, a chair, and a kerosene lamp, so you see, I have all I need. Meals are in common with the other officers. I daresay you would find the food very plain, but there is plenty enough and it will sustain me.

I have made headway in setting up my hospital, though the army calls it an infirmary. Considering I have only been here a day, I am quite pleased with my progress. My predecessor absconded with most of the supplies, but I was able to bring enough from St. Louis to stock my pharmacy.

The country is arid and harsh, with few trees, except along the river. A pitiless glare from the constant sun will take some getting used to and it is very hot for a New Englander accustomed to cooler climes, though I understand the winters can be severe.

The fort lies on flat ground. It is virtually unprotected, but I am assured that no attacks are expected. We will have to chastise the Navajo and Apache for they are very prone to raiding and stealing, but they don't attack frontally, or so I am told. I suspect this is an optimistic appraisal, for they seem very fierce.

I was somewhat shaken to learn that Indian women serve the men as laundresses, but in actuality they are slaves, since they are purchased from disreputable men who have stolen them from their flocks, and they are forbidden to leave. I assure you I shall not fall into this arrangement however, though some of the women are quite comely.

This evening takes me to a neighboring rancheria, guest of Don Fernando and Dona Eugenia Chavez. It will be my first experience with Mexicans. I will try to remember everything I see to share with you.

The mail packet is leaving, so I will close. Send my affections to Mother and Father. I pray that his disappointment in me and the manner in which I chose to pursue my fortune will ease in time.

I miss you all, but truly think I can find my place here. My regards to Kitty. I am sorry I will miss your wedding. You must write and tell me all.

Your loving brother, Nathaniel Cabot

"This is such a sweet letter, don't you think, Nicholas? He misses his brother and he's so far away." Cabot glanced over the letter. "Comely. Don't you love it! Am I comely, Nicholas?"

"As comely as they come."

"The letter closes with promises that he'll write again. But there aren't any more letters. I wonder why. I wish I knew who this particular Cabot was."

"Maybe your grandfather would know."

"Wait a minute. There are family bibles down in the library. Come on. I can remember family trees in front of some of them."

They found it in the second one, a big leather-bound book that looked well used. The cream parchment genealogy leaf in the front of the book began with the year 1810.

"This one ends with grandfather. Nobody ever put Daddy or Mother or me in it. Do you think I should?"

"Sure, since you're about to have issue yourself."

"Issue. It's a baby. You sound like a lawyer."

"I wasn't thinking," he said dryly.

"Look, here's Nathaniel and William, sons of John and Caroline Cabot. Nathaniel was born September 1st, 1828, dies...oh, no. He died the day after that last letter he sent. June 15, 1852. I wonder what happened."

"He probably ran into an ancestor of mine," Nicholas said pleasantly. "While he was out chastising."

"I won't believe that. There's got to be some marvelous reason you're called Kaab't, and I just know it's got to do with a beautiful Indian girl he loved. Maybe he bought a Navajo girl after all and just didn't want to tell his brother. That wouldn't have been something you admitted to your family back then."

"I wouldn't think you would want to admit that to your family today."

"Oh, Nicholas. Is this bothering you? I think he sounded very sweet. Not likely to exploit Indians. He was a doctor, after all."

"You're determined to romanticize this. Look, Cabot. We'll never know. We Navajo didn't keep written records until recently. The old singers who remembered genealogies are long gone."

"You *are* named after Nathaniel Cabot. Or the chief who was named after him. I know it. I have special vibrations. Pregnant women have extraordinary powers."

"If you say so." He pulled her to him and hugged her. "Pregnant women should be humored when they have wild fantasies about beautiful Indian maidens and handsome army doctors."

She made a face at him and bent over the Bible again. "Nathaniel never had any children according to this, but William and Kitty did. They had a daughter, Sara. Let's see."

Cabot studied the musty page and ran her finger down the generations.

She continued studying the family tree. "Stop laughing at me, Nicholas. I know I'm on to something."

He put his arms around her, nuzzling her neck. "I love my intense, romantic red-haired pregnant wife when she has wild fantasies…"

She looked around and made a face at him. "Don't be so sure it's all fantasy. Just look at these dates."

"…who is so sure that her new husband is, for God's sake, a relative."

She kissed him and went back to the bible. "Let's see…a generation is roughly twenty years." She ran her fingers down through the family tree. "Nathaniel died in 1864. Brother William married his Kitty that same year…" Cabot raised her head triumphantly. "William Cabot was my great, great, great, grandfather. Nathaniel was my great, great, great, whew, great uncle. If Nathaniel had a Navajo lover and they had a child called Kaab't, he could be your great, great...let's see...great grandfather." She closed her eyes and hugged herself. "It just gives me a chill. I think we're kissing cousins." She kissed Nicholas. "There isn't any incest going on here, is there? How incredibly erotic. Do you think we're illegal?"

"Well, it's too late to do anything about it now. The issue has already been decided."

"I am having our baby, not an 'issue'. Your puns are terrible."

Chapter Thirty-Nine

TÁÁ' NÁAZNILÍ' TÁDIIN' DÓÓ B'AA TSEEBII

August 1852

The ride with Chilhajin to Daago's familiar valley took twelve days. He stopped often for her to rest and made camp early in the evenings. He dressed her arm, pleased when her hand returned to almost its normal size. But in the aftermath of the snakebite, she was weak and debilitated. Chilhajin had wanted to find another Navajo camp, but Daago became so agitated at not continuing, so distraught at not going home, that he decided to forge ahead. When they had put some distance between themselves and the fort, Chilhajin hunted and caught small animals which he roasted and fed to her, along with a variety of herbs and vegetation. Slowly her weakness ebbed.

While she and Chilhajin were on the long trail back to

the Todachiinii, she told him everything that had happened to her in the terrible nightmare of her captivity. He had held her in front of him on the spotted horse and she was grateful that she didn't have to look into his eyes as he questioned her. Haltingly she described her terror, from seeing the shepherd dog's throat slit, to being bound to the horse. How the Ute had tried to mount her and the ugly white man had shot him. She told of her humiliation with the Mexican foreman, the lewd eyes of Don Fernando as he violated her with his eyes. The contempt the white men and the Mexicans had felt for her had been the hardest to bear she told him. She could feel Chilhajin's body tense with outrage.

She wondered if he would be jealous when she described the man with the beautiful red hair and the strangely-colored eyes, who was different from the others, the man they called Kaab't, who she had lain with before she killed him. But Chilhajin had only been grateful that the man Kaab't had been kind and treated her gently. He regretted that Daago had had to kill him, as well as the sentry who guarded the horses.

He told he she must not dwell on these necessities, but it would be expected there would be retaliation of some kind on the tribe for the killings, but that was nothing new. They would be vigilant. He would renew his prayers that this hateful scourge would leave Dinetah, the land of the Navajo, and they could all walk together in beauty and harmony again.

The Todachiinii, thinking Daago was lost to them forever, rejoiced when Chilhajin rode with her into their camp. The children were the first to see them and their squeals brought the adults. Chilhajin dismounted in front of Hezbah's hogan and eased Daago from the spotted horse and placed her in her mother's arms. Hezbah wept and carried her daughter into the Hogan.

"I can walk, Mother, truly I can," Daago protested,

dismayed that her mother seemed to forget Chilhajin in her joy at seeing her daughter again.

"Hush, Daago. Oh, you're so thin, you weigh nothing. Your hair has no shine." She settled her daughter on a pile of sheepskins, appalled at the ragged, foreign clothes she wore. "There is lamb stew on the fire. You must eat. Become strong again. We thought you were dead. Or a rancheria slave. When the men came back from the trading post, they tracked you, but it had rained and the trail disappeared. They found the dead Ute and circled and circled around. But it was no use. Chilhajin was beside himself. When they all came back, he prayed and sang. Then he took the root of the datura flower. When he fell asleep he had a vision. He knew he would find you."

Daago smiled as her mother rattled on, patting and arranging the bed of sheepskins and blankets, removing the torn uniform with distaste.

"We must bury these. Surely they are evil. Chezhin will arrange an Enemyway ceremony. Only then can you be cured of the infection that has befallen you."

"I want to marry as soon as possible," Daago said. "Do you still have my wedding dress? Are the preparations still ready? It seems so long ago that I was taken. Was it very long?"

"Twenty three days." Hezbah bowed her head and thanked the Holy Ones for this blessed return of her daughter. "Everything can be readied quickly enough. After the curing ceremony and you are restored, the wedding can take place. Your hogan has been finished. Chilhajin insisted it be done while he was gone. Our family is very beholden to Chilhajin. Already our clan looks to him to follow your father as leader. With your marriage our ties to the Deeschiinii clan will be stronger than ever. They helped us look for you as if you were already married to Chilhajin. It is a strong alliance between our two clans."

August 1852

After the four-day isolation period following her purification, plans for the wedding increased in tempo. Daago began to suspect she was pregnant. She was disappointed that her first child would not be Chilhajin's, but all children were blessings and she knew that they would both rejoice in the infant.

It was sunset when Daago was taken to the hogan of her aunt. Her mother and female relatives dressed her in the soft deerskin dress and wove shells and yarn through her hair. White deerskin moccasins and leggings matched the dress. The women chattered and admired their handiwork, then quieted and solemnly led Daago to her mother's hogan.

Daago, suddenly nervous, though she had awaited this day eagerly, stepped into the familiar hogan. Chilhajin sat on the northwest side in front of a small fire. He smiled with encouragement as she came in, escorted by Manases, who led her to Chilhajin's side.

Chezhin had set out the contents of his medicine bundle: pieces of wood from lightning-struck trees, a crystal, prayer sticks, a bag of corn pollen. And the most important part of the bundle: four pouches made from the skin of an unwounded deer, containing soil from the four sacred mountains of Dinetah. One of the prayer sticks, that Chilhajin would hold, was marked with a turquoise signifying its maleness. The female stick showed a white shell for its femaleness.

Daago sat beside Chilhajin, her knees to one side, her feet tucked under. Her aunt handed Manases a basket of corn porridge and directed a specific point in the basket's design toward the door, to the east. From a pouch Manases took a handful of corn pollen and made a cross, then a circle. He turned the design toward Daago and Chilhajin. They washed each other's hands in a bowl of water, moved at this ceremonial touching of each other. Chilhajin rubbed the still-tender scar on Daago's hand. He then took a pinch of porridge from the circle to the east, then bits from the south, west and north. Daago followed each time. The basket passed from friends and relatives jammed into the sweltering hogan, who repeated Chilhajin's and Daago's actions until the basket of porridge was gone.

A gentle rivalry ensued to see who would take the last mouthful. Daago's Uncle Chii smiled and scooped an extra large portion to take the prize. Laughing he presented the basket to Chilhajin's mother, pleased to be so honored by the bride's family.

Then came a series, almost endless it seemed to the bride and groom, of speeches and expostulations by the elders of the two clans on the duties and obligations of marriage. Some of their exhortations were so sexually explicit that both Daago and Chilhajiin found themselve blushing furiously as the crowd chuckled good-naturedly at their discomfiture.

A ceremonial drum began and chants and songs of the Blessingway filled the night air. The feasting began and, finally, as the first rays of the sun came over the Chuska Mountain peaks, the dawn songs were sung. The couple went outside, faced the east and breathed the dawn four times. Now they were allowed to leave for their hogan. Since they would not be living in the camp with Daago's family, Niyol and Chilhajin's black and white spotted horse were brought.

Daago and Chilhajin started down the trail, with the pink streaked sky in front of them, to their new home.

Chapter Forty

TÁÁ' NÁAZNILÍ' TÁDIIN DÓÓ B'AA NÁHÁST ÉII'

March, 1853

A raw wind that promised snow gusted through the door as Chilhajin sprinkled a layer of warmed sand over the hogan floor and watched anxiously as Hezbah and her mother and sister led Daago to the door. He tested the woven red cloth that had been suspended from the roof, then spread a blanket of sheepskins while the women gave her an herbal decoction to drink.

Daago smiled encouragingly at her distraught husband and knelt on the sheepskins. Chilhajin sprinkled the red cloth and Daago with corn pollen and sang a song from the Blessingway ceremony, the one sung by Changing Woman when she delivered the Twin boys, Monster Slayer and Child Born of Water. He would like to have done the whole ceremony, but Daago's labor had come on too fast and he had had to hurry with other preparations. It was bad luck to make too many early arrangements.

Daago had observed all the proper taboos to ensure the health of the child: she had not watched him make any sand paintings, watched an eclipse of the moon, or broken any pots. She had not woven any blankets upside down on the loom. She had not broken any weaving tools. He felt positive she had not violated any of the other taboos.

Chilhajin helped her undo her hair. It poured through his fingers as it fell around her shoulders. He did the same with his own. If her labor were protracted, all of the clan would wear their hair loose and all the horses and tied animals in proximity of the birthing would be let free.

He held her face in his hands, but her eyes were turned inward.

She handed him her jewelry: the symbolic gesture a Navajo woman's last will and testament. Childbirth was such a threat to her life, Daago willed her property to her husband.

Daago tensed and a contraction bent her body double. The women shooed Chilhajin out the door, clucking at his nervousness.

On her knees, Daago clutched the red cloth loop while the midwives encouraged her to push. Her aunt rubbed her heavy abdomen with corn pollen and massaged her gently, telling her to stretch as high as possible on the loop while the other midwives urged her to greater effort. She was sweating profusely and could feel the baby moving along the birth canal at every painful contraction. She swallowed her groans. A medicine man's wife should set an example.

After five hours of intense labor, the final pains approached and her aunt moved in front of Daago to catch the baby. The women glanced at each other briefly when the tiny boy was expelled, then her aunt cut the umbilical cord with a flint knife. She shook the infant gently and rubbed his chest until he wailed and began to breathe normally. The women took him and wrapped him in sheepskin and set him by the fire, careful to arrange the soft wool around his head so the skull would keep its shape.

Hezbah tied a stone around the end of the cord still attached to the placenta. A yucca had been roasting during the last contractions and was now peeled. Hezbah rubbed the slippery juices of the plant over her right hand. When the placenta was not expelled on its own, she inserted her hand in the birth canal and pulled it forth. It was handed out the door to the delighted Chilhajin, who hurried to bury it in a specially prepared place, where he had built a fire to thaw the ground, frozen hard by the long winter. The hole must be deep enough to discourage witches.

Daago's aunt was given the honor of cleaning the baby as soon as the placenta had been disposed of. The bathwater was disposed of as well, and the infant was wrapped in white cloths and laid to the left of Daago, his head pointing to the fire. Daago's aunt anointed his head with white and yellow corn pollen that had been shaken over a corn beetle, as Changing Woman had decreed long ago.

Then she began to shape the baby, pressing her thumb onto the roof of his mouth and pressing her fingers on the baby's nose so that it would be long and straight. Next she molded his arms and legs, then his tiny head. Next she fed the infant with corn pollen mixed with water, which he would have until Daago's milk came in strongly. The mother's early thin secretions were not to be trusted.

The exhausted Daago was made to lie on a bed of pine boughs and given juniper tea. All the skins and cloths used in the birthing were gathered carefully and given to Chilhajin to be buried to keep out of the hands of witches. The umbilical cord would be dried and buried in the corral so the boy would be good with horses.

The child was tucked close to Daago. He would never be more than a few feet from her until he was weaned, in about two years. Daago gazed drowsily at her firstborn. He was beautiful, with hair not truly black, but with a rich, reddish sheen accentuated by the firelight.

The women opened the door and called to Chilhajin, congratulating him as sincerely as if the child were his own.

May, 1853

Several weeks later, as Daago and Chilhajin sat on blankets in front of the fire in their hogan and played delightedly with their new son, Chilhajin turned the baby's face to him.

"His eyes are truly a beautiful color. The color of a mountain lion's. We will raise him to be a great leader," he said, then laughed. "All our sons will be great leaders.

Daago smiled. "What about our daughters?"

"They will marry great leaders and bear great leaders."

"Like I did?" She brushed his face with her fingertips, wondering why the faint scars had ever bothered her. What if Chilhajin had not persisted?

"Of course." He reached over and touched her hand.

"You must name him soon."

"Yes, I have thought of it." He took both of her hands in his own. "I want to name him Kaab't. What do you think?"

"Why, Chilhajin?"

"He is my son. I feel it in my heart. But I also know that I did not father him. The name will be all my son ever has of his sire. This boy may be the only child of the man who was gentle with you and whose life you took. It is sure the man will have no more sons. It is fitting."

Daago rested her head on his shoulder.

He touched her face. "So be it. We won't speak of it again."

Chapter Forty-One

May 15, 1993

"You know what, Nicholas? Do you remember?" Cabot gazed drowsily at the tiny mahogany-colored head that nuzzled at her breast. "It's almost a year ago that I saw you for the very first time. In the lobby of the hospital in Fort Defiance."

Nicholas held them both. He kissed her forehead.

"I remember. You knocked my socks off."

"It's absolutely amazing. You seemed so exotic to me, with your long hair and everything. Now, it isn't even quite a year and I'm in a hospital bed on the other side of the country nursing our son."

"I don't like to look at fate too closely. It scares me."

She brushed her lips against the downy fuzz. "I seem to do this rather easily. Let's have lots more."

"Well, how many do you have in mind? The manufacture I can take care of easily enough. It's the maintenance."

"I hated being an only child. Maybe four sisters for him would be nice. Like you have."

"I think I could handle that. When do we start?"

"Well, we probably should wait until we get home. One tumble on a hospital bed was enough."

Nicholas smiled as a tiny fist curled tightly around his finger. "Well, baby. What are we going to call you? You're four hours old. We shouldn't dawdle around about these things."

"We're going to call him Nathaniel Nicholas Cabot Nakai," she said dreamily.

"Had that planned all along, have you?"

"You don't mind, do you?"

"No, I don't mind. Nathaniel Nakai. Nate. I like it, though I sort of wonder if he needs four names. I got by well enough with only two."

"You have three."

"The one is private and doesn't count."

"Well, we cover a lot of ground. We can add Horseman, too, if you want. Your father is such a nice man. Would he be pleased? "

"I think my father will understand if we leave him off the list," he said.

But it would make a fine war name, Nicholas thought, when the time came.

~The End~

Please turn the page to read the Afterword and an unedited sneak preview of Virginia Nosky's next book.

AFTERWORD

Nicholas Begay, killed in World War II, died without children. Nicholas Nakai and his son are direct descendants, through his mother Agnes and his grandfather Franklin, of Daago. Daago and Captain Nathaniel Cabot were Nicholas' great, great, great, grandparents. Nathaniel's brother William's daughter Sara was Kaab'ts first cousin and Nicholas Nakai's great, great, great aunt. Daago was Lily Cabot Chase's great, great, great, great aunt. Daago and Nathaniel's son Kaab't was her cousin.

To a Certain Degree
Coming in 2008

Excerpt

The blazing Arizona sun shimmered off the pale concrete of the Scottsdale CivicCenter, making tiny rainbows in the plaza's towering fountain, center of a photoshoot now winding up. Shakira's beat throbbed from photographer Max's Street's boombox. It ricocheted around the Civic Arts complex., attracting the occasional bystander willing to linger in the oven-like August heat to gape at the photographer, assistants scrambling about with reflectors, fussing wardrobe and makeup people, but at especially at the tall, dark-haired model in the revealing black dress moving seductively in front of the fountain's glistening spray.

"Throw your head back a little more, sweets. Move your legs apart, tug that top down as much as it'll go, ha ha, without a wardrobe malfunction. We're selling seeeeduction here." The photographer cocked his head, his bright eyes appraising his dark-haired model, tucking a long, dishwater blond lock behind his ear. His diamond earrings glistened in the sun.

Iolanthe McKenna sighed and adjusted her position. "It's just a cocktail dress, Max, not an invitation for a hookup. Neiman's wants to sell this dress, not my boobs."

Max grinned and hopped around her with his camera

clicking at rapid-fire pace. "Evening clothes are sex, Io. That's what they're for. To soften up the guys." He let out a bark of a laugh. "Or I meant to say…"

"Oh, God, please don't," she said dryly, moving continuously into different flirtatious poses, moistening her lips, running her fingers through her heavy shoulder-length hair. She slanted her eyes through thick lashes and tossed her head, moving her body to the rhythms and whirrs of the camera shutter and pulsing, pounding music.

Max Street was fun to work with, she thought, and he certainly made her look good. But he had a one-track mind. He wanted his photographs to be sexy. Period. Even his dog food ads were amorous. His clients loved him. He could make a plate of spaghetti absolutely lascivious.

"Man, it's good to work with a New York pro. I could keep you busy every day, Io. Forget this school stuff. We could make a bundle. Do the studying when you're old and gray. Give me another series of fuck-me looks, please."

Iolanthe pouted and smiled enticingly into the camera. "We've been through that, Max. I'll be thirty in a year and a half…"

"Yeah, and into your most beautiful years. Baby fat's gone, the eyes are wise, you're sexually…" he interrupted.

"…*and* I promised myself at thirty I would begin the serious part of my life. I'll walk away from this with no regrets. Modeling's worked for me as a means to an end. It's paid the bills, but it's not what I want to do with my life." She reached down into the bodice of the strapless black lace dress and dabbed at a rivulet of perspiration. A trickle moved from under her hair and dribbled down her back. "I hope these shots are good. I don't want to roast again under this sun. Ugh. I'm soggy. I'm probably ruining this ruinously expensive dress."

"Just a few more, lovey. You gotta class or something?"

"At eleven, and ever-so-big-deal Dr. Byron Rossi nearly shriveled me with his annoyance the last time I ran late. He simply scorched me with a look when I tried to tiptoe into the room. He's utterly terrifying. I *can't* be late again." She checked the diamond watch she'd been given to wear with the wisp of a dress. "Oh, damn, I already am late. By the time I scrub all this stuff off my face…" She put both arms under her hair and let it spill over in glossy profusion as she flirted with the camera.

"Really, my dear, why you feel you have to frump yourself up to go to school I'll never know. You'd get straight A's if you just went the way you are now. Blow the doors off Hot Shit Byron Rossi. Why not? Maybe the big TV star is finding the action a little slow in Az. Get his mind off his Bunsen burners. Those guys blow themselves up."

She sighed, "He's a physicist, not a chemist, Max."

"His rocks, then."

"Didn't do too well in science, did you, Max. Hm?"

"Whatever. Don't move." He stopped to insert another roll of film in the camera, then continued clicking. "Good. That's great. Terrific!" He moved in for a close-up. "Y'oughta lighten up a little, Io. Life ain't supposed to be as serious as you're trying to make it…pull your hair away from those bling-y earrings more. Show them, show them! Sell it! That's it. Come with me to a party tonight. That'll loosen you up." He cackled. "Are we ever looooose, man. I gotta guy who gets me really good weed." He tipped her face at an angle. "Why you'd want to bury those eyes in some friggin' laboratory I don't get. It's a crime against humanity, that's what it is."

The photographer buzzed fussily around her, with his assistants crouching, swooping, scurrying up small step ladders to adjust silvery reflectors, another to run a brush through her hair. His foxy face glowed bright with excitement. "You've got great hair. Wanna do the Mane Chance ad series? Starts in two weeks? LuAnn Moffitt was supposed to be the image gal, but she went and got pregnant and her hair simply *died*."

"Sure, if the time's right. You know I'll do anything if the schedule fits mine. Give my agent a call with the particulars. Janice will fit it in for me if she possibly can." She licked her lips and stretched languorously, but glanced nervously at the diamond watch again.

Max continued to circle around her. "Hey! I love it. Do the impatient look at the watch again. Boyfriend is *late* and you are ready for it right *now!*"

She groaned, looked at the watch with pretty impatience for the camera. "Max, you promised me we'd be out of here by ten. The sun is burning me up. I swear I'm going to jump in that fountain in a minute, designer dress and all."

Max yelped. "That's it! That's it! Io my girl, get yourself under that fountain spray. Wet, clingy dress, wet hair, wet girl. Hot, hot, hot! We'll win the Nobel prize for a shot like that."

"You're joking, Max. This is a Dolce and Gabbana…over two thousand at least."

"Get in, get in…take the Manolos off if you want, but we're going hot to cool you off. I'll tell Neiman's you slipped and there was no point in not taking advantage. Hoo hah."

She moaned. "I can't, Max, I'm so late now."

"Wait! The watch. Give me the watch. I won't be able to bluff my way if we get those li'l diamonds wet."

This time Iolanthe wailed piteously, then unclasped the diamond watch, slipped off the strappy stiletto Manolos and waded out to the fountain spray.

"Look happy, carefree, splash, put your face up to the water, spin…ohmigod I can't stand it this is going to be so fabulous, I'm getting a boner…whirl, jump…oops, don't lose a boob....go, go, go." His camera clicked and whirred. "Hey, since you're wet, wanna get in the lake and swim along with that big swan over there, he looks kinda horny...."

As if in answer, the swan honked.

"Oh my God, Max, I'm going to scream in a minute."

"All right, all right," he muttered. "Don't go along with my artistic vision. Swan boy over there even liked the idea. You heard 'im." He tried his version of the swan. "Honk, honk."

"You sound more like a donkey, Max. And as far as the artistic vision? Ha! Your X-rated hallucinations, you mean. Get me out of here."

He grinned at her and lowered his camera. "Okay, babe. That's got it."

Iolanthe sloshed back out of the fountain. "I look like a wet cat," she grumbled, squeezing water out of her hair. Max handed her a towel. "Maybe the dress can be rescued." Then suddenly she grinned. "I admit it sure felt good. I'd love to be there when you explain to Neiman's about the picture of me frolicking in a fountain in their fabulous Dolce and Gabbana."

"They'll cream over the photos. They don't I'll get huffy and say *Vogue* does this sort of thing all the time. That always works out here in the hinterlands." He pulled the camera strap over his head. "That's a wrap. Go to your class, Einstein." He thought a moment. "Hey, maybe you could take me sometime. I concede I really do admire Rossi professionally. Those science specials are really well-done. The graphics are terrific and his photographer's just excellent. Your guy's got a gift for making all that scientific stuff look easy and fun. Plus he's a hunk."

"He's not my guy and oh, I know he's good. He just rubs me the wrong way. And vice versa. But sure, I'll let you know what he has coming up. Some of it can get pretty esoteric and dull. Other people have brought guests and he hasn't said anything. I think he enjoys as big an audience as he can get. His class is always full." She made a face. "His self-esteem is boundless. You may have to sit on the floor and annoy the Fire Marshall. Everybody at the university is just absolutely *cooing* over their famous TV star visiting professor."

"Great. I'll call your Janice about the Mane Chance job. Go do your quick-change act into Miss Mousie."

"Lipstick and blush aren't going to write my dissertation, Max."

"The very word makes my bowels congeal. We got some good stuff today. Should run in the next few weeks. I'll give you a call about the old Prescott Raceway shoot this weekend. I love the ratty dump. You had to step over horse shit and a few drunks. Extremely colorful. The shiny new track has no character. Looks like those places you get your driver's license. It'll be nice up there. Drive with us if you want. We'll stay overnight. Early morning and late afternoon light's the best."

"Great. I can study on the way up. See ya," she called over her shoulder as she disappeared through the big doors of the Scottsdale Museum of Modern Art, where she'd changed costumes in the museum's bathroom.

Jenny, Max's assistant had gathered the clothes and accessories the crew had used in the photo shoot. She eyed Iolanthe's soaking wet dress with horror, shaking it out hopefully. "I don't know what Max is going to say to the store people about that. They usually have a cow over any little thing. All I know is I don't want to be there."

Iolanthe laughed. "Max had an inspiration. See what you can do. Maybe it'll dry okay." She hurried to the bathroom vanity and began her transformation from sophisticated professional beauty to serious graduate student, moving with an economy of motion that spoke of years of quick changes in tight places.

Concentrating on her reflection in the wide mirror in the big, gray-tiled bathroom, she scrubbed away at the carefully made-up eyes, blushed cheeks and raspberry mouth. There was a hint of shadows under her eyes she noted critically. She'd better get some extra sleep before the next photo job, she fretted. Makeup wouldn't cover those dark circles if they got any worse. Oh, don't let there be a test in Rossi's class Friday she begged the exam gods. Why did so many hard classes fall in this semester? She felt absolutely inundated.

Jenny busily arranged the clothing they'd used into big garment bags. "I love your name, Io. Ee-oh-lahnth. I'm always afraid I'll say it wrong. You just used the one name in New York, didn't you?"

Iolanthe threw her special facial scrubs into the trash basket. "Yes, I did. It sounded unusual enough to stand alone. I thought that one name bit sounded a bit, like, too, too, you know, what I mean? But the agency insisted." She laughed. "And you do what the agency says."

"Did you make it up?" Jenny asked.

"No. Oh, no. It's my real name, all right. It was a fairy princess's name in an operetta my mother loved. The princess married a mortal, which really pissed off the other fairies. Mother thought it sounded very romantic."

"Oh, it is romantic." She sighed. "Not like 'Jenny'."

"But you are a romantic, Jenny, and that's what counts." She thought a moment. "When you have an odd name it sometimes causes more trouble than it's worth. People look irritated when they don't know if I made it up or how I pronounce it." She smiled at the girl, then bent to rummage again in her battered tote bag. A dark, nondescript T-shirt went over her head. She tugged cheap faded Levi's up over her hips and wiggled her feet into tan Birkenstock sandals.

Glancing at her big, men's Seiko watch, her stomach plummeted. Iolanthe had always hated being late. But her schedule was so tight she always seemed to be ten minutes behind, at least. A glowering Dr. Byron Rossi looming ahead didn't make it any easier. She quickly twisted her damp hair into a tight knot, crammed a baseball cap on her head, gave herself a final once-over and turned from the mirror and slipped on dark glasses. "Maybe if I make all the traffic lights and take my chances with a speeding ticket and a parking ticket I can just make it," she muttered, and grabbed her back pack. She called back to Jenny, struggling to get the big clothing bags zipped. "Thanks for the help, Jenny. See you Saturday. I'll bring some muffins from that great bakery near my place."

The small face peeped out from the loaded bags and grimaced, "Io you're going to self-destruct with the pace you keep."

The scrubbed down graduate student waved and swung through the door. *If Rossi doesn't do me in first.*

By the time she got to the parking lot her T-shirt stuck uncomfortably to her back. They'd started the shoot at six, but it was still August in Phoenix, and thanks to the seasonal monsoon weather, humid as well as blazing hot. She unlocked the door to her little blue Toyota SUV, ouching out loud as she hit the blistering leather seat. She'd taken a couple of courses the last session of summer semester in hopes of getting herself acclimated before the fall semester began the middle of August, but she still couldn't get used to the steamy waves that shimmered off the roads and sidewalks and assaulted her when she opened her car door. She had forgotten. She'd been back East too long.

Hellish, that's what it is. Trying to ignore the red hot steering wheel and furnace-like heat that seared her eyes and lungs, she screeched away from the parking lot, hoping the air conditioner would make the car bearable in a few minutes. She groaned aloud when the first traffic light turned red.

The corridor was empty as Iolanthe skidded through the heavy glass doors of Emerson Hall, and her thick sandals made scuff, scuff sounds in the empty hallway as she scurried to the big lecture theater. Her heart sank when she saw that the door had been closed. She knew from the last time that the door made a god-awful squeak, no matter how carefully you opened it. She winced as she pushed the door and slipped inside. *I swear I'm going to put a can of WD-40 in my bag and squirt that hinge. About a million kids would be grateful. Especially the ones who wanted to sneak out. Not that anyone dared sneak out of Byron Rossi's class when the line waiting to sign up for it had been a block long during registration. Physics majors working on advanced degrees got in, but after that they'd resorted to a lottery.*

Iolanthe knew she'd probably be late again. Inevitably, unless she quit her modeling jobs. But who'd pay the rent then? She could live off her New York savings if she absolutely last-ditch had to, but her carefully nurtured nest egg was her insurance. She knew all too well that when you lost your money, you lost your options. She'd grown up with that. Oh, yes.

Her eyes flew to the podium as she slipped as unobtrusively as possible into a back seat. Byron Rossi leaned casually on the lectern, talking about a display up on a big screen. Iolanthe flipped open her notebook and relaxed slightly. He didn't look like he'd noticed her.

"...as Michaelson's figure shows, the speed of light is

slightly higher in a vacuum than in air…the speed in free space generally accepted as the most precise is…" He turned to the whiteboard and began a rapid scribbling. "…c+2.997922458 x 10 to the 8th power m/c…"

Iolanthe slouched behind the student in front of her.

"…with an uncertainty…the young lady in the back row who came in late, please be good enough to see me after class…of 1.2 m/c. New laser experiments, however, may…"

Her heart thudded. He'd purposely acted like he'd not seen her, lulled her, then slipped that "would the young lady" crack in. He had a mean streak. She bent her head and began writing furiously, dreading the end of class, trying to tell herself not to be so intimidated by his curtness. *Byron Rossi's a man like any other.*

But she knew he wasn't.

After class, as she stood in a line of eager students in front of him, it surprised her he wasn't taller. She stood just a shade under six feet and he looked maybe three inches more. Yes, he was tall, but not a giant. Maybe because he had a powerful physique. Then the force of his out-size personality made him appear to occupy extra space. For the past three years he'd had a series of science specials on television, and that persona came across well on the screen. An assurance—yes, an arrogance charged the air around him—not a male type her most favorite, but she watched the programs, just like every body else.

Iolanthe shifted her weight from one foot to the other. She'd love to just leave, but she needed to ace this class. He'd singled her out and wouldn't take kindly to her ignoring his order to stay. It would be insanity to jeopardize the opportunity to study with this authority in her field. He'd been mentioned for the Nobel several times, and though he hadn't won it yet, everyone felt sure he would eventually. Arizona State had snared him for a visiting professorship and it would be a big plus for her to have studied under him.

Back at Columbia Iolanthe had heard there'd had been whispers in scientific circles that somehow Byron Rossi had prostituted himself and pure science with his beautifully produced television series explaining the mysteries of physics. He'd become a media star and made it all look easy doing it, plus he'd won a couple of Emmys.

It had all been very funny, she thought grudgingly. The scientific circles sniffed all they wanted to, but audiences and the media adored Byron Rossi. And, she thought sourly, were fascinated by whichever beauty he had on his arm at any given time. Iolanthe knew all too well the world of science had its celebrities and jealousies, just like any other.

Two more to go, will they hurry up? What did he say to that girl? Is she crying?

When he finally turned to her his dark eyes were icy, his deep voice tight with annoyance. "Miss, concepts I cover in this class are complex. When students come in late they interrupt my train of thought, as well as break the concentration of the students who bothered to get here on time. This is not an ideal set-up. The lecture hall is too big, the class is too big. Disruptions are hard on everybody, don't you agree? I would be very grateful if you would make every effort in the future to be here on time."

"I'm really terribly sorry, Dr. Rossi. I was detained at work. I know that's not an excuse...," she ended lamely.

"No. It isn't." With unmistakable dismissal he turned to a waiting student, who looked sideways at Iolanthe with sympathy for the tongue lashing.

Relieved of the ferocity of his gaze, she felt her knees

wobble. *I've had brilliant professors before,* she scolded herself. *Why am I letting this one intimidate me so? Is it because he's famous as well. That never bothered me in New York. Hah! I've gone out with bigger fish than this one.*

Cross with herself she slipped out of the lecture hall, glaring at the door as it squeaked mockingly.

"The great man on your case, Io?"

Iolanthe turned and flickered a cool smile into the bloodshot eyes of Peter Lessing. She'd heard he'd been an Olympic gymnast and it showed in the heavily muscled upper torso and arms. Trying not to be unfair to someone who seemed only trying to be nice, she made her voice casual, neutral. "How'd you find out my name? I don't tell anybody."

He smirked through scraggly facial hair. "I have my sources."

Iolanthe, indeed, filled out all her class registrations as "I. McKenna." Her first name was unusual and a bit dramatic. She'd argued at first, but at the agency's firm suggestion, she used it alone during her New York career. And now she associated it with the other part of her life that had nothing to do with her scientific studies. She kept the two lives totally separate. Iolanthe stayed in New York. An indeterminate, unisex *I.* lived and studied here. She wanted to at last melt into the gray world of scholarship.

"Excuse me, Peter. Gotta run. " She dodged around Peter Lessing.

He grabbed her arm. "Come for coffee with me, Io? I know you don't have a class."

She froze at the contact, then spun and jerked away. "I really have a tight schedule, Peter," she called over her shoulder. *How does he know I don't? And why does that give me the creeps.*

Iolanthe had learned her lesson about involvements at

school back East. Now, here, she pulled her hair into a severe knot under a baseball cap, scrubbed her milky, porcelain skin, hid her robin's egg blue eyes behind darkly-tinted glasses, and swathed her elegant angles in a variety of out-size T-shirts and drab, unfashionable sweaters. When the weather turned chilly she planned to wear hoodies and socks with her clunky sandals to make her personality as nondescript as her costume. She rarely smiled or chatted with classmates. Aloof, she didn't attract attention and fellow students rarely singled her out. When rebuffed they seldom bothered her again.

Now this monkey-like fellow graduate student wanted to ease into her shell. She felt him trailing behind her, so she quickened her pace and didn't look back.

Iolanthe surged out into the white noon sun with the crowd of students changing classes. On the horizon over the tips of the South Mountains, the sky showed the beginnings of the mountainous cumulous clouds of the dying desert summer monsoon season. Fed by the intense heat reflected off the desert floor, they might produce violent dust and thunderstorms by late afternoon, or collapse in the fading sun, only to renew the cycle the next day.

The air felt heavy with humidity. A storm would be a relief, she thought, as perspiration trickled down her spine and between her breasts. Great old olive trees spread heavily fruited wide branches over the walkway, a welcome respite as she crunched their hard green olives under her sandals. Later into fall the olives would ripen into glossy black—softer and squishier goo underfoot.

She would have to skip lunch today. Dr. Helms, her advisor wanted to see her about deciding on a subject for her dissertation. He was getting anxious, she knew. If she wanted to get her doctorate in a year, she'd have to get her outlines submitted. And get her committee together. He promised her he'd be as helpful as he could, but the final decisions were hers. She turned into the entrance of the old section of the Physics building, reviewing her plans in her mind.

Dr. Helms rose when she tapped on the doorframe to his office. "Miss McKenna, do come in. Here, let me move these."

Iolanthe did her best to hide a smile as Dr. Helms fussily scooped a stack of papers off a chair for her to sit in. He had been on the faculty for thirty years and she seriously doubted if anything had ever been thrown away. Bookshelves and filing cabinets groaned with their burdens. Mounds once recognizable as chairs and tables were stacked precariously with papers, books, publications, magazines, tests and theses. The big desk was invisible under a snowstorm of world-wide correspondence. The walls, may, or may not, have bulletin boards mounted on them. They had long since disappeared under a blizzard of posters, flyers, schedules and notices.

What could not find shelf space, or room on table or chair, spilled onto the floor. Boxes leaned this way and that, accordion files, ledgers, long-forgotten experiments were cast willy-nilly into corners. Testimony to the legendary character of Dr. Helms's office was a corner wall devoted to years of cartoons about disorderly offices, presented to Samuel Helms by three generations of students and faculty alike. Iolanthe suspected the good professor was secretly proud of the renown of his office and had, over the years, relished polishing the legend of this monument to academic chaos. His mind, she found, was clarity itself.

Gingerly she found a place to place her feet, disturbing a small tan spider that scuttled under a nearby teetering pile of scientific magazines.

"Ah, Miss McKenna. You've been on my mind this morning," he beamed, polishing his metal-rimmed glasses. "I've been recruiting on your behalf. I hope you will be as pleased as I." He carefully placed the glasses on his nose and adjusted the earpieces. "But first," he then rushed on, "have you come to any conclusions about the subject of your dissertation? That should be our first order of business."

Puzzled by his first words, she answered, "Yes, I think so. As you know, I've been interested in the knot theory and statistical mechanics. I studied with Joan Switzer at Columbia. My master's thesis touched tangentially on the subject. I'd like to pursue the aspects of the resemblance of the algebraic expressions of certain topological relations among braid formations, the mathematical properties or polynomial invariants. What do you think? I'll narrow the scope down, of course."

"Yes, yes. Fine ideas. Dr. Rossi..."

"I know. I would have been foolish not to use the opportunity to take the classes with him this semester and next. I hope to get into one of his smaller graduate seminars spring semester as well. Concerning my committee, I've not gotten any promises. Well, I haven't asked anybody yet. You're my chairman. Dr.Wheaton, maybe? Do you think he'd be willing?"

The little man rubbed his hands together with obvious satisfaction. "Oh, I'm sure. Dr. Wheaton would be most amenable. Oh, this is excellent. Excellent." He beamed delightedly. "Now, my surprise." His voice rumbled with excitement. "I have convinced Dr. Rossi to serve as your chairman." He held up his hand. "Now please don't think I wouldn't be honored to have you, but this opportunity is so outstanding, so rare. We have the dean's permission, since Dr. Rossi has just joined the staff. He is to be here only this school year, but you plan to complete your doctoral work in one year I understand, so that won't be a problem. You'll have to formally request him, but the dean agrees that his credentials...why my dear, whatever is the matter?"

Iolanthe's felt the blood drain from her face—her voice a weak croak as she tried to put together an explanation. "Oh, Dr. Helms, you can't really mean that. I mean...he couldn't know it's me you're talking about." She raced on. "We really haven't gotten off to a very good start in class. I don't think he's terribly impressed with me. I know he must think you're talking about somebody else. He's only just beginning to sort out who we are in the class because it's so big." She caught herself before she started wringing her hands.

Dr. Helms smiled benignly at her agitation. "Now, now, Miss McKenna. You're being just a bit star-struck is all. He's really quite a delightful man and it will be a most fortuitous addition to your Curriculum Vitae. I've presented him all your credentials and he quite agrees he can be of help. Would enjoy it, as a matter of fact. Says he's been away from academia too long. He says he'll be most pleased to have a graduate student to guide. And now, the focus you've chosen couldn't be more felicitous. He's doing important work there."

She felt numb. Dr. Helms had sprung it on her she would have to go into that man and ask him to be the chairman of her dissertation committee. He'd probably throw her out. She couldn't admit it to Dr. Helms, but she simply did not like Byron Rossi. Not only did he antagonize her, she sensed that, not only with her, but with the other women in the class, that the famous and supposedly charming Dr. Byron Rossi, scientist extraordinaire, thinking man's television star, did not think women were as capable as men. In scientific fields anyway. She could see it in his attitude toward the women in his class. An ever-so-slight condescension around his mouth and a certain edge to his voice when he questioned a female student's answers. Her mind went to the woman student that she'd thought might be in tears after she'd spoken to Rossi.

She tried again. "Dr. Helms, I'm terribly flattered, really, that you've given me your consideration. You're very kind. But I honestly don't think star-struck has anything to do with it. I sense, and I hate to say this, but I don't think Dr. Rossi takes women in the sciences seriously."

"Oh, my dear, not at all. You're quite wrong about that."

"If I do him an injustice, I'm sorry, but I can't help the feeling. I can't imagine why he would agree to this association. I can see by your expression that you're going to disagree with me. I wish you would reconsider and be my chairman. I'd be uncomfortable with Dr. Rossi. If you don't feel you can, I'd welcome another suggestion."

Iolanthe found she had to catch her breath.

"Now, Miss McKenna. This is the 21st century. That sort of attitude went out long ago. Can't think why you'd get that feeling with Dr, Rossi. He's a fine man, most respectful of capability. He's already agreed. Was impressed with your credentials. You've only to make the formal request. I'll go with you if you like. I know he can be a trifle brusque."

She knew she'd lost the argument, unless she became disagreeable, and Dr. Helms was too nice a man. She leaned her head back in the chair, her mind a flurry, weighing her choices. Maybe Rossi wasn't so forbidding when you got to know him. After all, she wasn't looking for a friend. The position didn't call for a friend. Rossi had agreed to be her chairman; he had seen her credentials. He knew her qualifications. Maybe her misgivings were wrong.

I made up my mind when I was twelve that I can handle anything. And I have. I'll handle this if it kills me. Byron Rossi isn't going to finish me after I've come this far. And Dr.

Helms is right. It will look impressive on my C.V. Since the man has agreed, I will have to be very, very good. But I know I am that.

But deep down, regardless of what Dr. Helms thought, she knew her instincts about Byron Rossi were right.

She considered his offer to go with her to see Rossi, but that would never do. With a heavy heart she knew she couldn't hide behind her advisor. "No, that's not necessary. You've been kind enough already. I'll talk to him. He'll be expecting me? I'll make an appointment today." She stood, trying to dislodge the weighted feeling in her stomach. The day had gone downhill from the moment she'd struggled out of bed, groggy and needing four more hours of sleep.

At the door, Iolanthe turned to smile, wanting to reassure the dear man and caught him putting back a clutch of papers on the chair she had just vacated. He grinned sheepishly.

After leaving Samuel Helm's office, she stopped at a snack cart on the mall and bought an apple and bottle of water and found a spot on the grass under one of the silvery old olive trees that shaded the campus. She sank down cross-legged and absently bit into the apple. She couldn't blame Dr. Helms. He didn't know an awful lot about her. She'd gotten him for her advisor when she had enrolled in summer school, had taken a class with him and had another this semester. She knew he sensed her reticence about her outside life and he hadn't pried.

She'd only told him why she hadn't continued her studies at MIT, though her grades had been excellent. Her tuition had been paid for one year, and when she had a chance at employment in New York, she transferred to Columbia, where she'd gotten her Bachelor of Science and Master of Science degrees. Asked about her job, she said she'd worked with photographers. What she hadn't told him was that her parents had been killed in a plane crash the summer before she left for MIT and when all her father's affairs had been settled, she'd had only enough to live on for one year at Cambridge. The modeling offer had been a godsend that allowed her to continue her studies in New York.

She knew Dr. Helms thought she was a very good student and now had taken a fatherly sort of interest in her and felt he'd done a special thing for her getting Byron Rossi to agree to be her dissertation chairman.

Well, life would go on. Didn't it always? Iolanthe finished her apple and stood, brushing the grass off the seat of her jeans. While she looked for a waste receptacle to pitch her apple core, she tried to picture Byron Rossi's mouth in a "charming" smile. His glowering face as he scolded her about being late swam into her head. *Huh, Iolanthe, babe, your imagination ain't that good.*